Praise for Faith O'Shea

Faith O'Shea is a contemporary women's literature writer who loves writing about romance, magic, conviction, and loyalty, with strong women and the friendships they build. She has created many series of stories to make us laugh, cry and feel empowered and writes in a voice that speaks to women of all ages. Faith believed there were subjects and life that needed to be written about. ~ Loyce M.

I truly love the Everyday Goddess series. The strong, leading women characters, in this day and age, are inspiring to me and keep me coming back for more! The books are light, fun, extremely relatable and I can't put them down! ~ Kathryn B.

I just finished the Fire and Ice series. It had romance, strong friendships between the women characters and complex stories that were clearly very well researched. Loved all of them and looking forward to the goddess series next! ~ Gail N.

Oh wow! I just finished reading the *Magic Bean Café* and I must say that I was hooked from the first chapter and loved every page. The characters were full and believable. The child, Willow, had my heart with her wild imagination, gift of laughter, and the way she melted Aisin's heart and helped him to realize that you can love a child that wasn't yours. Thank you for gifting me this awesome read. ~ Your newest fan, Carol F. ❤

Magic Bean Café is a fantastic book of compassion for others with realistic characters. Plus a generous millionaire to help fulfill dreams. ~ Belinda

Books by Faith O'Shea

The Greenliner Series
Four baseball players, one team on the rise

Thrown for a Curve
League of Her Own
Clutch Hit
Out in Left Field

The Scalera Family Series
Five boisterous Italian siblings, five ways to find love

Cold Sweat
Edge of Forever
Thin Blue Line
Coming Home to You
Finding Joy

The Fire and Ice Series
One law firm, six partners, friends to the end

Consumed by Fire
Skoli on Ice
Heart on Fire
Heart of ICE
Tendrils of Ice
Rekindling the Fire

The Everyday Goddesses Series
One extraordinary café and a circle of magical friends

Magic Bean Café
Once There Was a Tree
Tipping the Scales
Can't Be Tamed
Remains to Be Seen
Gardens of Eden
The Girl from Nowhere
Sweetwater Stables

Scalera Family

Five boisterous Italian siblings, five ways to find love

Cold Sweat

Johnny's the oldest, drummer for the heavy metal band Raging Thunder. The man knows how to rock and roll and thinks he's just the one who can teach Letitia Jones, a classically trained pianist, everything there is to know about life but when the tables are turned, he runs scared. Will he come to realize that settling down, isn't the worse thing in life that can happen?

Edge of Forever

Rissa's sketches of Luca Caroli, bassist for her brother's band, are uncovering edges, and revealing things meant to stay hidden. He's not what he seems and she's beginning to think he might be her forever. Problem is, he's stuck in the past. What can she do to align the stars in her favor?

Thin Blue Line

Lana, the youngest, never got over her father's death, and swore she'd never marry a cop. Her mother had paid the ultimate price for loving such a man. So how did she find herself married to Zachary Taylor, a cop, who's more than willing to put his life on the line every second of every day? If she sacrifices him now, will it save her grief in the end?

Coming Home to You

Tony is his father's son, with a badge and a gun, but he's not going to leave a widow behind like his father did. When he takes Tansy McPhail under his wing, and gives her shelter, he thinks he's just doing some community service. How long will it take for him to see, that his place isn't a home, without her?

Finding Joy

Dennis has been married before and has no plans on walking that aisle again so when he meets the sexy diva Artemis, under protest, he has no illusions. But as he works to produce her new record, he finds she's more than the tabloids have led the public to believe. She's warm and funny and down-to-earth, but she's still Artemis to him, not Joy Munroe. Does he have what it would take, to win her love?

THIN BLUE LINE

Scalera Family
Book 3

FAITH O'SHEA

Cover Design by Jaycee DeLorenzo at Sweet 'N Spicy Designs
Formatted by Woven Red Author Services, www.wovenRed.ca

Thin Blue Line/Sue Campbell writing as Faith O'Shea- 1st edition
ISBN eBook: 978-0-9987229-6-2
ISBN print book: 978-0-9987229-7-9

http://www.faithoshea.com

Printed in the U.S.A.

To My Readers

The Scalera series is composed of my first venture into publishing. Cold Sweat was never meant for Kindle. I was writing for me, as a means of self-expression, and perhaps some healing as well. It's intimidating to put your work of art into the public domain, and I wasn't sure I wanted to go that route. I am grateful to my friends and family who persuaded me to get it out into the world.

My writing is the means I employ to get the voices in my head into an organized format. Stories have percolated for years and once I retired from my job, they became the driving force of my days. I have never been happier or more fulfilled.

This series is about the Scalera's, a big Italian family, like the one I grew up in. They say write what you know, and this thread is one I know intimately. My grandmother didn't have as many children as Celia, but food was love and there was never a time I didn't go to visit that she wasn't telling me to sit and eat. Mangiare.

Thin Blue Line has Lana taking center stage. She had to be a chef, following in her mother's footsteps. It was a way to bring home the aspect of the culture that is my own. The lemon squares and escarole pizza were staples in Nana's house and just the other day my son asked if anyone had the recipe for the sweet and sour lemon treats. We're hoping one of my cousins were smart enough to get a copy and it wasn't lost with her death. My Nana was just shy of her hundredth birthday when she passed, and she is missed.

I have two series going at the moment and it's been nice alternating between the two. Fire and Ice is more contemporary, and takes place in the current political climate we're living in. They are romance novels, but women's friendship is also central to the storylines. I can't think of two things more important than friendship and family.

I hope you enjoy Thin Blue Line, and if you haven't read the ones that came before, I hope you check them out on Amazon.

Tony and Dennis are soon to follow and I'm looking forward to working with them.

Faith

CHAPTER ONE

Lana Scalera was sitting outside her parents' house, waiting for her mother, the sun not even peeking out of the January sky yet. They had a lot on their agenda today and their commercial kitchen beckoned. She looked over to the door, expecting her to run out any minute, her bags of staples swinging from her arm.

What was taking her so long?

Celia was the one who'd called, insisting she be here at this ungodly hour, the to-do list having multiplied overnight. There was probably a method to her madness, this time of year not one of Lana's favorites. Yesterday's family dinner, replete with birthday hats and streamers had done nothing to alleviate the ache and yearning her memories evoked. The cassava cake from her favorite Italian bakery was still untouched, taking up space in her refrigerator.

She honked the horn again, her fingers tapping on the steering wheel, and glanced up to see Paul in the doorway, beckoning her with a wave of his hand. While mumbling about being late, about the full day of cooking ahead of them, she pushed the clutch in, put the car in reverse, yanked on the emergency brake, and ran the short distance to the house. She slid through the opening, Paul stepping out of the way to let her in.

She went on red alert almost instantly. His expression was somber, and her heartbeat went into overdrive. She'd lived through something like this before and it had changed her life forever. She couldn't afford to have it happen again. She glanced in her mother's direction, hoping her instincts were wrong, but the look on her face did nothing to quiet her nerves. The twist of pain in the region of her heart sucked the air right out of her lungs.

She knew what they were going to tell her, why she was here.

If it were a more family-inclusive disaster, she wouldn't be the only one standing here. Her brothers and sister would be with her.

When Paul pulled out a seat at the table and said, "Sit, please," she collapsed into the chair, clasping her hands together to stop the trembling. Her heart was now beating like a horde of wild horses, trying to outdistance the impending doom.

Paul's silence was making it worse, so she stuttered out, "Tell me already. What...happened?"

The voice was gruff as Paul scratched out, "It's Zach."

She'd braced herself for this, or thought she had. Panic like she'd never known before welled in her throat. Her blood rushed and dizziness consumed her. It was hard to form the words, but she had to know.

"Is he..."

Paul was quick to reassure her. "No. He's alive."

Her eyes fluttered shut at that small miracle.

"But..."

Paul had taken a seat beside her, reaching out to hold one of her hands.

"He was beat up pretty badly last night, or should I say early this morning. He got out of the operating room an hour ago. He's stable but critical."

She felt the prick of tears as they filled her eyes. What was growing in the pit of her stomach was a scream, a primal one, directed at Zach, at whoever did this to him, his supervisors, the superintendent.

The noises in her throat sounded odd to her own ears as she gasped for breath.

"I knew this would happen. Didn't I tell you..."

Paul remained calm in the face of her agitation.

"Lana, he didn't go looking for this."

She replied in a small, frightened voice, "He doesn't have to. These things find him. I told you I couldn't deal with this. I...I hope he doesn't expect me to visit him."

She'd sat by his bedside once before, coaxing him back to health. It had gotten her a heart full of pain.

Paul said slowly, "I know very little at this point. He's in recovery. I'll be going over later to check in."

She'd gotten up, begun to pace, a finger in her mouth that she chewed with vigor.

"What are his odds?"

She stopped, held her breath, waiting for an answer, not wanting to care, but needing to know if he was going to live or die.

"The doctor thinks fairly good considering his constitution."

He'd been a Marine. Still boxed, still lifted weights. Apparently still had a death wish.

She pressed her palms into her eyes, holding back the pinpricks of tears that threatened.

Her mother, who was hovering nearby, closed the distance. Her voice was soft and gentle. "Lana, I think you—"

Lana threaded her hands in her hair as anger sliced through her.

"Don't Ma. I walked away for a reason. This reason. I don't have any inclination to walk back into it."

Celia took her hands. "Lana, he's in bad shape."

"His choice, not mine." Her voice quivered.

Now there was a bite in her mother's tone. "You're going to tell me you don't care about him at all?"

Lana stared right through her.

Yes, she cared. She cared too much. It was the reason she'd cut him out of her life.

Putting trembling fingers to her forehead, she announced, "I can't work today."

As she raced back out to her car, she whispered in a ragged voice, *I'm sorry, Zach. I can't do this. Not again.*

On auto pilot, all her thoughts on the man in the hospital, she drove home, pulled into her parking spot, and sat staring into space, not remembering how she got there.

There were too many images of him in her head, his smile, his rugged features, his broken body. The one she'd helped him rehabilitate after his last brush with death.

He was one of Boston's finest. The truth, according to her, was far different. He was a hot-dogger, with a freneticism that was un-reined and undisciplined, who did everything he could to get himself killed. One of these times he'd succeed.

A ripple of fear coursed through her, along with a ripple of something else she didn't want to name.

Once inside her condo, she ranted and raved at him as she cleaned, scouring everything, from top to bottom, the nervous energy needing an outlet.

Zach could hear sounds, murmurs, the beep of the heart monitor announcing he was still alive, felt a nurse checking his pulse and he forced his eyes open. Then closed them again. His mother and father were here, along with Lana's stepfather, Paul Catalano. He should be glad. No one liked dying alone, but the one person he needed to see had stayed away and he knew the reason. He'd been here before. Not the same room, but the same hospital, hurt, tattered, and in pieces. She'd helped him regain his focus back then, got him through the pain of recuperation and rehabilitation, made him laugh even as she cried. He'd seen to it that she was no longer part of his life and he'd proven her instincts correct with this latest disaster.

He swallowed past the lump in his throat, allowed the pain to have its way. Maybe he deserved it.

His mother sat by his bedside, and he felt her take his hand.

He licked his lips, tried to get the words out, but failed. His jaw hurt like hell, his body hurt like hell, but he had to ask.

He pushed the question out, his voice hoarse. "Does she know?"

"I told her this morning." Paul's voice sounded as if he were underwater, the reverberation pounding in his head, one of Johnny Scalera's drum solos going full out.

He rasped out, "And?"

He noticed Paul glance over at his parents before he admitted, "She's not coming. Said she couldn't."

He could feel his mother's tension in the way she squeezed his hand, but she remained silent on the issue, and he was grateful for that one small favor.

The nurse, who must have been hovering close by, announced, "I'm sorry but you're all going to have to leave. He's only been out of surgery for a couple of hours, and he needs to sleep."

He felt his mother's kiss on his forehead, heard his father's strong voice telling him they'd be back, before he opened his eyes to see the look of regret in Paul's. His lips were pressed thin, as if he wanted to offer some hope.

"Maybe she'll change her mind."

With a clenched jaw, Zach suggested otherwise. "We all know where she stands. She won't. Just remind her that I'm alive."

"I will. You take care."

Zach gave a brief nod, talking too painful.

He heard the door open and close, and he was finally alone, alone with the thoughts that could undo him.

When he'd been laying in the alleyway waiting for the grim reaper, there was only one thought that rushed his mind in waves, one word he'd said over and over. *Lana, Lana, Lana...*a mantra that focused all his thoughts in one place. Left bleeding and broken, he hadn't been sure he'd survive this time, thought he'd never see her again, never hear her laugh, never see her eyes sparkle when he walked in the door, never feel her muscles tighten around him.

Had he cried out her name with that last kick, the one he thought would finish him off? It wouldn't surprise him. He'd seen enough soldiers on the battlefield cry out for someone at the moment before death. Most called for their mother. But then most had been boys who hadn't lived long enough to find a love deeper than that.

⌐

He'd loved her down to the bottom of his soul, but he'd found out the hard way that her love hadn't been as deep as he'd thought.

It was ironic that the assault had come when it had. Last night, his body had been broken. Two years ago, to the day, his heart had been.

It was also ironic that he'd fought with everything in him in Afghanistan during his last battle, and in the alleyway where the thugs had jumped him, but he hadn't fought as hard for the one thing that really mattered to him.

Fact was, he hadn't fought at all. It was the first time in his life he'd simply walked away.

What had that told her? That the job *was* more important than her? That if he couldn't have it his way, she'd have to choose?

Well, she had, and he'd spent the last two years looking back. He still was.

As he drifted in and out of consciousness, the flashes of the past adding to the physical pain, he decided it was way past due to go to war for the woman who was more important to him than his life.

CHAPTER TWO

Almost a week later, Lana still wasn't right, still up at night worrying, not only for Zach's recovery but with a new concern. The reckless fool in the hospital was being partnered with Paul, who was a detective in the Homicide Department. It was at the personal request of the superintendent, who was a close friend of the family. Paul had mentioned it at their weekly Sunday dinner in passing, like it was no big deal.

It was a friggin' big deal.

The thing that always took her mind off worry was work. And she'd been doing that with a vengeance. It had helped that the catering service had back-to-back events, not a given during January. There was usually a lull during the cold winter months.

She'd be at her mother's this morning, going over the invoices and expense report for the wedding they catered yesterday, and making the final preparations for the functions being held over the next couple of days. If she couldn't be cooking, the next best thing to keep her mind occupied was making plans to cook.

After parking her car in the driveway, she collected her bags and fumbled her way up the stairs, not wanting to waste time with two trips. She stopped short when she saw a face staring up at her from the morning paper, the face she'd been trying to block out of her mind. The headline screamed *Undercover Cop Taken Down*. Her blood began to boil again, amping up from the simmer she'd been dealing with since she'd heard about the assault. Against her better judgement, she rearranged everything in her arms, freeing a hand to pick it up.

The picture captured a man covered in bruises, both eyes blackened, his lip swollen. There was a moment of panic, but she was able to shove it away as she scanned the article.

There was no mention of his name. If the newspaper contributors were trying to keep from blowing his cover, it was a tad too late. Whoever had done this to him, knew exactly who he was and what he'd been doing. As her eyes grazed the blurb of words, they picked out key phrases: brutal ambush, left for dead. Neither implied recklessness. She knew there had to be a missing piece to the story. She just didn't know what it was because she hadn't asked.

She shivered, the cold air sneaking in through the gaps in her coat. Unable to prevent herself from doing so, she glanced back at the face on the front page. A pang of longing shot through her.

She'd known him since she was a kid. Her parents and his were friends, part of an extended tribe that consisted of policemen and their families. Four couples and children merged every Saturday for barbeques or winter soups, it didn't matter the season. It was a network built to provide support, and she'd seen it in action, been a recipient of their largesse when her father had been killed in the line of duty.

Being five years younger than him, she hadn't had much interaction in those days, content to hang out with the kids her own age but there were moments she'd observe him, from a distance. Her twelve-year-old eyes appreciated his looks, and she'd even become tongue-tied around him as she got older. While her brother Johnny made fun of her, Zach had always been kind, his steel-blue eyes penetrating deep into her soul.

It was only after he'd been deployed to Afghanistan, almost ten years later, that she got to know him. At first, it was through conversations around the kitchen table when his mother, Jeanne would talk about where he was and what he was doing, the sadness and fear tangible. Then, one day, Jeanne asked some of the women at the friendly gathering to write to him, hoping cards and letters would keep up his morale, keep him safe. She'd taken her up on it.

Over the years, she'd heard most of Zach's war stories, begun to live with the growing fear he could fall at any time, re-learned what it was like to have anxiety take up residence in a corner of her mind. He wasn't the kind of man who did anything in half measures. He'd been stationed in Afghanistan by the time she began their correspondence, having already done a tour in Iraq and his father who had been disappointed that he hadn't followed in the family's footsteps became exceedingly proud of his service record, his Medal of Valor

a symbol of intrepid behavior. He'd won that for his actions during his last
battle, winning his release, as well, when he was gravely injured.

She'd waited for the call telling her he was coming home...in a box, and a
call had come but they had considered themselves lucky. He'd been alive, but
barely.

There was a homecoming, a long hospitalization. The choices she'd made
during and after, she was still trying to correct.

Or so it seemed.

This latest hospitalization was no less traumatic for her than his last had
been. Only this time she knew it was safer to stay away.

⌒

After taking her gaze off the picture, she pressed the latch of the glass-plated
red door and pushed it open, entering the familiar entryway of her childhood
home. She'd moved out the year she left culinary school, not long after her
sister, Rissa. The condo she'd purchased was small, but it was hers. The only
downside was the kitchen. So tiny she had a hard time testing any of her recipes there, and as a result, spent an inordinate amount of time here with her
mother, the recently remodeled kitchen more in keeping with chef status. It
had been gutted, right down to the studs and rebuilt piece by piece, according
to the design mother and daughter had in their heads. White cabinets lined
two of the walls, and a stainless-steel dual stove/oven provided the necessary
cooktops and baking capacity for the food prepared for the many events they
covered. The island was six feet long by four feet wide, giving them an abun-
dant amount of counter space needed for food preparation, leaving an area
available for packing the finished product and storing it for transport. They
had used poured concrete rather than granite or quartz even though it had to
be resurfaced every few years. Ceramic jugs held a preponderance of utensils,
spoons, spatulas, and tongs, and the Kitchen Aide blender was hidden in a
cabinet, stored out of sight when not in use. Since they'd rented a commercial
kitchen once the Cookery increased its client base, the double-door refrigerator had become the family way station. There was an unwritten invitation that
any Scalera who entered this domain could pilfer without fear of retribution.
And her family stopped by as often as they could for the comfort and love the
food offered.

She loved working in here, the room so light and spacious. Last night she'd
worked in her own cramped space, far into the early hours.

Exhaustion from lack of sleep was producing some serious side effects, and the picture of Zach was having more of an impact than she needed, and she told him so, mumbling under her breath as she entered the kitchen.

"Lana? Who are you talking to?"

Her mother's voice echoed down the short hall as she approached the room she all but lived in.

"No one. It's just me. I brought over the samples of the new recipes I tried last night."

She placed the bags on the cool surface of the island, set her pocketbook beside them, the newspaper still clutched in her hand.

Celia appeared, stopped and studied her, a concerned look on her face.

"Did you stay up late testing?"

A simple nod answered the question.

"Are you still going to tell me you don't care about Zach? From the looks of things, I'd say you're not only lying to me but to yourself."

Lana dropped the newspaper on the counter and pointed at the picture, shifting into a more confrontational tone.

"I'll admit it's his fault I've become a cooking demon."

Her mother took a step closer, craning her neck to see what Lana was referring to. Then sat on a stool to get a better look.

"Oh, my. They were supposed to bury this. George is not going to be pleased. Neither is Paul."

Paul joined the women, his voice gruff when he asked, "What am I not going to be pleased with?"

Following her stepfather was the man in the flesh who took up half the front page.

He looked worse than the image in print.

His arm was in a sling, his face was bloated, his eyes purple and yellow tinged, and he walked with a limp.

And he still looked intimidating.

Even the wounds couldn't hide the wide expanse of chest, the square face, the strong chin. Even the slouch couldn't disguise his six-foot-three-inch frame.

Grief ripped through her, but she tapped it down, saying almost flippantly, "You look terrible."

Leaning on his cane with his good arm, he said sarcastically, "Thanks for pointing that out. I hadn't noticed. My mirror must be on the blink."

He seemed to have a hard time getting the words out, his jaw clenched while he spoke.

His sarcasm only incited her further. She hated his total disregard for his life.

"What the hell did you do to piss someone off so royally?"

His eyes were shooting daggers right back at her, which made her retreat a step, but his tone held moderation.

"Working to break up a theft ring." He flicked his eyes away from her. "Something...went wrong."

Pointing her index finger to the article her mother was reading, she said, "You were undercover, weren't you? How did you blow that?"

"Shit happened."

She was staring at him, hoped that her eyes were menacing. She could tell from his expression that she was getting under his skin just as she'd intended, but she almost jumped out of hers when he barked, "What?"

She seethed with mounting anger.

"Why do you do this?"

"What?"

"Try to get yourself killed."

There was a twitch of a smile, but his eyes captured hers and didn't let go.

"Haven't you figured it out yet? I do it just to annoy you."

Scared, pissed that he took it so lightly, she narrowed her eyes dangerously, and she let him know that he'd just tipped her scale.

"This is no fucking joke."

"Watch your language, Lana. I won't have you talking to him like that."

She glanced over to her mother, whose eyes held a warning, then back to the man in question.

He was leaning more heavily on the cane, his shoulders slumped as if under the weight of her words. "I don't believe I'm laughing."

Lana spun away, the visible signs of his injuries making her weak in the knees. Washing her hands at the sink to keep from strangling the man, she felt his eyes on her, heard the bite in his tone.

"She probably wishes the thugs had finished the job. Then she could stand over my grave and say I told you so."

Her heart skipped a beat. She wasn't sure she could ever stand over his grave, knowing he was forever out of her life. She'd probably climb right in with him. Her mother would be the one saying those words.

When she turned back to the audience, she saw Zach rub the stubble on his chin, noticed his expression was not a happy one.

Going back to the storyline, Paul now reading it over her shoulder, Celia said, "I think this move to homicide is a good one."

Lana was watching Zach's expression, waiting to hear what he thought of the transfer.

"It was an order from up high. Seems my mother doesn't like my face to look like mincemeat. She holds a lot of sway with my old man."

Lana still had some fight left in her despite her mother's warning.

"I suppose you are stupid enough to want to go back."

"Sure. If I'm underground, they can't see me."

Desolation puddled through her and she all but rasped out, "Or so you thought."

His stark blue eyes glowered.

"It's what I do."

Paul was the one who stepped into the breach.

"Lana, give it a rest. He has a hairline fracture in his jaw, and he's not supposed to talk. The dumb shit refused to have it wired."

She threaded her hair back, her body language speaking volumes.

"I bet he's not supposed to be on his feet, either. Doesn't seem he listens much to authority."

"I listen fine."

His response was more a grumble than an answer.

Her words came out like bullets from an AK-15.

"You do anything to get Paul hurt and I'll hunt you down…"

Stooped over, his head down, he asked, "And what? If three thugs couldn't kill me, I don't know why you think you'd get the job done."

The thought of him dead in the alleyway brought the nausea back, chills raising the flesh on her skin, a definite complication in how she felt about him.

Stuttering, she said, "I'll…poison you."

"I've tasted your food. It hasn't worked so far."

His tone was as bland as the food he liked, igniting a fire in her belly.

She curled her hands into fists and was tempted to take the ungodly smirk off his face.

Paul grabbed his coat from the back of the bar stool.

"Come on, Zach. Your mother's waiting for you."

He'd asked Paul to give him some time before dropping him there. Fact was, he wanted to see Lana, needed to see her face and hoped she'd be at the Catalano's. When he heard her voice, he'd known where he wanted to convalesce. There was a definite upside to staying here and he was going to go for it. He moved in the direction of the door, leaning heavily on the cane.

"No. I'm going to my place."

Paul stopped in mid-stride.

"You know the doctor's orders. Stairs are out, and you need to be monitored. It was the only reason they let you go."

"I'm not going to my parents' house."

There was a finality in those words that Paul must have recognized and understood.

"Well, then we have a problem."

His eyes were trained on Lana when he said, "How about I stay here? We're partners now. Don't we have to take care of each other?"

He was busy watching the expressions moving across Lana's face when Celia stepped in. "Zach, your mother..."

He unlocked his gaze from Lana's and looked at Celia.

"My mother's been driving me crazy with all her coddling. I've recuperated at the old homestead before, and I don't want a repeat performance. If my place wasn't rented out for the next six months, I'd go there but...it is. I'll have to either find a short-term rental or give the guy time to move out."

He'd bought a condo a couple of years ago, when he re-joined the force but when he'd gone undercover, he'd rented it out, not wanting to shell out money for two places.

Noticing Paul's glance in Celia's direction, her nod of approval, Lana heard Zach exhale in gratitude.

Lana glared at Zach with reproachful eyes and her voice cut through him like a chef's knife, sharp and lethal.

"What if they come after you? I'm not letting you put my family in danger."

Celia asked calmly, "Do you think that could happen?"

Zach carefully shook his head and added, "If they wanted me dead, I'd be dead. They wanted to teach me a lesson, tell me I wasn't welcome back, which they did very effectively."

Paul stated, "He's right. It's not something we have to worry about."

Celia nodded. She seemed to agree with his assessment and let Lana know she'd lost the argument with the words, "He stays."

Lana felt tears prick her eyes. She'd been thrown off by the calculated way Zach had answered her mother's question. If they'd wanted him dead, he'd be dead, as if his life held no consequence. It made her temper flare, and the tears abate. Families shouldn't have to talk in terms of life and death, not as often as this one did.

Her head snapped up and she asked Paul, "Are you going after these guys?"

It was Zach who answered.

"If they'd managed to kill me, he would have had no choice, I guess. But they didn't. Someone else will be taking over for me underground. They'll get swept up in the eventual raid and then I'll testify against them."

His eyes closed in exhaustion, his face now looking sallow, etched as if in pain.

Celia offered, "Come on, there's a pull-out sofa in the back room. It won't be as comfortable as a bed but there will be no stairs to climb. There's a bathroom down here, so you should be fine."

As she led Zach out of the kitchen, Celia asked, "Are you hungry? I can fix you something to eat before you lie down."

"No. I can't really eat, anyway. They've had me on a semi-liquid diet, which I guess I'll have to stay on for a couple more days."

"I'll have Lana make you a healthy smoothie."

He turned, put his tired eyes on her, the smirk still settled on his lips.

"No thanks, ma'am. I don't want to take the risk of getting poisoned."

With her hands on her hips, she gave him the full force of her glower. His humor was back as he followed Celia down the hall. He was still under her skin.

CHAPTER THREE

As soon as Celia returned to the kitchen, having made up the makeshift bed, Lana spun around and asked, "How could you have agreed to let him stay here?"

She'd been stewing about it the whole time her mother was down the hall helping the man get settled.

Her mother's mood seemed to be in direct contrast to her own. Calm, patient, accepting.

"Because he needs time to recuperate and the best way for him to do that is to have some quiet. I know his mother. She hovers." Turning from inside the refrigerator, where she was one arm deep, rooting around for the ingredients for their first order, Celia gave her the mother look, eyes peering out over her glasses. It never failed to make Lana back down, but her back went up again when Celia asked, "Do you want to take him to your place?"

There was a snarl in her voice when she said, "Absolutely not."

"Well, then I guess that answers that."

Celia seamlessly went back to her task.

Without anyone to appreciate the glare, Lana began to unpack the glass containers of food samples she'd brought with her. Paul, who was getting ready to leave for work, dressed in suit and tie, came over to inspect them. While peering into one of the bowls, he sniffed. "What do you have?"

Lana showcased the mushroom-and-ricotta stuffed ravioli, the linguine with lobster sauce, lobster salad with micro greens and several desserts, explaining each as she went.

She pulled a fork out of a drawer and handed it to him so he could help himself. She was trying hard to maintain normal even though the man down the hall was making it hard to do.

Unable to sustain the curtness, she heard a tinge of sympathy in her voice when she said, "Maybe his mother wants him home. He came close to getting killed again. Cops are being targeted now more than ever."

The country seemed on the verge of a revolution, with five policemen just taken down by a sniper in Dallas, several more in Baton Rouge. And she was sure more violence against the men in blue would come.

Her mother's voice was surly, and the aim was a bull's-eye.

"Maybe *you* should give a shit."

Her mother was staring, waiting for a response, which she wasn't going to give her. Paul was picking at the lobster salad, a smile on his face, before he addressed the animosity.

"The job is the job. Everyone knows the risks. Everyone deals with them differently."

Slipping her hands into her pockets, Lana asked her mother, her eyes never straying from the furious glint, "How do you live with them? Knowing what you know?"

Her mother had lived through the nightmare of a cop killing, and as if that wasn't bad enough, married another one. Lana was still trying to understand her choice years later.

"Because Paul could be killed in a car accident, walking down Main Street, just as I could."

"Ma, the statistics..."

"I don't read statistics. It's who Paul is. Would you want someone telling you that you shouldn't be a chef? It's too dangerous, with the sharp knives and all?"

She rolled her eyes at the ridiculousness of that question.

"Chefs don't put their lives on the line every day."

Her mother admonished, "Someone has to, Lana. I'm proud of the work Paul does. He speaks for people who can't speak for themselves anymore. Now it's his job to teach that to Zachary."

Lana stared into space wondering...then shook her head.

"If the guy is willing to learn. Homicide will be kind of mundane compared to what he was doing before. He wants to fight the fight on the streets in a different capacity."

When Zach had rejoined the police force, just over two years ago, it hadn't taken him long to take on a more dangerous assignment. Walking patrol wasn't death-defying enough for him. When her brother Tony had told her he'd gone undercover, she'd been pissed but it hadn't been a surprise. She'd seen it as his driving need to return to the Helmond Province, where adrenaline fueled his life. The streets of Boston were no match for the black hell he'd lived through in the Middle East, an exterminator in the ratlines, the caves where the enemy hid. Until he'd found a way to embed himself with the low-life, put himself at risk of discovery, at risk of losing his life to the enemy. She shivered at the thought that he almost had.

Paul, who was on to another sampling, agreed.

"That's exactly what Zach said. He's not thrilled about the transfer. I hope he'll see that it's much more complicated and interesting than he thinks. Be willing to at least give it a fair shake."

Fiddling with the end of a dish towel, pretending indifference, Lana asked, "How long is he supposed to be off his feet?"

With fork half-way to his mouth, the spaghetti swirled around it in a caress, Paul said, "He should still be in the hospital. He signed himself out a couple of days early against doctor's orders. The concussion was severe. His internal injuries caused a loss of blood, which required a couple of transfusions. I'm not sure he shouldn't be at his folks house, with Jeanne looking after him."

Celia stole Paul's fork to sample the fare before disagreeing with her husband.

"I think he'll do better here. He called her while I was setting up the daybed, and although I think she argued with him, she must have given in."

They both looked up at Lana, but she pretended she didn't notice. Jeanne Taylor was not one of her biggest fans.

It was Paul who broke his concentration on Lana's expression first, agreeing with Celia's assessment.

"She knows he'll be well taken care of here, if you're around to do it. What's your schedule for the next few days?"

"An appointment this afternoon, a mercy meal on Friday, a wedding on Saturday. I'll stick around here, let Lana do the cooking. The staff and crew can pick up the rest. I'll make sure one of us is around to monitor him."

Lana interjected, "I accepted a staff meeting dinner order for tomorrow. And I hope you don't count me in as one of the us."

Celia shook her head, her glower directed at her daughter.

"We'll work it out."

Paul raised his eyes, part of the chocolate frosted brownie still to be eaten.

"Hope you're still thinking about opening a store front."

Lana was still humming with emotion but grateful that the conversation had shifted to a more neutral zone.

"I am. I just haven't found one yet that will work. Val's been checking some places out for me, but the prices are higher than I can afford."

"How is Val?"

"Great, and helpful as always."

Valeria was her brother-in-law Luca's sister. She'd become part of the family before the wedding and was the one assigned these kinds of things. She'd found a gallery for her sister, Rissa, and an artist enclave in Florence that Luca bought for their honeymoon.

It was just one big, happy Italian family. Almost like the Greek counterpart in the movie. The kids were coming fast and furious now, with another niece on the way. Johnny and Tish had added Dominic when Rosie turned two. Rissa and Luca had Jon Luc and Gabriella was arriving late next month. Dennis and Delaney had taken longer to get started but caught up quickly with twins Colin and Cora. Five kids and counting, kids she'd promised to protect as if they were her own. Babysitting duties weren't her thing, but family was family. When they called on her, she came through.

Maybe someday she'd have some of her own.

Or not.

The business had become her life.

Celia's Cookery had begun as a small-time catering enterprise when her mother wanted more from life than being a wife and mother. Celia's Italian cooking skills had been the impetus for the growing business, and Lana had gotten involved after her father's death, when she was only twelve. Her mother had been forced to take it from a form of personal expression to a business that could support her five children.

Lana had given up everything to help and then she'd given up everything to be a part of it.

Friends, fun, and family.

Not the big, rowdy family she belonged to but one of her own.

She'd gone out with someone for almost two years. When he got an internship in Pennsylvania, she had refused to go with him. It would have taken her away from the things she loved most, which told her he wasn't among them.

Almost everyone had been shocked, couldn't understand why she had turned him down. Her mother hadn't been surprised. Maybe because Celia was the one who'd noticed she never allowed Rafe to become part and parcel of the dynasty they were growing, never allowed him to fully merge himself with their lives. Lana had tried to convince them it was as much his decision as hers. It was Celia who had seen beneath the surface.

When she'd fallen for someone else, she'd included him in every phase of their lives, and he'd become embedded in the pulse of daily living. That her parents and siblings loved him as well had made it that much sweeter.

She hadn't gotten the happily ever after, though, as he'd dropped a bomb that shattered her dreams.

Now she was back to being alone. Most days it suited her just fine.

She had a new dream that she was counting on to fill the loneliness.

Celia untied her apron and turned it into a ball headed for the laundry.

"I'm sure Val will find you something. She's been successful so far."

Glancing up at the board where the day's events were listed, Lana concurred. "I know. It's just taking more time than I wanted."

Paul finished the sweet treat, took his suit coat from the back of the chair and shrugged his arms into it.

"I've got to get to the station. Some new information came in on the Brown case that I have to check out."

After kissing Celia goodbye, he winked at Lana asking, "Take it easy on him, okay?" before exiting the house, cooler in hand.

Celia was wiping her hands when she asked, "Do you think you could watch Zach for me for the next couple of hours?"

Lana's gaze flicked upwards.

"No. You're the one who offered. Where are you going? You mentioned an appointment. We don't have one scheduled."

"I promised Tish, I'd show her how to make cavatelli. I think she's ready."

Lana couldn't hold back the smile.

Her sister-in-law Tish had no prior training in the kitchen until she married Johnny. Over the last five years, Celia had been introducing her to the family secrets one dish at a time. It wasn't that Tish was a slow learner, just that her talents lay in another direction. A classical pianist, she spent most of her time practicing for her periodic concerts, the rest with her children and touring with her husband, who was the drummer in a popular rock band.

Petulantly, she gave in.

"Fine. I have a recipe I want to tweak so I'll do dubba duty. Give the kids a kiss for me."

Her mother slipped into her coat and left through the side door, leaving her alone with her thoughts.

Trying to ignore the man down the hall, she helped herself to the last dregs of coffee, sat down at the counter, and pulled the paper in front of her. It was soggy on the bottom from sitting on the front porch, but the top folded section was as dry as a bone.

The headlines still rattled her.

The image of his face in the flesh even more disturbing.

How could someone inflict that kind of pain on someone?

And sleep at night?

Taking a sip of the vanilla brew, she scanned the article, the reason for it becoming clear as she read on. With the spate of cop killings, the editors wanted to remind the public that police put themselves on the firing line every day to keep their communities safe. Zach had taken it for the city. In a brutal, vivid way.

As she read about his injuries, her eyes filled, but she brushed them off, refusing to feel bad for him.

He'd chosen this line of work.

Her eyes fluttered closed as she redefined her opinion.

Maybe there'd been no choice.

Maybe he'd been born into it, like her brother Tony.

Either way, he'd made the decision to protect and defend.

As she stared at the bruised face, wondering where the picture had come from, who had leaked it to the press, she also wondered who protected them, the men in blue?

Fellow cops?

The thin blue line?

Success wasn't a given.

She'd learned that the hard way, and she'd sworn more than once that was one line she wasn't crossing.

Gathering her wits, she pushed the paper aside and got busy, taking out the blender, opening the refrigerator to see what was on hand, tucking her hair behind her ears.

If he was here, she might as well feed him, although she knew it was probably a wasted effort.

He was one of those men who ate nothing but red meat and potatoes, French fries first choice, baked second. Neanderthal, all brawn, no brain, carnivore extraordinaire.

She should know.

She'd become chief cook and bottle washer when she'd made the colossal mistake of marrying him.

⌒

Zach eased himself down on the makeshift bed, yanked his shoes off and stretched out gingerly.

Every muscle in his body ached.

The reality of what had almost happened had hit him as he was being tended to by the doctors at Mass General.

He'd been pretty much out of it on transport, unconscious, bleeding, broken, but he'd woken to mind-bending pain that shouted out loud and clear that he'd almost been killed.

He didn't know why the thugs had left him semi-alive.

Not particularly grateful, either, until the pain had been removed with large doses of drugs.

He had taken himself off them completely yesterday morning, when he'd decided he didn't like the hospital, the zoned-out feeling, the ambiance of his surroundings. He'd called his new partner early this morning and signed himself out, although he wasn't sure whether it was one of his brightest moves.

At least his mother wasn't here.

She would have been determined to keep him in bed, medicated and subdued.

Her tears at his bedside had almost weakened his will, but then she'd gotten up, kissed him, tucked him in, held his hand just like she had when he'd been five.

He wasn't five anymore.

And he was not going to let this keep him from his job.

His new job.

The one he didn't want.

The one his father insisted on.

George Taylor had been standing next to his bedside when he woke up from surgery. And didn't waste any time reassigning him.

Your cover's been blown. I've talked to Paul Catalano, and he's agreed to take you on as his partner in Homicide. You've got the shield. You're going to use it.

He'd gotten his shield a year after he joined the force right out of college, wanting to rise in the ranks as quickly as he could. Those plans had gotten put on hold when his father made superintendent. Not wanting to work in his shadow, he'd enlisted in the Marines. Now that he was back on the force, he was determined to resolve the issues that still rankled.

Woozy from the after-effects of the anesthesia, he couldn't argue effectively until later that night when his father returned.

"I'll be bored out of my mind in Homicide."

"Trust me, it's not boring. Even if it was, tough shit. It will keep you alive."

"I'm not interested. I'll transfer. Move. I love what I'm doing."

His father had dropped into the chair beside his bed, looking almost defeated.

They had never had a close relationship, so this was something new. He'd almost looked concerned.

His father was out, patrolling the streets, moving up the ranks, most of his life, and he was part of a generation that held back emotion and was piss-poor at nurturing, George had stressed high standards and good manners and imparted words of wisdom like, "Suck it up. You're a man."

That had served him well in the Marines in Iraq and Afghanistan, served him while in rehab for his war wounds, and it would serve him well now.

"I know you love it, son. But you take risks that are not prudent. We almost lost you. Again. Will you just give this a chance? For now? If you're determined to go back undercover, we'll revisit this conversation in, say, six months, when you're completely healed."

His head had pounded, the nausea all-consuming and he wasn't in the right frame of mind for an all-out argument.

He had acquiesced, extracting a promise that they would discuss it further in a few months.

He still had a long way to go.

It had only been a week since the attack.

He thought he'd infiltrated the theft ring successfully and had been planted for close to nine months. All the time invested, was now wasted and he wondered who'd be next in line for the assignment. He didn't like it when he didn't get the bad guys.

Hated it more when the bad guys got him.

It was a doorway to hell.

A concussion, dislocated shoulder, internal injuries, a hairline break in his jaw, a few broken ribs, deep tissue bruises in his leg and back.

And he could feel every single one of their punches and kicks.

They had pretty much covered every part of his anatomy, but it could have been worse.

He'd been found in an alley by a homeless man who had the decency to flag down a police car, at risk to himself.

At least that's what he remembered.

From the report, the guy had stopped the cruiser, pointed to the narrow alleyway and then disappeared.

There were good people in the world.

He'd like to find him to thank him.

He let his eyes flutter closed.

Maybe next week, when he felt better.

CHAPTER FOUR

He came awake the instant he felt a presence in the room.

His gut never failed him when danger was near, and he instinctively roused himself.

The pain shot through him, and he collapsed back onto the bed, swearing under his breath.

Lana was there, tossing her hair off her face with a flick of her head as she moved into the room.

"Good to know I'd win a standoff."

He arched his brow and gave her an annoyed look.

"Not one of my better days.

"You're safe here, macho man."

He lifted his head an inch or two to see her carrying a glass of green shit.

"Are you sure? That looks like the poison you promised."

"That comes only if someone gets hurt because of your macho-ness. Someone other than you."

Clenching his teeth, he winced at the pain. He pushed the words out, trying to ignore it.

"I couldn't hurt a fly right now."

Baiting him, she said, "I have a feeling, if it was life or death, you'd somehow conjure up your magic powers and give it a go."

He dropped his head back onto the pillow, the ache in his jaw telling him to shut it.

She smiled at her win and advanced toward the bed.

"This is my witch's brew. Lots of vitamins, minerals, those healthy things you want no part of. They build bone and muscle."

"I have both."

"I remember but some of those bones are fractured and some of the muscle is crap."

"I'll give you the bones, but my muscles aren't crap."

"I could arm-wrestle you and win, Underdog. Which tells me that they are crap."

He had to give her that, too. He stuck the glass under his nose and sniffed. "What's in it, exactly?"

"I don't give away my recipes. If I did, I'd have to kill you."

He said smoothly, "As you can see more experienced people have tried and failed."

Her lips thinned, and he knew that point was his.

"Like I said. I'd go the poison route. It's fairly effective and doesn't take so much brawn."

Still eyeing the glass suspiciously, he thought he'd gag if he attempted it, but she wasn't going to let him by-pass this part of the operation.

"I expect you to drink it all down, like the not-so-good boy you are. I know you can grit it out."

"I am not—"

"Oh, but you are or you're heading home to Mommy."

"You can't—"

"I already got the go-ahead from both Paul and Celia."

He doubted that, but he wasn't going to let her get the better of him. He maneuvered to a sitting position, took the straw, and drew in a small sip.

He all but glared at her, testing to see if she was going to cave.

She wasn't.

"That's a start but I'm not waiting all day for you to finish it. Now drink."

It didn't taste half bad, but he wasn't going to give her the satisfaction of telling her that. He glanced up to see her standing, arms akimbo, a slight resemblance to Celia emerging, eyes a similar whiskey color, same profile but a few inches taller than Celia's five-foot- three-inch frame. With some hidden curvy assets. Her lips were full, but they were pressed into a thin line. Her booted foot was tapping. Dark hair was streaked with light blue and purple highlights, a chin-length bob that framed her face well. She could have been one of his informants, dressed in a pair of ripped jeans and a zip-up sweatshirt.

The booted foot began to tap faster.

Her patience seemed to have as short a fuse as his.

He leaned forward but then retreated, as if he couldn't take the plunge.

"If you could just change the color...it might be more appealing."

"Kale only comes in green. Otherwise, it would be genetically modified, and I don't use those kinds of ingredients."

"Kale? Maybe I shouldn't have asked what's in it."

"People pay good money for one of my smoothies. Feel privileged you're getting it free of charge."

"People pay for this?"

"Amazing, isn't it? There's smart and then there's...you."

The thought of drinking down something so vile looking brought the nausea back but he knew Lana didn't back down.

Putting the straw back between his teeth, he drank it all, slurping the bottom so she'd know he was done.

Wiping his hand across his mouth, he said, "Okay?"

"Yup. You get to stay another day."

He dropped back onto the pillow, the exertion of merely drinking from a straw wearing him out. He closed his eyes, giving her permission to leave.

She didn't want him here. It was obvious. He thought maybe...if she saw him...she'd...Shit, he should have known better. She'd made it quite clear, when he'd announced his decision to go back to patrol, that she wouldn't share her life with a policeman. And that's what he was down to the soles of his feet. It meant they'd never be able to resolve their differences. It's what had made him walk away without a backward glance. She was a stubborn woman and that sentiment seemed to be etched in stone. She'd moved on with her life.

It might be time for him to do it, as well, resign himself to the inevitable. And if he could forget what they'd had together, about the home they'd created, the love they'd made, maybe there'd be a chance of it happening. But he couldn't. He missed coming home to her, thoroughly enjoyed that aspect of a co-joined life. The other perk? Sleeping with a woman who set him on fire. It had only lasted a few short months, but he'd missed it every day since she demanded he leave. He'd had nothing but the job since and nothing he did, short of quitting, would bring her back.

He closed his eyes to banish her image, but she still lived in his cells.

He'd gone underground to escape her. It had been a fruitless endeavor.

He opened his eyes to see her still here, staring at him. She blushed when he caught her at it and when she swirled around to leave, he forced out a thank you.

"Um, the slime wasn't half-bad."

"Gee, thanks. Could you email that to my website? I never turn down a glowing review."

⌐

Lana walked away, her heart thumping in her chest, leaned against the wall outside his room and tried to breathe. She'd almost...crawled into bed with him. What the hell was she thinking?

Thinking had nothing to do with it. It was pure feeling that had her ready to jump back into the fire. Seeing him lying in bed, hurt and broken, pushed every button, anger, fear, love, pain and the overload had almost caused a meltdown of significant proportions.

No way was she going to get caught in that volcanic eruption again. Hadn't she learned anything? Being so close had risks, and she'd taken a big one by standing at his bedside. Why couldn't he have stayed at his parents'? She would have been able to pretend he meant nothing to her. With him here, she was being forced to admit...

Walking back to the kitchen, her palms sweaty, her breathing labored, she tried to push away the picture of him lying there. Of the brutal beating...

It should be a stark reminder of why she'd walked away. Instead, it was a like a twisted fishhook had snagged her and she was being reeled in.

She made her way to the kitchen, all but ripped an apron from the drawer, and tied it on. Her head snapped in several different directions almost at once, as if to familiarize herself with a room she knew like the back of her hand. How could he still have this kind of effect on her that she forgot where she was, who she was? The daughter of a policeman shot in the line of duty. Did she have to conjure up the grief, relive the sensation to keep Zach at arm's length? It had been one of the worst days of her life.

When the tears came, she squeezed her eyes shut, forced them back by digging her palms into them.

She had been home that Friday afternoon, rolling the tiny meatballs for the Italian wedding soup her mother was making for Sunday dinner. It was a staple, at least through the cold winter, a dish that could warm the bones, and the whole family loved it.

The doorbell sounded, and her mother had gone to answer it. The ungodly howl sent Lana running out to the doorway to see what had happened. As soon as she saw Captain Detective George Taylor, hat in hand, tears in his eyes, standing there beside a friend of Sal's from the patrolmen's association, her heart had seized. She'd known what it meant.

With trembling lips George had begun, "I'm sorry to inform you Celia that Sal was killed..."

Before he could finish his sentence, he'd jerked forward to catch her mother before she collapsed.

She could hear the scream, hysterical crying, a horrible retching sound, and as soon as she'd felt her mother's arms go around her, she'd known it had come from her own misery and grief.

They'd sunk to the floor together, mother consoling daughter, both sobbing, one pleading over and over again for it not to be true.

The pitiful sound had flung itself off the walls surrounding them. Her mother had offered soft words, comforting her daughter as her own world was skidding to a halt.

"It will be all right, my *capretta*. I am so sorry you were here for this."

"He can't be dead, Ma. He can't be. This is a mistake. I know it is."

Brushing her hair off her face, Celia had explained with gentle calm, "George would not be here unless it was true."

Celia had pulled her off the floor, her arm tight around her. She could feel George's shadow behind them as he followed them into the kitchen.

"Can I call someone for you?" he asked.

Lana could feel her mother's limbs shaking, but Celia had quickly gotten herself under control and told George, "I'll call my sister. She'll let everyone else know. We won't be alone for long."

She could do nothing but stand and stare, numb, her world shattered, her life forever changed.

She'd heard her mother's raspy voice ask, "How?"

Lana had noticed George's hesitation, surmised that they didn't usually give out details, but this was one of their own.

"Domestic dispute gone bad. The husband had a gun, was ready and waiting for them."

"And?"

George paused again before the telling.

"When the guy opened the door, he shot. Paul saw what was happening and pushed Sal out of the way, taking it in the chest. When he went down, he fired off a round. It knocked the guy off his feet, but not before he aimed at Sal...to kill. I'm so sorry Celia."

Celia's face was in her hands. The crying had begun but without the hysterics that were running rampant in Lana's own brain.

Her mother had looked up and asked, as if just remembering, "And Paul? How's he?"

"I don't know. He's in surgery. That's my next stop."

⌒

She didn't know how her mother had functioned after that because she hadn't let her go, hanging on her arm, following her every move until almost an hour later, the house was filled with family. Her brother Johnny had been summoned home, and she was his responsibility until the day of the funeral when he had stood beside his mother, holding Celia up as they went through the ritual of burial.

Tony was the one who'd held her hand in a death grip, the two youngest holding each other together. They would all be scarred in some way, some worse than the rest.

Her worse than all of them.

⌒

When Zach awoke again, the sun was no longer streaming through the curtains, and he wondered how long he'd slept. The scent of something good wafted down the hall and into the room. His stomach growled. He hadn't really eaten anything in days. He'd been on intravenous fluids for the first forty-eight hours, liquids and Jell-O after that, and the smoothie earlier hadn't filled his belly. He hungered for a thick steak and a baked potato. He had a feeling that wasn't what he was getting for supper but...the aroma wasn't unappealing, and his taste buds were beginning to come alive.

Was Lana coming back to feed him again? He geared up for another round of their banter and smiled.

The air lost all expectancy as Celia arrived with a bowl of chicken soup with tiny meatballs, rice and vegetables floating in broth.

Celia set the tray down on the bureau and went back to help him sit up, fluffing the pillows behind him to give him more support.

He gritted his teeth. He didn't like needing help.

Celia must have noticed the tensing of his shoulders because she said, "Keeping the coddling to a minimum, honest."

He blew out a breath. He knew Celia wouldn't try to suffocate him. This was what help looked like and he'd take it.

"Thanks. I appreciate it."

"How are you feeling?"

"Like I've been run over by a train."

She retrieved the tray and settled the legs on both sides of his body. He shimmied to a sitting position, and peered at the liquid

Celia offered, "This should be fairly easy to swallow. All soft without being mushy."

"If I can open up enough to get it in."

"Slurp. I won't complain."

Taking the spoon in the working hand, the one minus the sling, he awkwardly brought it up to his mouth, spilling the liquid onto the napkin strategically placed on his chest. He tried again. This time some of the liquid slid down his throat.

She sat down on the edge of the bed and watched while he ate.

"What happened, Zach?"

Zach closed his eyes, the scene returning, the image stark. He had been along for a pawn shop run. Routine for the band of thieves he was running with. He'd thought he had enough evidence for an arrest, and he'd suggested they take them down that day, but the higher-ups wanted another week to work out the details, possibly get someone higher up on the food chain. Maybe if they'd gone with his suggestion he'd still be out on the streets and in good condition.

He began to give Celia the play-by-play.

"We were driving in a beat-up old van, one I'd never seen before, TVs, computers, all kinds of stuff in the back that the guys planned to pawn, making deliveries. Come to find out, the plates on the van were stolen, which alerted the police. A cruiser signaled us to pull over. The driver and the guy in charge of the operation started arguing about what to do. IQ of about thirty between the two of them."

Taking a breather, his jaw beginning to ache, he had to push the words out.

"They were yelling at each other. All hell was breaking loose, then the driver sped ahead, the police car right on his tail. I could hear sirens in the distance, and I knew it was just a matter of time before they caught us. The moron in the back must have figured that out, too, because he pulled out a gun, opened the back door and aimed it at the cruiser."

He had held his breath, hoping the guy wasn't that much of an idiot. He should have known better.

"After the first shot was fired, I had a decision to make. Hope he missed or...take him out. When the second shot shattered the windshield and the cop kept on coming, several more sirens blaring from every other direction, the decision was an easy one. I jumped in the back and disarmed him. Told him I wasn't going to get arrested for a cop killing. I thought it sounded convincing."

"But they didn't buy it?"

"Seems not. Even though I was arrested along with them when the van was surrounded by police and finally pulled over. The next night I showed up where we hung out. One of the women told me to leave, so I did. Three goons were waiting for me outside."

He was still trying to figure out what had given him away. Maybe it was simply the bad guys knowing the way a cop moved, held his gun, alert and ready for a take down.

He attempted another smile, a wave of pain shooting along his jaw his reward.

"One of the women had been coming on to me. Thought she liked me, was giving me a warning. I was wrong. She set me up. Should have known better. The saying *thick as thieves* is a literal one."

"I bet that doesn't happen often."

Meeting familiar brown eyes, the crease suggesting age rather than youth, he responded, "I can't afford to let it happen often."

"But you're willing to go back...to that?"

"Like I told Lana. It's what I do."

It hadn't been the first time he'd said those words. They would always be a bone of contention between them.

Celia had been connected to the job for close to thirty-five years and seemed to accept the risks involved, seemed more appreciative of his efforts than her daughter but he was getting the impression that even she thought he might be tilting towards the side of foolish.

"And from what I hear, you do it well. But it's hazardous Zach. Isn't it time to get out of the danger zone or are you the adrenaline junkie Lana thinks you are?"

It was the war stories he hadn't shared with his family that might have proven that point. He should never have shared them with Lana. It had only hurt his cause.

"That was satisfied in Afghanistan."

She studied him cautiously before stating the obvious.

"It must be hard being the son of the superintendent."

"It's hard being the son of one of the best. I'll never live up to his reputation."

"Unless you take on the jobs that no one else wants."

His eyes shot up to meet hers. She was the first one who'd guessed part of the truth. He attempted another swallow and then put the spoon down, rubbed his forehead.

"The Taylors get better every generation. What does that leave me?"

"Your great-grandfather was killed on the job. That's not the road you want to take, is it? He left behind a family who missed him."

The first George Taylor had joined the police force after surviving the Spring Offensive at Belleau Wood during World War I, one of the most famous battles in American military history. The Marines had fought so fiercely they earned the nickname Devil Dogs, and as a member of the gritty fighting force, George was awarded the Medal of Honor for valor. Seemed he was safer on the war front than on the streets of Boston, because he was ambushed in an alley and gunned down by the suspects in a liquor store heist years later. He was thirty-nine years old and left behind a wife and three children, two of whom followed in his footsteps as Boston cops, one of whom was Zach's grandfather Thomas. He'd won the Medal of Valor for his bravery in dealing with the Irish mob. Zach's father was the current superintendent. The reputations that preceded him were tough to live up to.

"Unfortunately, some die in the line of duty. You already know that. Sal was one of them.

Celia patted his hand.

"Just wearing the badge seems risk enough to lose your life. You shouldn't go looking for it."

He leaned his head back, tired from spooning warm liquid into his mouth. Tired from the lectures he'd been getting about his undercover work.

Maybe it was time for a change.

Celia offered, "Paul's looking forward to working with you."

He was beginning to think that he might be looking forward to it, too. If only for a little while. It might be a good break from the grind of working alone. And it would get him out on the streets faster than going back to a beat.

"I'll give it a couple of more days before I ride with him."

"It should be longer than that."

"Can't just lie here."

He'd go out of his ever-loving mind. He was not used to being idle, no matter what his condition.

Hesitating she gave in. "I'll let you determine your timetable. But please don't force it."

His eyes fluttered closed, the need to sleep again too strong to fight.

"I won't, ma'am."

He didn't even flinch when Celia took the tray, with the half-eaten food, and disappeared.

CHAPTER FIVE

He sat staring into the distance, his mind frozen in another time and place.

Memories.

Not the good kind.

Holding his ground, his riflescope zeroing in on his target.

Gunfire exploding around him.

One of his friends dead beside him.

The rest of his unit pinned down awaiting rescue.

The ping of bullets off rock, the shards penetrating the skin on his face, one of the few areas exposed to wind, rain, and shrapnel.

A sniper shot felling an adversary, one, two, three, like ducks in a row at a carnival.

How many killed?

He'd lost count.

Then there was a shift in surroundings.

He heard the voice beneath the surface. It was one he knew well, missed with increasing futility.

"Zach, Zach." He was awake but zoned. She knew the difference.

Lana was sitting at the edge of the thin mattress, taking his limp hand by his side into hers.

The blurred image in front of him was in duplicate. His eyes fluttered shut, his brow creased.

"Yeah."

He squeezed the hand holding his, in tune with the drumming in his temple.

Gentleness creeped into her tone, something he hadn't thought possible anymore.

"I would think you'd be over them by now?"

He could feel the sweat on his brow but didn't want to let go of Lana's hand to wipe it.

"They don't come as often. The attack rebooted them."

He felt her fingers brushing away the moisture, the touch igniting a hunger that couldn't be quenched.

He opened his eyes, caught her penetrating stare as she wiped her hand on her pants.

"I guess I can understand that."

Pissed that those bastards had given Lana another reason to push him away, he disagreed just because—

"I can't. Nothing similar about them at all. In one I'm on the winning side, in the other, biggest loser."

Biting at her lips, her concerned expression telling, she stated, "You can't keep doing this to yourself."

He lowered his voice, all but begging her to understand.

"Lana, this wasn't supposed to happen. I didn't get careless. There was a cop's life at stake."

She was scrubbing her face, pushing her hair back. Her tired eyes had lost their luster. It appeared she was sleeping no better than he was. It also seemed she'd run out of patient understanding.

"You did it knowing it might blow your cover. Why do you always have to play the hero?"

Resigned that she'd always see him that way, knowing it wouldn't do any good, he countered, "I wasn't playing at anything. Trust me."

"There's something wrong with you Zach. A psychological disorder."

He shifted, wincing as he slid into a sitting position. Lying on his back was not going to advance his cause.

"I didn't know you had a shingle up."

"A couple of us were in therapy for a while, remember? You need it."

"You had nightmares? You never told me."

"No. Tony had them. I was forced to go because my mother worried that I...grew up too fast. She thought I became too serious."

"You were twelve."

He remembered the wake and the funeral. He was a senior in high school, had been in class with Johnny when he was called home. Found out from his parents after school. It wasn't until he was at the burial site, Sal's casket being lowered into the ground, that he'd believed it. Sal had been a big man, full of life. And then he wasn't. It had unsettled them all. He'd watched every member of the Scalera family that day, to measure how they were handling it. Celia was holding it together, but barely. Johnny had stood by her side. Dennis had his arm around Rissa, her head buried in his shoulder, his expression solemn. Lana and Tony had held hands, hanging on to each other as if their life depended on it. It was a horrible day, made less traumatic because of the strong friendships fostered over the years, the men and women in blue taking care of their own.

"It was tough."

"Any age is a tough one to lose your father."

He could still picture Sal holding her when she was a kid, her dresses frilly, her hair long and fine, the smile beatific, noticed because she looked so small embraced by her father's thick, beefy arms.

"You were his princess."

"According to the rest of my family."

"The baby."

"And then I wasn't a baby anymore."

Her eyes were boring into him, reminding him of what she'd told him the last day they were together. Sal's death had changed her, and she wouldn't spend her time with someone who could succumb to the same fate.

His voice had lost its steely edge and was so low she almost didn't hear him. "For as much as we knew about each other, we didn't know anything at all."

Staring out the window into the darkness of night, she agreed.

"Not the important things. It might have changed the outcome if we'd been more honest with each other. Problem is, I thought I was."

He pressed her fingers into his closed fist, and when she looked back at him, he asked, "The outcome would have been the same either way, wouldn't it? We wouldn't be together."

"We could have saved ourselves some pain." Her voice sounded wistful.

"Do you really believe we would have felt the loss less deeply? I think we would have felt that either way. At least—"

"Zach, it's in the past. Let's leave it there, please."

He let out a long, audible breath and laid his head back against the pillows, wishing he could do what she asked. He'd been trying for years but he'd never gotten there.

As much as he understood her fear, his own great-grandfather dying on the job, in the same kind of alley where he'd skirted death, his family had always accepted that death might be out there waiting. The job had been part of his family heritage, and they understood the sacrifices, understood the calling.

Lana's life was enmeshed, as well, but from a different perspective.

Needing to understand, he asked, "How do you deal with Paul...and Tony?"

"I don't have any say in what they've chosen. I just have to live with it." There was a bitter edge to her tone.

He continued to pursue her.

"You seem able to love them well enough."

"I do. They're good men but..."

"Cops." he said in a grudging voice.

She swallowed hard and met his eyes in a defiant way.

"Yeah."

"Do you think I'm going to get Paul killed?"

Her shoulders slumped as if a heavy weight had settled there. The truth didn't make it any lighter.

"It's not him I'm worried about."

He felt a small victory with her admission.

He let her fingers go, touched her cheek, brushed along her jaw.

"You still worry about me?"

He liked that she seemed agitated with the question but was unsure as to whether she'd answer it. He was surprised when she did, more surprised by what she said.

"Of course, I do. Just because I don't know where the hell you are half the time, or what the hell you're doing doesn't mean I don't..."

Grimacing, he shifted higher and whispered, "So, what difference would it make if we lived together? You'd at least know where I was nights."

He saw the slightest tilt in his direction, as if her body instinctively sought his out, but then she countered it with purpose. She was still fighting for self-preservation.

"I'm able to shut it out at times. I wouldn't be able to do that if I lived with it twenty-four-seven."

Her hand was back in his. His thumb was brushing her fingers, telling her something she didn't want to know.

"I wish it were that easy for me."

Snatching her hand away, as if the intimacy of the touch was too much for her conflicting emotions, she said, "Please. You were the one who chose this."

She always put their stalemate on him, but it had taken the two of them to get here.

"You're blaming me for what you feel? That's mighty childish."

Her cheeks flushed; her eyes blazed at him.

"You knew how I felt."

He replied sharply, "I thought you loved me enough to work through it."

Her nostrils flared in fury.

"And I thought you loved me enough to do something else with your life."

They were resurrecting an earlier argument that had gone in a similar vein. Nothing had changed.

His eyes met hers and he felt the heat of her gaze. But it wasn't the kind of heat he wanted from her.

"Looks like we're at a stand-off." Shaking his head at her, he complained, "No one wins."

Squeezing her eyes shut, she said in resignation, "I don't lose."

Taking her hand again, his voice scratched out, "I think we both did."

With a pinched expression, she reminded him, "You've still got your precious job. That's what you wanted."

Was it?

He wasn't sure at times.

But he also didn't know who he was if it wasn't a cop.

He'd tried his hand at the military, but he was on foreign soil, protecting the world when all he wanted was to be at home, protecting the innocent.

He still had to figure out how to do that without feeling insufficient for the job.

"I wanted a life with you, doing what I was put here to do. Was that asking too much?"

"Yes. You were asking me to live with a fear I've spent most of my life trying to overcome. I couldn't do it. I'm sorry."

He noticed the glassy sheen in her beautiful eyes, and he wished with all his heart he could give her what she wanted.

Instead, he gave her a promise of another kind.

"You don't have to worry about Paul. I'll have his back while I'm with him."

She gripped his hand.

"I know that. You'd put your life on the line for anyone. That's who you are. It's just not something I can live with."

They were at another standoff.

As if she was convincing herself rather than him, she stated, "Homicide's different. You have police doing your dirty work. They're the ones who will make the arrests once you've targeted your perp. You'd really have to go out of your way to get either of you killed."

She heard Paul's words coming out of her mouth. She only wished she believed them.

His voice was hoarse, his words forced out through a clenched jaw.

"Yeah, it's all paperwork, knocking on doors, canvassing, sitting on my ass waiting. Not my idea of exciting."

Her voice filled with contempt.

"God forbid you use your brains instead of your body."

His eyes were blazing at her now, his voice filled with animosity.

"You don't think it takes brains to go undercover?"

She gave him a hostile glare.

"I think it takes the scrambled kind. Less analytical, more fly-by-the-seat-of-your-pants."

He was going to argue with her, but it was pointless. Her mind was already made up about him, and what difference did it really make, anyway?

His voice was heavy with weariness when he asked, "Another topic please. How's the catering business?"

He was stroking the inside of her palm with his thumb, and she pulled at it again. He stilled his thumb, but his fingers hung on.

"What do you want to know?"

Trying to lighten the mood, he teased, "Do you make anything a different color or does every dish scream green?"

He noticed her shoulders relax, some of the tension draining away.

"All the colors of the rainbow. Knowing you have an aversion to all things green, I'm making it my mission to give you nothing but."

"Is this what I have to look forward to for the next week?"

"You can always go home to your mother."

"It's tempting but that's not my home and I won't ever recuperate there again."

"You don't have a home. Doesn't that tell you anything?"

"I have a place but I'm renting it out. I wasn't going to be there...Fuck, what difference does it make?"

He'd never thought of his condo as home, anyway. She was.

He held her eyes for a moment and noticed a change in her pupils.

When she pulled her hand out of his, he asked, not wanting her to go, "What's on your agenda for the day?"

"Sleep, then I'm meeting with some potential clients at nine and eleven a.m., both for weddings. I've got a teacher's staff meeting early tomorrow evening that I need to prep for. In the afternoon, I've got to be at the Boys & Girls Club at two p.m. for a lesson in nutrition, several twenty-minute sessions with a bunch of sixth and seventh graders."

"Boys & Girls Club. That's in a run-down area, isn't it?"

"Yeah. It's the inner city, you know, where the kids need a place to go to keep them off the streets."

"How often are you there?"

"Twice a week. Tuesdays and Thursdays. It's getting hard to schedule appointments around it, but I like working with the kids too much to quit."

"What kinds of things do you teach them?"

Her face glowed with the telling, giving him the impression that she really did enjoy it.

"How to read ingredients on a food label, what kinds of foods are good for you, and we prepare something easy in the kitchen there. I teach them how to eat healthy."

"Maybe I can attend one of those. See what to avoid."

"I think you're already well informed in that area. I'm sure nothing's changed."

"Guilty as charged."

The stifled yawn was an obvious indication she was tired, so he decided to let her go.

"I'm fine now. Get some sleep. I thought your day would consist of finding ways to incorporate green into my food."

"If only."

"Lana."

She was already at the doorway, but she turned when he'd called out her name.

"Thanks for checking on me. I appreciate it."

She bit her lip before she smiled weakly and disappeared.

⌒

When she'd left, he stared out of the open doorway.

He had to admit he enjoyed their repartee although it wasn't always pleasant anymore. Her tongue had become as sharp as her knives, and it was as cutting. Tonight, it took his mind off the residual pain in his chest, the headache that still plagued him, the shadows that still lurked.

Some might think she was a tough cookie.

No empathy, no sympathy, just cool and calm. He'd been told her heart was in a Deep-freeze.

But he knew that she was anything but.

His days as an undercover cop had taught him to read beneath the surface of things, read between the lines. That he knew her only added to the depth of awareness. All her antagonism meant she was still trying to detach herself from her feelings about him, refused to admit what they had was too good to throw away.

She thought she concealed her worry...but it was there in the furrowed brow, in her whiskey-colored eyes. The problem had to do with her fears. They were still too strong to overcome. She was afraid to put herself at risk. That she thought he was careless only added to it. Truth was, he was far from that. Every move was calculated, every word was spoken with care, and he was always alert to his surroundings. Immersed in constant deception, simulating the look of a junkie, hanging out in seedy bars, fending off sexual advances. It was difficult to remember who you were.

He'd worked hard to make sure that didn't happen, connected to reality when he could. Consistently boxed at a ring almost an hour away, grabbed a beer with one of his close friends in the suburbs, had the occasional lunch with his mother, took a couple of days here and there to recoup his energy and grab some normalcy.

His supervisors didn't usually force him to stick with something he knew wouldn't work. Something some of the undercover cops in other precincts had to worry about. He knew a couple of guys who'd turned into real druggies, who wanted to quit but were told to stick it out.

He wouldn't have let it get that far.

Or had he already done that?

Maybe it was time to get out for a while.

Now it was more than just a stress-filled life. It had gotten physically hazardous to his health.

He didn't have a death wish.

He just wanted to clean up the streets.

The drug dealers, the theft rings, the pimps.

Maybe he could clean up the streets in another way.

Get murderers instead.

Working with Paul might be the antidote to what his life had become.

He could give it six months. If it didn't suit, then he'd think of an alternative.

Maybe it was time to come out from behind the shadow of his ancestors and the underbelly of crime, live an authentic life. It might be time to rejoin humanity and to fight for what was important to him.

He'd have to learn to be satisfied with just being good at his job, without having to live up to being something better than what came before. If he could win Lana back, it might not even matter anymore.

Sleep didn't come right away. Instead, he lay awake staring at the wall, reliving the hell of war, over and over, retracing the thousands of steps across dry ground scattered with incendiaries that could blow men into smithereens.

It was better than living in the hell his life had become without her.

CHAPTER SIX

Lana arrived home later than she'd planned. Stopping in to check on Zach had been a mistake. He was zoning again, wide awake but back in the desert, firing, shooting in his own killing fields. When he'd first come back from war, injured, spending weeks in the hospital as his leg and foot were put back together, she'd sit with him, and he'd talk. Stream of consciousness at times, fleeting thoughts, images shared. Then he'd sleep but not sleep, flashbacks coming in the night to disrupt, dismay. Just when she'd nod off herself, she'd be interrupted by groans, yells, orders. She knew the reason. He'd shared so much of his military life with her over the years, the ups, the downs, the deaths, the victories, that it was as if she'd lived them right along with him.

Then he'd been released from the hospital, had gone to his parents' house, months of rehabilitation ahead of him.

Recovery duties were taken on by his mother, but he'd hated the way Jeanne had treated him, so he'd insist she come and pick him up, take him to rehab, get him away from the suffocation of his mother's presence. And she had.

And they'd grown even closer, the foundation built through their correspondence getting stronger and more solid.

She had glimpsed a future in his deep blue eyes.

He'd been the only man who had gotten in, gotten through her fears of attachment. The letters they'd written each other had been a way to communicate without filters. She had felt safe and allowed herself to become vulnerable, sharing her thoughts and emotions freely, without her usual reticence. He had slipped beneath her defenses, like vapor under a vaulted door, seeping in without warning.

And she'd been captive, falling more deeply in love with him with each rehabilitation session, the grit and determination, the courage, the heart so apparent in the way he fought back to health, she couldn't help herself. His goal had been foremost in his mind. A goal she'd never asked about, a goal that was hidden by the liabilities and frustrations of his recuperation.

When he'd proposed, she'd agreed. It had been a moment of weakness on her part. She'd thought she knew all she needed to make that decision. He was alive, had come home to her, and she loved him.

The ceremony had been small, held in the Taylors' backyard, the summer flowers in full August bloom. His full recovery was in the not-too-distant future. The months that followed were some of the happiest moments in her life, her gratitude that he was alive and hers fully expressed at night in his arms. He was her everything and she'd trusted that it would always stay that way. They ushered in the New Year with more in-depth plans, the kiss at the stroke of midnight filled with sparks and fire. Her birthday, the next day, was filled with family, who had welcomed Zach in with the kind of love reserved for their small but growing intimate group. They'd enjoyed cake, ice cream, jokes and laughter. The gift basket Zach had presented her with was filled with delectable kitchen items ordered on-line and it convinced her that he knew her well. She was blissfully happy.

Then the bombshell, right after dinner the following day.

His goal all along had been reinstatement to the Boston Police Department.

She'd felt a punch to the solar plexus, like the one she'd felt the day her father died. Numb, disbelieving, and confused, she'd forced him out of her life. Waiting for the phone to ring, telling her he'd changed his mind, had been delusional thinking on her part.

He still hadn't come to his senses, and he was still choosing the job over them.

And like before, she immersed herself in work, the hole inside an ache that she was beginning to think would never be healed.

Maybe it was time to stop pretending it would.

The alarm beside her bed went off, rousing Lana from her uncensored dreams.

Sitting with Zach last night had brought it all back in a torrent of emotion, and sleep had been elusive. A few hours of unsettled slumber weren't enough for the day ahead, but it would have to do.

She could be pissed at herself for giving in to the need to see him, pissed at Zach for being who he was, pissed that the pull was as strong as ever.

When he had taken her hand, as if she was still his anchor…

Don't go there.

Shaking her hands to get rid of the prickling feeling, she crawled out of bed, clicked on the coffee maker, and headed for the shower. With only five hundred square feet of living space, she didn't have far to go.

Her condo was small, not much bigger than a studio, but it was hers. She wished she'd had more confidence in her future earnings. She would have bought bigger. She'd had no idea that Celia's Cookery would expand to what it had become, although she'd had to bring Celia along kicking and screaming. Once the grandkids started coming, Celia had wanted to spend less time at work, not more, so Lana had taken on all phases of the new enterprise. Over the last few years, she'd hired numerous staff, servers, and set-up crews, cutting her role down to one, that of chef. But it was her mother's cooking skills that had earned them the stellar reputation and was the business's trademark, although great customer service had always been a priority. Her mother let her attend the initial customer meeting, to go over the food options available, allowed her to tweak as needed. It was one of the ways she could put her own stamp on something that wasn't entirely hers.

The first meeting today was at the home of a bride and her mother, the site of the wedding that was four months away. April was a tricky month for garden nuptials, New England weather being so unpredictable, so she had to have several plans of actions to cover any eventuality. Sylvia, her-right-hand woman, was accompanying her, being assigned the go-to person for the event, who'd see to every detail of the meal. Sylvia had been with the company for a little over two years and was taking on more responsibility as Celia took on less, and she didn't mind working Sundays. It meant one less day of child-care with her husband at home to look after the kids.

Sunday was the one day Lana took a few hours off. They were devoted to the family dinner table, where the Scaleras would gather, something that had become a weekly staple in a life with too few personal connections.

⌒

After slipping into a loose turtleneck dress, her matching black boots perfect for the crisp winter day, she applied her make-up, blow-dried her hair, and sat down for her first cup of coffee for the morning. She'd need a lot of it today. She was tired and had a full schedule. At least she could come home later and throw on some jeans for her work with the kids at the center. They were making trail mix and she had picked up the ingredients yesterday after making the soup for her mother's houseguest. She made sure to get the types of food the families could afford. Always sending home the recipe, knowing some of the parents could barely afford the basic necessities like bread and milk, she included affordable staples like Cheerios, Cheez-Its, raisins or cranberries, pretzels, mini-marshmallows, and pumpkin seeds.

She smiled as she remembered her first class with the ten-eleven-and-twelve-year olds. Coerced by her mother's friend Lillian Barone, the head of the volunteers at the Boys & Girls Club, to replace a woman who'd quit, she had arrived with a vague sense of unease. She wasn't exactly good with kids, her nieces and nephews the exception and had no idea what to do with them. But she'd learned quickly and was amazed at the interest level and how much the kids enjoyed cooking. Lillian told her the class on nutrition was the kids' favorite and was the first one chosen out of dance, computer, karate, band, art, and sports.

Today she looked forward to it with a deeper sense of enjoyment. She needed to banish the uneasy feelings that came from Zach being paired with Paul.

And the feelings of love that had come back in an unexpected rush.

⌒

"Good morning, Zach. How did you sleep?"

He hadn't, not after Lana's visit. Memories of her in his arms had come back with a vengeance. Celia didn't need to know that. He gave her a smile as he limped into the kitchen. He moved to the coffee maker, poured himself a cup and retreated to the breakfast bar.

She looked busy, a couple of pots on the stove, big ones that could hold enough food to feed an army.

"It's not the best accommodations we have but the one that works. Maybe when you're better at managing steps, you can move upstairs."

She had her back to him, stirring, seasoning, doing her thing.

"It's fine. Honest. I've slept on far worse."

Celia gave a brief nod, knowing his history. She put the wooden spoon down and turned to face him.

"What can I get you to eat?"

She was wiping her hands on a dishtowel, an apron around her waist, a portion of the counter area behind her lined with foil containers.

"It is all about food here, isn't it?"

"I could apologize for being Italian, but I won't. It's a good way to grow up."

"I don't want to bother you. It looks like you've got your hands full, so coffee will be fine."

"Don't insult me. We have eggs, bacon, pancakes, waffles, crepes…I'd offer you some frittata, but it's got zucchini in it."

He gave her a clenched but mischievous smile and a chuckle to go along with it.

"It's a good thing Lana's not here. She'd insist on the zucchini."

He heard the side door open, and the voice he loved to listen to entered the bright sunny kitchen, before she did.

"Of course, I would. But that's only because Ma makes a mean frittata."

She walked right over to where Celia stood and kissed her cheek in greeting. She was dressed in a black dress that fell a couple of inches above her knees, black heeled boots, and a tight smile. He appraised her with hungry eyes before asking, "Do you always get here so early?"

She dropped a folder, her phone, car keys, and a notebook onto the counter and grabbed a mug and some coffee. He noticed the two sugars and cream that followed.

She took a sip and sighed before answering him.

"Earlier some days. I wanted to check to make sure Ma had the ingredients for tonight's staff meeting supper. When she's babysitting you, and we're cooking for less than fifteen people, she'll make everything here."

She walked over to the refrigerator, opened it up and began to poke around the drawers and shelves, checking the inventory against the list she had in her hand.

Celia had taken a pan out and was frying up some ham and onions, the omelet she was making him halfway there. Whipping the eggs into a froth of yellow, she asked her daughter, "Check the sauce. Make sure it's defrosted. I took it out yesterday, but it was a solid block."

Removing the plastic containers, both gallon-size, Lana pried off the covers and stirred.

"Looks good. It should be more than enough for what we've got planned. You might want to use it up for supper tonight."

"I've got supper already planned. The sauce can hold until tomorrow."

Out of curiosity, Zach asked, "So what kinds of food are you serving tonight?"

After grabbing a plate out of the refrigerator now that her checklist was complete, she broke off a piece of the frittata and popped it in her mouth.

"A tray of macaroni with meatballs, a tray of chicken parmigiana, salad, bread, and a spaghetti squash dish for vegetarians. Dessert, of course. Drinks."

Zach's ears perked up.

"Dessert?"

"Yes, Italian wedding cookies, macaroons, and pistachio crunch."

"If you have extras, you might want to leave a couple for those you leave behind."

As another piece of yellow and green was popped into her mouth, her head tilted towards him. When her hair fell over her eye, she fingered it back. "Pistachio is green, you know."

Celia placed a steaming omelet in front of him, napkin and fork along with it. He thanked her before he offered his opinion to Lana.

"I think I could choke them down."

"Good to know. In fact, if the choking part is true, I'll make sure you have a half dozen."

Ignoring the barb, Zach opened the file folder that Lana had placed on the bar beside him.

Lying on top was a contract, signed by the director of the school they were catering. Fingering that up, he found the menu, prices, and invoice. Taking a small mouthful of eggs, he flipped open the brochure and started reading.

"Just like I suspected."

"What's that?"

"Not as much green as you've implied." It took her a moment to understand what he'd said, his jaw still causing some speech impediments. Moving to stand behind him, she looked over his shoulder and pointed.

"Here, spinach and ricotta ravioli, vegetarian lasagna, salads, spaghetti with kale and tomatoes, wedding soup..."

He tried harder to make his words coherent.

"Yeah, but it's, what, maybe twenty per cent of the menu? There's lots of meat options, too."

"I'm sure they were the first thing you noticed."

He turned his head to look up at her and hesitated, a flicker of desire holding him hostage.

In a flash, she had stepped away, and he knew she must have felt it as deeply as he did.

They had been good together, and even though it had lasted less than five months, it should have been strong enough to carry them to their golden anniversary.

Lana rinsed off her plate and stacked it in the dishwasher, grabbed her file and her keys, and without another word fled, from the scene of the erupting fire, the evil eye she gave him not dousing it in the least.

⌒

Seemed she was still running away from him. The piercing look of desire Zach had given her made her blood boil. If it had been in anger, she could have stayed, dished out more insults but it was in need, something she couldn't give in to. Right after their final argument, after he had left, she'd filled her days with work, cried into the lonely hours of the morning. She'd missed what they'd found together, had hoped it would last a lifetime. It had been hard the last couple of years. Not knowing where he was or what he was doing was like a nightmare she couldn't wake up from. Now that he was here...

The friggin' flame burned even hotter than before.

She'd give anything to feel his kiss again, feel the steamy heat flow through her blood at his touch. She was coming to the dreadful conclusion that it would never fade, no matter how much time had passed.

The way she kept immersing herself in the memories proved she hadn't been able to let it go. That Zach had chosen his blasted career over her still had her ready to spit bullets. He'd had options.

But he hadn't used them.

It was something she should have known, which made it more ridiculous that she had agreed to marry him. Fourth-generation cops didn't quit. It wasn't in their DNA, just so hard-wired, they had no choice.

She would have chosen him over anything.

Well, that wasn't the exact truth. She refused to choose widowhood, which was how some wives ended up. Her mother, for one.

After turning the key, the engine straining against the cold, she shifted into reverse, needing to shove Zach out of her mind, focus on a less flammable subject.

Her first appointment did that.

The family was friendly, no bridezilla antics and they chose the meal for the fifty guests with ease. Sylvia took notes as they went over the menu—pizza dip, antipasto, and fried ravioli as appetizers, salad, garlic roasted chicken, and skirt steak with pesto, asparagus with pine nuts, garlicky mashed potatoes, broccoli with red peppers and corn for those not inclined to go green. She'd stuck to the Cookery menu, not veering off course.

Celia was still the commander of the ship, her fingers always in the pie and she hadn't passed Lana any decision-making honors.

Lana knew she probably never would. And didn't really blame her. It had had been her baby for a long time and she was afraid that Lana would start dismantling her menu, adding more and more of her own favorites.

That was the reason she wanted a storefront. One with a kitchen, where she could sell some of her signature dishes as take-out, test recipes with counter space to spare, have a tasting station, so potential customers could taste what they were ordering. It was her short-term goal and would happen when and if she found something reasonable in an area that was conducive to this type of enterprise.

⌒

After her classes at the Boys & Girls Club were over, she headed to her mother's, to let her know how the earlier appointments had gone, start the binder that would hold all the pertinent details of the affair, and to pick up the food for tonight's delivery.

As she entered the house, the kids at the Boys & Girls Club having given her the break she needed from all disturbing thoughts, she found her mother in the kitchen, bending over the open oven, a roasting pan visible.

"What's for supper?"

"Plain fare tonight. Need to keep it bland and chewable for Zach."

Her stomach shifted but she kept her tone neutral.

"Still here, huh?"

She thought for sure he'd be stir-crazy and leave for parts unknown. Or was it hope? Not that out of sight kept him from occupying a lot of head space.

"Yes, and he will be for a while. Get used to it."

Knowing that wasn't going to happen, she opened the refrigerator, retrieved a bottled water, twisted the cap and took a sip.

It didn't do a thing to wash down the lump in her throat.

"Is everything ready for tonight?"

"It is. The garlic herbed spaghetti squash is warming in the other oven, the salads are packed and ready to go, the desserts are boxed, the paper goods are in that bag. All that's left is heating up the pasta and parmigiana. I added a couple of pizzas to the list, and they're ready for packaging."

"Did I hear the word pizza?"

The gravel voice preceded the man.

Lana looked over to see Zach leaning on his cane, standing at the threshold. He was dressed in sweats and a long-sleeved tee, and his face was covered in a five o'clock shadow. His coloring was still pallid, but his eyes looked clear and focused.

"Why don't you sit down macho man? We wouldn't want you to fall over."

She watched him limp over to one of the kitchen chairs and settle into it. He rested the cane against the ledge of the table and pronounced for her benefit, "Due to the lack of good food."

She leaned back on the counter, her arms crossed, the bottle of water still clutched in her hand.

"Ha. You've probably gotten more nutrients in the last twenty-four hours than in the last month."

"Just confirms what I thought all along. It doesn't make a person feel better."

"Oh, right. The thrashing you got has nothing to do with your lack of energy."

"Nothing a thick, juicy steak won't fix. Lots of iron and protein."

"I'm impressed with your vitamin knowledge, but it might be a bit tough chewing it with a wonky jaw. Or have you been miraculously healed?"

"If only."

The memory that he'd almost been killed came back to grab her heart. And squeeze. Moving away from the counter, she cast her eyes in her mother's direction to avoid looking at him.

"What are you doing up, anyway? I thought you'd been confined to bed rest."

Hoping he'd be sleeping when she got there, knowing the likelihood of that inconceivable, she had stayed in her car for an extra five minutes to get her emotions under control.

"Paul's going to take me over to my place to get my things. I'm moving out."

Her heart hammered in thunderous applause, and she spun around to face him.

"Of here? Let me get the balloons."

He quirked a smile as if knowing she'd be disappointed.

"Of my apartment. I only had another couple of months until the end of the lease and I'm paid up, so there's no problem vacating those premises."

She needed him to go away, far, far away.

"There really is, a problem that is. You can't stay here forever."

His eyes wandered to her mother, who was taking the baking pan out of the oven.

He seemed intent on not looking her in the eye.

Rubbing his chest as if in pain, he admitted, "I don't plan on it."

The ache was back, but she refused to let him see how vulnerable she was around him.

"Work quickly, won't you? For all our sakes."

"Lana, stop it. Zach is welcome here for as long as it takes."

Frowning at her mother, Lana busied herself with the appetizers, the large foil trays filled to overflowing with the square pieces of pizza, covered with zucchini, ricotta and sausage, crust topped with escarole, spinach and cherry tomatoes.

She noticed his neck was strained, his eyes peering into the tray.

He asked, "What's wrong with pepperoni?"

"Not good for you."

"My taste buds don't agree."

"Your taste buds need a refresher course. It's full of additives and preservatives."

"Spoil-sport."

"According to you. Not worth the effort to argue."

Celia, taking the roasting pan out of the oven, said, "Could you stop the bickering, please?"

Lana made a face as she boxed up the meal.

Celia turned to Zach and almost in apology said, "The nights we're out, it's everyman for himself. If you want, I can make a plate up for you before we leave. Otherwise, you can wait for Paul. He should be home soon."

"If you don't mind, I'll have something now. The soup didn't fill me."

He wasn't sure he could use his jaw the way it was meant to be used, but he was going to do his best to get something into his stomach. He was sick of being hungry.

He had started to get up when Celia said, "You stay right there."

It was more a command than a request and Zach followed it to the letter.

As Celia scraped the spoon against the pan, she told him, "There are smashed potatoes, chicken, and carrots." Lana noticed the smile when she added, "I tried to stay away from anything green."

Lana went over to inhale the aroma of the steaming meal, pulling a piece of chicken from the bone and popping it in her mouth before going to freshen up. She had to change out of her jeans, but she wasn't going dressy for just a drop-off. A nice pair of fitted pants and a sweater would work, and she had those in her old room upstairs. Keeping some of her clothes here prevented her from wasting her time traveling back and forth between Allston, where she lived, and Melrose, where her mother lived. She brushed her hair, applied some lip gloss and checked her eye make-up in record time, and returned to the kitchen.

Zach wasn't eating alone. Her brother Tony had come in, and with plate in hand, he was helping himself. He looked up from his task and smiled.

"Hey goat. Good to see you."

Suspending the hand on the way to his mouth, Zach asked, "Goat?"

Her nose went in the air when she informed him, "It's *capretta*, actually."

Tony sat down at the table, his smile even broader at Zach's inquiring look.

"English translation: goat."

"Where the hell did you get that name?"

Celia walked in on the threesome and explained. "She's my *capretta*."

"Why? She eats everything and anything?"

Coming to stand beside her daughter, she stroked the back of her head.

"No. She was always so lively, always moving this way and that."

Lana heard the regret in her mother's voice. Her liveliness had ended the day they'd buried her father. Maybe she needed a new nickname...

Tony must have noticed their mother's tone as well because he offered, "I'm *Lupo*."

"Lupo, like the werewolf in *Harry Potter*?"

"Yup."

Celia explained, "It means wolf, strong, family-oriented. Dennis is *orso*, bear. He's big, cuddly and lovable."

Zach attempted a smile, but still was unable to carry it off.

"More interesting than *dear*, which is what my mother calls me."

"Hmm, maybe I can start calling you *daino*, which is buck in Italian. A male deer."

Giving Lana a once-over he said, "Certainly better than goat."

"I hate to interrupt your fun at my expense, but I have to get going."

She began to gather her things, while her mother hovered at the table probably to make sure the men had everything they needed before she left. That was a part of her ethnic heritage that still surfaced every now and then that demanded women take care of their men.

Tony asked, "What movie tonight, Ma?"

"Some comedy. You know I never remember the titles."

"Or who's in them. Let me know whether it's good or not and I'll try to figure out which one it was. I have a date this weekend and going to the movies might be an option."

The women put their winter coats on, Lana adjusting the scarf she wore everywhere, before lifting the heavy boxes laden with food.

Zach inched out of his chair. "Let me help you with those."

Celia waved him off.

"Don't be ridiculous. We do this all the time."

Zach looked at Tony, his eyebrow arched.

"Yeah, they do. Feminists in action. Who am I to keep them down?"

And when Paul stepped into the house as they were leaving, earlier than anticipated, he merely kissed Celia good-bye before shedding his coat and hanging it on the hook at the door.

He rubbed his hands together, got a plate and joined the men doing exactly what Lana had told him to do as they passed each other in the foyer.

"Enjoy the meal."

Zach could only shake his head.

"I was taught to help women carry things."

"Try it with the females in this family and get your head bitten off."

"Why? It's just...common courtesy."

"Lana would tell you it's an indication you don't think she's capable. Like I said, off with your head."

"Does she ask when she needs help? Or is she too stubborn?"

"She asks. She's independent, not stupid."

Zach shook his head again, still not understanding.

His sisters loved it when he took the lead. Expected him to open doors, drop them off at the entrance, especially if it was raining, carry heavy things...in short, use his brawn, or take it for the team. The guilt of not being able to offer his services to Celia and Lana was not an easy thing to displace.

Paul had sat down to the still-warm dinner, and began to eat, explaining the mindset to Zach through forkfuls of chicken and potatoes.

"Sal wasn't home a lot, so Celia taught her kids not to expect help for the things they could manage on their own. Then when he died...I think it made them better able to handle everyday life."

Tony disagreed. "Not Lana. She changed overnight. She went from goat to turtle."

"Turtle?" Zach mumbled, his diction still off from his jaw injury.

Tony glanced up and explained, "Hard shell, solitary, keeps her head tucked inside."

Tony and Paul continued to satisfy their hunger Zach less able to open wide and chew, held a piece of chicken and thought about Tony's assessment.

After Sal's death, the Scaleras had still come to the house for the Saturday get-togethers. His mother was one of Celia's best friends and wouldn't let Celia isolate herself, insisting the rest of the family join in the weekly gathering even if it was without Sal. When Celia had married Paul, the friendship expanded to include him.

Soon after the shooting, he'd left for college, attending Villanova and majoring in criminology. Living out of state for the next four years, he hadn't seen the transformation in Lana's personality.

She had been lively as a kid, always wore a smile, dramatic, expressive. It used to light up her face.

Today none of those things were true. She was more reserved, no longer smiling openly.

Her letters had had him fooled. They were filled with anecdotes, pieces of her daily life made humorous, and he'd read life in them.

It was when he got back from Afghanistan that he'd noticed a change, thought it was his war wound that had prompted it. She'd become the constant in his life, an anchor keeping him grounded while he went through the hideous rehabilitation workouts. Her face often reflected his own struggle with getting back on his feet, the pain of his exertions marring her face in sympathy. She was encouraging, nurturing, loving. He had come to see them as a united front, and he'd asked her to marry him. He was floored when she'd agreed so quickly. He had forced her to set the date for the ceremony while he was still convalescing, before she could change her mind. He should have told her what his plans were, but he knew what she'd do. Turn him down flat.

He thought she'd stick with him when she found out, what they had was so good, but he'd been wrong.

In one second, he'd lost all her precious smiles, along with the blissful nights spent in each other's arms.

She'd been sharp-tongued since he got here. Yet there were times when she'd look at him with an open heart, her love shining brightly in her eyes. Did she regret where they were, and maybe the reason for it, as much as he did? Or was her fear still too strong to let him back in?

CHAPTER SEVEN

Zach got up slowly and limped to the sink, rinsed off his plate, stashed it in the dishwasher.

Paul was making short order of the food. "Why don't you go into the family room, relax. Let me just finish supper, get changed, and then we'll head out to your place. Are you sure you want to come with me?"

After retrieving the cane, Zach hobbled to the threshold and answered, "I'm sure. Take your time. I'm not going anywhere without you."

He made his way into the family room, the two men still at the table, bringing each other up to date on life on the streets. The room was small but homey. The sectional was the same one he'd seen as a kid, when it was the Scaleras' turn to host the weekly gathering. It was old but still in good condition. The TV was mounted on the wall, the chairs re-upholstered in a flowery print, and pictures adorned every flat surface. He went from one to another studying each member of the family. Johnny playing drums at one of his concerts, a rainbow strobe of lights flashing in the background. He'd been to one a couple of years ago and knew Raging Thunder's popularity was well earned. Tish, in an evening gown, seated at a baby grand, her fingers fluttering across the keys. Rissa and Luca's wedding portrait, Tony in his dress blues, Dennis and Delaney each holding one of the twins. He picked up the one of Lana who was sporting a nose ring, her hair highlighted in rainbow hues, her facial expression in direct contrast to her outward appearance. She should be wearing a sprite smile, proving her personality demanded the ring and the foil.

Hearing footsteps approaching, he looked up to see Paul enter the room dressed in a pair of jeans and his work shirt, but with the sleeves rolled up.

Zach couldn't help but ask, "Nose ring?"

Paul chuckled.

"She got it senior year in high school, got rid of it right around the time she began to cover appointments."

Zach glanced up to see Paul walking toward him.

"Celia allowed it?"

"Celia allowed them to be self-expressive, as long as it didn't hurt them."

"What did she think would hurt them?"

"Drugs and drinking. Those weren't the problems she had with Lana. Lana withdrew from the world. One day she was giggling at the mall with her girlfriends, the next she was shut up in the kitchen with Celia devoting all her time to cooking."

"The need to stay close to the survivor?"

"Maybe. I think it had more to do with her father. She adored him, thought he could do no wrong, that he'd always protect them, keep them safe. He'd failed at that, and she's been angry at him ever since."

"Thus, the trust issue?"

"She has an incessant need to keep everyone at arm's length. Except the rest of the family which is strange. You'd think she'd be afraid of losing them..." He shook his head, before adding, "That wouldn't be a problem if she had more to her life than cooking."

"She has a wall up."

"More a protective shell, like Tony suggested. Her armor. Worse since...She doesn't seem to trust love anymore."

Paul glanced over at him, hesitating. "It got worse once...you were gone. You should have told her, Zach. Let her make a life-altering decision based on the facts."

"She never would have married me."

"So, it was worth the four months you had together?"

Zach met Paul's eyes and said with conviction, "Yes. It was."

"She'll probably never forgive you. You betrayed her. Which is what she still feels her father did."

"By getting killed."

Paul nodded grimly.

"How did she take your marriage to Celia?"

"She wasn't happy, but she never said so outright."

"She'd known you for years."

"This family became my own once my wife sued for divorce. She told me I'd abandoned her for the job, that I gave everything to the force and had nothing left for her. I learned not to do that with Celia."

"My dad would refuse to admit he brought it home with him, but he did. I don't think it's possible not to. Always thinking about how to get the bad guy."

"Maybe you're right. Maybe Celia was just more in tune with what I did. Didn't mind being left alone so often, didn't mind when I zoned out thinking about the crime, the murder, the victim."

"She had her own life. My mother was often at loose ends. I think that's why she mothered us so tightly. It was her job. But it was annoying. I couldn't wait to get away from her."

"This time around, she had cause."

"She had cause to be worried, not hover. If she only knew some of my close calls in the Marines, she'd have a stroke. It was good she was thousands of miles away."

Placing the picture of Lana back on the table beside the chair, not wanting to linger on memories of their time together, he asked, "Ready?"

"I am. After you."

⌒

It was slow going up those four flights of steps, but Zach took his time, one step leading to the next, his brow becoming covered in sweat from the exertion. Because of his slow progress, he became aware of the peeling paint, the stained carpet on the stairs, the grimy railing, things he'd never noticed before. Usually sleep-deprived or in a hurry he'd take the stairs two at a time, missing the decrepit surroundings. He was relieved he wouldn't be coming back, even if it meant he'd be working in another department. He was coming to respect Paul's easy manner, even the companionable silences, and thought he'd make a good partner. The Homicide Unit was composed of seasoned professionals who worked as one. There'd be a primary, but everyone else would work toward closure.

It was one of the aspects of the military that was life altering. *Band of Brothers* might not be accurate because there were men who didn't pull their weight, men who were angry, men who were crazy, but it signified how close the unit became in terms of survival. He'd made sure the men he picked for his platoon were men of character, integrity, who were willing to die for their fellow Marine. And they had proven their worth time and time again. That was the one plus about moving to Homicide. He'd be part of something bigger than himself, could count on his peers to have his back. Undercover there was no one to count on, only your own instincts, thinking skills, and luck.

Coming to the top of the staircase, his breathing labored, he inserted the key and opened the door, the smell of sweat and mold hitting him head on. It was more than unpleasant, and he winced as he stepped inside, Paul following close on his heels.

"God, this smells disgusting."

He couldn't disagree.

He threw the key on the kitchen counter, limped through the kitchen into the bedroom. The twin bed was unmade, a threadbare blanket curled at the foot of it, a bureau scarred and worn standing against a wall, a small TV sitting atop it. There wasn't much to take with him, no personal effects. He'd never really considered this home, just a place to grab some sleep when he was able.

He pulled at the strap of a duffel bag sitting on the top shelf of his closet. He lost his grip, and it came tumbling to the floor. Paul was quick to pick it up and place it on the unmade bed, unzipping it for him. One-handed, Zach riffled through bureau drawers, packing away a few items of clothing but leaving everything else. He had nothing of importance here and there was little he wanted to take with him. In the bathroom, he threw all the toiletries away. His mother had purchased all he'd need, thinking he'd be staying with her. Celia had picked them up when they'd all agreed he'd be staying with the Catalanos'. After pulling his laptop from under the mattress, he placed it next to the duffel, relieved that it was still here, before heading to the kitchen. Paul already had the refrigerator door open, displaying the empty interior but for a few beers, some empty take-out containers, and an expired carton of milk. It all went into a large green bag that Paul tied up to deposit in the dumpster before they left.

As he stood at the threshold, he shook his head.

"I can't say I'll miss this place."

"I can't say I blame you."

"Seems I've agreed to a whole new way of life."

"Seems it's about time. Are you going to ask your tenant to move out?"

"I don't know. I'd hate to break our agreement, but I'll need someplace to go after I leave your house. I'll call him tomorrow, see if we can't work something out. Otherwise, I'll have to rent something short-term."

"Hope it's in a better section of the city than this."

"It will be. That's one of the upsides of working with you."

Paul took the duffel and the garbage, leaving Zach unencumbered except for the cane.

The descent was slightly easier than going up and it was good knowing he'd never come back. He let the relief have its way.

As soon as Paul was behind the wheel of his car he stated with distaste, "I still can't believe you lived there."

Shrugging his shoulders, Zach replied, "I wasn't there much so it didn't seem to matter. It was part of the cover."

"I couldn't have taken it that far."

"Better than the makeshift sleeping quarters in the desert. At least I had a bed. And there weren't any bullet alarm clocks."

Paul almost chuckled.

"I guess it's all relative."

After settling in, the roads cleared from yesterday's snowfall, Paul said, "You know you can stay as long as you want."

He attempted a smile, but his jaw just wasn't cooperating.

"I believe there's someone who can't wait to be rid of me."

Paul was stopped at a light and looked across the lanes to make sure no one was running a red before he accelerated through the green.

"I'm beginning to think it's for a different reason than she's letting on."

Zach looked out the window, the lights of the city sparkling in the distance. Paul seemed to be picking up Lana's mixed signals, but they weren't really garbled to him.

"There's no doubt in my mind, she loved me. Still does, if I read it right. She just wasn't strong enough to stay."

Maybe if he was in a different department, different capacity...Would she at least be willing to discuss it?

"I'm still not sure that Homicide and I will mesh, but I'm willing to give it a chance."

"That's good to hear. It's not boring, Zach. It's like working the pieces of a puzzle. Sometimes they slide in; sometimes it takes years to find them all."

Glancing over to his new partner, Zach had a good feeling about this. It was just a flash, but it gave him some confidence in the decision made for him by someone else.

"We'll see. From what I understand, there's a lot of down-time. I got used to that in the service. There were long stretches where we played a waiting game. Sitting, always on standby for a skirmish, a battle. Then shit would hit the fan and it would go flying."

Once on the highway, Paul sped up, not going more than ten miles over the limit.

"What was it like over there?"

"Hot."

"That's all I get, huh?'

Zach adjusted the jacket sleeve that was thrown over the sling, hoping he could take the damn thing off soon. He liked being unencumbered. No bullet-proof vest, no flak jacket, no crutches, no sling. He'd had to wear his fair share of them all.

"First year was the worst. You have no idea what you're getting into. By then, you're trapped in this no-man's-land with no means of escape. You learn to deal and adapt. It was the only year I was in Iraq. They were downsizing the number of troops by then, shifting them to Afghanistan which is where I spent most of my service."

"As a sniper."

"In one way or another, yeah."

"What did you use?"

He gave Paul a half smile.

"Interesting question. One Lana never asked."

Paul chuckled.

"She never liked guns. Even before Sal died. They made her skittish."

He knew that. It had probably gotten worse after her father's death.

"I carried an M40A3 and an M16. Sometimes a grenade launcher."

"What was its range?"

He knew Paul was asking about the sniper weapon.

"A thousand yards. Or more."

"How accurate?"

"Depends on the gunman."

"You?"

He shrugged his good shoulder. He was very good at his job but never liked to crow about it.

"I got familiar with my rifle fairly quickly. Shot thousands of rounds, knew exactly where they'd land. Every shot is significant, so your goal is to take the enemy out with one bullet."

"Does it haunt you?"

Paul was referring to the deaths he'd caused, not the ones that took out the men and women in his platoon.

"There's a lot of things that do. Seeing your friends die, maimed, seeing innocent children and women blown up, but not the kills. The more accurate you are, the less likely it is the target will come back to *haunt you* by killing your men."

Paul had just taken the exit that would take them back to the house, his concentration on the black ice that might line the curve. Then it was back on him.

"Any PTSD?"

"Not in the way it's portrayed on TV. Flashbacks, yes, but no anger, no increased stress. I rejoined the human race without issue."

Lana had helped with that. Her love had kept him grounded; his rehab kept him focused.

"Except for the injury."

"Yeah, except for that."

It wasn't that he'd forgotten about it. The ache was a constant reminder.

"Your father was very proud of you."

He froze, somewhat incredulous at the information.

"He told you that?"

"He did."

Sitting back, he asked, his suspicious nature taking hold, "Before or after the medal?"

"There was more than one if I remember correctly. It was well before any of them."

Shaking his head, Zach said, "Son of a bitch never let on. All I got was the anger of not following in his indelible footprints."

"He framed the article that was printed in *The Post*. The one for the Silver Star. It's hanging in his office. I think they called you a beast in the face of high-risk situations."

He scrubbed his face with his free hand.

"Please don't let Lana see that one."

"Too late. Johnny Googled it, read it at one of our Sunday dinners."

He immediately tensed.

"What the hell for?"

He'd been awarded that medal a year after they'd separated, the wheels of the government grinding slowly. It had taken that long to process the paperwork. She'd probably heaved a sigh of relief that she'd gotten out.

"You became their brother when you married Lana. It didn't change when she left you. They were proud to be part of your family."

Zach looked out the window. He'd missed the family, every single one of them. He used to hang out with Johnny back when they were younger, back when the families used to get together. They were the same age, and although they didn't have a lot in common, they liked each other.

"You went to the White House to receive it, didn't you?"

In his Marine blues, along with a couple other members of the unit. It was an honor, especially meeting the president. He was a good man, one who the military respected.

"You don't turn down an invitation by the commander-in-chief."

"Johnny watched it on C-Span. He was glad you got out, although not the way it happened. He didn't want you over there. Too many stories. Too many deaths."

"Not as many as here in the States in any given year."

"You don't have to tell me. I get to solve too many of them."

Now he would, too. Might be better than bearing witness to them, than being the cause.

"I went over the notes on Povitch. Very detailed. It looks like you covered everything."

"Couldn't have or we'd have caught the killer by now."

"You followed every lead."

"I did. But Mr. Povitch hasn't been vindicated."

"There were a couple of interviews I keyed in on. Might be worth revisiting them."

"Take a go at it. I could use another set of eyes."

"I'm not sure I've got the best interrogation skills."

He tended to be direct, wasn't known for his subtlety.

"It's a learned talent. You'll make some mistakes and hopefully they'll teach you something."

"From what I hear I've got a great teacher. How many cases you working on?"

"Got several. They're not usually resolved quickly. One of them is Clarence Brown. Drug dealer extraordinaire. You might have heard of him."

"I have. Drug dealer to the guys I was working with. His reputation preceded him. Happened a couple of months ago, right? Drive-by?"

"Hate drive-bys, always collateral damage. A sixteen-year-old girl was hurt, hospitalized. She was walking her dog. Wish we could get the damn guns out of the hands of criminals."

"Easier to do it in the Middle East than on the streets of America. NRA's more powerful than Al Qaeda."

"Fool thing is, Congress knows that."

He looked out the window, then back at Paul.

"Did you ever solve that Anderson case?"

Paul fiddled with the controls, jacking up the heat.

"You were on patrol back then, one of the officers who showed up after the call, weren't you? I remember. No, we didn't. Stockett was lead. He retired last year."

"Do you think anyone would mind if I looked at it? That one grabbed me. The woman had most of her face carved off. The husband had an airtight alibi."

"He was the primary suspect for the first twenty-four hours. Left all sorts of vulgar and threatening messages on her phone. Wasn't until the daughter got back from a daytrip that we were able to confirm his alibi. He was home with her. Couldn't have done it. We got some DNA from under the vic's fingernails but could never match it."

Paul looked over at him.

"You handled yourself well that night. You asked good questions, made astute observations. I was impressed. That's why, when you father approached me about working with you, I agreed. I knew you had what it takes to do this."

"What you're saying is I didn't throw my guts up."

"Your father would have passed out with that one. Pretty gruesome."

That fact still surprised the shit out of him.

They pulled into the driveway, and he stumbled out of the car, his breath evident in the frigid air. The winter had been especially harsh, and the night he'd been ambushed had been no better. He could have frozen to death before morning if things had worked out differently.

When they entered, Zach listened for sounds coming from the kitchen, something he was getting used to only forty-eight hours in. Celia's and Lana's voices would echo down to his room. He loved hearing one of them, the one that used to make his heart stutter, still did.

There was nothing but silence.

CHAPTER EIGHT

Lana was tucked away in her condo, curled into the corner of her loveseat, munching on a pouch of Pirate's Booty. It lacked the grease and salt she craved, but she'd eaten every last crumb in the bag of chips last night. That this was healthier was a minor consolation. In for the night, a long, busy day behind her, she checked her star channels, and was rewarded with one of her favorites, *To Have or Have Not*. She wanted to work on one of the movie baskets, and this was just the kind of romance she was looking for. No one better than Bogart and Bacall. The sexy chemistry between the two sizzled...Picking up her notepad, Lana scribbled down a possible menu for the two characters...sizzle meant bacon, steak seared in a hot pan, French fries spitting in hot oil...the kind of meal that Zach would enjoy. And she could see him sitting at the table, his knife slicing through the tenderloin, bringing the fork up to his mouth, hesitating while his eyes met...hers. Yup, she was the one who sat opposite him.

Sizzle.

And they'd had it once.

Problem was, it was still there. She felt it every time he merely entered a room. He had a way of making her feel...shaky inside. She was still fighting it with every ingredient in her arsenal.

Bogart was playing the role of a man who lived dangerously. Bacall, the only kind of woman for a man like him. The simplicity of the plot was in stark contrast to the on-screen chemistry, and it's what made the movie a classic.

Zach fit the role, going where danger beckoned. Iraq, Afghanistan, then undercover. She, however, was no Bacall.

She closed her eyes, going back to the day Zach had returned from Germany, stable enough for the transfer, his foot in need of reconstruction. His parents had flown to Landstuhl, where he'd been taken after his injury, stayed with him until he was out of the woods, and escorted him back to the States. Lana had rushed to Mass General to wait, Jeanne giving Celia an estimated time of arrival. It had taken hours, and plenty of check-ins with the front desk, until the receptionist finally gave her a room number.

She'd needed to see for herself that he was still alive.

When she'd walked into the room, Jeanne and George were standing by the bedside. Zach's eyes were closed. He looked so thin, his skin tinged green and the impact of what he'd survived nearly made her weep. But she hadn't. He didn't like coddling, so she'd held herself in check, stood on the periphery of the room, nodding to the Taylors when they acknowledged her presence. Zach had opened his eyes, the blue as startling as always, and he'd zoomed right in on her. He'd given her a crooked smile.

"I was hoping you'd come."

He held out his hand and she'd walked over, gripped it in her own.

Jeanne, looking exhausted herself, had asked, "Will you be staying? I'd love to go home for a couple of hours..."

Zach's expression had looked hopeful, and her heart had fluttered.

"I will."

She'd watched as Jeanne kissed her son, heard George issue a gruff, "See you later," and when they'd left, she'd taken her place where his mother had stood, taking in the buzz cut, the gaunt face, the weathered skin. His leg was in a cast suspended in the air; the foot covered with gauze.

She'd been ready to push away the need to touch him, feel the warm flesh beneath her fingers, and her heart had skipped a beat when he lifted the covers and invited her to lie beside him. As soon as she was tucked into the curve of his arm, her hand on his chest, she'd felt like she'd come home.

Pointing to the bag dripping liquid into his vein, he said, "This wasn't how I expected us to meet again."

Her heart had gone to her throat at the off-handed way he was talking about his injuries. But her words didn't reflect what she was feeling inside. With more bluntness than she'd intended, she'd stated, "At least it wasn't in a body bag."

Closing his eyes, he'd shaken his head, the lop-sided smile back.

"That wouldn't have been any fun."

"Zach, don't trivialize..."

Cold, steel blue eyes had blazed.

"Lana, I'm going to be okay. The kid who tripped the IED won't."

She knew that the IED that had exploded killed the person beside him, a nineteen-year-old from Nebraska. He'd spent days conflicted over the death, anguished that he hadn't been able to protect one of his men. She knew too much about brain tissue and blood and fragmented body parts. Zach had described the firefights, the hand-to-hand combat, the grit and heart his men displayed, the deep sorrow he felt when one of his men fell at the hands of the enemy, during their correspondence.

She was witness to another side of him the day he called the kid's parents to give them his condolences. He'd cried in the telling, quiet tears that the kid's parents couldn't see or hear. He'd said all the right things, all the important things, and she was moved by his sensitivity. It was another step taken on the short road to loving him.

Zach hadn't gotten away unscathed. The explosion had taken part of his foot, the flying shrapnel piercing his leg, partially severing an artery. After self-applying a tourniquet, he'd given orders to those who were scrambling for cover. Even with his injury, he'd been able to direct the fight, killing his fair share of Taliban, not wanting to fail his men, not willing to go down until there was no way out. He'd accomplished his goals, securing the perimeter, extinguishing the rapid fire of machine gun and rocket launcher with his sniper skills. Evacuated by a helicopter when the battle was won, he'd spent time in a MASH unit and German hospital before being sent Stateside.

Zach hadn't told her any of it. Her brother Johnny had read the account at the dinner table one Sunday, over a year after they'd separated, when he was awarded a medal for bravery. She had sat through the telling with as much stoicism as possible but had gone home and cried that night, endless tears of regret.

⌒

She often wondered what would have happened had she not sent that first letter. Would she have ever found someone else who would have opened her heart?

She'd struggled with setting a tone, not knowing what to say, yet wanting to reach out and say something. There were dozens of crumpled pages before she was done, until she thought she'd gotten it right.

She'd sat on this very love seat, her legs curled under her, the pad of lined paper resting in her lap, as she put ink to the words, she hoped would seem worthy yet light. The one thing she hadn't wanted to sound was worried or somber, mainstays of who she was now, so she'd reached inside of her to find remnants of the girl she'd been once.

It was in August...Her cynical laugh cut through the small space. August seemed to be the time for beginnings...and January the time for endings.

Closing her eyes, she remembered the words she'd written him. They were etched in her mind.

Dear Zach,

Your mother asked a bunch of us to write to you. It was hard to say no with the tears streaming down her cheeks. She cornered a lot of the wives on the force to find willing participants, unmarried ones if you want to know. I think she has an ulterior motive but please don't tell her I mentioned that. If you find you have an abundance of pen pals, just pass this along to someone who might enjoy a few words from home.

I'm not sure what to write–don't know what to ask. How's it going or are you alright seem dumb-ass questions for someone on the borders of...far away, dressed in fatigues and carrying a gun. I'm pretty sure I can answer those questions, anyway. The Marines suit you. The best of the best or be the best that you can be...Whatever the slogan is, you'd fit the bill. You could be the poster boy for it.

It's hot today but according to my Google search, it's not as bad as it is there. What's it like in Afghanistan? Shopping malls, tourist attractions? A place to visit that should be on my bucket list?

I keep seeing you outside your parents' house, playing touch football with Johnny and Dennis and your other friends. I couldn't have been more than six or seven, but thought you were the fastest and smartest out there. That's the way I'll keep you in my thoughts. Laughing while you scrimmaged.

Lana

It had taken a couple of months for him to write back, and she had all but given up hearing from him. She had gotten home one day and there in the mailbox was a brown envelope, the address giving away the sender. After racing inside, she'd dropped her bag, ripped it open, and stood at her kitchen counter reading what he had to say. There was a prickle of fear, along with some other unknown emotion that she came to realize was the early blossoms of love. She still had that letter and all the others he'd sent. Over the years, they'd shared private thoughts and feelings. After he'd become the leader of his unit, he would agonize over his role. He'd had no one else to talk to about his responsibility; he had to lead by example. He couldn't show doubt, be indecisive, cry in front of his men. She had somehow become his sounding board, a position she didn't necessarily like, but one she took on willingly.

She knew his darkest secrets, his innermost thoughts, and when she walked into the hospital room that day, she hadn't known what he'd say.

He'd made it easy and over the next couple of months, made loving him easy. When he'd proposed, she'd accepted.

Looking back, she had to wonder why she'd agreed so quickly, why she'd let him talk her into marrying him half-way through his recuperation.

Maybe it was his injuries, maybe it was because he made her feel like she was important to him, maybe it was because she was madly in love with him by then.

They'd had barely five months together when it came to a screeching halt. She was still reeling from the hurt it had caused.

The blaring music brought her back to the present, and she watched the ending credits of the movie scroll on the screen. She wiped away the sniffles, her body's way of telling her the tears were coming. Not wanting to continue to grieve for a situation that was dead and buried, but being unable to put it behind her, especially now that he was close enough to touch, she was mired in reminiscing. She got up and went to retrieve the box she kept his letters in. It was originally meant for jewelry but as these were her most precious items, she had put every envelope carefully within the blue silk folds. Flipping through the pile, she took out the first one he'd sent, fingering the faded ink before slipping out the single page.

Dear Lana,

It's no surprise that my mother is still trying to exert her motherly duties, even from so far away. I appreciate your willingness to reach out. Not too many took her up on her request, so I guess the marriage tack didn't work as well as she'd hoped.

The Afghanistan I know is like a land before time, we're talking pre-civilization. No roads, no cars, no phones, no electricity, no running water. As hot as it may be there, you have water to cool your face, air conditioning to give you some relief. Me—I'm sitting here in the dirt, my face caked in grime, hacking up the dust that you can't help but breathe in. Sunset is fast approaching, and we'll be leaving soon for our mission. We do our best work at night here. The one thing I can't complain about is the stars and how bright they shine in an unadorned sky. Some nights I just lie on the ground and take in the beauty. Most nights I don't have that luxury.

How are you? How do you spend your days? Still dating that guy? I can't remember his name. I think my mother told me he was going to be a doctor. Maybe I'll get to meet him one day. Hopefully not for his services. I intend on staying in one piece.

The Humvees are lining up. Time for patrol, so I'll be off.

Different scrimmage line out here and I don't think I'll be laughing much, but I'll smile when I think of you.

Zach

Zach.

Just his name had the power to bring it all back into stark focus. She'd once overheard someone say that when you love someone and they leave, the missing never ends. They were right. It didn't. She knew first-hand. It was even worse for the one who'd caused it. She could blame only herself for her misery.

Clutching the letter to her chest, she wished with all her heart it could have ended up differently. They'd lived apart for more than two years, but she'd never been able to break the connection, no matter how much she bent and twisted it.

Now that he was physically back in her life, she was letting all the buried feelings out. They'd become a Pandora's box of swirling emotions. She was just beginning to process them for the first time since that awful January day when he'd walked away. Would hope be the emotion left when she was done?

Hope. It was such an iffy proposition. It spoke to possibility and expectation, not surety, and it demanded trust. Could she trust a future with him?

Did it matter? She'd almost died the day he announced he was returning to the police force.

It had broken her heart. She refused to wake up one day wearing widow's weeds.

I'd say you're already wearing them.

⁓

When the men returned to the house, Paul carried the duffel bag down to Zach's room, shrugging off his coat as he went. When he re-joined Zach in the kitchen he asked, "Want a snack? I'm sure Celia left something for us."

Zach limped over to the refrigerator, where Paul was taking inventory. It was chock-full, container stacked on container.

"I'll never starve while I'm here, that's for sure."

While pulling out a row of glass-covered bowls, Paul explained, "Food says love in Italian. There is always a great-tasting snack to be found. You didn't notice that when you were living with Lana?"

They hadn't been together long enough for his focus to be on anything but her and the endless nights of feeding the fire that burned in her soul.

Paul slid a foil tray out and chuckled as he uncovered it. "This must be Lana's latest attempt. She's working on creating romance baskets, tying a menu to a love story. She wants to sell them at the storefront. This one's marked *Avatar*. Never seen it, have you?"

No, he hadn't, but he didn't get to watch much while undercover, too busy staying one step ahead of the criminals. If it was out before that, he'd been too busy fighting the enemy, or loving Lana.

Paul returned the tray to the back of the shelf before pulling out a pie plate and checking the contents. He closed the door, obviously finding what he was looking for.

Zach was still trying to process what Paul had just told him.

Romance baskets? Love stories?

"Did I hear you right?"

Paul had a broad grin on his face.

"You did."

"What kind of movies?"

"*Casablanca, Gone with the Wind,* stuff like that."

He shook his head as if his brain was addled.

"I can't see it."

For as playful as Lana was in the bedroom, she was more of a realist than a dreamer.

A smile tugged at Paul's mouth.

"How long did you live with her?"

"I guess not long enough."

No guess about it. It wasn't nearly long enough. Not only because he didn't know these little details but because he missed her more now than after those first few days without her.

After taking the aluminum foil off the plate, Paul pulled a knife from the drawer and cut himself a slice.

"She's loved them for as long as I can remember. I'd come in from work when she was a teenager to find her completely absorbed in a black-and-white movie from the '50's. Clark Gable is one of her favorites."

Zach was more than surprised. He just couldn't picture it.

The '50's screamed man taking care of woman. The old days when men knew how to behave, things weren't so confusing, and you didn't have to scope out how a woman felt about things before you acted.

"Those kinds of films are a far cry from feminism."

"Not when you think about it. Usually, the movies she liked had a strong feminine lead. Katherine Hepburn, Vivien Lee. Out of the norm for that time."

He gave Paul a look of incredulity. "And you would know this how?"

It wasn't something a man would think about.

"She pointed it out to me once when I sat and watched one with her."

He looked over, the big man not one he'd take for a romantic.

"You sat through a chick flick?"

"Don't think that's what they were called back then. They were very successful at the box office. Anyway, she had had a restless night, couldn't sleep right after–" he took two plates out of the cabinet and put a piece of pie on each before looking at him– "...you two broke up. She stayed with us for a while. I don't think she liked going home. She looked like she needed some company, so I watched. *African Queen*. Humphrey Bogart. Was pretty good, actually." Holding the plate up, he asked, "You do want one, right?"

Zach went over to see what Paul was holding.

Inspecting it closely, he couldn't decide whether he wanted to try it or not.

"I don't know. Maybe. What is it?"

"Something like cheesecake, only better."

He contemplated that for a moment before agreeing. He very rarely had issues with dessert.

"Why not."

Paul brought the dishes to the table and put one in front of the two seats and then sat down. Zach joined him, forked off a sliver, and put it up to his mouth, licking the creamy texture before taking a sample.

Paul was already halfway done. "This is a family favorite. If you don't like it, don't tell anyone. You'll only be insulted for your lack of taste."

Finally submitting to the smooth cheese flavor, Zach slid the fork into his mouth and let it melt on his tongue. His mother didn't cook like this. She did okay in the meat and potatoes category, but her idea of a dessert was store-bought pie, cake, or ice cream.

"I have to admit I could become addicted to this."

"Don't get too addicted. It doesn't last long around here. I'm surprised Tony left some for us."

"I thought he told me he had a place in the city. Has he moved back in?"

He talked to all of Lana's brothers regularly. They'd kept in touch even though they were technically on Lana's side of the estrangement.

"No, just eats here any time he can. Like the good Italian mother, she is, Celia spoils him in the food department. What he doesn't eat here, he takes with him."

He mustn't have taken much when he left tonight. There was still a full reservoir of food, three containers deep.

"Where is Celia, anyway?"

"Still out with her friends. It's movie night. She'll be home in an hour or so."

"It sounds like movies are an inherited taste."

Paul pushed the dish away after he'd scraped every crumb off.

"You want a beer?"

"Sure."

Paul got up and retrieved two, handed one over.

"I'm not sure Celia even likes the movies. She usually comes home complaining about the plot, the writing, the acting, or the violence. And she can never remember the name of it. I think it has more to do with being out with her friends."

"Sounds like my sister's book group." He'd been privy to one. One night he dropped by to hang out with her husband in the basement while the women took over the family room. "They drank lots of wine and got around to discussing the book at some point, but it didn't appear to be the reason they got together. Only the excuse."

"Women like that sort of thing."

Men did, too. They only difference were the things they did when they were together. They didn't talk, they grunted. They didn't read, they played.

Paul said with a laugh, "Now me, I like my poker games. Every Friday unless I get called out. Most of the guys are cops, so they understand. You're more than welcome to sit in if you want."

"Thanks. I might take you up on it somewhere down the road. What I'm looking forward to is getting back in the ring."

Paul crossed his arms over his chest and sat back in his chair

"That's right. You're a boxer. Don't know why anyone would willingly take a punch in the face."

Zach gave what might have been a smile if his jaw worked right.

"We wear head-gear, teeth guards, gloves. It beats getting into it on the street."

Paul took a swig of his beer, paused before asking, "What made you go under cover?"

Celia had already figured out part of it, one of several reasons he'd taken the assignment.

The first and foremost reason? Lana had left him, and he wanted to disappear. Undercover gave him the necessary ingredients for surviving the loss, or so he'd thought.

He gave Paul another.

"Afghanistan."

"You mean you did miss the adrenaline rush?"

He shook his head, fiddled with his bottle.

"Being in command meant I was responsible for the men and women under me. I only wanted to be responsible for me."

Undercover meant he didn't have to project confidence in the face of terrifying circumstances to calm his troops. There was no burden of responsibility to keep every man and woman alive. Any one of his actions back then had grave consequences. Any command given would be followed without question no matter the odds of survival. He had to put the mission before all else, which meant checking his humanity at the wire gate. "Undercover there's no chain of command. It was a change I needed."

But if he was honest, he'd missed the camaraderie. In Homicide, he wouldn't have to make decisions that affected other lives. He'd be giving a voice to those who'd died, something Paul did with regularity.

Paul leaned his crossed arms on the table, his face taking on a somber expression.

"I'd say your background was what kept you alive the night of the attack. You gave as good as you got."

Using his fork to scrape some of the graham cracker crust that stuck to the plate, Zach said, "Not sure about that. None of them were lying in an alley when it was over."

"Three against one isn't the best of odds."

Looking up, Zach admitted, "The odds of my surviving it wasn't great either. They would have killed me if that was the goal."

"Lana was beside herself when she heard."

Paul made such a smooth transition it took him a moment to catch up. Zach paused, thought about that for a moment and asked, "How did she find out?"

"She was supposed to pick Celia up that morning to take her to the commercial kitchen. After we got the news, Celia called her, telling her to get to the house as early as she could. I told her when she got here. You were just out of surgery at that point."

Lowering his head, taking the last bite of pie, dejection thick in his voice he told Paul what he already knew.

"She never came to see me."

He had waited, hoped, prayed that she would. But after the third day, when he was transferred out of ICU into another ward, he'd given it up. She'd shown him her word was like steel. Unbendable.

Zach looked up to see Paul studying him.

"She was downright pissed. She holds herself so tightly that any emotion would have told us it struck a nerve."

"Yeah, and it all but confirmed her fear that I was out to get myself killed."

"From what I heard, she was a zombie most of the day." Paul added, "The next day, she looked like shit. Puffy eyes, furrowed brow, choppy movements. She could have given Johnny a run for his money in the banging department."

Closing his eyes, Zach asked, "Tell me what I could have done differently?"

"Wasn't there so I can't."

"That cop's life was on the line. Damn fool. He should have pulled over once his windshield was shot out."

"That's not what we're taught to do."

"Yeah, right. We go in when everyone else runs out." Shaking his head, he added, "She'll never let me back in. I don't know what I was thinking. My asking to stay here was a mistake. It won't get me what I want."

"Is that why you asked?"

"I was not going to stay with my parents. And I wouldn't have stayed at my place, even if I could have climbed the damn stairs. But with her standing there, looking...I've missed her, Paul, and I thought maybe close quarters might bring back some fond memories. There had to be some."

"Celia and I still hope..."

"I know she still loves me. I can feel it in my bones. But I'm not sure she'll ever change her mind. Too many things are against us. My job, my driving need to give it everything I have, my inability to do anything else, her fear."

"Now that you're in Homicide..."

"That's what I thought, after my initial blow-up, that maybe she might be okay with that. Told my father that I'd give it a try."

"What did he say?"

"He told me if I could do it, I'd be the first Taylor to make it in Homicide."

Paul laughed. "He admitted that?"

"Yeah. Said he had to transfer out after six months."

Zach still couldn't believe George had told him he was too squeamish. Vomited at some of the scenes, had to leave the morgue or pass out. He made his mark as superintendent but not by way of Homicide. He said he'd rather be shot at any day of the week than deal with the dead. He left solving murders to the big boys.

Paul had to agree. "It was not his calling."

"I thought he was all-knowing, all powerful."

"None of us are that."

"It made me feel better about taking this on. Maybe I could make a mark after all."

Thinking of where the conversation had begun, Zach came back to Lana.

"She thinks I have a penchant for trouble. That it will find me even if I don't go looking. There's no way for me to counter that. Not in my present state."

"She hasn't found anyone else. Doesn't even date."

"We're still married. She wouldn't."

"What are you going to do with that?"

"I'll never file for divorce, so if she wants one, it'll be up to her."

"That means..."

"Yup, celibate."

"But for how long, Zach?"

Paul had gotten up, cleaned up the late-night snack, and was standing against the counter.

Zach rose from the chair, picked up his cane and leaned on it.

"Maybe I can convince her that even if she doesn't want to stay married to me, we can still be more than friends."

"Good luck with that. Lana can be somewhat stubborn."

Zach laughed for the first time since their conversation had begun. It hurt but felt good.

"That's one thing I learned while we were together. But so am I. We'll see who gives in first."

"And that will satisfy you?"

"It'll have to. I'd bet my life she'd never willingly give birth to another generation of Taylor cops which means family's out."

"Think it through, Zach. Family is important. I never had my own kids, but Celia's might as well be mine. I'd do anything for them. Someday, you might find someone who doesn't have the same kind of...aversion to what we do."

"Yeah, and maybe pigs will learn to fly."

"Keep your options open, Zach."

"No matter how hard I look, Paul, I'll never find anyone like her again. I'm not sure I want to waste my time."

They let the silence eat away the next few minutes until Paul said, "I'm heading up. I left two files for you. Get to them when you can."

Still hobbling, Zach returned to his room, overstuffed files in his hand.

He'd take a look, wanting to be up and running, ready for his new assignment. He also wanted to review the cold case he'd talked to Paul about, the one he'd worked as a patrolman. He hoped he'd get the green light to open it back up, work on it in his spare time. That woman deserved some justice. His insides were thrumming in anticipation. It felt good knowing that in a few days he'd no longer be trapped in a house with nothing to do.

CHAPTER NINE

Lana dedicated Friday to calling potential clients back, answering email, checking Facebook and the website for any problems to solve. She also wanted to update the reviews for the brochures. They were running low, and she was going to have to re-order. There was nothing worse, or lazier, than a vendor keeping the same information year after year. She'd had to change linen companies once when the successful company with glowing reviews she used, changed hands. Their reputation had been sold along with it. Their brochures had stayed the same, the acclimations old, and she'd only found out about the transfer when she'd had problems with them. Now she Googled her vendors regularly, wanting to make sure Celia's Cookery used the best around.

Sitting at the small desk that was cozied up against the wall in her living room, a pencil in her mouth, she worked on a couple of estimates and jotted down some notes in her daily journal. Paper pushing wasn't her thing, but her mother didn't like it any more than she did, and Celia had let it slide onto her shoulders when she was still too young and immature to argue. It had become routine, and there was no way her mother was going to take it back. Just as she finished adding up the figures that would give the Freemonts' an idea of how much the wedding they were planning would cost in catering terms, her phone vibrated across the small space.

Her breath hitched when she saw who the caller was and was forced to pick it up when it almost fell off the edge of the desk.

"Hey, Zach."

When he spoke, the deep baritone voice sizzled through her.

"Whatcha doing?"

Thinking about you again, something I had finally stopped doing maybe a couple of seconds ago.

"Crunching numbers."

"I hate to ask, but can you do me a favor?"

After pausing, trying to anticipate what it could be and whether she could get out of it, she asked, "I don't know. What is it?"

"Can you swing by my parents' house, pick up some of my stuff? I'm going to need some dress clothes for work and would love another pair of sweats and jeans. My mother offered to bring them by, but I don't trust her to bring everything in one trip. She'll probably forget some things on purpose, so she'll have a reason to come back."

Lana began to flick her pencil on the top of the desk.

"Why are your clothes there?"

"When I went underground, everything went into storage. I left the clothes at my parents' house in case I needed them."

The doodling she'd begun on an empty envelope began in earnest.

"Why can't my mother do it?"

"She's babysitting Johnny's kids this afternoon. Besides, I'd prefer she stay out of my sock drawer."

There was another long pause before she said, "You do know your mother hates me, don't you?"

"She doesn't hate you."

The tip of the pencil broke off, she was pressing down so hard. She flung it aside and began biting her nails.

"Bitterly disappointed in me, then."

"My mother's very well-mannered. She'll be civil."

"Thanks. That helps a lot."

There was a pause, and when his voice came back over the line, there was a hint of annoyance in it.

"Lana, you can't blame her, can you?"

She squeezed her eyes shut as a wave of regret washed over her. Jeanne had loved her like a daughter, and it had hurt when the woman shut off all feeling. The switch had been turned the day she told Zach to leave. She'd stayed away from any interactions with her mother-in-law and had meant to keep it that way for the next hundred years or so. By then maybe Jeanne would let bygones be bygones.

"My showing up at her door is not going to make it better."

"If things stay the way they are, you'll never have to see her again. Unless you want to view the body when I'm dead."

A cold knot formed in her stomach when she thought about that possibility.

"Zach..."

"Well, according to you, it will be any day now."

That was a gross exaggeration. She didn't expect it to come any time soon, only that it would come when she least expected it.

"If I show up on her doorstep, my body may hit the slab before yours does."

His chuckle reverberated in her bones long after she'd agreed, and he'd hung up.

It had taken lots of procrastination, busy work, piling paper in stacks, re-stacking them, doodling on her scratch pad, until she'd convinced herself the sooner she got there, the sooner she'd be out.

After dragging on her coat, she drove across the bridge hoping this would be quick and bloodless.

Listening to some of her sister-in-law's CD's, in the hopes the classical music would calm her nerves, Lana tapped her fingers on the steering wheel as she sat at a light, coming closer to the face-off. She had always liked Jeanne, always felt welcome in her home when she was a kid and during the short term of her marriage. When Zach had announced their engagement, Jeanne was ecstatic, patting herself on the back at having put the pen pal idea into her head.

When Lana had disengaged from the family, Jeanne cursed herself for being a meddling mother. She'd tracked her down at her condo one night soon after the separation, and her blistering attack hit Lana right where it hurt. Almost crippled by Zach's betrayal, she could do little to defend herself against the onslaught. She'd stood there and taken it, the cracks in her heart widening, the fissures long and deep.

The falling-out had come precariously close to damaging the friendship between mother and mother-in-law. Jeanne was one of her mother's best friends. She was one of the first to come to the house in the aftermath of Sal's death, had organized the household, had made sure there was food to eat, and brought a sense of normalcy to a chaotic situation. She'd held the mercy meal at her house, opening it up to hundreds of mourners who had come out for a policeman's burial.

To this day, she still felt the residual guilt for causing the disruption in the age-old relationship. Jeanne had been overly generous, laying the blame for the break-up solely at Lana's door. Celia had let her, so angry with what she'd done.

Lana wished she could go back to how it used to be. Even if she reunited with Zach, she was sure there'd be some level of distrust that would continue to mar the relationship.

Her mother-in-law had made it known she would be quite content to never see her again. She'd hurt her son and Jeanne was always his most fervent protector.

It should have been his wife.

Lana exhaled, gearing herself up as she pulled into the driveway.

She still had time to change her mind, could pull right back out and hit some stores, buy Zach new clothes, or she could pick some of his stuff up—

Oh, no, you don't. What Zach doesn't know can't hurt you.

Still procrastinating, she sat outside the Queen Anne's carriage house where Zach had grown up. It was an old home, nestled in one of the most reputable areas of the city, just blocks away from Harvard Law School. It was the house she used to visit with her family, the backyard generous but deceiving from the front, where she'd stood facing Zach, vowing to love him forever. That part was true. It was the living with that was tripping her up.

Taking a deep breath, she opened the car door, took the cardboard box she'd brought along from the back seat, and made her way to the thick wood front door that could have protected a fortress.

When she rang the bell, the chimes echoed out to her, and she gulped, knowing she'd soon be face-to-face with a woman who had treated her as one of her own once upon a time.

When the door creaked open, Jeanne stood there, impeccably dressed, a stony look on her face.

"Lana. Come in."

After slipping into the gleaming wood-floor vestibule, she mumbled, "Thanks, Jeanne. I'm sorry my mother couldn't do this."

The frown lines told her she was sorry, as well.

"As you are probably aware, I'm not happy with this arrangement. I don't think it's good that Zach is in proximity to you. You've caused him nothing but grief. I wanted him here and if he'd gone along with my wishes, this visit would be unnecessary."

Lana bit her tongue. It wasn't wise to let Jeanne know the real reason Zach wanted to be at the Catalanos'. It would only hurt her feelings and she'd done enough of that to last a lifetime. She also failed to mention how much she liked him in that proximity. She was reveling again in his living flesh.

Glancing up at the stately woman, Lana stood stock-still waiting for Jeanne to give her permission to do what she'd come to do.

It didn't come as soon as she would have liked. Jeanne had to get something off her chest first.

"This is your fault, you know."

Lana's hands fisted. There was no way she was accepting the blame for his beating.

"What are you talking about?"

"He wouldn't have gone undercover if you'd stayed with him."

She was tired of being blamed for *his* recklessness.

"If I'm not mistaken, that was his decision, not mine. And it might not have made a difference where I was. He didn't think it necessary to tell me about his life plans."

Jeanne dipped her eyes to the floor, almost contrite now that the anger had flared and gone out.

"I have to admit, he should have talked to you about it. But how could you think he'd do anything but? He was born to it."

Jeanne was right. He was. Inherited all the right traits for making it his life's work. Intelligence, self-discipline, physical prowess.

And he had heart, the drive that prevented him from ever quitting under any circumstance. He always gave everything he had to his mission and had the inherent will to accomplish what he set his mind to.

That was one of the glaring reasons she thought he cared more about the job than her. He'd given up as soon as he walked out the door, never looked back. If he'd loved her, wouldn't he have fought long and hard to keep her with him? If he had made her his mission, she might have—

With lips in a thin line, Jeanne finally said, "Why don't you go on up. You know where his bedroom is. Take what you want."

Stepping around her, Lana climbed the carpeted stairs that led to the second floor, then proceeded to the room she had often visited while Zach was incapacitated after his tour ended.

His was the smallest room, and he used to joke that his sisters had gotten all the good ones before he arrived. He was the youngest of the three children, and the last. Male heir finally achieved.

The ceiling was slanted, and the bed sat under the eaves. There was a bureau, a closet, a bookcase, but not much in the way of personal belongings. There were only two things he cherished, and they were always with him. At least they had been.

Would he have taken the chance that his great-grandfather's pocket watch would be safe while undercover? Or his grandfather's medal?

She didn't think so.

He hadn't said anything about them during their earlier conversation, so she doubted they were here.

She went to the closet, bent down, fingering two pairs of shoes that she placed in the box on the floor. Next, she went through his drawers, packing away jeans, socks, underwear, tee shirts, a couple of sweatshirts, and sweats before picking through the closet. There wasn't much here, just a couple of old suits and two shirts, a blue and a white button- down. It didn't look like he'd replaced his wardrobe, but he wouldn't have needed to. He'd worn his uniform when on patrol and then he was undercover. The result of that made her weak in the knees.

As she took the hangers off the rod, she brought the shirts up to her face and inhaled.

His male scent still clung to them, and she wanted him back with every beat of her heart, wanted to go back to that time when everything was heaven between them. Her mind was playing a game of ping-pong, thoughts racing back and forth on why she should back down, why she shouldn't, his close brush with death putting the added spin on the why she shouldn't.

This was too intimate a task for her, and she needed to get out of here. After dropping the shirts in the box, she pulled out the suits and folded them on top.

She refused to glance at the bed where they'd sat, talked, and planned. Didn't want to see the books by his bedside that she would have read to him as he struggled to fall asleep.

Everything would be in the same place and the haunting memories were phantoms that shadowed every emotion. The ache for him wouldn't stop.

And it was only getting worse.

He'd left a mark on her soul that she couldn't seem to erase and leaving him had paralyzed her.

Or had it been the fear that had done that?

How could she unlock the door to a more fearless kind of love?

Embrace him and the future she knew she could find in his arms?

She wasn't sure she could, but she was beginning to think she had to try.

⌒

As she entered her mother's house to drop off Zach's belongings, Celia was there to grab the box that was almost falling out of her hands.

Her mother arched her eyebrow and asked, "So how did that go?"

"Better than I expected. I escaped alive. Jeanne let me in and disappeared."

"I spoke to her a little while ago. She wasn't pleased we sent you."

"I wasn't pleased with that, either."

Dumping the box on the floor by the entrance to the hallway, Celia said with a note of apology, "Tish was meeting with Arturo this afternoon and with Johnny in the studio, she needed me to watch the kids. I told Zach I could get over there tomorrow but for some reason he was adamant about getting the clothes today."

"Probably to stick it to me."

"No, although that was a rewarding side effect."

The man had a habit of sneaking up on her, and she all but jumped at the sound of his voice. He then explained the reason for the exigent circumstance.

"I'm running out of clean clothes."

Celia stood, her hands on her hips. "Why didn't you say so. I could have thrown some of your things in the wash when I did ours."

"You're doing enough. I don't want to impose any more than I am."

Leaning against the counter, her coat still on although unbuttoned, Lana asked, "Are you waiting to do laundry until you move? I don't think I took enough to last that long, and I took almost everything that was there."

"No, I was going to figure out the machine before long."

"Right. You once told me you'd move heaven and earth if I could just do your laundry. I don't think you ever did one load of wash."

"The offer still stands."

The sheepish look on his face almost made her laugh, but she reined it in, in time.

"I tell you what, seeing that you're not up to the task quite yet, I'll do it for you this once, then you're on your own."

He pressed his hand down on the cane as he made his way farther into the kitchen.

"And you won't make everything pink just to spite me?"

She gave him a lop-sided smile.

"Now would I do that?"

Taking a seat at the table, he admitted in a grave tone, "Yeah, I think you would."

"Well, I guess you're just going to have to trust me."

Meeting her eyes, he asked, "That's risky, isn't it? You've already threatened to poison me, and you went back on that promise you made, you know, to have and to hold."

Blue steel bored into her, and all humor disappeared from her face as she stepped away from the counter. She felt the agitation of his last statement rile through her. She had let him down. But he'd let her down, too. No one saw it as clearly as she did.

"Let me take the box to your room."

He was up out of the seat like a jack-in-the-box.

"No, I've got it."

He placed the cane against the table, picked up the box that was topped off by the suits and shirts still on hangers, and limped into the hall.

Why could this man make her weepy? She hated seeing him hurt, hated the way it made her feel. Willing to coddle and care for him, cry over and kiss all his booboos better.

That thought gave her a flash of heat.

Spinning away from the spot she was standing in, she needed something to do to take her mind off those various parts of his body that were calling to her.

Her mother was busy carving the roast beef. Everything else was on the table ready and waiting for Paul's appearance and dinner to be served.

"There's nothing left to do?"

"Are you staying?"

She'd planned on dropping the clothes off and leaving, but there was a pull to stay.

It happened every time she was in the room with him. It's why she hadn't come anywhere near her mother's house yesterday.

"Is there enough food to go around?"

Celia gave her a look that spoke to the ridiculous nature of the question. Her mother cooked enough to feed a small army, used the leftovers to pack lunches, doggy-bagged it for Tony to take home.

As Lana took her coat off and hung it on the rack, undoing her scarf and placing it on top, her mother suggested, "Why don't you throw some of his clothes in now while you're here? Or are you planning to take them home with you?"

"I can take them home."

"That was nice of you to offer doing his wash."

Reining in her thoughts, she answered, "He hated that chore. He swapped off anything I was willing to swap to get out of it. I often wondered who he got to do it before and after me."

"Military takes care of its own. Undercover probably meant he didn't have to."

"Hmm. Maybe that's why he went that route."

"I can think of a couple of reasons, one of which had to do with you throwing him out."

She flinched. This was the second time today someone had told her that.

She didn't want to believe it, couldn't. Pushing him into a more dangerous situation had not been her goal. Her own safety had been.

"Why would our separation have anything to do with that? He had a penchant for that kind of work before I arrived on the scene. You know, Iraq, Afghanistan. He was a sniper, for cripes sakes." Lana cleared her throat. "Who told you that anyway?"

"Tony."

That caught her off guard. She'd never thought they'd continued their friendship, which if she thought about it was another ridiculous assumption.

"When?"

"Tony boxes with him sometimes, when Julian can't."

Had he explicitly told her brother he'd gone undercover because of her? Or was Tony reading between the lines? Knowing her brother, he could have read it wrong.

"What did he say, exactly?"

"Who? Tony or Zach?"

"Ma. You know who I'm talking about."

"Why don't you ask him yourself? You're getting it third-hand from me."

She didn't want to ask him. He might guess where the question was coming from, concern for his well-being, which she should have given up by now.

"What's going on with you, Lana? Are you having second thoughts about your decision?"

"No."

"I feel something."

"Then your radar is off."

"My radar is fine. I always thought you two would get back together once you realized you'd made a mistake. I had hopes..."

"My mistake? Why am I the monster here? He omitted a very important truth, but the blame for our break-up always lands squarely on my shoulders. It's so not fair."

"You should have stayed. You promised to love him..."

"Yeah, till death do us part. I was afraid that would come before I got a shot at the others."

"Oh, for goodness sakes Lana, grow up. Life isn't a picnic. It's good and bad, up and down. You can't run away from it."

"You keep saying that. But you put me in therapy because you thought I grew up too soon. Which one is it?"

"You got too serious about life. You were like an old lady before high school. Seems you still let your fear get in the way. You can't let the past dictate your present."

"It doesn't. I have an aversion to cops. Okay? That simple."

"You don't like Tony?"

"I love Tony. That's different."

"How?"

She had begun to pace, her hands talking along with her voice.

"He's my brother. Not the father of my children. The ones who would grow up without if something happened to him."

"Which tells me it does have something to do with your feeling abandoned by your father. You think Zach will do the same thing."

She spun around to face her mother.

"Have you met the man? Maybe if he was a different kind of cop, a different kind of man. One who wasn't so dead set to fight for right and justice."

"Then you wouldn't love him. It's who he is that drew you. How *do* you feel about him?"

Her heart did a butterfly flutter. There were a half a dozen wings beating. It happened every time she thought about the way he kissed her or held her or looked at her. A crack widened every time she told herself she didn't want him, couldn't live with the possibilities.

Could it hurt any more if she lost him another way?

She was beginning to doubt it, especially since they'd been thrown together so much the last week. He was the whole package, good looks, killer body, heart-rendering smile, gentle touch and a heart so big it could embrace the world. It wasn't good for her to be so close. She was sneaking her head out from her shell to peek any chance she got.

"Well?"

Biting her lip, she hesitated. Then decided to tell her mother the truth. Maybe she'd leave her alone.

"I feel too much."

Taking steps to cover the distance between them, Celia hugged her daughter.

"My *capretta*. To love someone and not be able to be with them…That is truly sad."

She flashed her mother a warning.

"You don't have to pity me. I made my decision and I'm living with it."

"I can feel your heart beating for him."

"I can't do anything about it, Ma. I can't. My life would be filled with worry every second of every day. I can't, won't live like that."

"Are you saying you don't worry about him when you're apart?"

Lana felt her composure slipping away. She replied in a low, tortured voice, "Hold my breath every time I think about him, wonder where he is and what he's doing."

Celia threw her hands up in frustration.

"I should have kept you in therapy. I never realized…Seems like you are suffocating from fear. It's no way to live. If, God forbid, something happened to Zach tomorrow, you wouldn't regret your stubborn resistance?"

Her heart did a total flip and her lungs seized at the thought. She might not be willing to share her life with him, but she couldn't imagine a world without him in it, either.

Would it be worse? Would she regret it?

It gave her food for thought. Her mother gave her another serving.

"Having his children would be a way of keeping his memory alive. It helped me. You gave me a reason to keep moving."

"We never talked about having kids. We were too busy getting him well."

"There was something between you ever since you received your first letter from him. You never stopped writing to him, not once. That wasn't like you, putting something before work. And from what I'm seeing, nothing has changed."

"It doesn't matter."

She could taste the lie and it had bitter undertones.

"Regret crushes the spirit. You don't want to look back years from now and see the mistake for what it is."

"The regret would come if I gave in, and something happened."

Celia took her by the shoulders and shook.

"Maybe you were the bullet, Lana. Maybe you killed whatever you could have had together. It didn't take someone with a gun. You did it all by yourself."

Her mother's tone wasn't gentle, it held all that she'd had held back for close to two years.

She let her go and went back to her task without another word.

But the words spoken were swirling around, creating a lather of emotion. She did love him, heart and soul, head and body, and it was slowly shredding her resolve.

If she could just figure out a way to push the mind-numbing fear aside, she might lower her defenses. It niggled when he'd been in the military, when he wasn't part of the fabric of her life. Living with him, lying in his arms every night, sending him off with a kiss every morning made it a much more dangerous situation. He would be an integral part of her life. What would happen to it if he was no longer the centerpiece?

She'd seen her mother struggle with it, a witness to her mother's journey through the horror of murder and the aftermath.

Her own journey was just as difficult. For several weeks after her father's death, she would wait for her father to get home, yelling out, "Where's my welcoming committee?"

It was her cue to run out and greet him.

When she was small, he'd lift her high in the air, enveloping her in a bear hug. When she got older, he would pull her close, kiss her forehead and ask her how her day went.

But the clock would tick right past the time for his arrival, his absence a huge hole in her heart, the silence heavy. She finally had to accept that her father was gone. The man who had promised to protect her couldn't protect himself. A door had closed in her heart that day. The hysterics were replaced by a total detachment from anything emotional, and there was a dark sense of foreboding that still hovered over her today.

When she'd abandoned the daily vigil, she began working with her mother, making dinner some nights, helping pack up the meals that would be transported to an event. She waitressed, cooked, began experimenting with different recipes, burying herself in the work, leaving childhood behind.

There had been just one foray into a relationship. She'd met Rafe at an event. He'd asked her out, and against her better judgment, she'd accepted. After a year and a half of dating, they'd broken up. She'd held him at arm's length, so the disruption wasn't major. Work had always come first, and she had barely seen him, which suited them both. Or so she'd convinced herself until he asked her to marry him. She'd declined, her heart in cold storage, and he hadn't warmed her enough to defrost it.

Then that first letter from Zach had come and she'd once again become someone's welcoming committee. And as the letters had continued to arrive, her heart had begun the slow process of melting.

He'd become her sun, and she'd found herself rising more and more to the challenge of loving someone.

Until Zach had told her he would be returning to the force.

She'd never been able to temper the memories of this man, as she had her father.

Zach had been the recipient of a woman's love, not a daughter's.

She'd reverted to the shadows once he was gone. With him here, the sun was back out, and she wasn't sure she wanted to continue to live in the gloom anymore.

CHAPTER TEN

Zach unpacked some of the clothes that Lana had brought back from his folks'. There wasn't much, a couple of suits, some shirts, ties, a pair of jeans. He'd worn a uniform his first six months back on the force, and then scuzz clothes when undercover, which he'd thrown away, should have burned. He'd walked out of Lana's condo with just the clothes on his back the day he left and had never replaced his wardrobe.

He'd have to get out and pick up some new things, something he'd put off for as long as possible.

After showering, he threw on the clean pair of jeans and one of his long-sleeved tee shirts. It had the Patriots logo emblazoned on the front. Lana had bought it for him right before he attended his first Sunday family dinner. The whole gang crowded into the family room for the Pats game, watching it with as voracious an appetite as they had sat down to one of Celia's meals with. Every member had some kind of jersey on, from Johnny's authentic Brady shirt to Dominic's onesie, Luca's Edelman game shirt to Tony's age-old sweat-shirt. The women were attired in fan logos as well. He had gotten to experience the whole season with them, and it had been the highlight of his year. He had talked to Lana about going in for a game but was told it wouldn't be as much fun as sitting with the Scalera fans and she had been right. He'd gone once with his friends, after the break-up and he'd had a good time, but it had only made her absence that much more glaring.

He'd been wearing the shirt the day he left her. It's why it had been hanging in the closet at his mother's house.

Did she remember? He was surprised she'd included it.

It wasn't the only memory that haunted him.

The day he'd told her he was rejoining the force was the blackest of his life. It was a Friday, and they were at the condo, had just finished eating. He was out of time and had to get it over with. After putting the last dry plate away, he'd faced her and let it spill out.

She'd gone quiet, her expression haunted. Her eyes had shone with dark pain, then gone cold.

He'd taken a step to embrace her, but she'd pushed him away and croaked out, "When do you start? Can we still talk about it?"

Walking a fragile line, he'd said, "I start Monday."

She'd begun choking on her tears. "What? How long has this been in place?"

"For...a couple of weeks."

He'd never forget her eyes, darkened with emotion, or the way she'd looked at him, as if he'd just sliced her with one of her kitchen knives.

"And you're just telling me now?"

He could hear the edge in his voice when he admitted, "I knew you wouldn't be happy about it. But Lana, this is what I do."

She'd run her hands through her hair, her eyes downcast as if avoiding eye contact.

"I thought..."

Folding his arms across his chest, he'd closed himself off from what she was feeling.

"Thought what? That I'd find another line of work?"

"Yes. You've given enough, haven't you? Why can't you do something normal?"

"What do you consider normal, Lana?" He was exasperated, and he heard the heavy sarcasm in his voice.

"Anything that doesn't include guns and bullets."

Her hand had gone to her forehead as if in deep thought, her steps choppy as she paced her living room.

He'd been too stupid to know any better and asked, "You'll come around, won't you?"

She looked at him through tear-filled eyes.

"No, I won't *come* around. I can't stay with you if you go back to the department."

His heart had stopped beating. He'd never thought she'd take it to that extreme. He'd also thought she knew him better than this.

"I have no choice, Lana."

"Yes, you do." Her voice a broken whisper.

He took a step toward her, wanting to calm her fears, needing her to understand.

She cowered away from him.

"Lana, I wouldn't know how to do anything else."

"Then you have to leave."

There was a tortured expression on her face. It seemed as if her words were killing her, the way they were killing him.

"Please, sweetheart. Let's talk about it."

"There's nothing to talk about. You knew how I felt about this. You knew. How could you have kept these plans to yourself? We should have had this discussion before you talked to the department, before you agreed to go back."

Fear could so easily flow into other emotions and his turned to anger.

"This is who I am. You knew that going in. Don't pretend ignorance now."

"I'm not asking you to stop being who you are."

He should have kept the volume of his voice down, but he couldn't believe she was going to throw what they had away. Because of some childhood fear.

"Yes, you are. There's a threat here that if I don't become who you want, I have to go."

"It's not a threat. I can't ignore a part of who I am, or what I want out of life. It's not this."

They were at a standstill, neither willing to budge and when she'd shoved his coat at him, shown him the door, he had walked away without a backward glance.

The whole thing was his own damn fault. During their correspondence, he'd shared things with her he'd never told anyone else. His barriers had broken down and his innermost thoughts were on the page before he realized it.

When she had first begun to write to him, a couple of years into his deployment, he'd thought it would just be a novelty and that she'd stop at some point. But for close to four years, her letters had arrived like clockwork. Well, a clock that was set to military time. It took forever for the mail to get from one place to the next and find its way to him. He had come to look forward to them, tidbits from home, pieces of her embedded in every line. He'd trusted her with parts of himself that he kept buried, had to, to keep the morale of his troops up. She'd become his sounding board, and he'd poured out the pain of losing friends, the frustration with the higher-ups who were unable to communicate their goals, the threat of death hanging over him as he moved up in rank, knowing that in the lead, he would become the target.

He'd found out just how adverse she was to his life in the military one of the first nights that they talked until dawn, after he'd been shipped back to the States. And he knew when he'd asked her to marry him it was a risk. He'd hoped that she'd get used to the idea. A cop's life was safer than a Marine's, wasn't it? She'd be able to trust him to stay alive, right? Love him enough to overcome her fears?

Wrong, wrong and wrong again. He should never have led her blindly to where he wanted to go. Paul had been right. She'd never forgive him for betraying her like that.

He should have made her aware that he'd gone in to talk to Human Resources weeks before his grueling rehab was over, that all he'd need was clearance from his doctor before he could rejoin the force. He'd never quit the department when he enlisted in the military, but took a leave of absence instead, probably knowing deep down he'd be back. He should have told her that when the torture of leg presses, squats, leg lifts, balance work was behind him, as soon as he had clearance from the doctor, he was rejoining the force.

He'd made a grave error in judgement. There was a different kind of torture ahead of him. He should have been honest even in the knowing that she'd walk away.

But she'd never been far from his thoughts.

Not when he was walking a beat, deep undercover, or in the alleyway thinking he was going to die.

He went to his duffel bag, unzipped the innermost compartment, and took out the bundle held together with an elastic. Leafing through the envelopes, he pulled one out at random.

It was dated May 2011.

Nothing special about the day or the year that he remembered. It was the same grind every day. Engaging the enemy was a regular occurrence, the troops spread out with no real cover, just small mounds of dirt they could hide behind.

Peeling back the flap, he slid out the paper and unfolded it.

January 2011

Dear Zach

I didn't realize it would take forever for these letters to make it back and forth between us. So much can happen from one month to the next. You could be hurt, and I'd be here making lasagna, thinking everything was still okay, the world was still spinning on its axis. I don't even know where you are. Someplace, Afghanistan. Middle East.

Every time I write, I want to say thank you but find those words seem meaningless. I don't know why you are over there, or what you are protecting me from. I just know that my freedom somehow depends on you and others willing to fight the fight. You are a warrior in every sense of the word, but, I have to admit, for as much as I respect your courage, I don't applaud the heroics. More important than how well you fight, is your safe arrival home. I've got a vested interest in that now. I've gotten to know the person you are, the integrity that is at the core of your being. I want to know that you will be alive in the world when your tour of duty ends. So please, be careful, don't take risks that seem unreasonable, give me the opportunity to continue our friendship in the years to come. Am I assuming too much? I don't ever want our connection broken and hope you feel the same way.

Rafe and I broke up a couple of months ago. He's living in Pittsburgh now, doing a residency. I've been filling my time with work. Mom added one of my recipes to the Cookery's menu. Will wonders never cease? We've been up to our eyeballs in clients since New England Lifestyle Magazine had an impressive write-up. Seems like one of the editors went to a wedding we catered and raved about the food and the service.

It might sound crazy, but I've been watching YouTube videos to see what a battle looks like. As much as your letters hold vivid accounts of AK fire, and rockets flying across the night sky and my imagination can conjure up those images, I'm at a loss as to how it must feel to be caught up in it all. The ratt-a-tatt of the gunfire, the beep of the Geiger counter, the static of the radio create a backdrop to the logistics, the orders, the maneuvers that I couldn't have heard in the telling.

The sounds I hear are so different. The ding of my timer telling me my casserole is done, the soft hum of the dishwasher as it cleans my cooking utensils, the beat of my heart as I read your letters over and over. They calm me and make me crazy all at the same time. The worry about your safety is consuming at times, but otherwise my life placidly goes on.

I'm here if you need to unload. Feel free to tell me things you might not want anyone else to know. I'm good at keeping confidences. You must get scared or lonely or tired. Keep the letters coming. I have an overriding need to hear from you, a need you will never understand or appreciate. Losing my father was the worst thing that happened to me, an ache I still feel. Losing you would be no less unbearable.

Keep yourself safe for me.

Love,
Lana

Interesting that this was the one he pulled out. It was all here, her worry, her wanting him to keep himself safe, her father's death. *Losing you would be no less unbearable.*

How had he missed the signs?

Maybe he'd been too focused on the part where she said she didn't want their connection broken. It had caused no shortage of smiles that day. Whistling while he worked, gunning down a number of the enemy. He'd found pure joy in every written sentence and had come to count on them to lift his spirits, to make the relentless drive of the troops into occupied territory worth it, to lighten the grief of those fallen comrades. She had become his anchor to the real world, the one outside the barren place where nothing was real.

He had wanted to get back in one piece for her sake.

And he had, barely.

He hadn't known it then, but it was the first strike against him. Now he had two, and the chasm between them had grown even wider.

Staying here had been a mistake. She was still in his blood. He was back to seeing her face every morning. It was a thing of beauty, but she was still pretending that there was nothing between them.

The pretense was driving him crazy.

⌒

Lana couldn't get her mother's words out of her head. *Maybe you were the bullet.*

She'd been afraid, deathly afraid that she'd find herself in her mother's shoes, with a husband dead and buried. Celia was stronger than she was. She'd handled it, had taken all five kids through the next day, and the day after that until the trauma was behind them and life found a new rhythm. She did it with the help of her friends, with the hours she spent working to support her family, and because her children needed her to. Glancing up, she watched Celia's movements as she scurried around the kitchen getting the rest of the dinner on the table. She was happy today. She hadn't let the past take control over her, had even married another policeman, although Paul went into Homicide not long after Sal was killed. He said he didn't want another partner, at least not on patrol. The men had been best friends for as long as Lana had been alive. When Paul's wife divorced him, he'd all but lived with them, coming to the house for dinner most every night. They had all loved him, looked to him as a second father, and when Sal died, he'd taken on the care for them before he and Celia even got together. How had her mother been willing to risk her heart again? She hadn't understood it when the two announced they were getting married. She didn't understand it today. What she did understand was that it was hell living without the man you loved. Maybe she'd been too quick to cut him out. Maybe if he'd talked it over with her, she would have been willing to give it a chance, see how she functioned. When he'd taken it completely out of her hands, made the decision without any input...that had been unforgiveable.

In the past two years, she'd never let herself analyze her decision, was never willing to open the door to take a second look. Hadn't dared to. Since the second Zach walked into her mother's kitchen the day he was released from the hospital, that's all she'd been doing.

Maybe...

She jumped as Paul came in and stomped his boots on the rug by the door, so engrossed in her thoughts.

"Smells great in here. But then it always does."

He went over and kissed Celia on the cheek, nuzzled her neck. And Lana grew green with envy.

Zach must have heard Paul's voice, because he was soon filling the doorway. The sight of him never failed to make her quiver and she drank him in.

⤙

At dinner, conversation lagged as they dug into the meal, and then out of the blue, Zach asked, "Can you give me a ride later?"

Zach was directing his question to her, but it took a minute for her to process it.

Her fork stalled as his blue orbs held her spellbound.

"Why?"

The word had come out with a croak attached.

"I got a call from my tenant. He saw my picture in the paper, wanted to see if I was all right. We talked. He'd said he'd just gotten engaged, and he wouldn't mind moving out if I could give him a couple of weeks. I wouldn't have forced the issue just because my face was rearranged, but when he offered, I took him up on it."

She narrowed her eyes at him, his strange sense of humor offending her sensibilities. The smile told her he was just trying to rattle her again. She didn't know why he liked doing it. Maybe it was to give as good as he got.

"I asked him if I could drop by at some point to take an inventory because I don't remember what I left and what I put in storage. He asked if I could make it tonight. He's on call for the next two weeks and this is his only free day. If I couldn't, he said we'd figure something else out. Seeing that I still can't drive, I'll need a ride. If you're not up to it, I could always text Uber."

Biting her lip, she considered it. This would mean he'd be leaving, and if he did, maybe her thoughts wouldn't be so muddy. She could return to her pre-jitter days when her body didn't betray her, only her mind did.

Besides, she was interested in seeing where he'd lived in the days after their break-up. Tony had told her he'd bought a place. It'd only made the whole ordeal worse. If he bought, he had no intention of coming back to her.

"Yeah, sure. Why not."

"Great. Is seven-thirty workable?"

"Yeah."

"Good. Thanks."

Apparently satisfied, he went back to eating but not before telling her mother, "This is the best meal I've in in years, Mrs. C. I don't even have to chew. The meat melts in your mouth."

Celia smiled at the compliment and then asked, "So, what did you do all day? Other than talk to your tenant. You didn't come out of your room once."

Lana let her mother take over the conversation, her stomach in knots at the thought of being alone with him soon.

"Went over some of the files Paul gave me. I would have loved to sit in on the interview he had today with one of the witnesses, but my father put a quash on it. Says it's still too soon."

Paul informed, "I would have done the same thing in his position. You're pushing by coming back Monday."

Zach opened and closed his mouth, probably unwilling to go there with Paul. After the pause, he pulled at his ear and asked, "Did you get anything of value in the Half Bit case?"

"Twenty long days in and we finally figured out who sold the perp the gun. It was a guy I interviewed at the beginning. Pisses me off I miscalculated his involvement. I thought he was being up-front, being honest with us. His name came up yesterday, when we interviewed one of the victim's friends, as the one who sold the gun to Polo. When we pulled him in this morning, we had him dead to right, so he didn't deny it this time. Instead, he pretended to be surprised that it was the gun connected to a murder. Like he didn't know. I hate it when they think we're stupid."

"Didn't you tell me the perp didn't even kill the right person?"

Paul finished chewing the piece of bread and butter before he answered. "If any one of them had a brain, they'd be dangerous. He'll do time. That's all I care about."

"Save some action for Monday."

"We just caught another one last night. I thought you might have heard me leave. New father got shot multiple times outside the housing projects. Naji's primary but we'll be doing some grunt work on that, I'm sure. No witnesses have come forward. There'll be a lot of door-knocking over the next few days. While you're tied to a desk, you might be stuck with the tech piece."

The frown told Lana he didn't like the role he'd be playing. It led her to doubt he'd be hanging his hat in Homicide.

She pushed away from the table, got up to rinse off her plate, unable to finish her meal. Listening to the baritone voice had almost mesmerized her, and she had to shake the hypnotic spell. It was so easy on the ears, and there was a trap in following his every word. One she couldn't afford to trip. Her body was rigid, her back against the counter.

Then he rose, following her routine, scrape, rinse, place the dish in the dishwasher.

Then he was beside her.

"We should probably get going."

She wasn't sure anymore that it was a good idea. He was too close, too much of a temptation, one she been fighting off with all her good intentions. "Do you really need me?"

There was an underlying sensuality in his response.

"More than you know."

A shiver of panic coursed through her, his words holding a double-edged meaning that could slice through her resolve, a resolve that was already holding by a thread.

"I should help Ma clean up."

The betrayal was immediate as her mother scoffed, "Don't be silly. You two run along. This will take me no time at all."

After pausing, still not sure of the brilliance of this move, she removed her coat from the rack and shrugged into it.

Feeling his hand on her back as he escorted her out to the car, she scurried ahead and took her place behind the wheel.

CHAPTER ELEVEN

The ride to Somerville was done in silence, the nervous tension building. As they approached Union Square, the pangs of regret were back. If they had stayed together, this might be the kind of place they would have purchased together. It was in a great location, and they had talked about finding something bigger, after they'd settled into married life. He'd told her he had some money saved, all those paychecks while he was in the Marines being socked in the bank. He hadn't needed much back then.

When she pulled up to the three-decker house, he directed her to park in the back.

"This is it."

She followed him silently, around the front of the house, to the outer door, where he rang the bell.

The man who greeted them was tall and thin, his glasses giving him a professorial look. That he was a doctor was a surprise.

He stepped aside and let them enter. Lana stood there spellbound before shattering the silence.

"Oh, my God. Look at this kitchen!"

Zach scanned the room, taking in the white and grey granite counter, the white cabinets, stainless steel appliances. There was an island which he knew she'd think was a good work prep area. He'd never been inclined to cook. He'd bought it because he hoped...

"Zach, you have a wine cooler."

He watched as she opened it up to peer inside, followed her movements as she swept through the space, enjoying her enthusiasm. He hadn't seen her cheeks flush like this in a while. There was a broad smile on her face when she glanced over at him. He couldn't prevent himself from smiling back at her.

"And it's so open. I bet the place is flooded with sunlight during the day. Not that you care about any of this. I can't see you cooking."

There was a bay window that framed an eating nook, two bedrooms, one with an en suite, and a generous walk-in closet.

Dr. Jones stayed behind in the living room while they toured the rest of the place, Zach ticking off things he'd need when he finally moved back in.

Lana had peeked into the bathroom off the master, and he heard the exhale.

"A soaking tub." She said it as if she might be in heaven. Then her tone turned cynical. "It'll be wasted on you. I can't see you lounging in a bubble bath."

"What about my lady friends?"

Her eyes jolted to his.

She obviously hadn't thought of him entertaining women here. He didn't have any plans of doing it, but he liked the fact that her complexion was suddenly tinged with green.

"Something bothering you, goat?"

"Don't call me that."

"It's your nickname, isn't it?"

"When I was little."

"You're still little."

She shifted her stance, so she was her full height, and disagreed.

"I am so not."

"You only come up to here on me."

His hand was placed horizontally a couple of inches below his neck.

"Although I have to admit it always felt right when you were tucked against me."

The flush returned to her cheeks, and he chuckled before returning to the living room.

"I appreciate you letting me come over, Scott. It's been almost two years since I was here, and I almost forgot what it looked like. And don't feel like you have to move immediately. I have a place to stay in the interim. I'll give you as much time as you need."

"I've already talked to my fiancée and we're good with the first of February. I'll be moving into her loft until we figure out where we want to end up."

"You've been great. Kept the place looking good. If you ever need a reference, give me a call."

"I will but I'm hoping I'll be buying next time. Liv and I are talking about starting a family and we'll want some room."

"Congratulations on your engagement and good luck. And just leave the keys on the counter when you leave. I have another set."

They shook hands and Zach led Lana out into the night.

"You liked it."

He felt her stiffen but it was too late for her to curb her interest, although she tried.

"I have nothing to do with it."

"What if I want to cater a party someday? You'd have the room to cook here."

"I wouldn't agree to cater an event here."

"Why not?"

"Because."

"Your answers are always so reasonable."

She sputtered but nothing more was forthcoming. They'd reached the car when he said, "I'll be out of the house in less than a month. You can start blowing up the balloons."

His expression grew serious when he noticed what she was gazing at, his lips tingling in anticipation.

And he took advantage.

His hand snaked around her neck, pulling her close, his lips hovering over hers.

And then he dipped his head, kissing her with firm insistence. Without the resistance he'd anticipated, he continued the surge, flicking at her bottom lip with his tongue until she opened for him. Their tongues danced as in days gone by, as if synchronized, moving as one, taking and giving, advancing, retreating, and the rush of adrenaline was making his ambush feverish, uncontrolled passion in its onslaught.

His body convulsed at the heat, and he roughly pulled her to him. There was nothing else that felt this good. For as much as he told her she was little, she fit, in every way possible, although there were a few ways he still hadn't tested. He knew her enthusiastic participation wouldn't last, couldn't. She was too entrenched in her animosity for his job, but he would take every morsel she'd throw him, relish it, be consumed by it.

Then he felt the push, her hands against his chest, pummeling in anger.

"Don't. You don't have that right anymore."

Her lips were swollen, her breathing shallow and the flush in her cheeks told him she had enjoyed it as much as he had, needed it like air, like blood.

But where he'd accept it for what it was, she refused.

She brushed by him, scrambled back into the car and waited for him to join her.

There was nothing he could say, so he did nothing except let the residual impact of her kiss keep him tight, hard, and throbbing.

When they arrived back at her parents' house, she sat in the silence until he got out. He heard her peel away, a little too fast for his peace of mind.

She might still be running away, but she still wanted him. And he wanted her right back. Not just for what she did to him, although that could have satisfied him for life, but for who she'd become to him, a safe place to hide himself. If she'd open her heart a bit wider, he'd gratefully climb right in.

⁓

With shaking fingers, she opened the door to her condo, stumbling over the threshold, still frantic from the kiss. And what it had done to her.

She'd tried hard to forget how good it was. But the tingles at the first brush of his lips on hers had turned to jolts of electricity and flashed in psychedelic colors. It was the same today as it was when he'd stolen those first few kisses within weeks of his return from Afghanistan. She'd never realized a kiss could be so potent.

He'd been out of the hospital a couple of weeks and had started his rehab, pushing himself like he always did when he had a goal. She'd cleared her schedule for the daily hour-long sessions so she could get him back and forth to the physical therapy center. Forcing herself to watch, the pain evident in every feature of his face, the tight-lipped expression, the creased brows, the clenched jaw, she'd suffered with him, needing a respite but not allowing herself one.

After one of the grueling treatments, she'd helped him to the car, the crutches scraping the asphalt as he hobbled along. His mood was somber, his body beaten.

As they stood by the passenger-side door, he'd surprised her with a kiss.

His lips had been so soft, his stubble rough. The contrast in textures arousing.

Placing her hands on his face, she'd leaned in and returned it in kind. He'd welcomed it with a parlay of tongue on tongue.

And then he'd rested his forehead on hers.

"I don't think I'm up for this right now, but my body needed a reward for what I just put it through."

"I'm sorry...I..."

The brush of his lips quieted her.

"I've wanted to kiss you since the first day you showed up at the hospital. Thoughts of you were the one thing that kept me safe."

"Oh, Zach."

"That's why I wanted you with me during this torture, so I could focus on you, push myself to get better so... I want a future with you Lana. I can't see my life without you in it."

⌒

She had wanted to believe him, had believed him to the point she'd married him when he asked. She'd been living in a bubble of naiveté and had bungled her future by not asking him the questions that would have saved them from what came after.

The separation would have come sooner if she had known, so maybe...

If she had known, she would have missed the months of bliss she'd found in his arms.

Nothing had felt that good. She didn't know that kind of happiness existed or make her crave something so badly. The pain she felt in the aftermath was of equal measure.

Her fingers went to her lips. They still tingled.

After throwing in a load of his wash, she moved to her bedroom and changed into her pajamas. Clicking on the TV, she hoped there was a movie on to make her forget her explosive reaction to him, but there was a part of her that wanted to remember, so she pulled the box of letters onto her lap and pulled one from the bunch.

October 2012

Lana,

I guess I should wish you a Merry Christmas now seeing this letter will probably arrive just in time for the holiday.

I'll be leaving this part of the world on temporary assignment, probably by the end of the month. I'm heading to Virginia for sniper school. I was one of four selected out of the twenty esteemed members of the Marines who began the indoctrination. It took four days for the battalion leader to make his choices. There was a physical fitness test, which I aced (ha ha), a written test, followed by classes on sniper tasks like first aid and medivac procedures. From what I hear, all I need is good eyes, good behavior, and strong body. Oh, and the stamina to survive the training. From what I hear, it's a bitch. More stories to come, I'm sure.

After the eight-week course, I'll be heading back to this part of the world.

I was sorry to hear about the breakup of your relationship. From what my mother wrote, you hit every benchmark on the road to matrimony.

What happened?

How do you feel about it?

I know I'd have a hard time letting you go. Even as just a pen pal. I can't imagine what life would be like if you stopped writing.

You've become my anchor in a very choppy sea.

I know I tell you more than I should, but there aren't many people I can talk to about the feelings that surface out here. My mother would have a stroke if she knew what I faced on any given day. My father would tell me to man up and get the job done. My commanders only talk to people up the chain, not down, and the men and women under me wouldn't want to know how scared I am at times. The immense responsibility I carry every step we walk is like an over weighted backpack that gets heavier every day.

What are your plans now?

I can't think about a future out here. The main focus is on making it back to camp, never mind Stateside. The enemy do all they can to spoil our short-term goal, but we trudge ever onward.

Say hi to your family for me and think of me while you're opening your presents. Mine will be the one that's not there yet.

All my best,
Zach

She fingered the letter that was years old.

Her present had arrived right after Christmas, just in time for her birthday. It was an Afghani scarf with a red paisley print. She wore it every winter, had it on this morning.

Had he noticed?

She would have. She noticed everything about him, knew exactly what kind of toll the beating had taken. While he was talking to the renter, she'd studied his profile, although she knew it by heart. His strong jaw, his classic-shaped nose, his thick dark hair. His deep blue eyes were hooded but she knew the power they had over her. The muscles hidden beneath his button-down shirt had lost mass. She could feel the difference when he had pulled her close. Knowing him it wouldn't take time to build them back up.

He'd be back in the boxing ring as soon as he could be, she was sure of it.

She'd gone with him once, to sit and watch as he sparred with a friend of his. He'd decided he needed another form of therapy, one he enjoyed, so he'd hit the boxing club on the weekend.

He was primal in the ring. Strong, disciplined, overwhelmingly male.

It was ironic how safe she felt in his arms, as if the world could blow up around them and she'd survive. The problem was her heart. It had cracked into pieces when he left, but if he was killed in the line of duty, it would have been demolished.

She had done the only thing she could to protect herself.

But what had it gotten her?

A life half lived.

An empty bed.

A heart that still hadn't healed.

She wondered if it ever would.

After jamming the letter back in the box, she rushed into the kitchen. She had to put all this demoniac energy to use so she began to pull out the ingredients for lemon squares. Baking was her go-to when she was agitated. The mixing and measuring calmed her; the aroma soothed her senses.

After setting the oven at three-hundred and fifty degrees, she blended the softened butter, sugar, and flour and pressed it into an ungreased pan.

As it baked, she transferred his clothes to the dryer, holding each piece of clothing as if it were sacred, wanting to cry at the feelings still festering, the effects of the kiss shredding her resolve. His hand had caressed her neck, his fingers had stroked her skin, his lips had been insistent, and something deep within her had spiraled out of control.

She couldn't stop herself from falling into him, so she had let him consume her, his tongue velvet, working her masterfully, and she followed his lead as if an apprentice in the art of love. It had been like that from day one. She didn't have much experience with that kind of kinetic emotion. Rafe's kisses had been good, but there hadn't been this kind of electric spark between them. A spark that could ignite into a full-blown inferno.

She'd let the knowledge fade or so she convinced herself. She'd tried to put him out of her mind, but he lurked on the fringes, always there beyond reach, on the outer edges of her fear. A fear that seemed to know no bounds. At least when it came to him.

But what had it served her?

Her solitary life was a dead end. She knew it down to her soul.

The kiss had upset her equilibrium, made her consider new possibilities. It had also sent the fear running, pure attraction filling the space.

Could fear and love live in the same dimension? Or would they always run parallel, making it impossible to merge the two?

The buzzer jolted her out of her thoughts.

After scurrying back into the kitchen, she took the browned crust from the oven and began the next phase, whisking together the rest of the flour and sugar, adding the eggs and lemon juice before pouring it over the crust and placing it back in the oven.

The hint of lemon in the air quieted her roiling emotions, stilled her hummingbird-like heartbeat.

A calm acceptance came over her.

He would always be the one.

The last few years had done nothing to alleviate her need for him.

Maybe it was time to work from the other side of it.

Instead of letting her fear keep them apart, maybe she could let her fear of losing him forever take the upper hand.

As Scarlett O'Hara would say, tomorrow was another day.

She'd wrestle with it then.

It was quiet when Zach entered the Catalano-Scalera house, the only light on the one over the oven, and it cast an eerie glow around the room. Maybe the strangeness came from the emptiness. This was the heart of this house and it seemed odd when life was absent.

Maybe it was Lana's absence that made it feel dark and soulless.

That's what his life had become since she left.

The kiss had told him what he'd thought since getting here.

She still loved him.

It was a mixed curse, because the knowing didn't necessarily mean a thing.

After settling into his small room, he flicked on the TV needing sound to supersede the thoughts rattling around in his head. Thoughts of her always caused the most suffocating need, his body tortured by the images of her in his bed.

How could he get her back there?

And would it be enough if he did?

He had wanted a family, kids, house, the whole nine yards, something he knew she wouldn't agree to.

The last year he'd spent in the Marines had been tolerable only because she was here, waiting for him to come home. There had been inferences that she might be willing to take it to a new level when he returned.

If he'd known this thing between them existed, he would have quit sooner, before Afghanistan, before the injury, maybe would have stayed on the force instead of immersing himself in war. He'd left only because his father became superintendent. He didn't want that hanging over his head, didn't want the comparisons that would have come with it, or to live in his shadow. He'd thought by joining the Marines, he could live on his own terms. He'd wanted to set the world on fire.

His genius for setting up structures, his marksmanship with a rifle, the qualities of leadership had set him apart and sent him up the ladder. Direct to the point of rudeness, he could outline the mission in detail so that everyone knew their job and what was expected. He had done well and could have spent his life there. Then Lana came into his life and the pull to return was too strong to ignore. If the injury hadn't brought him home, he would have left the service in one piece months later when his enlistment was up. If only—

He shook that thought out of his head. It couldn't have gone any other way.

If he'd never enlisted, he would have been a cop and Lana wouldn't have given him the time of day. The time served had given them a means to an end. But it wasn't the ending he wanted.

He'd wanted a life with her, but her insecurities ran too deep, the complexities of emotion multi-layered, due in part to what had happened to her father. The police department represented loss on a visceral level to her, and she didn't want to live that kind of life.

But she hadn't shut him out as much as she wanted him to believe.

This morning, she'd been wearing the scarf he'd sent her for Christmas one year. He'd seen it in a bazaar during his first week in Afghanistan and thought it would suit her. He'd been right.

He'd almost said something but thought it better to keep it to himself.

He'd sent her other things over the course of their correspondence.

One of the treasures was an authentic Afghani cookbook. During their four months together, when he lived in her condo, she had offered to make him some dishes. He'd laughed about it, telling her he never wanted to taste spicy goat again.

Goat.

Her nickname.

He'd be more than willing to taste that spice again.

Maybe once he moved, he could lure her to the condo to cook for him. Eat goat if he had to. She seemed to love the kitchen, had been enthusiastic about the space. The way to Lana's heart just might be through that route, one he'd be more than fine following.

CHAPTER TWELVE

Lana pulled up to the commercial kitchen and was out of the car before she put it in park. Getting a call just an hour earlier that her delivery team had gotten in an accident with the catering van and wouldn't be able to get the materials or food to the wedding venue on time, she had scrambled into action. Showered and dressed in record time, she alerted her mother about the disaster, asking for the cavalry to be called in. This was when family counted, and she knew from experience that they'd be there for her. They had only a few hours to get service tables, linens, warming trays, food for close to two hundred people packed and transported to Quincy, where the banquet hall was located, and then set up for the reception.

Inspecting the cars sitting double-parked along the short street, ready to breathe a sigh of relief that her mother had done her Houdini act, she tensed instead. None of the cars looked familiar.

Approaching the open area where the aluminum accordion door was hidden behind the sleeve of the building, she noticed a rental van squeezed into the bay, its back doors open. There was a bustle of activity as people carried equipment out, but they weren't the usual suspects. Instead of her brothers coming out to greet her, it was a few of Zach's friends, Julian, Ed, and Andy. She had met them during his recuperation, befriended them before and during her short marriage, and she could feel her cheeks flush in embarrassment.

Flustered and tongue-tied, she asked "What are you doing here?"

Julian grinned at her. "This is what we do. Someone in the family needs help, we help."

"But...I'm not..."

"Whether you like it or not, you're a part of mine. It automatically makes you part of theirs.

She jumped as the voice that was coming closer, registered.

Zach's jaw was still clenched, although his words were still discernable. He was limping, his cane missing from his hand, as he carried several clean bus pans that held dry goods, utensils and flavor extracts, handing them to Julian, who had taken up the position of packer.

Her eyes widened as she watched him manipulate the heavy bins up and into his friend's waiting arms. Even though he had lost some muscle since the beating, his strength was still impressive.

Shaking herself out of her reverie, the magnetic appeal unabated, she snapped her eyes off his flexing muscles as they worked their magic. As he leaned against the side of the cab, she knew the hefting was taking a toll on his bruised body.

More cutting than she'd meant, she barked, "You're supposed to be resting."

"Your mom said you needed help. Part of my job description lists for better or worse. It seems I've hit a bit of worse, but I'll live."

She exclaimed in irritation, "There is no job description anymore."

"That's right. I was let go."

Although his words sounded playful, the meaning was not.

Their eyes met, and she caught a glint of steel in his.

It seemed they were at another stand off until he pushed away from the van and said, "I've got some stuff to move. If you'll excuse me, we can take this up later."

And with that, he gave her his back as he hobbled into the space where the stacks of good to be delivered, were waiting.

Julian was now taking a few other boxes from Andy and lining them up against the wall of the van.

Julian's voice reached out to her.

"Why do you bother? You know him as well as any of us. Do you think he would have just stayed behind?"

Julian gave her an easy smile, although she couldn't understand why. The guys should be aggravated that they'd been pulled away from their Saturday to help a woman they couldn't possibly like anymore.

Her hands closed into fists, her irritation making a leap towards anger. She couldn't believe they had let him risk his recovery for this, that no one had stopped him.

But Julian was right. She did know Zach, and this didn't surprise her, just affirmed her opinion that he was reckless.

Striding into the kitchen, she went directly to her mother who was directing the flow of workers, organization one of her strengths.

Arms akimbo, Lana asked, "Why did you bring them?"

Celia was busy getting the chickens ready for transport and she didn't look up.

"Johnny and Luca are in the recording studio, if you remember correctly and Dennis and Delaney took the kids to the mountains for the weekend. When Zach heard about our dilemma, he called his friends and here we are. Tony should be coming along with his partner. Paul is already on his way to Quincy with the service tables and linens but then he has to get to work. Now, you can stand there glaring at me or you can help us. Your choice."

She knew she should be grateful. Her mother was in a bind, or rather the Cookery was, and Zach had given her the gift of his friends' brawn. Her concern over Zach's injuries overrode it. Like it always did. Knowing she'd never be able to change it, she tried to lighten up. He had saved the day, just like the cartoon heroes did. The problem was he was flesh, and blood and he'd spilled it far too often.

Staring at her mother's back, she gave it up although her voice still held an edge.

"Fine. What do you need me to do?"

"Start packing up the ravioli. The food will be the last to go in, but they're working faster than I'd anticipated and I want it ready ASAP. I'm just glad the bride decided to go with a cake from one of the local bakeries."

After moving to the back of the container-like room, Lana opened the refrigerator and withdrew the sealed container that held the lobster ravioli. She had made them yesterday from scratch. It was becoming one of her signature dishes, one she'd definitely have on hand once she opened the store front. Chicken pieces were packed away in Rubbermaid containers, freshly butchered yesterday after the pasta was sealed away. Knowing her way around the kitchen, Lana soon found a rhythm. All while thinking about the men who had come here to help.

She had liked them. A lot.

It had been years since she'd seen them. They were Zach's best friends and they had become an important part of her life, if only for a while. They'd been there for him when he was rebuilding his body, with a hand, a shoulder, or conversation. Once he was well, they'd all gather on Saturday nights for a house party, alternating between the four homes where wine, beer, food and conversation flowed freely. She had become part of the intimate group upon her marriage, and she'd come to appreciate the affinity of the men in blue.

They always had each other's back. This would be no exception.

Stacking the two chicken bins one on top of the other, spraying the disinfectant along the stainless-steel counter she tried to keep her mind busy. When she retrieved the salad pouches and tucked them safely in another container, she couldn't help but smile at the thought of Julian, commandeering the van, as much of a leader as Zach. He was a member of the Special Operations Unit, assigned to the SWAT team right before she'd met him, but he'd known Zach since they were partnered as beat cops right after Zach graduated from college. He was Zach's sparring partner at the gym and matched him in height and weight. And temperament. Julian's wife, Aurora, or Rory as she preferred to be called, had married him right out of high school and the term *sweethearts* still applied almost fifteen years later. She worked at Petals, a local florist and they had discussed referring clients to each other in the way friends did. It hadn't become an actuality until later, but Petals was now her go-to for anything floral.

Ed was a member of the Drug Control Unit and his wife, Chris, had become a stay-at-home mom when the kids started coming. They had three and she remembered how good a job she was doing given the time constraints of her husband. It was another friendship Zach had formed at the community level during patrol days.

Then there was Andy, a member of the Crime Against Children's Unit. He was the sweetest man she'd ever met, and she could never understand how he could tolerate the conditions he dealt with. Investigating any crime against a child had to be horrifying, but from what she'd heard, he did it well, with calm and patient care. His wife Mona, a social worker who'd met him on the job, was good at compensating for his nature with an acerbic wit that had them laughing along with their tears as he told them stories of the kids he rescued.

Lana had allowed Zach to lead her into friendships in a way she'd never allowed herself, unwilling to take the time away from work to make the connections that would buffer her when the going got rough, when she needed a shoulder to cry on. But they hadn't been there when she needed them most. She had cut them out of her life right along with Zach, not wanting to keep friends who would remind her of what she had given up.

⌒

She'd reached out to Rory a couple of days after what would have been her and Zach's first anniversary. Depression had hit her hard. She'd needed a friend, someone not in the family, someone who might not place all the blame on her shoulders. As soon as she'd heard Rory's voice, she'd broke down, apologized for letting the friendship go, for taking so long to call.

"So am I Lana. I should have called, checked up on you. I was just so surprised. Stunned really. You guys seemed so good together and Zach loved you so much. It was hard for us to see him so devastated."

That had shocked her. He'd been devastated? She'd never seen that, only felt her own soul-deep distress at his betrayal. She knew he was pissed from the way he'd slammed out of the condo without a backward glance, and she'd never heard from him again. Hadn't seen him until the day he'd walked into her mother's kitchen, bruised and beaten.

Once the door to friendship had been re-opened, she'd talked to Rory every couple of months. She was the first person to tell her Zach had gone undercover because of the break-up.

"That's how upset he was. He wanted to disappear."

"All he had to do was quit the force, Rory. I would have flown back into his arms."

That he hadn't, hurt almost as much as his leaving.

"Which means you loved him."

Of course, she did. How could people suggest otherwise? Zach had been the only person she'd let in, and agreeing to marry him, so soon after he got back, spoke volumes about her feelings.

Rory didn't understand; neither did anyone else.

"How could you have left him then? There's no way I could have just walked away from Julian. My happiness is colored by my love for him."

She'd wanted to explain but didn't have the words to express what she felt. She still didn't.

"We're ready for the food. How's it coming?"

She turned to see Zach standing there, pale and stooped.

And her heart squeezed in her chest.

Wanting him to think it was anger egging her on, rather than fear for his condition, she kept moving without giving him a glance, keeping her tone curt.

"You need to go back to Ma's. You look like you're going to fall over."

He found support with his hand on the counter as he gave her a smile.

"I've got a couple more trips in me. I'll rest on the way over."

She was holding the slotted spoon, which stopped in mid-air. She looked up to glare at him.

"What do you mean?"

"We're driving the van over and setting up for you."

The spoon clattered to the counter, her fingers shaky.

"You can't."

He nodded his head in Julian's direction.

"They're taking the brunt of it for me. I'll be fine."

She gave up the pretense of irritation, her face contorted in concern.

"Please..."

He leaned towards her, fingered the pink and blue strands of her hair.

"From what I hear, you don't ask for help often, so I assume you really need it. Let me do this for you. You'd be doing me a personal favor."

He dropped his fingers when Tony rushed into the space to see what the holdup was.

"Come on. Let's get this show on the road. Adam and I have to be at the station in a couple of hours."

Her mother's voice had lost the strain that had been evident when she'd arrived.

"With all this help, we'll be able to set up in record time. We'll get everything cooked and then Sylvia can take over. There's nothing like a little adrenaline to get you moving."

Zach followed Tony out, a box of staples in one hand, a tray of food in the other. Lana watched the slow progress as he made his way to the van.

Lana grabbed hold of her mother's arm and implored, "Please, get him to go home. He looks like he's hurting."

Celia glanced back and took him in, the scowl first-rate.

"He's as stubborn as a mule. Julian and I tried to get him to stay at the house, but he refused to listen."

Lana's anger was back at his insistent desire to fix things.

"He always pushes himself. Sometimes beyond his limits."

Celia asked with sarcasm, "You've noticed he has limits?"

Lana glared, telling her without words Zach's relentless drive wasn't a joke. She'd seen those limits even as he tried to hide them from her.

Lana began collecting pots and pans to put through the clean cycle.

"Everyone does."

Her mother was standing there now, arms across her chest, glaring.

"Some are easier to detect than others. Like yours."

Celia winced at the racket being made by the banging as utensils were all but thrown into the dishwasher.

"I'm not good at hiding mine."

With a cool stare, Celia stated, "Your limits are too confining. They are ruining your life."

Slamming the door closed, Lana jabbed at the power button.

"I'm not going there. Here, take a box."

Lana stormed out of the kitchen, heading for the exit, her arms full of food bins.

And when the last crate was packed in, Julian swung down from the back of the van and closed the doors.

Stepping close, Lana said, "I can't thank you enough."

As he brushed his hands back and forth against each other, he said easily, "No thanks needed."

He paused before adding, "When Rory heard where I was going, she asked me to say hi."

Biting the inside of her lip, Lana said in a bashful way, "Say hi back. How is she?"

"Good, great. She probably would have come with me but she's in the throes of morning sickness."

Lana's eyes lit up. She hadn't talked to Rory in a few weeks, but knew they were trying to get pregnant, knew how much Rory wanted to start a family.

"Julian, congratulations. That's great."

He laughed.

"Not so great right now but she's gaining on it."

Sincere interest prompted her to ask, "When is it due?"

His hands went to his hips, his stance casual.

"Call her and ask. I know she'd love to talk to you."

Her eyes slid to Zach who was leaning against the van. She wasn't sure he knew she'd kept in touch with Julian's wife.

"Would you mind?

"Why would I?"

Her eyes were holding Zach, when she said, "The guys are your friends. I don't want you to get pissed at me for stepping into it."

"I know you've been seeing Rory. I think she has enough love in her heart for both of us."

There was an invitation there in those deep blue orbs, a sense of forgiveness and she lingered in it, but when Zach looked away, the spell was broken.

Julian must have been watching them because it was only then that he responded.

"You hurt one of our own, Lana, so Ed, Andy and I took sides. We couldn't help ourselves. It seems Zach is willing to let you back in, so we'll just follow suit."

Turning to Zach, he demanded, "Okay bud, in the truck and sit still. If you so much as lift a finger, I'm going to put you back in the hospital. And it won't be the case of just dropping you off."

After helping Zach gain his seat, he hopped in behind the wheel and backed out of the space.

Barking out the window, he said, "See you there."

Lana's heart filled to overflowing. Julian would make sure Zach was okay.

CHAPTER THIRTEEN

Once the guys finished unloading the truck at the wedding venue, it was time for Lana and her mother to get moving in the small kitchen. As the chefs in charge, their job should have been just beginning, prepping the courses instead of starting from scratch. The set-up crew should have gotten the hall in perfect order, tables set with linens, silverware, flower centerpieces, chairs tucked in around them, but it had fallen to the owners to pick up the slack.

Celia was coming down from the adrenaline high.

"I'm already exhausted."

"I'm just glad that we had the time we needed to get everything in place."

"You can thank our volunteers for that. They're nice guys. Zach has good taste in friends."

Celia was right, and the longing was back.

As she stared into space, her hand stumbled with the zipper of the storage bag that held the crostini.

Celia snapped off the lid of the container holding the chicken. Placing the pieces in a roasting pan, adding the garlic and rosemary, she asked, "They're one half of the couples you hung out with every weekend, aren't they?"

Lana was making up the trays of hors d'oeuvres, gloved hands arranging the finger food along the centered doily.

"Yeah. We alternated houses. Ours was the smallest, so it was kind of cramped with eight of us, but they never complained. Said it made it more intimate."

After peeling off her gloves, and pulling on another pair, Celia began setting up the coffee urns that would pump out the hot, steaming brew in time for dinner.

"I bet the food was better, though, so it compensated."

Lana laughed, and it felt good. They had a way, even now, to lighten her heart.

"They always had an excuse as to why I had to bring something edible with us."

Glancing over, a smile on her face, Celia asked, "Like what?"

Lana returned the smile. They were in their zone, her mother's movements in flow with hers. They had always worked well together. Maybe because she began her life in the kitchen at such an early age, maybe because they just liked each other. Conversation while they constructed the meals was always seamless.

"Usually dessert. Lemon squares, cannoli, cream puffs, chocolate mousse."

"What kind of meals did you serve at your place?"

Taking an empty tray, she lined it and began decorating it with another type of appetizer.

She could hear the regret in her voice when she admitted, "We only got to host four. Then Zach dropped his bombshell, and they were over."

Her mother must have heard the regret, too, because she let silence fill the space for more than a few heartbeats before saying, "We did the same thing, as you well know. We'd use any excuse to get together knowing we might need each other someday, and it helped to have those friends around me when your father was killed."

Lana had been too young back then to realize the why behind the weekend gatherings, thought it was just the way extended families behaved. Being Italian with their own rituals made it easy to see it that way. It shouldn't have surprised her to see the support after her father's death, the casseroles, the nighttime visits made to console, women helping women lift the burden of widowhood.

Lana knew it had helped her mother cope.

"I don't think there's any other profession that bonds that way. Well, maybe the fire fighters."

"Not many other professions lose so many to death, either."

With the last pan of chickens placed in the oven, Celia peeled off her gloves and washed her hands.

"You're probably right."

Checking the time, Celia gathered the twelve pitchers, filling them with ice and bottled water so the waitstaff could begin their finishing touches on the table settings.

"Tell me what you served the times you hosted."

She had been so nervous, wanting so hard to please. Zach had upped the game, telling everyone what a great cook she was. Not that he'd know. He wouldn't even taste some of the things she put in front of him. But she'd learned which meals were his favorites and she'd recycled the meat and potatoes every way she could.

"What Zach wanted. Meat, meat and then some meat. The first time I made a balsamic steak with Lyonnaise potatoes and asparagus. Well, he didn't eat the asparagus. It's—"

"Green."

Her mother chuckled as they said it in unison.

"You never got to go exotic cooking for him?"

"Italian is exotic for Zach's palette."

"He eats it at our house."

"I didn't say he didn't eat it, just that it's foreign. It was never first choice."

"Why do chefs end up with such finicky eaters?"

There was a downward tilt to her lips, and she felt her heart dip as if it was frowning, too.

"We didn't end up together, remember?"

The words wedged in her throat; the fact still able to bring tears to her eyes.

Having the memories scattered on the floor had to be better than having pieces of her heart littered there.

Didn't it?

The problem was her heart was shattered. Did it really matter where the pieces were?

Her mother told her something she already knew.

"It's hard for me to forget. There's an empty seat at our Sunday dinners. I liked it better when he filled it."

So had she.

Dusty, one of their senior waitstaff, came over and announced, "The guests are beginning to arrive. Are we ready to go?"

Celia nodded, pointing to the trays of appetizers that would soon make the rounds.

While the photographer worked with the bride, groom and ensemble, waitresses cut through the crowd offering bruschetta, gorgonzola polenta rounds, asparagus-prosciutto crostini, and sausage-stuffed mushrooms. On the individual tables sat flatbread slices, pizza dip, and arancini for those who wanted to socialize from their table. It was a full Italian menu, and once the reception was in full swing, the courses came out timed with precision, the food a mix of old and new. Salad, the wedding soup, the lobster ravioli, chicken with rosemary and garlic, Tuscan white beans, spring peas with pancetta, and roasted fennel and tomatoes served by a superior staff, all directed by one of their managers.

Celia made the rounds, making sure everything was going smoothly, checking the tables for potential refills of water pitchers, bread and butter servings, bottles of wine. Very rarely did she find anything amiss. Once the last course was served, the dishes already being rinsed and placed in the kitchen's multiple dishwashers, Lana heaved a heavy sigh.

"I think that does it."

"You run along. I know you've got to follow up on the crew and the van. I'll close us out."

"Thanks."

And when Lana shrugged into her coat, put on her mittens and wrapped her scarf around her head, she walked out into the late afternoon, breathing in the smell of bitter-cold air.

⌒

Zach's eyes were closed, his body aching.

Even he'd have to admit he probably pushed himself too far today, but there was no way he was going to let his friends carry the load for a woman they didn't trust.

"You need help getting in?"

Julian had pulled into the Catalanos' driveway and was waiting for an answer. Being the good friend he was, Julian had kept his counsel to himself during the ride back to Melrose, which only took about twenty-five minutes. Not wanting to take any more time away from his friend's day off, Zach said, "No. I'm good."

"You sure? Rory's at work so I have a couple of hours to kill."

It was close to noon, and when he'd roused everyone with his SOS, he was sure no one had had time for breakfast. He, for one, was starved. Figuring there'd be something in the refrigerator to eat, he offered, "How 'bout we grab lunch. I could use a beer and I know I shouldn't drink on an empty stomach."

"You sure Mrs. C wouldn't mind?"

"If I've learned anything over the last week, it's these people live for food."

"You didn't know that from living with Lana?"

"I didn't realize it was a family disease."

"Right. None of those Sunday dinners you used to tell us about gave you a clue."

Climbing out of the SUV, awkward in his movements, Zach slid his feet to the ground and hobbled along the driveway to the side door. Taking the key out, he opened it, feeling more at home here than he did at his parents' house.

There was life here, laughter, not the stilted polite demeanor expressed in tight lips and pinched brows.

He missed those Sunday dinners Julian had mentioned.

The whole family would be seated around the table, enjoying each other's company. Manners were mandatory but there was no walking on eggshells trying to avoid a confrontation. It was a free-for-all where no topic was off the table, a varied group of musicians, artists, and wildly creative people, who were curious about life and interested to know the meaning of things. Luca was a science geek, albeit a very successful bassist, who could discuss the meaning of the universe in ways a novice could understand. Delaney was a nurse in the emergency room at one of the Boston hospitals and brought to the table another kind of story. Tony and Paul were on the force and spoke his language. He'd always felt part of them, a member in good standing.

When he was no longer welcome, he'd sit and brood on Sunday afternoons. Julian, Ed, or Andy would come to his rescue, invite him over to one of their houses, try to make him feel a part of a whole he thought he'd never be part of again.

They were his friends and they had come through for him again today.

As he opened the refrigerator, feeling a bit awkward about making himself so at home, he let Celia's words about helping himself counter it.

Taking two beers out, he offered one to Julian, who took it, looking over Zach's shoulder to see what treasure lay within the gleaming stainless-steel appliance.

"What you got to offer?"

Labeling containers with date and type of food, a health code necessity, was followed here as well as at the commercial kitchen they cooked out of, so it made it easy to tick off what was available for consumption.

Zach reached in and read off the choices.

"Spaghetti and meatballs, chicken and potatoes, lentil soup from Celia's kitchen."

Taking three glass containers out and putting them on the counter, he said, "These are Lana's containers, so they must be her testers. Chicken gumbo, Mediterranean vegetables and lamb casserole, and beef and vegetable casserole."

"Didn't she test some Afghan dishes on you?"

"Um, she offered. I didn't make a good guinea pig. Refused to even try them."

"You are so lame. She's a great cook."

"Yeah, so people tell me."

Rolling his eyes, Julian said, "You get first pick seeing that I'll eat any one of them."

Taking the cover off the beef dish, Zach put it to his nose and sniffed.

"Oh, man. You've got to be kidding."

"Hey, she threatened to poison me. I'm not taking any chances."

"She wouldn't just leave it in there for anyone to take, she'd add it before serving, I'm sure of it. Now give me this one. I'm in the mood for some heat."

Julian took the gumbo and looked around for the microwave. After placing the glass dish on the swivel tray, he punched in the time and let it turn.

Zach got out silverware and heated his dish up as soon as Julian's was finished.

Seated at the table, Julian took several mouthfuls before announcing, "This is gooood."

Zach picked at the mix of meat and green, forking out a piece of beef and tasting it.

One never knew what kinds of spices Lana would add to any given dish, and he'd been sorry in the past that he dove right in. This didn't seem to have any hidden traps for his taste buds, so he began to eat with more gusto.

Julian took a swig of the beer before asking, "So when are you thinking about going back to work?"

"Monday."

"Zach. You need more time."

That's what his father had said. After the argument they had about it, the superintendent had given in.

"No, I don't. I'm going stir crazy."

"But..."

"I'm not going undercover again, remember? I'll be in a car, at a desk. Dad said he wasn't okaying the field for another week. I can sit there as well as here."

He'd somehow finagle his way out of that restriction, as well.

Julian almost agreed, *almost* being the operative word.

"I know you. You won't be able to take it slow. There'll be someone who tries to flee the scene and you'll be the one taking off after him. Or her."

"Why does everyone think I have some kind of death wish?"

"Because you act like you do?"

"My leg took another beating so I'm not sure I'd be able to chase down even a slow-moving perp. Besides, according to Lana, Homicide is *special*. They don't do the dirty work."

Scraping the side of his bowl to extract every last smear of the gumbo Julian said, "No, just inspect dead bodies that no one wants to be witness to."

Wiping his mouth, Zach was nonchalant in his response. "Nothing I haven't seen before."

"Kids, Zach? Can you stay detached if the kid that dies is a...kid?"

Looking up and into Julian's eyes, he asked, "How old do you have to be to be a kid? Four? Ten? Eighteen, nineteen? Been there, seen that shit."

Rubbing his hands together, Julian posited, "I think this might be good for you. Everything that went before brought you here."

Leaning back in his chair, his hands flat on the table, he admitted, "I'm beginning to think so too."

Julian got up from the table and cleared it, placing both bowls inside the deep farmer's sink.

Then as an afterthought Zach stated, "I should be back in Somerville soon. My tenant offered to move out. I'll have my place back."

Julian's head snapped in Zach's direction.

"What? You're not going to live in that flea-bitten pesthole anymore?"

"God no. That was one of the positives about transferring to Homicide."

"That means you can host a Saturday night or two again. Can you convince Lana to cook?"

He gave his friend a broad smile. "She did like the kitchen, so there might be a chance."

Taking back his seat and another swig of beer he asked, "She saw it?"

"Yeah, I needed a ride."

"And she went?"

"Yeah. I think she wanted to make sure this was going to happen."

In a more serious tone, Julian asked, "How's that been?"

"Tough."

"What made you ask Paul if you could stay there?"

"No way was I going to my parents' house."

Julian gave him a quizzical look.

"Okay. I guess...I'd hoped... Things didn't work out like I wanted."

Julian let that settle between them before asking, "When you moving?"

"Beginning of the month."

"I suppose you'll want help."

"Of course. I've helped you a couple of times. You can call it payback. It's not far from you. And I won't have much."

"Can we find a new gym?"

"You didn't like driving to Framingham?"

Zach couldn't risk being seen locally with a cop, so Julian had accommodated him.

"Not so much. Now that you can be seen around town, it might be nice to hit one closer to where we live."

"We can go back to the one in town."

The first gym they'd boxed at was in Somerville, convenient to both.

"I never left."

"You went without me? I'm hurt."

"Then get over yourself."

Julian leaned his elbows on the table.

"The fact that you've agreed to Homicide...does it mean you're giving up, moving on?"

Julian didn't have to explain what he meant. His friends knew he'd been holding out hope that Lana would change her mind. Two years later he had to take another look at the impossibility of that.

"Don't know. Maybe. I...I'm trying to show her I'm...not reckless, that I can settle down like normal people. I kissed her the other day. She kissed back. I keep thinking...she still loves me. It might not be enough."

Zach worked his jaw, trying to get the kinks out. Julian must have seen the hidden sorrow in his expression because he said, "Look, why don't you come out to the house tonight. Spend some time with us. It's been a while since you've been able to."

"Don't tell anyone of consequence but I've got to lie down. My body is a throbbing mess. I'll see how I feel when I get up."

"Sounds good. Don't push it. If we see you, great, if not, there's always next week."

"That's one of the upsides to living above ground. I get to see my friends more."

Seeing Julian out, he thanked him once again, then limped down the hall and into his room. Sinking down on the bed, his head in his hands, he knew he had to talk to her. A serious-where-are-we-going kind of talk. They'd never really had one. Then, if she wasn't willing.... Being partnered with Paul was going to make it harder.

He lay down, and before he could begin to analyze what he could say to make it better, he fell into the sleep of the dead.

CHAPTER FOURTEEN

Lana walked through the door of her condo. Flicking on the light as she entered the kitchen, the cloudy January day preventing the sun from cascading across her tiled floor, she rummaged through the refrigerator, pulling out the container of spaghetti and clam sauce she had left over from the other night.

She heated it up in the microwave, and sat at the small table, the dish in front of her. Her mind took her back to this morning, her fork twirling strands of pasta around and around.

Zach had saved her from disaster.

At least had saved the Cookery's reputation from taking a hit.

The van had been towed to a repair shop; the insurance company had been called. It would be out of commission for over a week, the repairs bad but not fatal. Her crew was fine, with no injuries reported, so the apologies were easy to accept.

The three-member team had been with the company for a few years and did their job so well she'd forgotten things like this happened.

Accidents.

They could hit at any time, always without warning.

Different than things done with intention.

Like leaving your husband.

Leaving behind friends who had come to mean something.

She placed the pasta in her mouth, but it tasted like sawdust, so she pushed the plate away and sat back staring at the clock on the wall, the ticking sound a reminder that time didn't stand still.

Two years had flown by.

And what did she have to show for it?

Her job, her family, her life.

She hadn't added anything to it, had subtracted from it if truth be told.

Wasn't time supposed to provide you with growth, expansion?

It hadn't done either for her.

That had been done with intention, as well.

Uncorking the wine bottle she'd brought to the table, she poured herself a drink and swallowed it down in one gulp.

It was a fruity blend with crisp acidity.

Zach had introduced her to it when he'd started living here.

He'd introduced her to a lot of things.

Good love was one of them.

After pouring another glass, she held the stem and twirled, listening to the emptiness of her surroundings, her thoughts taking her back to one of the nights they'd spent time together without the insistent commands of his physical therapist or the hovering presence of his mother.

They'd left the rehab center, and she'd been ready to drive him to his folks' house when he asked if he could hang out with her for a while. Eying him, gauging if he was physically spent and needed rest, she'd decided to leave that choice to him.

"Sure. Do you want to pick up something to eat? You must be hungry."

"I thought you were a chef."

"I am, but not your kind."

He leaned his head against the back of the seat, but he turned, the beginning of a smile tipping the corner of his mouth up.

"You're just my kind."

She fed on his words like a person starving for...affection, love?

Whatever it was, she wanted more.

"The only leftovers I have in my refrigerator are testers."

"What are they?"

"Recipes I've tried out to see if I like them."

"What was the verdict?"

"A couple I liked a lot, one not so much."

"I'll probably like the one you didn't."

He hadn't, turned his nose up at all of it so she'd made him an omelet, leaving out all the things she would have loved enfolded in the yellow creaminess.

They had spent most of the evening in silence, watching TV, sitting together on her small couch. With him the silence hadn't been awkward. It had enhanced the easy way they had of being together.

It was only when they were getting ready to leave that he showed her that the quality of their silence could be improved.

He had pulled her close, tucking her against his chest, rubbing her back up and down with his hands.

And then he dipped his head, his lips covering hers. She'd been hoping for a repeat, and the shot of adrenaline that came with it, that blended all her other hormones together in a rush of feeling.

"I've wanted to do that all evening. I want to do other things, as well."

Initiating another kiss, she felt the quiver intensify and molded herself to his body.

He took advantage, bringing her even closer, his mouth now taking the lead, his tongue probing, hers exploring, his hands molding to her body and quickening the coil that tightened inside her.

They didn't take it to the limit that night.

That had come later, after they had spent many hours enjoying the feel of textures, tasting to their hearts' content.

He wanted to make sure what she was feeling was real, not just the result of pity or sympathy.

She must have convinced him, because he proposed before they ever made it to bed.

Their marriage had taken place two weeks later and he'd moved in until they could purchase a bigger place that would accommodate her cooking dreams. A condo, a house, here in the city, out in the suburbs. They'd discussed all of it.

Prematurely it would seem.

For all the questions she'd asked, she hadn't asked the important one.

What do you plan on doing with your life Zach? Now that you're back and healing.

The why not still bothered her.

She got up and walked into her bedroom, opened a drawer in her bureau that held some of her most cherished possessions. Opening a small box, she took out her wedding ring, put it on, and fingered it. It was gold, thin, and felt too familiar.

She'd been happy the day Zach had slid it on her finger, but she wished she'd known what was around the next bend so she could have appreciated it more, cherished it more.

Not that she hadn't cherished him while they were together.

He was a man she could lean on, trust. He had integrity and stood for all the things that were important to her.

Or so she'd thought.

He'd ultimately betrayed her, and she was left standing in the cold, hard truth of who he was at his core.

A policeman.

Today he'd proved she could still lean on him. Willing to put himself through pain to do it.

She wished she could be more like him.

But she wasn't that strong.

She could lose him too easily to a stray bullet, to a crazed perpetrator.

So instead, you lost him to your fears. What's the difference?

Spinning around, the emptiness becoming too confining, she raced out of the room they'd once shared.

It had taken weeks, no, months, no, years to put his ghost to rest.

Maybe it would never be put to rest because she wanted him here.

To comfort, to help heal, to love.

In sickness and in health.

There had been too much of the first and too little of the latter.

She seemed destined to be with him in times of trouble, his body wracked in pain. First after his return from Afghanistan, and now in the aftermath of the ambush that left him broken and bleeding.

What would it have been like to be with him in good health?

Even scarred, his body was amazing. His lovemaking tender, passionate, thrilling.

Nothing like she'd ever felt before.

Love did that.

Made everything more intense, more vivid, more real.

And she loved him with her full heart, no part of it void of him.

⌐

Picking up her phone, she scrolled through her contacts and found Rory's number.

She punched it in and listened to the rings.

Then the voice.

"Lana? Is that you?"

"Hi. I heard congratulations are in order."

"Can you believe it? I wasn't sure it was ever going to happen."

"When are you due?"

"August. It seems so far away but each step is exciting. Except this one. The morning sickness has been pretty rough."

"Is there anything I can do?"

"Um, if you have any leftover desserts...I grew a sweet tooth and it's calling out for something gooey, chocolate, tart,...anything. Maybe you could bring it over tonight. Our turn for dinner, so everyone's going to be here if you want to stop by. It'll be good seeing you again. It's been months."

The Saturday gathering. She would love to be part of that again. It had always been so much fun.

She looked down and fingered the ring again, her heart sinking like a stone.

"No but thank you. I wouldn't want anyone to think..."

"We all know the score. And I doubt Zach will be here. And maybe you can bring that dessert?"

"What you're saying is you want my desserts. I can messenger one over if you want."

"No. I want you *and* your sweets."

"I'd have to make something. What did you have in mind?"

"Chocolate. Decadent. Satisfying."

"Are you sure that Zach won't be there?"

It would be the first time she joined the group since she'd let Zach go. She wouldn't want to interfere with the core group dynamics.

"Julian said he was pretty beat up when he dropped him off at your folks'. He did ask him to come but it didn't sound like he was going to take Julian up on the offer."

He was pretty beat up.

That wasn't a surprise. He'd pushed himself again, for her, and she didn't like the way that felt.

Maybe she should drop by her folks' house to see how he was.

After she made the cake.

On her way to Rory's.

Zach looked at the clock.

He's slept a couple of hours and had to admit it had helped. The joint pain wasn't as bad but maybe it had been the aspirin he'd taken before the nap.

Pricking his ears was the sound of the front door opening and closing.

Was Celia back?

He forced his legs over the side of the bed and sat for a minute, the ache in his bones, the throbbing in his leg making it hard to stand up.

Then a picture stood at his open doorway. Her jeans were an upgrade over the ones she wore the other day with the ripped threads and holes in the knees. Her sweater was tunic- style and covered a nice butt that curved perfectly in his hands.

She had moved with the kind of stealth he'd found in the Marines, although he'd always been one step ahead of the enemy.

Was she the enemy?

"How are you feeling?"

"Been better but not as bad as I'd thought I'd be."

"You got some sleep?"

Scrubbing his face with his hands, he wiped away any evidence that's what he'd been doing.

"Yeah. Is that why you came over? To see if I rested?"

He looked up to see her stance had shifted, her arms crossed tightly over her chest.

What was she trying to protect herself from?

"Me? I'm not a coddler and I'm not your mother. I wanted to check in to see if you're going to Julian's tonight."

He didn't like the way that made him feel. He wanted her to care, to check in, to coddle. A spark of anger flicked through him at his need, or the fact that she didn't feel the same way.

"Why? You never cared where I went before."

Her lips thinned, and he knew there was a scream waiting to be unleashed. She surprised him when she kept her voice modulated.

"That's not exactly true. The police department was always off-limits."

He scowled and then stood on shaky legs but solid feet, as solid as possible on his damaged foot.

"I haven't decided whether I'm going. Again, why?"

Her arms dropped to her side, and she took a step towards him as if she expected him to fall flat on his face.

Eying him, her mood recalibrated, she replied, "I talked to Rory this afternoon. She invited me over, but I think it was more for what I had to offer than my company."

His anger had shriveled when he looked up at her. Her transformation was a stark one. Gone was the animosity. Now there was a softness about her that ignited his heart, a fragility that always drew him. It was in direct contrast to who she was at the core.

"I can't say I blame her. It was always what you had to offer that did it for me."

"And what was that?"

She was chewing the inside of her cheek which told him she was off-balance, as if she was afraid of how he'd answer her question.

"Your independence, spirit, empathy, courage."

She pushed her hair off her face and tucked it behind her ear.

"Me? Courage? I think you have me confused with...you."

He took a step toward her, and he was surprised she stayed in place and didn't retreat.

"You took a chance on me."

"And chickened out not long after."

"That took courage, too. The courage of your conviction."

He reached out his hand to cup her chin, his thumb tracing her lip.

This time she did retreat.

"Rory asked me to make something chocolate. Which I did. If you're going, I'll send it with you. If you're not, I'll drop it off myself."

He asked without thinking it through, "Why can't we go together?"

Her eyes flew up to meet his.

"A terrible idea. They might get the impression..."

"That we decided to be friends. Is that too hard to believe? It's how we started out."

It was but she'd forgotten how to do that. All it had taken was a night in his arms. Or maybe it was their first kiss.

Could *he* go back to that place? If he could, he didn't feel what she did.

Was that why it was easy for him to choose the job over her?

She gave him a skeptical look.

"Friends?"

His eyes were piercing, and her skin felt the ripples that came with it.

"We were the best of...once."

It seemed forever ago.

"I'm not sure I can do that."

"Why not?"

She struggled with an answer to that question. She couldn't tell him the truth. That it was outside her realm of comfort. Or sanity. She lobbed it back.

"You can?"

"If it's the only recourse left to me? Yeah. I can."

His eyes met hers. Need was written in the bluest ones she'd ever seen. She fell into them, wanting to fall into his arms, pledge her undying love. But she'd already done that, and it caused the kind of suffering she'd never known existed. Was this the alternative?

Being with him was better than being with anyone else.

That was a fact she couldn't change.

"Are you up for it? I know you worked hard this morning."

"If you drive, and I sit while I'm there, I can't see a problem."

He watched as she decided, her mouth to the side, her brow furrowed.

"This isn't a good idea."

"Lana, do you want me completely out of your life, or can we find a way to...make the connection work again?"

She slid her eyes up to meet his and she was welcomed there. It made the decision even harder.

"I don't know."

"I like having you in my life. Is that too hard a concept to accept?"

"I like having you in mine. It's just...the worry is the same now as it was then."

"I don't think we can go back to when it didn't matter. Can we?"

She shook her head.

"Then let's find a way to move forward."

"Maybe."

His hand linked with hers as he led her out of his room and down the hallway.

Throwing caution and all good sense to the wind, she shrugged on her coat and picked up the cake bin.

Maneuvering through the light traffic, she glanced over from time to time, to admire him, his head back, his eyes closed, He was rugged, good-looking. His hair was longer now than it had been when they had gotten together. It made him even more appealing, the shaggy locks that held a slight curl. She'd often wondered what their children would look like. Dark hair for sure, maybe his dimple, maybe her oval face. They'd never talked about having them, too busy getting him back on his feet, then it was too late for it to matter.

She felt so small sitting next to him. He had a big personality that took over a room.

It was one of the things that made this so impossible.

Her father had made her feel the same way.

Small but safe.

With his death, that had blown up in her face and *safe* became a word that had no meaning. She was left with a fear so strong she choked on it.

It hadn't mattered until Zach came barreling into her life.

Through the letters, she had let down her guard, had let him in. With his survival came gratitude that he had outwitted fate.

She couldn't count on his luck lasting.

But what had that gotten her?

An empty bed and a broken heart.

She looked over again, a ripple of desire becoming a torrent of regret.

He opened his eyes and she was sure he could read what was in them. The blue pupils darkened and burned into her.

He found her hand with his and stole it from the steering wheel.

Bringing it up to his lips, he kissed it, sending tingles up her arm and down into that cavity that he'd once filled. Her mind shifted to a tangle of sheets, a deep thrust, and the satisfaction they had found in each other.

She gave him a penetrating look.

"If you ever want to pick up where we left off...let me know. It's been a while for me."

Snatching her hand away and gluing it back on the wheel, she tried to stop the erratic beat of her pulse.

What was a while?

He couldn't have gone two years without...anything.

The thought of him in someone else's arms caused a rumble that started in her toes and skyrocketed up.

"Yeah, for me, too. I kept my marriage vows."

She could feel him bristle as he bolted upright.

"You mean there was one you kept? And here I thought you broke them all." His voice was heavy with accusation.

She stiffened at the tongue-lashing.

She had no right to be angry that he'd found release in another bed. She'd given him the okay the day she told him to get out of her life.

Then why did it feel like the ultimate betrayal? Her heart felt like it had been pierced with a dagger.

"I'm sorry. I have no right to judge you."

Shaking his head, he turned to stare out into the night.

"Lana, I kept all my vows. It makes me feel less like a fool to know that you kept that one."

"You never...took anyone else to bed?"

"Crazy, isn't it?"

Crazy, maybe. Mind-boggling, yes.

"It's been two—"

"I know down to the minute how long it's been. So please don't look at me like that."

"I'm not looking at you...well, not like that."

"We might not have been together long, but I know *that* look."

Scrambling to find solid ground, unable to with him right there beside her, she exclaimed, "I'm going to drop you and the cake off. I'm not doing this tonight."

"Does that mean there's hope for the future?"

"No. I told you this was a bad idea."

He dropped his head back again and gave a loud exhale.

"I'm sorry. I promise I'll keep my hands to myself. Let's enjoy ourselves tonight with good friends."

She wanted to, wanted to be part of the community they offered. Wanted things she shouldn't want.

It corroded her good sense and she found herself standing beside Zach in front of the door.

As they waited, the bell ringing inside the house announcing their presence, she swallowed the lump in her throat wondering what the hell she was playing at.

CHAPTER FIFTEEN

Julian was the one who opened the door, as the bell was still echoing beyond the wall, the look of surprise on his face almost priceless.

"Well, this I did not expect. Come in."

Rory was approaching, her arms extended, and before Lana was engulfed in a hug, she passed the cake to Zach, freeing up her hands so she could reciprocate the full embrace.

She watched as he handed it over to Julian, a smile on his face.

"I think this is for your wife."

"And we can only hope she shares."

Arm in arm, Rory and Lana walked up the stairs, following the men into the family room where Ed, Chris, Andy and Mona were seated, a tray of appetizers on the coffee table. A fire was blazing, the warmth of both friendship and ambience a reminder of what she had found here, what she'd been missing. She'd been with them a half a dozen times. At first it was as chauffeur, sticking around to make sure he got home okay. Then she became an official member of the group, married to one of the men. It was why she had given in so easily to Zach's suggestion that she accompany him inside. It hadn't been the promise he'd stop trying to seduce her.

Here, with these people, she was incapsulated in a spirit of camaraderie and open affection.

She sniffed the air.

"It smells great in here."

The aromas always caught her attention. It was the chef thing, although at times it did more damage than good. She could tell how a meal was going to taste before she even knew what was being served. On the upside, she could prepare her taste buds for the eventuality of a bad dish.

Tonight, there was going to be a good one.

There was a scent of mustard that was not too strong, and Brussels sprouts, which was a good pairing.

It would be interesting to see what Zach was going to do with it.

Rory was back from hanging up their coats and there was a skeptical look on her face.

"I'm trying a new recipe. Although if I had known for a fact Zach was coming, I might have planned something else."

Zach was moving toward the appetizers even as he said, "I keep telling you guys, I don't come for the food."

Andy joked, "How many times did you serve pizza and beer when we first started this?"

"Every time?"

"That should tell you it was never about the food for us, either."

She watched Zach take a seat next to Mona and noticed the kiss Mona deposited on his cheek.

"It's nice to see you're up and around. We were worried."

Lana knew the guys had visited while he was in the hospital. The women must have kept tabs on him through them.

"It's nice to be up and around. The Scaleras' know how to take care of a man in distress."

Ed joked, "So when did you become a damsel?"

Julian guffawed, "The night he let someone beat the piss out of him."

His hand went over his forehead. "Woe is me. Even in pain, they abuse me."

Lana reached over to take a cube of cheese and a cracker. She hadn't eaten anything, the spaghetti and clam sauce finding its way into the garbage disposal once it was hard and cold.

Julian placed a glass of wine in her hand, and she sipped while she listened to the playful banter.

Rory had been moving back and forth between the family room and kitchen and had turned down her offer to help.

"You'll intimidate me."

"I don't do that."

Chris was the one who said, "Um, yeah, you do."

"I'm sorry. I never meant..."

Mona was the one to assure her, "Oh, it's not anything you say or do, it's just who you are."

Rory was smiling when she asked, "Yeah, how would you feel cooking with Julia Child in the house?"

Lana was almost tongue-tied and a bit embarrassed.

"I'm no Julia Child."

Mona laughed. "You are compared to us. I don't even cook during the week, Andy does."

Lana could feel the blush.

"I don't want you to ever feel like that. I've enjoyed every single dish you guys have served."

Mona disagreed, a cheese and cracker in her hand. "Not true. That disaster I made with the Cornish game hens was a...disaster."

Lana stifled a laugh.

"I forgot about those."

"It was the last time you were at my house, and I blew it. The next meal I served was so good I wanted to call you and ask you to come over, so I could redeem myself."

"Everybody has a bad night."

Andy laughed. "Don't let her fool you. I was the one who cooked after that."

Mona punched her husband's arm in a good-natured way as Rory announced, "Okay guys. Dinner is served."

They all got up and walked to the dining room where the table was set as if the company was special. Cloth napkins, good China, and an arrangement of flowers decorated the tablecloth, and Zach had come behind her to pull out her chair.

"Thanks."

He was too close, and the tingles were back. Then he whispered, "What are those?" and she had to laugh.

She whispered back, "Brussels sprouts."

To the table at large she said, "You'll have to excuse him. He just sees the green and all else fades away. Like good taste."

As if pouting, he yielded.

"I'll try them. I've had enough green over the last couple of days to know that some of it isn't all bad."

The platter of chicken and sprouts was passed around, followed by the bowl of rosemary potatoes.

Lana dropped a warm roll on Zach's plate.

"Here's one kind of food I know you'll eat."

"You can give me two if you want."

"That bad?"

"No, the chicken looks good. And the potatoes."

Conversation flowed around the table. Discussions about the upcoming election, the Black Lives Matter movement, Boston politics. Each male represented a different division of the BPD, so the stories about the job were varied and interesting.

The one thing she noticed was that each male had his phone right by his plate. They laid in wait for the call that would beckon them to work.

Just as they were finishing up with the meal, Julian was the one who got it.

The wail of the phone stopped all dialogue.

He pushed himself back from the table and retreated into the family room to take the call.

The only noise was his muted voice and the forks that continued to move food to mouths.

He reappeared at the threshold and said, "Sorry. Gotta go. Hostage situation at Bunker Hill."

Zach rose to his feet as if he were going to join him.

"I didn't hear your phone ring."

"If there's a hostage, then..."

"No murder yet, my impatient friend. And if I have anything to say about it, there won't be. You stay and enjoy the rest of the food. I've got to change and get going."

He came over to kiss his wife. "Don't wait up."

"Okay. I love you."

"I love you, too."

"Guys, later."

Lana knew the code. The *I love you* was to make sure it was the last thing said if...the worst-case scenario happened.

There wasn't anything worse than having a loved one die after a fight.

She knew that for a fact. She'd had one with her father before he got killed. There had been a concert she wanted to go to. He'd said no. They'd argued, she'd said things she'd give anything to take back.

During therapy, she'd come to understand that her father knew she loved him despite the last words spoken between them. He had expected arguments like that. Had them with her older siblings. But the remorse had never fully healed, and she doubted it ever would.

The conversation became muted as the group finished their meal, helped Rory with clean up. They bypassed the dessert that had gotten her here and disbursed into the night, each carrying a silent prayer that their friend would be okay.

⌒

Sunday dawned with a fresh batch of snow. Lana cringed as the weatherman forecasted another few feet over the next couple of days. She didn't mind the white stuff; it was the ice and cold that was coming with it that had her shiver in anticipation. The breaking news this morning gave a recap on the hostage taking and thankfully it seemed the good guys had won the day.

She had worried into the night about Julian and the other SWAT team members, and she was relieved to know he was safe and sound, probably catching up on his sleep as the on-air reporter droned on about traffic safety.

Taking a sip of her now tepid coffee, she couldn't believe she had found her way back into a zombie world, one she thought she had escaped.

The tossing and turning at night were becoming the norm. Finally giving up any attempt at sleep, she'd accessed Netflix, scrolling for a movie that would take her mind of the situation...and Zach.

Why she had chosen the one she had still didn't make any sense.

Or did it?

She had wanted to crawl into the underbelly of Boston, living the life of a mole, and Leonardo DiCaprio took her there. Lies, deception, and danger were at the heart of the story, and she shivered at what an undercover cop had to do to stay alive. She'd clicked it off only halfway through, the seamy side of life making her quake with aftershocks of what Zach had done for close to two years.

She was glad she'd never known what the job had involved. It would have been too terrifying to think about, never mind live with.

The abstract was bad enough; she didn't need the details.

Zach must have known Julian's call would upset her, because he didn't speak to her on the ride home last night. Probably knew it would only make the waiting to hear about their friend that much more difficult. He'd said, "Bye," without even glancing in her direction, and as she watched him make his way to the house, she had wanted to call him back, so she could tuck herself inside his pocket.

She wanted to feel safe, not this edginess that always came when someone she loved was at risk. She thought by releasing Zach from their vows, she'd be able to go back to a feeling of normalcy. Normalcy for her. Where she stayed detached, when she didn't let a job undermine her ability to function.

But she'd been wrong.

Whether she was with him or not, she worried. Maybe she even worried more when she didn't know where he was or what he was doing. Knowing she could get a call telling her that...her world had truly ended.

Once she'd realized the depth of her feelings, the door to sanity was closed forever. She'd been banging on it, trying to get back in but all she got for her efforts were bruised fists.

She hadn't expected that or maybe she would have....

What, stayed?

Glancing around her small kitchen, the emptiness clawing at her, she had to admit she missed him. Missed the life he brought into her home, missed the way he loved her.

Forcing herself up and into her bedroom to get dressed for the day, she stepped into her black jeans and a long sweater and pulled on her socks and boots. Looking in the mirror, she asked herself, "Why?"

But she really didn't know what she was asking so she had no idea what the answer would be.

She sat back on the bed and riffled through her box again.

The envelopes were worn around the left corner edges, from taking them out so often, from reading about the life he'd lived before she was fully a part of it.

She gingerly pulled out the onionskin paper, knowing exactly which letter this was. He'd written it the night before shipping out to Afghanistan, holed up in the airport hotel after leaving Quantico.

October 2011

Lana,

Just finished up sniper training.
Glad to tell you that I am still alive, but barely.
These last two weeks were more difficult and more dangerous than the Middle East.
Suffering is the name of the game and our instructors had that down to a science. Bad weather, hunger and fatigue, long movements added to the purposeful punishment. They put every setback they could think of in front of us, pushing us to our limits.
They seemed intent on undermining my strengths and abilities, but I fooled them all. I'm now an official PIG, professional instructed gunman.
The next step is HOG, but I need to be out in the field to earn that label. I'm sure I'll have no problem once I'm on Afghani soil.
We train in pairs and the guy I partnered with, Cooper Ivans, is heading out with me. We're hoping to stay together. It's not easy to trust someone with your life, but he can call with accuracy, and I came to depend on it.
I didn't get to see much of American soil while I was here. The hours were long, and we were so exhausted we fell into bed for the few hours they gave us. I wish I could have gotten home for a few days. Maybe we could have grabbed a coffee, caught up in person on what's going on.
How's working with your mother?
Is it all still going well?
I'd love to taste some of your food, on the condition that it would consist of meat. Real meat. Not like the kind I choke down out in the desert. Dried beef jerky is the closest I come to the delicacies I took for granted at home. Some of the guys get care packages and they share on occasion. I just wish I had something to swap with, you know like cookies or canned fruit. Then I'd get to barter for some of the bounty.
Coop and I are going to head down for some food before we bed down. It's up and at 'em early tomorrow, and who knows when I'll get another taste of a pink slab of steak?

Stay well and keep those letters coming.
Zach

She had started sending him care packages as soon as she got his new mailing address. Somewhere Afghanistan.

Middle East.

～

She ran up the steps to her parents' house, the white stuff still floating down around her. Stomping her boots on the covered landing, she pushed open the door to hear her mother telling Zach, "Of course you're coming. You're still part of this family and you will always be welcome."

All conversation stopped when she entered the kitchen.

Her mother gave her a look that challenged her to argue the point.

She declined.

She knew her mother loved Zach and had been on her case to rethink her decision for the whole time they'd been separated.

She had refused.

Or had she?

She'd never even given divorce a thought.

Maybe that was one of the whys that needed answering.

If she ended up doing that, she might find herself at his gravesite wishing she had listened to her mother's advice. It was the specter of the children holding her hands at the burial that kept her resolute. She'd held her brother Tony's hand while they lowered Sal Scalera into the ground, and she didn't want her children to have to deal with a loss so consuming.

Zach's latest disaster had only strengthened her resolve.

Your resolve is shit. Don't kid yourself.

Pretense was becoming the norm since his arrival, so she announced, "Doesn't matter to me in the least."

"I thought you were meeting us there. Why are you here?"

Another why.

She didn't know.

Tish and Johnny were hosting the dinner this Sunday. Cavatelli was on the menu, Tish wanting to test her cooking skills. She was trying her hand at braciola, as well, which should satisfy all the meat eaters of the family.

"I called Tish to see if there was anything she wanted me to bring and she suggested dessert. I thought I'd come by for the cannoli I made yesterday. If there's still some left."

"You could have called. I would have brought them."

Not wanting to admit she came by to see Zach, see how he was doing, maybe stay with him for an hour or so so he wasn't alone, she should have known her mother would have invited him along.

The whole family would welcome him.

Shocked that the two had gotten married, so soon after Zach's return, they'd also been over the moon about it.

When she had all but thrown Zach out of her condo, they had been angrier than she'd ever seen them. Each, and every one of them.

She couldn't argue that he wasn't a good man. He was one of the best. She could only reiterate what she'd vowed with her father's murder.

They didn't think it was a good enough excuse.

Her mother had told her to grow up.

John had told her that some vows, the stupid kind, were made to be broken. They restricted choices, made for dangerous bedfellows. The one he'd made had almost kept him from Tish, and he warned her that she would be sorry about it one day.

Tish asked her how she could just let love go that easily.

Rissa had all but stopped talking to her. Having taken so long to find her husband, almost turning her back on the relationship because of her own fears, she'd argued that Lana had found something too good to throw away. She was distraught the month it took Rissa to get over the breakup.

Tony had been the most vocal.

"You're the one who should have stayed with the shrink. It wasn't that you grew too serious, you had bigger issues than I did. You've given up a great guy, all because you're afraid. Well, Lana, law enforcement is what we know. It's who we are. You've got it in your genes and so will your kids no matter who you marry...or divorce."

Once he joined the force, he thought maybe she'd betray him along with Zach.

"You going to divorce me from the family, as well?"

He was her brother and she had to deal with the possibility of his death every day.

How many men would she have to worry over?

There were two she couldn't do anything about, but the third? She had a choice there and she'd made it.

Tony had kept her in the loop for a couple of months, telling her about Zach's life. He'd gone back to routine police work and with his detective shield, was ready to rise in the ranks. Then he'd gone underground, and Tony had nothing to report. Or refused to. She'd since learned he'd boxed with him, so he would have known... How would he know she worried? Or that her fears grew deeper? His move had frightened her to death.

She was staring at him now. He was dressed in jeans, and a button-down shirt that matched his eyes and her whole body began to shake.

"I won't go if you don't want me to."

His voice was conciliatory, and she knew he meant it.

Fumbling with a smile, she said, "It's fine. They liked you best, anyway."

And they proved it once he was inside Johnny's home.

The welcoming committee comprised all adults in her family and most of the kids. They still called him Uncle Zach, and the only one who didn't come and jump into his arms was Dominic and that's because he was in the bathroom. He wanted his privacy when it was time to go.

The voices comingled with laughter and Tish went to set another seat at the table, at the place that had been his for dozens of times he'd been here. Right beside her.

"You look good, bro."

Johnny was inspecting his face, the blotches still not faded.

"You should have called us, man. We would have had your back in a second."

Luca was the brainy one, but with enough brawn that he would have been one of the ambushers' worst nightmares.

"Wish I'd had the time to do that. Three against three would have evened the odds."

Lana couldn't help but laugh.

"You three would have brought the force of ten to that fight. Those guys wouldn't have had a chance."

Johnny gave her a grin.

"That's what family's for."

Lana gave him an arched eyebrow in return.

"So say you now. Seems there were years we didn't exist."

"That's when I was stupid and careless. If I remember correctly, I was your age. You got to love adolescence."

He kissed her nose and gave her a hug, whispering in her ear, "You can't bullshit me, goat. I know what's hiding here." His finger jabbed her in the heart region of her chest.

"You should let him know so we can get him back in the fold."

Her eyes met his. His held laughter. She felt something else entirely.

Then she looked over to where Zach was standing, in between Dennis and Luca as if they were his bodyguards.

His blue eyes shone like cobalt, and they were studying her face.

And the electrical phenomenon that was him caused her blood to race through her veins.

How would she ever get her body to behave again, now that it had been re-awakened?

Maybe the question was, why would she want it any other way?

Sitting around the enormous dining room table, they laughed and joked, as if the last two years had never happened.

CHAPTER SIXTEEN

On Monday, a week after he'd arrived, Zach was ready to go back to work, although there'd been limits put on him by the superintendent. He couldn't go out on a case yet. There'd be too much standing around, and his father didn't think his body was ready for that. Maybe he was right, but it rankled that he was living under his thumb. He still limped but refused to use the cane any longer. His jaw no longer throbbed, his ribs ached less, and his shoulder was no longer creaky. His face was another story. It still bore the brunt of his run-in with the thugs. He hoped they were still wearing the physical reminders that he hadn't gone down without a fight.

He was dressed in a suit and tie, some of the clothes Lana had picked up for him on Friday, and it was a stark change from his undercover clothes. He was making his re-entry into the world of public police work, and he was looking forward to the new challenge.

Hoping Lana had already arrived, he was pleased to see her standing in the kitchen, coffee cup in hand.

There was a bemused expression on her face.

"I forgot how well you clean up."

He was freshly shaved, his shaggy hair trimmed by Celia, his suit pressed, his shoes shined to a fine gloss, a remnant of military discipline.

He couldn't help but admire the way she looked. She was dressed in a grey skirt, a lighter grey cardigan over a blouse, belted at the waist. Grey boots complemented the outfit and the weather.

"Thanks. I didn't forget that you did."

She had great assets, rounded bottom, shapely calves and impressive bust line. He'd sampled them, and he hungered for another full-on taste.

"First day at the station?"

"In this capacity. I know where it is and what it looks like."

"I didn't think cubicles would be your thing."

"Caves weren't my thing either, but it's amazing what you can get used to."

He watched her bite her lip, knowing he could silence her with the mere mention of his service.

"Coffee?"

Her exhale of breath and question told him they were off the subject.

"Yeah. Thanks."

The bemused expression was back.

"Help yourself."

He smiled and moved toward the counter, where the pot was steaming with the dark brown brew. There was a tray with several mugs sitting beside it, a bowl of sugar and a container of creamer, the latter two unnecessary.

"What do you have planned for the day? You're all dressed up, so you must have an appointment."

"I do."

Celia swept into her domain with a flourish, outfitted in a dress and heels. Zach was surprised. She was usually dressed down, her kitchen her place of employ.

He assumed she'd heard Lana's succinct answer when she embellished, "We're going to check out a store front. I'm along for support. We need to look like we have the money to invest."

"Do you?"

Stepping away from the counter, Lana drained her cup, walked to the sink to rinse it out.

Turning, she looked him straight in the eye and said, "I do."

The sparks flashed between them, and he was sure she felt it as strongly as he did because her eyes dipped away.

"Where is it?"

"Arlington."

She was shrugging into her coat, car keys jangling in her hand.

"Nice town."

Picking up her pocketbook, she glanced at her mother to see if she was ready to follow and then proceeded to the side door.

"It is."

And then she was gone, Celia giving him a short wave as she closed the door behind her.

He watched out the window as Lana slid behind the wheel. When she glanced up to see him standing there, there was a pause, and the world stood still. He felt it begin to rotate again as she pulled out of the driveway and headed south.

She was making him feel they weren't at a dead end. They'd just gotten stuck along the way.

⌒

"Ready to go partner?"

Paul had poured some coffee into a travel mug and was waiting for him to come back to earth.

Glancing at his watch, Zach moved back into the center of the kitchen.

"Yeah. Might as well get this over with."

"What over with?"

"The looks, the mumbles. Dad pulled rank and I'm there because of him, unable to even field a call. Not sure how that will go over with the rest of the force."

Rubbing the back of his neck, Paul said, "It went over fine. They're all looking forward to working with you. You saved a cop's life, got beat up for your efforts. You've got your detective shield. You've earned your place."

He'd earned his shield before joining the Marines, earned a couple of medals there for his sacrifice. Now he was back.

Out in public, not hiding undercover.

How he'd perform was anybody's guess. He had a history to uphold, and it rested heavily on his shoulders.

Could he do it with the mundane task of finding murderers?

Maybe just doing his job to the best of his ability was all he could ask of himself.

Or his father could ask of him.

He was the one who had assigned him the task. Maybe all his father wanted him to be, was alive.

He could almost live with that.

As they drove to the police station, Zach looked around, the congested streets rubbing against the seamy underbelly of life, something he could compare to the life he'd grown accustomed to in Afghanistan. There he'd been embroiled in battle and his strength, courage, and loyalty were called on daily. One of the supporting reasons for going underground was to get away from the heavy burden he'd carried over there, but he'd missed the singularity of purpose he shared with his unit, the cohesive attachment to members of the group. As an outsider whose higher purpose was in taking down the bad guys, he was unable to fulfill the true spirit of service.

Glancing over at Paul, he thought maybe he'd find it in Homicide. Aligning himself with the elite seekers of justice, he could find a sufficient sense of community and a shared sense of justice. It wouldn't take strength and courage, only a sense of logic. Instead of leading men into the valley of death, he'd track down the people responsible for crimes against humanity. Maybe it would offer a small amount of retribution for what he had lost. What he had taken.

Paul found a parking spot just outside the building, this precinct located in Dorchester, an area of the city that held a full spectrum of ethnic culture and diversity. It also had one of the highest homicide rates in the state, so he knew he'd be busy. He looked up at the brick façade. It wasn't new but both exterior and interior had been updated. When they moved inside, it was no longer the snarl of dirty corridors and small spaces he remembered as a kid when he visited his grandfather.

The only thing that was the same was the cubicles.

Paul had a small office, as befit a lieutenant. He'd cleared out an enclosed cell right beside it. They would be within talking distance.

"Whose space am I taking?"

Zach was looking around, getting nods of greeting from the men and women already working in the confined areas.

"My former partner. He's been reassigned to Narcotics, his request. He didn't like seeing dead bodies. Said he'd rather work with druggies than corpses."

"Okay. Good."

He liked knowing that Paul's partner hadn't been bounced from the detail because of him.

Taking a step towards the desk, Zach scanned the surface. There was a computer, the phone, stackable trays collecting dust, a stapler, paper clips. After pulling out the seat, he sat down in the swivel chair. He slid the case binders Paul had given him along the desktop, consciously marking his territory.

He pushed back and took in the rest of the room. Small TV screens lined one of the walls where he assumed the detectives could watch an interview in progress. A white board lined another, where they listed murder victims in black, describing in short detail the method of death. The accused once arrested was documented in red and most of the murders, from what he could tell had been solved.

Clocks hung above each desk. The cubicles near him held personal effects, pictures of loved ones, kid drawings, name plates, coffee mugs, cell phones. One of the detectives had a stuffed monkey hanging from his wall, another an award plaque.

He wasn't into showcasing his achievements.

The only artifact he'd want was a picture of Lana.

He chuckled.

She wouldn't be thrilled about that but seeing that she'd never know, he made a mental note to pick up a frame for the picture he had in mind.

Once he'd cased the place he swiveled over to Paul's door and asked, "Now what?"

Handing over a brown file folder, faded and worn around the edges, Paul said, "I got this out of the basement. It's the one you asked about. Got the okay for you to look at it. It'll give you something to do while you wait for the doctor's clearance to be out in the field."

"It's not the doctor who has to clear me. It's the old man."

"He'd be doing the same for anyone here. Part of his job is to take care of his people."

It was probably the truth, so he shouldn't take it personally. George Taylor would probably go down as one of the best superintendents the city had seen. He had a cool head, a sixth sense about things, and he would always have a cop's mentality. He should just give in to the pride, instead of fighting it.

"There's an empty cubicle on the other side of the room you can use to scan through it. Take copies of things you might want to review at the house."

"Good. Thanks. I appreciate it."

"No problem. That's one we'd all like to close. Before you get to that, I'd like you to go through the Braxton notes."

"Old case?"

"Yeah. Happened last fall. Fight erupted outside a nightclub; shots fired. One guy dead, one hospitalized. A couple of witnesses said they saw the victim arguing with someone earlier that night. Seems it was over a woman. We interviewed her right after the murder, but she said she didn't know anything. One of her friends just came forward saying she knew a lot more than she admitted. We're talking to the friend this morning."

"What happened to the guy who was hospitalized?"

"Lost his memory along with a fair amount of blood."

"Afraid of retaliation?"

"That's my guess."

With that, Paul disappeared around the corner, and he began to digest the well-organized information, reading the notes taken at the scene, studying the pictures that told a grisly story. There must have been a half dozen entry wounds, one taking off part of the head. Not pretty.

He'd seen worse.

⌒

While Zach couldn't go out and work an active investigation quite yet, he was allowed to sit in on an interview, and the one they held with the woman in question had been a satisfactory one. It was conducted off-site, at a precinct closer to her home and after it was concluded, they drove back to the station.

"Can you grab me a sandwich from the cooler in back?"

Zach looked at Paul speculatively, then glanced at the well behind Paul's seat.

"You bring your own lunch?"

"Celia or Lana packs one every day. My wife got tired of hearing me bitch that I didn't have time to eat anything except pizza and doughnuts. My daughter didn't like the quality of my food choices. They call it my travel pack. Always add extra so my partner is fed, as well, so help yourself. I'm hoping Lana didn't hold back because it's you."

After lifting the small Igloo cooler and bringing it in front, Zach slid off the top to see sandwiches wrapped and organized neatly around freezer packs, a couple of waters, and cookies bagged individually.

Working at it, he smiled and joked, "You'd get laughed out of the station if you brought this in with you."

"I do, and I do. Tough. They don't like it, what do I care? I eat well; they don't."

There were probably men who envied Paul his lunches, or suppers or snacks...whatever he called them. He knew for a fact that detectives sometimes worked around the clock and didn't have time for anything more than a fast-food delivery or a stop at a grease pit. This was taking it to a new height though, and he couldn't help but smile at the old coot's attitude.

Shaking his head, Zach asked, "What do you want?"

"Top is fine. They know what I like."

Zach took the top one, unwrapped it, and handed it over before picking out one for himself. It was way past lunch, and he was hungry. His jaw had lost some of its rigidity and his mouth was working better, so his food choices were expanding every day. A sandwich shouldn't be a problem. The problem would be what Lana stuffed the bread with.

Unwrapping the tinfoil, he studied the contents from the side. If Lana had made it, there must be green stuff hidden somewhere.

Paul laughed.

"I got used to green a long time ago. It's not so bad."

"Lettuce I can do. It's the tomatoes that need to go."

"Honestly, Zach I've never met anyone so finicky."

Zach gave him a sidelong glance. Finicky? Damn straight. The things he'd eaten once, out of his backpack, he'd had to choke down. He swore he'd never eat anything he didn't want to, ever again.

He pulled out the offending tomatoes, leaving the lettuce and wrapped the offending red pieces back up in the discarded foil and took a tentative bite.

Plain ham and cheese, which surprised him. The roll was soft and gooey, the mustard a bit tangy and he began eating with relish.

They ate in companionable silence until Zach asked, "Who have you been partnering with since your old one transferred to the drug unit?"

"No one, routinely. Whoever's around comes with me when I get the call. They're all good cops, so I have competent help but it's nice when you're with someone you've gotten to know. Quirks, strengths, gut instinct."

"Good cop, bad cop routine?"

Scrunching up the foil and baggie, he leaned over the back to deposit the trash in a small plastic bag behind Zach's seat.

Laughing, he said, "I'm always the good cop. Just so you know."

"I think I can be your Jekyll."

"I have no doubt."

Gruffly, Paul admitted, "I think we're going to make a good team, Zach. I like you, what you stand for. I admire what you've done with your life. I hope it works out for you, as well."

"Thanks, Paul. I won't know until I'm up to speed whether it moves fast enough for me."

"You'll get your chance to find out. There's no shortage of murders here."

"I don't want to say it can't come fast enough. That would imply I can't wait for someone to get murdered but..."

"You'll be out there soon enough. Don't you worry."

CHAPTER SEVENTEEN

Lana approached the façade, her mother following in her stead. From what she could tell, it appeared to be an attachment to the building beside it and it was small but with lots of windows, fresh white exterior paint, the location perfect for what she planned. It had been a dry-cleaning business, the owners at retirement age and moving to Florida. It was cheap. Something she liked because it meant she could put most of her money to improvements.

"Lana."

She turned to see her sister, Rissa, Val, and the real estate agent striding towards her.

"What are you doing here? Not that I'm not glad to see you."

"Luc was around and willing to watch John Luc so I ran out the door before he could change his mind. I only have a little time left of relative freedom and I don't want to squander a minute."

Her protruding belly gave her words meaning. Rissa was expecting her second child with her sexy husband, the bass player for Raging Thunder. The fact that Rissa and Luca had ended up together was still a mystery to all concerned. Rissa had sworn off players, not the musically inclined but the sexually active and Luca had spent years being bullied, so his sexual conquests fed his need to be wanted. Both had a dim view of relationships but had been able to overcome all of that falling head over heels in love with each other.

She was often envious. Her brothers and sister had found their soul mates.

Hers had come already but he'd made it impossible for her to stay.

Cookie Carter, the real estate agent waited for the hugging to end before getting down to business.

"This just came on the market yesterday and Val had asked me to call her if something like this came up. I don't want you missing out on the deal of the century."

"So far, so good. It depends on what's behind the door."

"Let's see."

After opening the door and stepping inside the dim interior, Cookie flicked on the lights and stepped forward into the square open space. There was a counter, silver poles crawling across the wall, scattered plastic bags hanging with abandoned suits, sweaters, and dresses. She could envision herself behind the counter, ringing up a sale. It was cramped, but there would only be one person working the register, so it could work.

They skirted around the counter and headed toward a narrow passageway that took them to the core of the store. It was long and narrow and there were presses, more metal poles snaking across the space, an ancient sewing machine against the wall, the scent of cleaning solution hanging in the air along with the dust motes dancing.

Cookie asked, "What do you think?"

Lana was studying each square foot, imagining what would go where, professional stoves and oven, storage for all her pots and pans, the dedicated area for allergen-free cooking, sinks, dishwashers, utensils, freezer storage, commercial refrigerators to store available goods for sale.

"If it works the way it has in my mind, I'll take it."

Turning to Celia, she asked, "What do you think, Ma?"

"Show me."

Lana began to draw a diagram with her finger, pointing out where the ovens would go and all the rest of the appliances, she'd need to perform a daily cook fest. She would glance back to her mother from time to time to see a nod of her head as Celia followed the description.

Rissa added, "You'll have to be very efficient at placement. It's not very big but it could hold all you need if you do it right."

Lana was still examining every inch when her mother added, "I agree. The front won't need a lot of renovation. Clean-up for sure, but it's well positioned. The poles have to come down, refrigerated cases with shelves put in."

Lana's brain was churning with seismic activity.

"I'll have to work out the cost. Although I've got a general price list, now I just have to add these variables. I actually think it's perfect."

"Nice windows, lots of light, well trafficked, safe location, business district close by. It ticks all your boxes, Lana."

Val had a broad smile on her face, hopeful that she had found what Lana had been looking for.

Lana beamed back.

"You work magic, Val. You did the same thing for Luca when he was searching for an art gallery for Rissa."

Rissa flushed, still uncomfortable with her talent so publicly exhibited, but Lana knew she was proud of what the gallery offered the community.

"Hiring Penny to curate it, we were able to expand the talent pool to other local artists looking to showcase their work."

Celia all but crowed, "So much talent in the family."

Cookie asked, "So do you want to put in an offer?"

"Absolutely. Can we write it up today?"

"I brought an offer agreement with me, so let's put it on paper and see what happens."

Lana's stomach fluttered with nerves. It was a big investment; one she'd been saving for years. And it was about to become a reality.

She hoped it would be as successful as she'd envisioned. There was a lot of talent in her family, and she wanted to be part of that.

～

Once Cookie had left to put in the offer, Celia suggested they grab lunch at a delicatessen close by while they waited for an answer. Lana loved the idea. It would give her a chance to spend some extra time with her sister. They'd always been close but since the falling- out over her decision about Zach, they'd lost something, didn't talk as much. Maybe it was her fault. She'd put up a wall to keep Rissa's opinions from getting in, refused to share her feelings, the heartache still palpable. Johnny was the only one who listened and kept his counsel to himself, not that she talked about it often. She missed her sister, and she didn't spend nearly enough time with John Luc. Her fault, as well.

Rissa was bubbling over, her opinion about the storefront a positive one. Lana wanted to pinch herself. If this worked out, she'd be buying the premises, which she would dismantle as soon as the agreement was negotiated.

The pastrami sandwich was half-way to her mouth when her mother asked, casually, "What are you naming the business?"

She released the sandwich back down to the plate.

"Huh? I...don't know. I haven't thought about it as a separate entity."

"This is yours now. A new beginning."

She studied her mother's expression. There wasn't anything to suggest she was upset by what was taking place.

"I've been part of the Cookery for so long, I...don't know."

Rissa offered a suggestion that piqued her interest.

"I like the word *Piatto*. It means—"

Celia finished her sentence. "—dish in Italian."

Lana had one hesitation. "But I've added so many other types of food to the menu. I won't be offering Italian fare exclusively anymore."

"True but a dish is a dish is a dish."

She let it slide over her tongue a couple of times.

"I do like the way it sounds."

Rissa said eagerly, "I can already see the sign out front...a plate with the name imprinted on it hanging from the front, a stencil of it on the window."

Lana could see it, too, and she loved the idea.

"Would you draw what you have in mind? Then I can take it to a sign company."

"Of course. I'd better get to it soon, though. Gabby is making some noise about joining us."

"If you can, fine. If not, it can wait. I've still got so much to do."

Her mind was busy, creating a brochure in her head, the emblem on the front of a black trifold. She'd been working on it while searching for the location. Now that she'd found it, she had to put the finishing touches on the mailer she wanted out before the opening.

She was still deciding whether she wanted to offer customized menus based on personal preferences or if she was going the prepackaged route. Her recipes were recorded in her journal, and she'd been adding to them with each test she'd made. She was also wondering if she should offer a delivery service.

She had learned about the business end through the Cookery, so she had a depth of knowledge on spread sheets, budgets, and cost efficiency.

Val was the one who asked, "What are you going to do about a website?"

"I'll have to get someone to design it and get it up and running but I should be able to pick up from there. I don't want the monthly expense for maintenance, and I've been updating the Cookery's, so I know my way around." She looked at Rissa again, the artist in the family, but didn't have to say a word.

"I'll see if I can work up something that ties in with the sign."

"Thanks, Riss."

She liked having common ground again, a reason to touch base with her. She knew it wouldn't be for long, with the baby due, but it might be a way to open the channels between them. The guys were working non-stop on their upcoming album so Luca would be available to take care of their son while Rissa was bonding with the newborn. She was going to make it a point of getting over there to relieve them. Her sister had asked her to be godmother and she was going to take the duties seriously.

Val offered, "I have a friend who is good and reasonable if Rissa doesn't have time. You don't hear those words often, but she does a flourishing business because she is both. I could give her a call."

"That would be great. Thanks, again, Val. How did we ever get along without you?"

"Quite well. I owe the Scaleras' big time for bringing my brother back into the world of the living. Rissa especially for giving me the nephew and niece I've wanted. I thought for sure my brother would never give himself over to a woman and my kids would be the only ones in the family."

"Once Rissa got involved, you didn't have to worry. We're good at procreating."

Celia laughed. "I don't think any of you are willing to have five."

"I wouldn't bet the farm on that. Johnny and Tish want to keep going. Who knows when they'll stop."

"I'll take all the grandbabies I can get."

Rissa sat back, lightly massaging her stomach.

"Two's it for me, Ma. I know my limitations. I don't know how you did it."

"I had a lot of help. And you kids stepped up when you had to. I'm proud of all of you."

Just before leaving, Lana got a call saying the offer had been accepted. She was buying the dry-cleaning business, which she would dismantle as soon as the financing was in place. She'd already been approved, so it was just a question of moving ahead.

All but squealing when she got off the phone, she did a happy dance, the others joining in.

As soon as they were on the road, Lana and Celia started chatting about all the work that needed to be done in the coming months, Celia willing to help any way she could.

⌒

Zach was exhausted after his first full day at work, achy and sore, but it had been more interesting than lying in bed again, more interesting than he'd thought it would be. They'd stayed late so Paul could go over the entire caseload. There was a lot to digest, so much to study, and he never realized there was such a mountain of material involved in tracking down a murderer. Or the connection that had to be retained with the families of the victims. Some families called every day, making sure that their loved one wasn't forgotten. He had a feeling Paul didn't need any reminders. There were pictures of all his victims tacked onto a cork board in his office. They only came down with resolution. There was one photo that had been hanging there for ten years. Paul told him he still pulled the file out from time to time, went over the particulars, to see if he'd missed anything. It seemed he never gave up the search.

On the way back to the house, they'd made a stop so Paul could update one of the families on the most recent progress. He'd been able to get a warrant on one of the suspects in the Flanagan murder and they'd made an arrest. The evidence was compelling, and Paul hoped that it would hold. Until there was a conviction, the suspect was assumed innocent, and until the jury came back with a verdict, anything could happen. The family was relieved that someone was going to pay for the murder. Knowing the guilty party would be punished would go a long way towards the healing. Paul had told him the worst day of the case was informing the family their loved one was dead, and the best was the day he told them an arrest had been made.

It had been his job as sergeant, during his last year with the Marines, to contact the family of the deceased serviceman. There was never a good day that followed. At least now, he might have that to look forward to. Zach had been surprised at the level of respect and caring between the detective and parents, and he gained another level of understanding about what the job entailed.

Celia and Lana were busy in the kitchen when they walked through the door. Zach smiled at the scene. They were chatting like magpies, and it didn't seem like they even noticed the men's arrival.

He watched as Paul placed the Igloo cooler on the counter, gave his wife a kiss and leaned in to see what they were cooking, then his eyes gravitated to Lana, an apron around her waist, her hands busy at chopping...something green.

No surprise there.

He sauntered to where she stood and looked over her shoulder, his head brushing against hers. He felt a spark shift through him before he heard the warning.

"Never crowd a woman with a knife."

Her scent was too much of an aphrodisiac, and he couldn't back off for the life of him. He had a feeling it was dangerous.

"You know I live to take risks."

The chopping stopped, and Lana spun around, knocking him back, her arm still holding the sharp instrument. The angle was perfect for a jugular slice.

He didn't retreat, proving his point.

Her trembling fingers gave him hope that she felt the same spark even as her words told him something different.

"I don't."

"I've noticed."

"Nothing's changed, so back off."

Giving in to the glower, he took the necessary step away from her.

She resumed her chopping position, and he could hear the staccato beat of the knife begin again.

When he glanced over, he saw both Paul and Celia studying him, Paul's brow arched in question.

Not wanting to answer it, he shrugged and said, "I'm going to change. What time's dinner?"

Celia was slow to answer, her expression one of interest.

"It should be ready in about an hour."

"Okay. Thanks."

Paul added, "I'm going to do same, then catch the news. Call when it's time."

Zach limped down to his room and collapsed on the bed, foregoing the change he'd planned on. He couldn't move. His body was on fire, his leg throbbing at the seam of his original injury. The beating had aggravated the parts of him that he'd thought were healed. Massaging the muscles that had atrophied in places, he contorted his face as his fingers pushed and squeezed. His groan as he yanked off his shoe suggested his foot wasn't in any better condition than his leg. Having lost a portion of it to the IED, he'd had to learn to walk again, which was the most brutal part of the rehab, but he'd been grateful that the foot had been saved. Otherwise, there would have been no way he could have joined the force again.

Thinking of Lana, he mused that the gratitude might be misplaced.

CHAPTER EIGHTEEN

"Are you all right?"

He looked up, a grimace on his face.

"Yeah, why?"

She softened her voice and it filled with concern.

"It sounded as if you were in pain."

"I was on my feet too long and..."

She looked at the sock that covered the mangled appendage. He'd been worried that she'd find his foot and the scar on his leg disgusting, but he'd had nothing to worry about. Any inch of his exposed flesh gave her goose bumps. He was a powerful specimen even scarred and she'd taken on the role of masseuse willingly.

She missed her hands on him, and before she could think it through, she was moving toward him. After kneeling, she all but caressed it, her thumbs applying pressure along the scarred flesh that lay beneath.

The groan was even louder this time and anxiety spurted through her.

"Am I hurting you?"

There was an indefinable emotion in his eyes. She didn't know if she was reading it correctly, because it looked like hope.

"No. I... You always knew just how to massage it."

Her hands, experienced from months of servicing him this way, reclaimed his flesh and advanced up his leg. He closed his eyes as if savoring the feel.

Parts of him were coming alive under her ministrations, and for a moment she thought about moving higher, like she used to after they were married.

The massages began the foreplay. After warming the therapeutic lotion, she'd grease her hands and begin at his foot, working her way up his calves, thighs until she was massaging a part of him that she reveled in.

They would make such passionate love her world exploded. Every time.

She closed her eyes in remembrance.

She wanted to feel him again, inside her, filling her.

It was getting harder to keep him at a distance, the need to be part of him again compelling her to throw all her fears out the door.

She clenched her jaw to keep the words buried, the words that would lead her to promise him forever again, still unsure she could keep it.

She sat back on her haunches, her fingers itching to go back, finish their work.

"You need some rest. You're pushing yourself again. I'll bring supper to you, and you can eat in here."

"An hour should give me all the time I need to get back on my feet."

She found his eyes with hers, and there was entreaty there.

She was sure the look was a familiar one, but one he still defied.

"I'll be fine, Lana. I promise."

He traced her cheek with his fingers, the skin smooth, the texture familiar. Then his thumb found her bottom lip and he caressed it.

Instead of retreating, she leaned her cheek into the palm of his hand and seemed to breathe him in. It was his breath that hitched.

"Please take care of yourself. Your body can't take much more abuse."

Combing his fingers through her hair, he said, "I will. Like you already told me, Homicide is the place to be if you don't want to put yourself on the line. Just like I told you, all paperwork."

She lifted her head, and her cheek felt the loss, but she slid onto the pull-out bed, sitting close beside him.

"It's better than you thought, isn't it? Paul said that you dived right in."

"I don't know how to do it differently."

She gave him a tentative smile.

"I know."

Her gaze didn't waiver and the incessant streak of lightning she felt shooting through her system didn't, either.

Reluctantly, she rose and made her way to the door, looking at him once more, asking, "Are you sure you don't want to eat in here?"

"And miss your company? That would never be my choice."

She chewed on her lower lip and then whispered, "I wish it could've been different, Zach."

His expression stilled and grew serious.

"So do I, Lana. You don't know how much."

They paused in each other's eyes, and she backed out of the doorway.

"I'll let you change. See you out there."

⌐

She stood in the hallway and breathed.

Being with him always made her feel this way.

Light-headed, tingly, trembling.

It was why she'd all but assaulted him with the knife. He'd gotten too close for comfort, and she'd needed him to back off, refusing to let him affect her senses. She felt heart-sick when she heard his groan, and the bubble of tension she felt at his nearness in the kitchen popped. Knowing what he needed, she'd put down the instrument she threatened him with and all but ran to see if she could help. Without a word, she took up her task, moving the knots that had formed, smoothing out the tendons and muscle. She needed it more than he did. It was a way to coddle him without making him feel coddled. Her hands were always looking for ways to touch, to tantalize.

To heal.

⌐

He stared at the empty space.

His body was still on fire but now it was a different kind of flame. The burning desire to have her back in his arms was growing stronger by the day and he needed to believe he could find a way to make the marriage work.

Would she be willing to give it another go seeing he was in a more reasonable place?

He couldn't risk the answer, so he hadn't posed the question.

The decision wasn't his to make. If it were in his hands, she'd never have left him.

He'd have to leave any kind of renewed relationship to destiny and hoped it favored him.

But he'd show up, be with her as often as he could, not wanting to miss a sign if it came.

And when he showed up at the table, she was sitting there, watching his every move and it gave him hope for the future.

The lamb roast was so tender he didn't even need to chew.

"This is delicious."

"Glad you're enjoying it, Zach. I'll probably be making spaghetti tomorrow so eat while you can."

"Your spaghetti is good, too."

Lana gave him a quizzical stare.

"You are so lying right now."

"Am not."

"Well, then you like hers better than mine."

"Yours was too...."

"Spicy?"

"I guess you could say that."

Looking up at her mother she said, "I had to make two meals some nights. Otherwise, I would never have eaten what I wanted."

"I used to do the same thing when you were young. Dennis was our picky eater. It was peanut butter and jelly or grilled cheese. Still isn't crazy about red sauce."

Zach's fork had stalled on the way to his mouth.

"I didn't realize that."

"What?"

"That you made me a dinner of my own every night."

Her eyebrow arched when she asked, "What did you think? I had carnivore central on speed dial?"

"I thought you brought leftovers home from the catering jobs."

"You thought I gave you leftovers every night?" She was shaking her head as if she couldn't believe it. "Did it look like leftovers? You had your own roast beef some nights. All that hard work and it went unappreciated."

He looked almost contrite, and then his eyes darkened with emotion.

"I appreciated the fact there was food on the table, food I'd eat. I wish I had known you went out of your way to do it." She was exhausted when she came some nights and if he'd known...

"Thank you for not making me eat the weird meals you made for yourself."

"My weird meals are another's haute cuisine."

He almost laughed at the haughty expression on her face.

"I'm sure that's true. I've seen my friends devour them."

Celia said off handedly, "She was one of the top students at school, and then she quit, wanted to take the Cookery in a whole new direction. I had a hard time controlling the beast. She enjoyed cooking those extra meals. Don't let her fool you into thinking she didn't."

Giving her mother a sour look, she said, "Now that I'm opening the storefront, you won't have to put up with the beast anymore."

Paul asked, "You'll still bring by your testers, right? That lobster-filled ravioli is one of my favorites."

Zach finally processed what Lana had said. "You got the storefront?"

Lana's cheeks flushed in excitement. "I did. It needs to be completely renovated and I'll have to get an architect to draw up some plans, but I know exactly how I want it. I probably won't be able to open until summer, but there'll be a lot to do between now and then."

Zach asked, "Have you decided on a name?"

Celia took a sip of the wine before informing, "Yeah, Rissa came up with it. Piatto. It means dish in Italian."

"You're still going with the Italian roots?"

Lana thought for a moment and admitted, "No. I like the way it sounds."

"It's catchy. What kinds of things are you going to sell?"

Her eyes lit up and he could tell she was passionate about the undertaking.

"Everyone seems to be in the package food mode. More and more people like knowing they can pick up dinner on the way home and not have to cook. Something I just don't get."

"Prepackaged doesn't seem to be your style."

"It won't be prepackaged in the way you mean. Everything will be freshly made that morning. Meat, vegetables, potato dishes, casseroles, soups, salads, desserts."

"Just a general menu so far?"

"It'll probably change seasonally. Local buys at the farmers' market will determine some of the dishes."

"I bet Mona will be one of your first customers."

"She already told me that she'll be picking something up for your Saturday night dinners."

He didn't miss the word *your*...the meaning clear that she wouldn't be a part of them. Trying to turn that around, he said, "Julian asked me if you'd cook at my place for them on my night. Maybe I'll do the same thing as Mona. Unless you're willing to be my personal chef?"

"It is a beautiful kitchen. And I suppose someone should take advantage of it. I'll think about it."

He took another heaping of the mashed potatoes, another couple of pieces of the lamb.

"Will you still work for the Cookery?"

He glanced up at her silence, noticed the look she gave her mother as if guilt was eating away at her.

"Not in any major capacity. I'll help out when needed, but..."

Wiping her mouth with her napkin, Celia pushed her dish away and took another sip of wine.

There was a critical tone to her voice when she spoke.

"It took you seven years to tell me this is what you wanted. I'm not going to let you take time away from the new business to help me."

Resting her arms on the table, Lana leaned forward.

"I didn't want to let you down. I've been part and parcel of the business since I was twelve."

"But I never wanted you to give up your dreams."

"You also said you wanted to work less so you can be with the kids more. I feel like I'm abandoning you."

"I am planning on cutting down. Maybe even selling but that's for me to decide. Paul takes good care of me, and I want to be a grandmother today. Not a cook."

"I could—"

"No, you won't. I'm hiring a new chef and that's the end of it."

⤳

Lana helped with the clean-up and then took off. She couldn't take a chance that she'd stay and enjoy Zach's company, something she still did with too much ease.

Monitoring his movements after dinner, when he and Paul were talking on their way into the family room to watch a hockey game, she'd gazed too long in his direction, consuming him with her eyes. He'd get the wrong idea...or maybe it was the right one. He knew the look.

The look that told him she wanted him.

And that look had been gaining more and more ground over the last couple of days. She gulped in one last dose of his masculinity and slipped out the door.

When she entered her own, her feet were free of the boots in two steps. Her coat and scarf made it to the closet. She padded in her white socks to her bedroom, and slipped under the covers, the chill of both the weather and her heart creating goose bumps all over her skin.

Bone-deep cold.

She reached over to her box and pulled out another one of his letters, needing him here in some small way.

It was the last one she'd received. He'd been hurt soon after and the next time she'd heard from him was in a hospital room his body torn and damaged.

December 2013

Hey, you.

> *Your last letter couldn't have come at a better time.*
> *My sergeant was killed yesterday, which makes me next one up.*
> *The thought of being the leader of the pack is frightening. Not because I'll be the bull's-eye but because it will be my job to keep everyone else here alive.*
> *I needed to hear about the mundane and the tick of the daily clock in another part of the world, where life and death isn't so in-your-face.*
> *Your story about the waitress who called in sick was humorous, although it sounded like you had to amp up your game, working with two hats. I picture you racing around like a scrappy point guard, running rings around everyone else in the kitchen.*
> *You seem to have scored a lot of points for the team.*
> *And your question "What is a hamburger?" got me thinking.*
> *Of course, it's one of my favorite meals.*
> *But what makes a good one?*
> *Salt and pepper for sure. Ketchup probably wouldn't be a good answer, because that doesn't go in the burger but on top of. Is it to kill the taste or enhance it?*
> *It's got to be juicy, and pink. The roll's got to be soft and gooey.*
> *And I better stop thinking about it. Can't let my team see me salivate. It will be almost a year before I can sink my teeth into one, and my taste buds are beginning to scream for it.*
> *Maybe you can promise me it will be my first meal when I get back to the States.*

Maybe by then you'll have figured it out. What did you call it, the Socratic method of cooking? You must have learned that in school, because who talks like that?

While you work on that, I'll just concentrate on the taste, texture, aroma, and what it will feel like in my mouth.

Anticipation is making me drool like a fool.

My jerky is calling me to dinner. Our mess hall attempts to cook American food, but they have to buy local at times and it means lentils and rice. The rice I can stomach, but lentils? Come on.

I hope you like the bracelet. I was at the bazaar on R and R last week and thought of you. I remember when you were younger you used to wear all kinds of bangles. If they're not your thing anymore...give it away, I guess.

Until next time,
Zach

She'd been worried.

But she hadn't wanted him to know that.

If she remembered correctly, she had begun the next letter with the salutation, "Hey, yellow dot..."

It was what she thought of when she saw a bull's-eye on a target.

She'd been going for humor but looking back it had been a gross mistake. She wasn't sure he ever got it, hoped he hadn't. Never realized how close to the truth it would come.

She'd spent years walking on eggshells, not knowing if he'd come home, not knowing if she'd ever get to kiss him, something she wanted as much as he hungered for that hamburger.

They had both gotten what they wanted upon his return.

A hamburger was the first thing she made for him.

And the kiss was a sensory overload of exquisite texture and delectable taste.

And she could never get enough of them.

Sleep never came to claim her. She was still racked with dreams of wanting a man she couldn't risk.

CHAPTER NINETEEN

As Lana headed to the Boys & Girls Club the next afternoon, the sun was high in the sky, and she hoped the packed snow that had become ice would begin to melt. She'd picked up the ingredients for the lemon squares, made a copy of the recipe, and hoped the kids liked them. She'd had one this morning for breakfast and still felt the zing of the sugar rush.

Entering the glass doors, she greeted the receptionist, who she had become friendly with since joining the staff. Anna was the mother of one of the kids who came here after school, and he had told her how much fun he had in her class.

"What's on for today? It's all Elio's been talking about this morning."

"An old family recipe. Probably too much sugar, but every now and then we have to have fun."

"He now has me reading labels in the grocery store. You're teaching me things too."

Smiling, Lana admitted to herself it was one of her objectives.

After lifting her bags off the floor, she strode across the lobby and made her way to the hallway on the right. The cafeteria was at the end, a large room where the kids ate their wares, the kitchen off to the side. There was plenty of room for the fifteen she had in each class, but she had to do some of the classes in shifts. She found trouble came, even at twelve, when you were waiting for your turn. One of the teachers had suggested she create word searches, which the kids loved so she made sure to always have a new one ready and waiting. She placed them on a pile on one of the rectangular tables, she carried her gear into the kitchen and began her set up. The radio in the corner was set to a station she didn't often listen to but clicked it on knowing it was one of the students' favorites. Hip-hop had the kind of beat that made cooking even more fun, and her spirit lightened as she collected bowls, set out the butter, flour, lemons, eggs and sugar on the stainless-steel countertop.

Glancing at the clock, she knew she'd soon have fifteen sets of eyes on her. Here she was in her element. Loved every aspect of culinary work from creating recipes to cooking favorites, figuring out what drinks to pair with them, even buying ingredients always taking care to buy healthy and wholesome.

"Hey, Miss."

She looked up, recognizing the voice.

"*Hola*, Berto. *Como estas esta manana?*"

The young boy was one of her favorites with a fun personality and who asked lots of questions.

"Fine."

"Just fine?"

She had explained to them she didn't want to hear they were just good or fine. It meant adequate when what we should feel was happy to be alive.

He added one word, but it was enough.

"Extra fine?"

She smiled into his sparkling black eyes.

"Me, too."

She could hear the shuffling of feet as the kids came down the length of the cafeteria to join her in the kitchen. All the students straggled in, the voices rising in volume as they surrounded her at the counter. She usually broke the group up into two segments but the time constraints due to baking allowed for only one group today. It meant everyone was crowded in the space, but there was no jostling, only deep concentration. After greeting each one of the students by name, she set the objective, giving them a list of the ingredients and explaining the steps they'd take to make the bars. She generated a conversation about what was good for them and what wasn't. Surprised once again with their serious expressions and animated conversation, she relaxed into her role. After the measuring and mixing, she joined them at the table, chatting about the aroma that wafted out, and what they expected them to taste like. She had explained about the palate being broken down into sweet, sour, acid and bitter, and most of them anticipated a sour taste due to the lemon. They also asked her questions about her job, her love life and her friends. For some reason, she could commit herself fully to the connection and couldn't wait for the next group to join her. Leaving most of them to their taste test and conversation, she was joined by a few others who helped her clean up and get ready for the next lesson.

⌐

After the first class was over, she had a few minutes to herself as kids shifted from one activity to the next. Walking over to the window that faced some green space, she watched as the snow continued to settle on the ground, accumulating more than was anticipated. She loved this aspect of New England weather. Always had, but more now for the silence you could find beneath it than the sledding she'd done as a kid. The trees were dressed in a coat of white, the bushes wearing a hat of it. Coming out of her reverie, she noticed a boy, who looked vaguely familiar, running towards the building. He was running fast, as if his life depended on it. Pressing her nose to the glass, wanting to get a better understanding of what was going on, she saw a couple of bigger boys chasing him, one of them waving something she couldn't quite make out. Suddenly, the parka-clad male was seized back, his arms jerking into the air, his body arched. His face held a look of surprise. He fell to the ground, flat against the snow.

Her brain was trying to process what had happened, and her eyes lingered on the prone figure, her mind swirling with questions. Then her gaze snapped up to see the boy standing over him, holding a gun, a hoodie covering his face. When his friend went over to him, looking down at the prone figure on the ground, he seemed to panic, his feet moving in skip steps, dragging his friend along with him.

It took a few seconds for her brain to catch up with her eyes, but when it did, she bolted for the exit, pushing through the throng of kids in transition from class to class, running, her goal to even the odds. Her feet slid on the wet tile floor as she made her way towards the room next door where she knew there was an exit.

She raised her voice, and the alarm, as she hit the door with both hands.

"Call 9-1-1. There's been a shooting."

As she left the screams and shouts behind, the chaos signaled a lockdown being put in place, the rest of the kids being secured within.

Out into the cold, her steaming breath coming in gasps, she raced towards the boy, falling to her knees, taking his hand, not knowing what to do but not wanting to do nothing. Her gaze was drawn to the sneaker lying three feet away, and his hat, which had been flung off, that lay in the snow by his head.

His eyes were closed, his face was pale, his breathing shallow. There was a spot on his back that was oozing red.

If they wanted me dead, I'd be dead.

The words became a freeze-frame in her mind as she struggled for calm.

Trying to keep the hysterics out of her voice, she whispered, "I'm here with you. I'm here."

There was a rattle of breath, and she almost didn't hear the salutation.

"Miss."

Her stomach churned as his eyes fluttered open, and the glassy pupils acknowledged her presence, then they closed, and her heart stopped just as his labored breathing did.

Squeezing the hand she held, wanting him to hang on, she knew, on a deeper level, there was nothing she could do to save him.

There was nothing anyone could do to save him.

She sat petrified in the snow, afraid to move him, so she hung on to his hand in desperation. His had curled around hers in a death-like grip.

The blare of sirens worked through her fog, bruising her ear drums. The metallic smell of blood was pungent and sickened her. His hand had gone cold, but she didn't know whether it was death or frozen temperatures that made it feel that way.

All she could do was hold on, knowing that help was on the way.

Mumbling to herself, she begged, "Please. Hurry."

⌒

The reverb of the speaker scratched the air.

Shooting at the Boys & Girls Club. All available units respond.

Zach snapped his head in Paul's direction and asked, "Isn't that where Lana is?"

His heart stopped as he asked the question.

Paul uttered one word.

"Fuck."

Paul called the station and let Blue-tooth take over from there, freeing his hand to put the siren on top of his car.

The several seconds it took for someone to answer felt like hours.

"It's Catalano. We just heard about the shooting. I'm up next and my daughter might be there. I'm on my way... She did?... Get her back in, now."

Then he punched the button and the call ended.

Zach looked over at Paul and asked, "What's going on?"

"Not sure yet."

Zach was asking a stream of questions.

"Is Lana..."

"She's the one who told them what was happening, ran outside before they could stop her."

"What the hell was she thinking? Did she know the kid got shot?"

"I don't know anything more than you do. Hang on."

As he threw what was left of his sandwich in the trash bag bin behind him, Paul's foot pushed the accelerator to the floor, and the car shot off down the street, the flashing light now atop, the siren warning traffic to get out of his way.

Zach's mind raced right along with the car.

What if the shooter came back? What if she had become a target?

God, no, don't let that happen.

A feeling of dread settled over him.

Is this what she feels like when you put yourself on the line? What she feels every day because of your job?

It was an overwhelming sensation of fear.

⌒

Grabbing the dashboard, his silent plea stuck in his throat, he steadied himself as Paul maneuvered at breakneck speed, in and around the traffic that was a mainstay on the streets of Boston. His siren forced some off to the side. Others ignored it as if it was just a nuisance along the way.

The agitation was thick in Paul's voice when he yelled out to the man in front of him, "Move you fucking moron."

With a few extended beeps of the horn, Paul wiggled and weaved through the bottleneck.

Finally, with tires squealing, Paul pulled up to the front of the building and was out of the car the second he put it in park. Several police cruisers already lined the drive, uniforms surrounded the area, running back and forth to secure the perimeter.

Zach beat Paul out of the car by a step, limping in the direction pointed out by one of the officers standing by the front door. He could hear Paul's voice asking, "Lana Scalera? Where is she?"

Zach didn't hear the response, went on instinct, and as he rounded the corner, he stilled at the scene in front of him. A man in blue was on his haunches, talking to Lana. She was kneeling beside the victim, holding his hand, her body wracked with sobs.

He'd been petrified at what he might find as he moved to the back of the building, but his heart started beating again as soon as he knew she was alive. But to see her prostrate like this, knowing what this might do to her, didn't allow for the exhale that was paralyzed in his lungs.

He hated the fact that she'd witnessed a death.

It was nothing that could be described.

He'd been warned, in the academy. Told it wasn't anything you could prepare for, could only be aware of. And his first experience with it had been mind-numbing. She'd not only be dealing with the murder but with the lifeless form in front of her.

He made his way over, winced as he squatted down beside her, glancing around for blood spatter, trying to gauge what she'd been exposed to. His leg ached but he needed to comfort, and he couldn't do it on his feet. Nick Katsaros was there, as well.

"I've been trying to get her to move. It's like she doesn't even know I'm here. I'll leave her to you."

He watched Nick rise and step back a couple of feet.

"Lana?"

As if frozen in time, she didn't answer him, her heaving shoulders the only part of her that moved.

Placing his hand on her shoulder, wet wool beneath his fingers, he said her name again.

Her face finally registered recognition and she leapt across and into his arms. She gripped the back of his coat and she hung on for dear life. So did he, the prospect of losing her hitting him like a punch to the gut. The guys who had worked him over had nothing on what he felt right now.

Her tears trickled down his neck, so he did what he could, placing his hand over her skull, holding her close.

Her grip tightened as she cried, "I saw him get shot, Zach. I saw him go down. Breathe his last breath... I...I..."

Finally looking up into Zach's eyes, she repeated, with a sob, "I saw him get shot. He didn't have a chance to defend himself."

She was so pale it frightened him, her eyes glassy, her limbs shaking.

He brought her back against his chest, repeating over and over, "It's okay, Lana. It's okay. I'm here. I've got you."

"Why? Why did they do that? What could that boy have done to make someone want to kill him?"

Her voice was thin, and it sent shivers through him.

"I don't know, Lana. We'll find out, though. Paul and I will find out."

In that instant, he wanted this job, wanted to get justice for the kid who was lying at their feet. Wanted to punish someone for what Lana was feeling, for what she'd been forced to witness.

He gentled his voice before he said, "You shouldn't have come out here, Lana."

She looked him the eyes, the sheer terror of what she'd witnessed still visible.

"I didn't touch anything. Just his hand. Honest. I wouldn't have moved anything. I just didn't want him to be alone."

Stroking the back of her head as he might an infant, he said in a soft and measured tone, "It was a dangerous thing to do. The shooter could have come back."

Her eyes now held a tinge of horror.

"I...I didn't think. I wanted to see if I could help him, then...I didn't want him to die alone. Is he dead? I think he's dead."

He heard hurried footsteps and looked back as Paul was running towards them, the ice making it difficult to find traction.

Paul yelled out in a gruff voice, "Lana, are you okay?"

He slipped and slid his way over to where they stood, the tread-like soles unable to keep a steady grip on the freezing ground beneath them.

When Lana looked up, Zach noticed the pale face, the haunted eyes, the quivering body, and if the murder hadn't been enough to cause the trembling, the words that followed were.

"I saw his face, Paul. When he got hit. Like he knew he was going to die. Is that the look Dad had on his face? Did he know he was going to die, Paul?"

Paul's eyes closed. It gave Zach the time to get Lana to her feet, but she stayed glued to his side, now gripping the front of his coat rather than the back.

Even as Paul stepped forward, she didn't let go. And he hung on to her in return.

"I...don't know, Lana. I didn't see his face."

Zach looked at Paul in speculation, as if he didn't believe him and the return look confirmed it. It didn't surprise him that Paul wasn't going to add to Lana's already overstressed system.

Lana didn't pursue the topic, let the statement hang in the air.

Zach pried Lana's fingers away from him so that he could shrug off his coat and wrap it around her shoulders. As soon as it was done, she regained her hold on him.

Paul glanced at him with relief in his eyes. They hadn't known what they were going to find when they got here. It could have been a shooting inside the building, and anyone would have been at risk. That Lana was alive was all that mattered now. But they knew there'd be deeper wounds. She already had so many issues regarding death, guns, and bullets. This was another loss, although not one as emotionally charged as her father's, but one they both knew would affect her psyche in an adverse way.

Zach pulled Lana closer, hoping to protect her from the time warp she was locked in, a past that held the loss of her innocence. Murmuring words of comfort, he held her steady against him, her grip not letting go.

Then her hands flew to her ears as the wail of the ambulance announced its arrival, the blaring howl quivering through her, and she bent over as if she were going to be sick, tears still streaming down her face.

The ME's wagon would be next.

CHAPTER TWENTY

Zach was here. Had he heard her screaming for him? It hadn't been out loud, but her mind had become an echo chamber of one word that symbolized everything she wanted or needed in the world.

Zach.

Feeling his arms around her insulated her from the gaping wound that threatened to bleed out. Why couldn't she escape the madness of guns and bullets? Death? Her father's face seen so clearly through the prism of time. Zach in the hospital, his wounds not the result of a gun, but a much more violent form of weapon that tripped men into another dimension. And she knew that fists, could work as well. The horror was waging a battle in her mind. Had this become the norm of daily living? Was it something she'd have to accept? Could she allow the vulnerability a space in her consciousness?

She clung even tighter to the man who had become her anchor. And she was not going to let go.

The wail of the ambulance was deafening as it got closer, but she knew it had been a wasted trip. The boy was gone and there was nothing anyone could do to resuscitate him. He was just a kid. Too young to have lost his life.

The bustling activity only agitated her further. Men and women in blue were swarming the area, stringing yellow tape around the dead zone while steering clear of the scene itself. Some were searching the surrounding area, while others stood over the body.

Paul was shouting out directives to the men and women gathered, resuming his status as lead on the case after making sure she was taken care of. He'd been deathly white when he'd approached her, all but running across the snow and ice to get to her. He'd been her father in every sense of the word since Sal had died. She knew he still carried the guilt that he hadn't been able to protect him, even though he'd been willing to give up his life to do it. She'd almost forgotten he'd been shot the same day. Consumed by grief over her father's death, she'd never visited him in the hospital, never asked what kinds of injuries he'd sustained. He hadn't even been fully recovered when he took over care for the family. She'd thought at first it had to do with his loyalty to his partner. It had taken years for her to realize he'd done it out of love for all of them.

As she watched him take command, a flutter of pride spread its wings in her heart. How could she have kept him at arm's length for so long? The stark truth. She was unwilling to embrace another possible loss. She'd missed out on an important part of life by building a wall of fear between her and so many others. She should have embraced the love...

As she felt the solid body beneath her hands, the protectiveness of the arms around her, she knew the toll it had taken, and the price she'd paid. It had cost her the man she loved more than life. She tucked herself closer to him, letting the steady beat of his heart calm her ragged nerves. Her eyes trailed the detective Paul introduced as Naji Prem as he walked over to the victim. After kneeling beside him, his hands encased in gloves, he checked the area for anything that might have fallen out of the victim's pockets, something that might give them a clue as to who he was. She knew they had to wait for the ME to show up before touching the body. Then Naji held up the phone he found before placing it in a plastic bag provided by one of the officers who'd been first on the scene. It would become part of the evidence that would be stockpiled as they built their case against the shooter, whoever that turned out to be. Would it give them the victim's identity? She had a desperate need to know his name, having shared in the most intimate of circumstances. The death rattle penetrated the memory she was desperately trying to shut out, losing the balance she'd tried so hard to find.

When one of the detectives shouted above the din so all could hear, "Medical examiner is here," she felt another ripple of anxiety.

She buried her face into the solid wall of Zach's chest, and she knew he'd protect her, not from what she'd seen but from what those lingering images could do to her. He was alive, and she could hear the thud of his chest beneath her ear, steady and strong. She let it hypnotize her, and once entranced, she was almost able to shut out any awareness of the world around her. At least that of the body that lay only a few yards away.

Zach felt her body shudder against him, and he stroked her back, needing to touch her in any way he could. She had come too close to danger, and the thought of her being gunned down as a witness all but choked the life out of him. He grabbed her close again, felt her bury her head in his chest. With her secure in his arms, he began to pay attention to the detectives working the field, knowing it would be his job one day. Paul had given him a run-down of procedure one night after dinner, explaining in detail the steps taken to solve a murder. It was a slow and tedious process. Purposeful documentation of the conditions was imperative. He knew Paul would take his time processing the scene, verifying and corroborating any information found here with any that came in from another source. They couldn't afford to overlook anything. Sometimes it was the smallest piece of information that led to an arrest. They would go over this area with a fine-tooth comb, documenting everything methodically. There would be no shortcuts taken, no evidence subsumed. He'd heard that Paul had amazing powers of observation and could stay focused even as the investigation was pulling him in different directions. Zach's father had praised Paul for his dedication, his organizational skills and his gut instinct. "There's no better detective in that department. Learn from him and you'll be one of the best homicide detectives, as well. Something a Taylor has been unable to do to this point."

It made the initial resentment about being transferred more tolerable.

Prem continued his search of the area, bent down to examine the ground, Paul beside him now, eyeing the hole made by the weapon.

"Not much blood spatter. Looks like a .38. We'll have to wait to hear what the ME has to say."

The forensic photographer was one of the first on site, and he was already capturing the scene and the body on video. Several officers were still clustered around the body, as if protecting it from contamination. Others were walking the perimeter looking for evidence, anything that might help with the investigation. The local police would do the grunt work, as the more elite members of the Homicide Department got to ask questions and jot things down.

Paul came back to stand beside them. "Not much in the way of physical evidence. I hope the phone gives us something."

Kade Anderson, one of the other detectives, came up and said, "I hear we might have a witness."

Paul hesitated and decided to bypass the question.

"You and Jerry can start questioning the kids inside. Maybe someone saw something."

Kade glanced to Lana, then said, "Sure thing, Paul."

Paul was silently watching the two detectives head inside the building before turning to him. "Your father insisted you be given another week before working in the field. It's just as well. I have a more important task for you. Wait here."

What did Paul have in mind? He wasn't sure he could accomplish any task right now, so consumed with the one he was already involved in.

Holding Lana.

Zach watched as Paul delegated, utilizing all his resources.

Coming back over to him, he said, "One of the most important managerial duties is finding the right man or woman for the job, assigning the right personnel to the right task. This is a no-brainer for me. I want you to take Lana to the station and take her testimony."

Zach felt Lana all but crawl into his skin.

Meeting Zach's eyes, the veteran detective said slowly, "I'm sorry you won't be here to learn protocol, but this is as important an aspect of the investigation as what I'll be doing. And you're the only one I trust to handle this...with kid gloves."

One of the officers approached asking, "Is this the witness? Do you want me to take her down for questioning?"

"She's my daughter...and Zach's— He'll be taking her statement. I want you to take the phone to the station, give it to one of the other detectives. They're waiting for it."

Zach said quietly, "What do you want me to do?"

"Go to the station and handle it yourself. There will have to be another detective in the room with you. I don't want the appearance of a conflict of interest but I'm not allowing anyone else to question her."

Zach felt the pressure of Lana's hands tighten on his jacket lapels. Pulling her closer, the need to make her feel safe a demanding one, he asked, "You won't get any flak?"

"Not if you do it well."

"I'm not going to press her...just so you know."

Paul's eyes went to his daughter. Licking his lips, he said, "Advice? Draw her out with patience. She's not the kind of witness who needs a heavy hand."

There was never a question that he'd be gentle. Paul's most important person might be the victim. His was the woman in his arms.

"I will."

Paul leaned forward and kissed Lana on her head.

"I'm sorry sweetheart but you have to answer some questions. Zach's going with you. I'll call your mother. I'm sorry I can't..."

She nodded before she wrapped her arms around Zach's mid-section, as if she were hanging on for dear life. Her clinging movements told him she wasn't going with anyone else.

He asked Zach, "Can you drive?"

"If I have to, but it might be better if I go with one of the men in a squad car. I can sit with her in the back seat...keep her warm."

Lana was soaking wet from the snow, her clothes sodden, and they had to be making her colder still.

"You're right. I'll tell Celia to bring clean clothes."

Lana, eyes still glassy, said in a whisper, "Mom is busy. She's got an event tonight, getting ready for it... She'll have to cover for me. I just...can't." The wobble of the last word struck a nerve.

Zach was as shaken as Lana.

"She'll figure something out."

Zach glanced down at the body before leaving, the child who lay in the snow killed before he had time to live. The snap of the latex gloves told him Paul was back in detective mode, squatting by the body, examining each wound, then getting up to scan the ground for any evidence the killers had left behind, as he continued to fire off directives with each step.

Zach guided Lana to one of the police cruisers, looking around to see who rode the vehicle. A young female came scurrying over, her blue uniform visible under her overcoat.

"Detective Taylor, can I help you?"

Everyone seemed to know who he was. He didn't like that his reputation preceded him, his ancestral one, anyway.

"We need a ride to the station. We need to take a witness statement and Lt. Catalano asked me to see to it personally."

"Sure. Let me tell my partner. I'll be right back."

Before she left, she unlocked the car, started the engine and opened the back door so they could wait inside, out of the snow.

The heater was just beginning to throw some warmth their way, the interior still holding the chill of the blustery afternoon.

Lana was hugging herself against the door, her glassy eyes looking out to the ice packed landscape. The trembling of her body was visible from across the seat. Not sure how to proceed, he moved his bulk beside her, carefully wrapping her in another embrace. After wrestling his phone out of his suit coat pocket, he searched for a number. He hit the call button and waited for his mother to answer.

But she skipped over the hello.

"Your father just called. How is she?"

"As you'd expect. We're on the way to the station. She's soaked and needs some dry clothes. Can you do this for me?"

"Of course."

"Call Celia..."

"I'll grab some of my sweats and a sweater. It will save time. I'll be there in fifteen minutes."

"Thanks. I know—"

"Don't. I'll see you soon."

He ended the call and slipped the phone back in his inside pocket.

Lana's hands were still curled into his side, clutching at his shirt. The grip got tighter as they got closer to the police station, and he had to almost pry them off after they'd arrived.

Keeping her tucked against him, he got out of the car, acknowledging the driver.

"Thanks, Officer."

"No problem, Detective Taylor."

⌒

He escorted Lana through the back door, and up to his new home away from home. Still new to the department, he was at odds as to where to take her, where the interview rooms were, where he could take up residence.

His father made the odds a bit more even when he met him at the elevator.

"How's she doing?"

George Taylor seemed genuinely concerned, which was a surprise. His family had turned their back on Lana the day she asked him to leave her life. Demanded he leave it.

As if reading his mind, his father admitted, "We're not getting any satisfaction from this, Zach. No one should have to see what she saw today. And it took guts for her to run out like that. Follow me."

And he did, down a narrow hallway until they came to a group of four rooms that were used for interviews. The room had nothing more than a table and a few chairs, a surveillance camera attached to the ceiling, and a waste basket in the corner, and he stepped through, depositing Lana in one of the chairs.

She grabbed onto his hand with both of hers, keeping him at her side.

Zach looked over at his father and asked, "Has Mom shown up yet?"

"She's about five minutes away. You know her and her lead foot. I had to call off the cops. She never would have waited around for an escort."

"Can I wait until she gets here and Lana's warm before we start?"

"Absolutely." Turning his attention to his daughter-in-law, he asked, "Do you want something Lana? A drink, something to eat?"

Zach could feel the shake of her head in response. He looked up into his father's eyes, sure that his raw emotion was evident.

"A coffee with some sugar would be good, Dad."

"Good idea."

He called out to one of the detectives and gave the order. The coffee arrived within less than a minute.

Zach placed it in Lana's hands and asked her to sip at it, which, to his relief, she did without question.

He wanted to ask George what to do, how to ask the questions, how to keep Lana from hurting but he wasn't sure anyone had the answers.

He'd just have to go with his gut and hope he didn't make matters worse for her.

⌒

A rap at the door signaled Jeanne's arrival. She didn't wait for an invitation but stepped into the room as if she owned it, handing the bag of clothes off to her son.

"Is there anything else you need?"

His witness was still numb, and he was afraid when she came out of it, she'd come face-to-face with what had happened. It would only make it worse.

"A redo of the day?"

"Sorry. I wish I could... There's several things I'd redo—"

When he saw Lana glance up, he caught his mother's attention with his eyes. She must have noticed as well, because she stopped mid-sentence. Her eyes flicked in understanding, and she gave him an apologetic frown.

One of the female detectives entered the room, introducing herself. Zach had seen her around yesterday but hadn't made her acquaintance yet. Slim and blonde, she seemed right at home with the procedure.

"Zach, I'm Martha Howe. Paul called, asked me to sit in with you. You okay with it?"

"Sure. Paul knows what he's doing. But we're going to get her changed first."

Martha nodded in understanding and said, "Good idea. Let me show you to the ladies room."

Lana's head gave a vigorous shake, looked up at him.

"I'm not going without you."

"Lana, I can't go into the ladies room."

Jeanne interrupted and asked, "Would you like me to come with you, Lana?"

His mother's tone was soft, and he was surprised by Lana's choked response.

"Thanks, Jeanne but if Zach can't help me, I'll stay as I am."

He saw the droop in her body, as if gravity was beginning to wear her down. The adrenaline spurt was evaporating, and sheer exhaustion would soon take its place. He wanted her home before that happened.

Zach gave his father a quizzical look, which George answered with, "My office?"

Zach countered, "Too many curious eyes and too much glass."

Martha was the one who suggested, "How about Paul's office, then?"

Zach knew that it was small, but it had walls and a door.

It would work.

Stroking Lana's hair, he whispered, "Come on, sweetheart. Let's get you out of these wet clothes."

Then he stilled. He glanced up at Martha and didn't know how to explain this. He was a detective who was about to interview a witness and now she was asking him to help her change, from the bottom down. In other words, see her nude.

Martha gave a nod, as if she understood.

"I know about...you two. A lot of us do. It won't be a problem."

It shouldn't have come as a surprise. Between Paul and his father, the detectives here would have known about the small ceremony.

He couldn't worry about that now.

He thanked his mother for bringing the clothes and followed as Martha led the way back out and into the office.

CHAPTER TWENTY-ONE

As soon as Martha retreated, Zach closed the door.

Lana was standing there, in a stupor, her body visibly shivering.

He stepped forward, unwound the coat from around her shoulders and then hesitated.

He hadn't seen her body in two years, but he'd never forgotten what she looked like. It was embedded in his brain, like a tattoo on his heart.

This was not the way he'd wanted to undress her, if he ever got the chance again.

He wanted it to be in passion, in love, in pure feeling.

But he wanted a lot of things. This was just another in a long line that wouldn't be met.

He touched her cheek, which was death-like cold.

"Are you sure you want me to do this, Lana?"

Her glazed eyes met his, but she made no move or gesture that told him what to do.

He fingered the hem of her sweater and stalled as he gauged her reaction. When he got none, he guided her arms up and lifted the sodden material over her head, letting it drop to the floor. Her skin was covered in goose flesh, and he warmed her by rubbing his hands down her arms. He was also stalling for time. Soon she'd be naked under his gaze, and he needed to temper the hormones that might mistake this for something else.

Slowly, he reached around her back, unclasped the bra, and peeled it away from her body. His breathing had become labored, and he pushed down the longing to touch. This was not the time or the place to take her in, her breasts such a thing of beauty.

But what he'd uncovered was so startling his fingers were drawn to it. A dragonfly was inked over her left breast, purple with a fine netting of wings. Over her shoulder, another fine netting as if her arm had taken on the wing as her own.

Her eyes flicked up to meet his and he read pain, sharp and clear.

"When did you get these?"

"A couple of days after you left. I added another one every year on the anniversary..." Her voice was fragile and shaking.

That statement slammed into his chest with the force of a bullet. She'd marked herself, to mark the anniversary...

"Why?"

It sounded more like a croak than a word.

"To feel a different kind of pain."

Her eyes were vacant. He assumed she was too much in shock to filter what she gave him. Her admission gutted him and his heart, beat faster in his chest. She'd been as affected by the separation as he'd been, something he'd never known. He had assumed she couldn't possibly feel the same kind of emotion as him if it had been so easy for her to end it. It had been the wrong assumption... If he had known...

Needing to cover her, cover the evidence that she had loved him as much as he loved her, he pulled the sweater out of the bag and worked her arms into the sleeves.

He braced himself, knowing there would be a third tattoo somewhere. He wasn't sure his heart could take it.

After removing her boots on bended knee, he stood back up, unsnapped her jeans and began to peel them away. The heavy and stiff material made it difficult, so he went behind her, his hands sliding between the jeans and her skin. He pushed them down, past her thighs, knees, down far enough so that he could help her step out of them.

He stilled when he found the third inking. It looked fresh, shiny from the lotion she must have applied, so he assumed it was the latest, done just a little more than two weeks ago.

His thumbs lightly brushed the words written in black scroll across her lower back, at her hip line.

Death might not be the greatest loss...it might be what dies inside when love is gone

His heart almost stopped beating. His breathing was labored, not from any sexual tension at seeing her exposed but from the psychic one.

The day she'd told him to leave, his soul had withered. Life had become uninspired. Death had become inconsequential.

Was he just finding out she had felt the same way?

Could she have loved him more than he thought?

It had been so easy for her to force him out. Or so it seemed. Seeing this...suggested something that had hope flaring in his chest.

With unsteady hands, he retrieved his mother's sweats, went back to the task at hand and helped her into them, his heart trembling at what she'd done to her body.

She stood deathly silent, her remoteness scaring him, until she was fully clothed. When he pulled her against him, her face in the crook of his neck, she held on as if she'd never let go.

And he hung on for dear life as he guided her back to the interview room.

⌒

She'd known there'd be no way to hide what she'd done once she was undressed. It's why she could never have let Jeanne help her. She didn't want anyone knowing...Would he be repelled by the ink? She'd never thought about covering her body that way. Johnny was the one that did that. The first one she got, a couple of days after his leaving, a small dragonfly, was a test. She always loved them as a kid, would visually follow its flight when she saw one. It had come to symbolize Zach in her mind, a creature of the wind. He refused to be held down, by her or anyone. On her second visit, she'd wanted to expand on that theme, covering her back and arm with the wing. He was underground by then, having flown away from her and her obsessive need to keep him whole. She might not have his body, but she would always have a part of him deep in her heart. She'd planned on doing something similar for the third one, until she read the quote. She didn't even remember where she'd seen it, but the words had become indelibly inked in her mind. She'd marked the truth of that sentiment on her body as well. She'd always thought that death was the absolute separator, but she'd been wrong. A bullet hadn't taken him away from her. It was her own fears that had done that.

Would he understand what the words meant? Would he finally understand that his leaving had all but killed her inside?

He'd stilled when he saw it and her breath had held. Then she felt his fingers brushing against her skin along the scrawled line. It had sent shivers racing through her body. His touch had always done that to her, made her feel alive and vulnerable at the same time. She didn't dare move, didn't dare let him know that she wanted what she'd denied herself. He didn't say a word. Just continued to dress her, covering up what she'd wanted to say to him for too long now.

But when he pulled her close, his arms wrapped tightly around her, she clung to him. This was where she wanted to be, always, or until his last breath.

He guided her back to the interview room. Thankfully, Jeanne was gone, and they were alone. He got her settled, pulling his chair close, his hand never leaving hers as they waited for Martha to rejoin them. She entered the space soon after, clutching her notepad and pencil.

He wished he knew what to do, what to say. He was an expert at many things, HOG in the Marines, Hunter of Gunmen, the bullet hanging from a thin silver chain still around his neck, scout, medic when needed but asking Lana questions about the murder was way out of his comfort zone.

He scooted his chair closer.

"We have to ask you some questions. Are you ready?"

She looked up at him. He read stark pain along with the glassy-eyed expression of someone who'd just been traumatized.

Taking a breath, his voice low and steady, he coaxed, "Can you tell us what you saw?"

She stared into space before she answered.

"I was waiting for the next class to arrive. It looked so pretty outside I went to the window."

Tears filled her eyes as she described the scene, the boy running, being followed, the shooting, someone else dragging the shooter away.

"It made me think of you. How unfair it was to be outnumbered. How badly you were hurt."

She looked up at him. "I'm sorry I didn't come see you."

His heart seized at the expression on her face. He finally understood how torn she was. It hadn't been easy for her to send him away and he'd never given her the patience she needed to overcome her fears.

"It's okay, sweetheart. I understand."

Finally.

Taking a deep breath, he asked, "Could you recognize any of them if you saw them again?"

"I didn't see the shooter's face. The hoodie was hiding it, but I saw the boy who led him away."

His breath caught. He'd been hoping she wouldn't be able to identify the assailants, God forgive him. He didn't want her to be any more involved in this than she already was.

"Can you give us a description?"

"I'm not sure. All I could think about was the boy lying in the snow."

"Okay, let's start with height."

"Um, maybe my height, a little taller."

"Age?"

She blinked at him as if she didn't understand the question, so he repeated it.

Her voice had a catch in it when she answered.

"Young. Maybe fifteen, sixteen."

"Coloring?"

"He might have been white, maybe light brown. Sometimes it's hard to tell."

Her eyes held an apology as if she wasn't giving him what he needed. He squeezed her hand and told her, "That's okay. You're doing fine.

As he looked at the hand that still held his, a fierce sense of protectiveness came over him. He wished he didn't have to do this, keep up the questions. All he wanted was to get her out of here, to someplace safe, where she could collapse and begin to heal.

He didn't have that luxury, so he prodded, "Did you notice what he was wearing?"

"A zipper sweatshirt, grey, dirty white, a pair of jeans, sneakers."

"Anything that might distinguish him from somebody else?"

She began to shake her head, then her head shot up.

"Chuck Taylor sneakers. They were grey. A boy in one of my classes pointed them out, said he wished he could get a pair."

Martha said quietly, "They are the designated footwear for one of the gangs in the area."

Lana looked up. "I thought it was because he couldn't afford them. He couldn't get them because..."

Zach finished her sentence, "...He didn't want to be associated with the gang."

Martha gave him a long look. "Or he knew the repercussions if he started wearing them."

This was the kind of clue that might get them resolution.

Zach picked up the line of questioning, trying to correlate the information.

"Did you recognize him as one of the boys who comes here?"

Her eyes narrowed.

"No. They were older. But maybe he has a brother who comes."

He looked over to Martha and asked, "Something to look into?"

All she gave was a nod of her head.

He kept the interview going.

He had started with the person she could identify but knew it was time to touch on the shooter.

"As to the boy with the gun, how tall?"

She paused, shook her head and then met his eyes.

"About the same as his friend. When they started running away, they were pretty evenly matched in height and weight."

"Anything about him look familiar, anything that stood out?"

As she slowly shook her head, closing her eyes, the pain crossed her features and Zach was sorry he had asked the question.

"I can't get the picture out of my head. The gun, the kid pointing the gun. It was surreal. I couldn't believe it was happening. Didn't know what he had in his hand until the other boy went down. Then it was obvious."

He was about to ask about the gun when she whimpered.

Opening her eyes, she said, "He held the gun in his left hand. Is that important?"

"It could be very important. Anything else stand out?"

"He had a grey sweatshirt and wore navy running pants. No coats, neither of them had coats. It's so cold outside and they had no coats."

That wasn't necessarily of import. The kids who came here were from lower income households and probably couldn't afford jackets.

"Can you give us a description of the gun?"

"I...don't know guns. Dad never took his out, always locked away. Same with Paul."

"That's okay. If we find the shell casings it might answer the question."

The glistening moisture in her eyes made him want to hold her but he couldn't. Not yet. Her next words shot right to his heart.

"I was with him when he died, Zach. He was alive when I got to him. I couldn't do anything to help him."

"You prevented him from dying alone, Lana. That was something."

She squeezed his hand, as if she needed the connection.

He brushed her wrist with his thumb, his heart still seizing from the sight of her outside sitting next to a dead body.

"How did you get out? The center went into lockdown pretty quickly."

"I saw it happen, ran right for the exit in the gym, I think I told them to get help, to call 9-1-1, but I got out before anyone else realized what had happened. I heard them going into lockdown, but I was already outside by then."

He shuddered at the thought that she could have been shot. And for a second felt what she must when confronted with his possible death.

He studied her then, her face, her expression, her huddled form hidden by his jacket, which he had draped around her shoulders again.

And realized the depth of his loss if she had been...

He felt the spasmodic trembling as she put her other hand on top of his. He clutched both in his before she asked, "What was his name? Do you know?"

"The victim?"

"Yes. What was his name?"

"We left before they IDed him."

In a small voice she said, "I'm sorry I took you away from your first case."

He wasn't going to tell her he was barred from the field for another week although he was going to get involved whether his father liked it or not.

Giving her a lop-sided smile, he reassured her.

"Isn't this part of it? Interviewing witnesses?"

A tortured expression took over her face and she croaked, "I don't want to be a witness. I don't want to have seen what I saw. How will I ever get this out of my head?"

Had something else died inside her today, as witness to death?

He glanced down at her small hand enclosed within his larger one, then closed his eyes.

"I can't lie, Lana. It will take time."

There was a sharp rap on the door which Martha answered, cracking it open to see who was there.

Celia was on the other side of the door, and he expected Lana to rush into her mother's arms, but she didn't. She merely looked up and stared into space.

"I came as soon as I could. I called one of the chefs I've interviewed, the one I'm leaning towards. She was able to take over for me."

Her gaze met his, the question in her eyes not one he could answer. She asked another he could.

"Can I take her home?"

"We've got a sketch artist coming in. As soon as that's done, yes."

It took an hour for the sketch to be complete, but when it was done, he thought they might have a very good likeness. He wouldn't know for sure until they caught him, but Lana remembered a lot more than she'd thought she could, seemed confident as she described the kid's features once she began the process.

When the police artist had left the room, Celia asked, "Can we leave now?"

"Yes. Get her warm, give her a shot of whiskey, get her to bed."

Lana's eyes flashed up to meet his.

"I don't want to leave you."

He took her face in his hands, couldn't help himself, and kissed her lips with a soft caress.

"I have to stay here, sweetheart. I've got to help Paul catch the kids who did this. I'll come back to the house when I'm done."

Lana's voice was thick with anxiety when she asked, "Can I stay with you tonight?"

His eyes shot up to Celia's.

There was deep grief etched on her brow, and he knew she wouldn't answer for him even if she wanted to.

He lifted Lana out of the seat and put his arms around her.

"I'll stay with you all night if that's what you want."

Her hands went up to cup his face and she leaned in and pressed her lips to his before tucking herself against his chest.

"I need you to."

"I'll be there as soon as I can."

She took a tentative step out of his embrace and said, "I'll be waiting for you."

Celia looked up at him then, total disbelief on her face.

He met it with a disbelieving look of his own.

They both had thought with the death would come another round of distancing. Instead, she was clinging to him. He had the feeling that Celia didn't understand it any more than he did.

They were gone before he could say anything else.

CHAPTER TWENTY-TWO

"You did a great job, Zach. She gave you some good information. That wasn't easy."

Martha was leading him out into the common area, and he was relieved to be out of the confining space of the interview room. He needed to get back out to the Boys & Girls Club. Let Paul know what they'd found out, see how they processed the scene, but his thoughts were still on Lana and what she had witnessed. For someone who had an aversion to guns and bullets to see firsthand what kind of damage they could do, it had to be gut-wrenching. He wished he could wipe it away from her memory. Even as a seasoned vet, he'd never gotten used to mangled bodies, lost limbs, death stares. Or the way death came.

Some men stood frozen, then collapsed as the pain registered. Some deflated like a balloon as the air rushed out of them, and some started running, as if they could outdistance the grim reaper, dropping unconscious from loss of blood. Then there were those who twitched in place, expiring with a shriek on their lips.

It was the victim's facial expression that she'd noticed. It was one of shock to be sure. And now that image would be burned in her memory, another connection to the loss of her father that couldn't be erased.

His phone vibrated against his waist, and when he swiped to answer, Paul was already asking, "How is she?"

"She's gone home with Celia. She's staying at the house tonight."

"Good. We can keep an eye on her that way. Did she give you anything?"

"Yeah. Several key points. The shooter was left-handed, the kid who dragged him away was wearing a brand of sneaker that's popular with one of the local gangs. She gave us a good description of him, I think. We have a sketch that we can start passing around." He hesitated before giving away one of his concerns. "I don't like her as witness, Paul. These kids don't have a problem with killing."

"That's worrying me, too. Just makes it more important that we get them behind bars. I'm just heading back. We processed the scene. The body's been transported to the morgue. I've got to notify the parents."

"I want to come."

"Zach—"

"I'm going to talk to my father. If he knows what's good for him, he'll ease up on the restrictions. There's no way I'm watching from the sidelines on this one."

As soon as he tracked him down, Zach had a brief but heated conversation with his father. George finally relented. He didn't want to bring his son up for insubordination, although he'd threatened to before he gave in.

"Let Paul know when you call and tell him that I'll be outside waiting."

His father had merely nodded to him before pulling out his phone.

Zach hurried out to the front of the precinct, and as soon as Paul arrived, they headed to the victim's house.

Even though he thought he'd prepared himself for the interview, it was heartbreaking. The mother keened, collapsing into her husband's arms, asking questions that were difficult to answer. The why might never be discovered.

Adrian Cruz was fourteen, a freshman at a local high school. Loved sports, the New York Yankees more than any other. His Yankees cap was found close to the body.

Paul discreetly asked questions about his friends, any enemies, trouble he might have been in. The parents had nothing to report other than the names of a few friends.

No, he didn't attend the Boys & Girls Club although he had when he was younger; no, they didn't know what he was doing there.

They questioned the brother, who added very little to what his parents already had told them.

When they left, Zach heaved a heavy sigh.

"We have to do this every time we catch a murder?"

"All part of the service. It's the part that sucks."

By the time they left the Cruzes', night had fallen. The temperatures hovered below freezing. The blanket was still pristine on the sidewalks, glistening in the moonlight.

They got back to the station, with several more things to scour through before they could call it a night, one of which was examining a video taken from the camera attached to the Boys & Girls Club building. Naji had talked to the tech guy and had it copied. They weren't optimistic about finding anything. It was angled away from the scene and after an hour of scrutinizing the DVD, several detectives sitting around the computer hoping to see evidence of the crime, they were all disappointed.

Zach sat back, threaded his hands through his hair.

"Why the hell have a camera up if it doesn't show you anything but the woods across the street?"

Paul gave him a smile that had a sardonic twist to it.

"At least it was working. There are some that are just up for show. That's a waste of money and effort. It galls me every time."

Zach was feeling the effects of being active all day, but he wasn't anywhere near ready to call it a night.

"What next?"

"We have a copy of Adrian's phone records. Your father cut through some tape and they're on my desk. Come on."

Zach hefted himself out of the chair and followed in Paul's wake. He glanced up at the clock and was surprised to find it was just after ten. They'd been at this for over eight hours, but it seemed they'd just started. Paul had schooled him on how important the first forty-eight hours were. If they didn't get a lead within that time frame, it made the case much harder to solve. Thanks to Lana, they had a jump on it. They had a face which might make all the difference.

Lana.

How was she doing?

He'd told her he'd be back as soon as he could. Did she think he'd gone back on his word?

"Have you talked to Celia?"

"About an hour ago. Told her I didn't know when we'd be back."

"How's Lana?"

"Waiting for you."

He worked the kinks out of his neck and took a seat. Paul was already going through the phone list that Howe had put together for him.

"This looks like a dead end. Sometimes it's the last caller who turns out to be the murderer. His was to his mother. The only other thing we found was a running text with his girlfriend. Last one told her he was running late. We'll talk to her, but not tonight."

After packing away the records into his file folder, he snapped the elastic in place, pulled his coat on, tucked the folder under his arm and said, "Let's go home."

Zach sighed in relief.

⌐

Paul drove carefully through the dark night. The black ice was hiding and the last thing they needed tonight was an accident. As they wended their way north and onto the highway, Zach asked, even though he knew he didn't have much more juice to give it, "Why are we waiting until tomorrow to investigate? We have some good leads."

Glancing over to him, Paul said, "We've done all we can for now. Most of the kids have been interviewed. No one other than Lana saw anything. It happened at the back of the building and the only windows are in the cafeteria. The gym had been closed due to lack of supervision, and that was the only other access point they would have had."

"Lana said that's how she got out. Through the gym door."

"I still can't believe she did that. Nearly caused me a coronary."

"I almost called her out on it. That was something she'd accuse me of doing, taking unnecessary risks. Decided it wasn't a good idea."

"Like I've said, you've got a good head on your shoulders. You know when to remain silent."

His chuckle turned somber.

"I've talked to Celia. She said Lana refused to eat but that she's resting. Rissa stopped by with John Luc and Luca, but no one was able to get her to talk." Looking over at him, Paul added, "She wants you."

He'd been waiting years for her to want him again. Now? It was a sad excuse for it, but he'd take it any way he could get it.

After exiting the highway, Paul took a right onto Route 28, the roads better now that they were out of the city.

"She's not going to sleep well for the next couple of days."

"And I hope she doesn't ask me again about the look on Sal's face when he got hit. It still sends shivers through me if I think about it."

"He knew?"

"He knew. The last thing he wheezed out was, "Take care of my family.""

"Fuck."

"I don't want them to know that. It might make them think I asked Celia to marry me because I owed it to Sal."

"But you didn't?"

"They were my family for over a decade. I loved those kids like they were my own. Celia, she's a good woman. I guess I'd always respected her, but once Sal was gone, I began to spend a lot of my free time there. I came to love her, as well. I wanted to spend the rest of my life with her. I was lucky she agreed. As you know, losing someone on the job can have long-term consequences."

"Firsthand."

"Yeah."

Paul pulled the Ford into the driveway behind Celia's car, reached into the back seat to retrieve the cooler, hefted it up and out with him. It was almost as full now as when they'd started out this morning.

"I hope there's something to eat. I'm starved."

Zach shook his head. He hadn't reached that level yet where the night's events were routine. Food had been the last thing on his mind since midafternoon, when they got the call.

As they entered through the side door, they wiped their feet before moving into the kitchen, where Celia was sitting at the island, drinking a glass of wine.

Paul asked, "Did Tony come by and shovel?"

"No. Luca did it before they left to go back home."

"How is she?"

"I don't know. She hasn't said much since we got here. Got her night pants on and crawled onto the couch. I sat with her for a little while, but it seemed to upset her more than calm her. She said she wanted to be alone. She keeps asking if Zach is back yet. Like I wouldn't tell her."

"Is she watching a movie?"

"Watching an empty screen."

Zach listened as he undid his tie, pulled it down from around his neck. Not saying anything, he moved to the edge of the darkened family room to see Lana sitting on the couch, a box of tissues beside her. The box didn't look like it had been touched. He wished she'd release some of the horror. It wouldn't do her any good to keep it bottled up.

He stepped in, walked over to where she was and sat down.

Her eyes were still vacant.

Closing her lids, she furrowed her brow, her lips tilting down. If this was her way of telling him to leave, she shouldn't have bothered.

"Adrian Cruz."

Her head spun in his direction, her eyes now opened wide, a live spark in them for just a second.

"His name. Adrian Cruz. We spoke to his parents a little while ago. They were grateful he didn't die alone."

Biting her lip, she said, "Thank you. For telling me that."

"You asked. I thought you'd want to know."

He couldn't keep his eyes from drifting to the patch of skin, the one with the fine- threaded tattoo. Her tee had fallen off her shoulder and it made his mouth water. This wasn't the time to let his mind wander in that direction. She'd been traumatized...again and he should be thinking with his head, not his...

"I did what you would have done, didn't I?"

She pulled his mind from the gutter, but he didn't understand her question.

"What?"

"The instinct to run to help someone, not even thinking about what kind of harm might be waiting for you."

Rubbing his neck, he thought carefully about his answer before replying, "Sometimes. Sometimes you go even when you know there might be an IED out there with your name on it."

He had gone out on a combat patrol every day knowing...knowing the potential was there for someone to get killed. His chances were as good as anyone's.

She gave him a glassy glare before stating, "That's real courage."

It was interesting that tonight she was calling it courage. She'd often used the term reckless.

"Both instances require a certain type of courage."

"I'm not sure I could have gone out there if I knew the shooter was ready and waiting for me."

He leaned over and brushed her hair off her face, his thumb caressing her temple.

"I'm glad you didn't have to make that decision."

Silence filled the space and he let it linger for a few minutes before suggesting, "Shall we watch a movie together? I hear you're trying to come up with meals around a theme. Maybe I could offer macho suggestions. You know, what a guy would expect to eat if he had to sit through a chick flick. There has to be a payoff."

"I would think the sex would be the payoff."

His eyebrow arched.

"He would get sex from this sacrifice?"

Lightening the mood had been his intent, but he hadn't expected the low rumble of something in his gut when she mentioned that three-letter word.

"A woman needs romance. The movie creates the mood, puts a smile on her face. Pulls at her heartstrings."

Her voice was devoid of emotion. She was stating facts that should have held a deeper meaning. Did. It was something he'd remember. He'd never romanced her. Hadn't needed to. Not at the beginning. It was something he'd take into the future with him on the off chance she let him use it.

"This puts it in a whole new light. Let me get changed. You pick the movie and I'll watch with interest."

Her eyes flashed up to his "Zach...don't expect..."

He read the panic there and he turned off his light-heartedness and reassured her, "Trust me, that's not on the menu tonight. I just figured we could sit together for a while, take your mind off things."

She grasped his hand and squeezed.

"I need you to sit with me."

"You figure out what you want to see, and I'll be right back."

⌐

She watched him go, a glimmer of longing flickering in her heart.

This was what safety was supposed to feel like. She'd felt it for the first twelve years of her life and then she hadn't. Until Zach, but only for a few short months. There wasn't any expectation to act or be a certain way.

Rissa, and her mother...They were trying to wade around her feelings, which made them that much more difficult to deal with.

Zach dove right in, had offered the boy's name, a connection, talked about mundane things that had nothing to do with what had happened today.

She wanted to fall into his arms, let him hold her, protect her from these jumbled emotions that were overwhelming her. Could she risk it?

She'd let her father do that once although she was young and didn't know that it could end in a second of madness.

Zach didn't back down from things, charged straight ahead. Ran into danger without thought for himself.

There had to be odds against surviving when someone did it with such consistency.

He'd done it in Iraq, in Afghanistan, had done it undercover, would do it tomorrow if the circumstances warranted it.

She couldn't let the feelings she had for him overcome her better judgment.

But maybe tonight, just for one night, she'd let him carry some of her pain.

Wrapping the afghan around her more securely, she waited for his return, giving in.

⁓

He re-entered the room, in sweats and a tee, carrying a tray.

His feet were bare, and she didn't know why that was having such an effect on her. One of them was only half there. What they had gone through bound them in a symbiotic way and the connection was still strong.

Her toes curled beneath the blanket as the electric current coursed through her.

"Your mother insisted I take this."

Bending over, he removed a plate and held his hand out for her to take it.

"Something green for you."

The wine glass he placed in front of her on the coffee table.

Holding up his own plate and a beer bottle, the tray discarded on the floor, he said, "And meat for me. Win-win, wouldn't you say?"

The escarole pizza, one of the family favorites, almost looked appetizing. The gurgle of her stomach suggested she was hungry, but she hadn't gotten beyond the nausea of the shooting yet. Maybe she could get a few mouthfuls down.

He took a seat beside her, his sandwich stuffed with mashed meatballs, mozzarella cheese gooey from the oven.

She peered at his plate. It was another one of her favorites.

"I think we should share."

"Absolutely not. I didn't know that you're a one-way kind of person. I'm sorely disappointed."

He smacked her hand as she reached over to finger some of the cheese off the meatballs.

She gave him a hard stare.

"I'd be willing to have it go two ways. It's you that's on a one-way street."

"Live with it."

And with that, she watched as he took a huge bite, the sauce dripping down his chin. She almost put her finger in another dangerous predicament. Instead, she picked up one of the square pieces of pizza and took a small bite, measuring how it felt before taking a bigger one.

Her stomach seemed to have settled, and the bits of sausage, red pepper flakes and black olives satisfied something she hadn't known she'd craved.

"What are we going to watch?"

"I'm not in the mood for romantic tonight, Zach. It wouldn't feel right."

A boy had died today, and she didn't think being lightsome was fair to his memory.

"Something else then?"

He had wiped the sauce that continued to decorate his chin with a swipe of his hand.

Her eyes wouldn't behave. Going from his chin to his fingers then to his feet. She didn't understand what was so erotic about them. There was a curl in her belly, then an undercurrent of magical juice boiling in her blood. She felt her cheeks get hot from the heat.

"So?"

She slanted her head at him.

He was conversational, relaxed. Wasn't feeling the buzz that was shooting off inside of her. She should still be feeling the effects of the murder, but with him sitting beside her, she was feeling the effects of him instead.

It was wrong.

And she got pissed at herself for not giving...Adrian a period of grieving.

"Maybe I should be alone."

Placing his empty plate on the coffee table, his feet going back up to rest there, he pulled her on to his lap and said gruffly, "I'm staying. Live with it. Now if you don't pick something out, I'll have to."

His blue eyes pierced the core of her, probing her to her very soul, and his smile faded.

He leaned in, and hesitated.

The hesitation always caught her off guard. It was a sensuous moment that held anticipation and outright wanting.

She placed her hand on his cheek, her thumb rubbing the shadow of a beard, the texture coarse yet soft.

Then he leaned in and took her lips in his, a gentle kiss that made her need even more urgent. She kissed him back, pulling him closer, wanting to become a part of him and fade into nothingness. He cradled her head with his hand as he explored the interior of her mouth, the thought that he didn't match her desire falling away with all her barriers.

Neither one of them heard the footsteps, but the voice, so close, had them scurrying back to their original positions.

Celia stammered, "Sorry. I didn't mean to interrupt. I just thought I'd collect the plates if you're finished and get them in the dishwasher before I head up."

Zach said easily, "We're finished. It was great Celia. Thanks."

Her mother must have noticed she'd eaten the pizza because a thank you, emphasis on the *you*, echoed back. She left the room without a backward glance, but Lana knew her mother, knew there'd be a smile on her lips.

"Where were we?"

He reached out his arm to curl her back against him and she sank into him. "Just hold me."

"Forever if you need me to."

CHAPTER TWENTY-THREE

He gave into the quiet, breathed her in, grateful that she was alive, she was here, and she needed him. After escaping death in the desert, he'd wanted to get on with his life, and live it. He'd thought, for all those months of struggling through rehab, the countless hours of pain he'd endured to get in shape, thinking that when he rejoined the force, their future would begin. Instead, he had signed its death warrant.

He'd like nothing better than another shot at this. He just wasn't sure which way it was going to go.

He felt her fingering the bullet around his neck. He'd put it back on the day he'd taken off his wedding ring. He'd needed to feel a connection to something. If it couldn't be her, then it would be the men and women in his unit.

"Tell me what it's like to shoot someone."

He pulled at his ear, considering her question, wondering where it came from.

"Is that really what you want to talk about?"

Her hand was resting against his chest, and it felt like a brand on his heart.

"You never said anything about what that felt like. I heard stories about the battles, the caves, the men who died, but you never told me how you felt pulling the trigger knowing that you were ending someone's life."

"Are you trying to understand what the shooter is feeling right now?"

"Maybe. Maybe I want to know what it felt like for you."

Could he explain it?

He wasn't sure he had the words to describe it accurately.

But when she looked up at him, he knew she was waiting for an answer.

Resting his head against hers, he pulled her closer, needing her warmth for the telling.

"Every face I saw in my scope still haunts me. It was easier when we were in the middle of a crossfire, if there were bullets flying our way. If I had to take someone out, one of their snipers, I couldn't think about what it would feel like. Or I wouldn't have taken the shot."

"It never gave you...satisfaction."

He'd looked at it as business. Snipers had to stay calm and collected, take a casual approach to the killing while being precise and professional.

"If it had, Lana, I would have begged them to take me out of the field because no one's life would have meant anything, and I could have easily turned on my own men."

He's seen it happen once. An argument, simmering anger, a man without a stable temperament. It had ended in the death of two good men before someone was able to take the sniper out. Three men down because they'd put a gun in the wrong man's hands.

"Why do people kill each other for no reason?"

He kissed her forehead, her skin tasting like honey. He'd prefer to sit in the quiet again, wanting to savor the feel of her, but she'd started the conversation, so he'd oblige her.

"There's always a reason. It just might not be a good one. And it's an age-old question, I think. Didn't it start with Abel? Or was it Cain?"

She lifted her legs, so they were straddling his, pulled herself into his lap, wrapped her arms around him. It was as if she wanted to become part of him. He closed his eyes and breathed her in.

"I know why you did it. You were trying to save your men. Our way of life."

He opened them to see her studying him. What was she looking for? Answers? The truth?

"I'm not sure we were there to save our way of life. I never did figure out why we were there. I did it to protect the men and women on my right and left. I was glad to get out."

"You still carry a gun."

He dropped his head back, knowing they were entering dangerous territory. He didn't want an argument.

"I do. Part of the job. Besides, according to you, I need protection. You've told me dozens of times I tend to get into sticky situations."

"Because other people don't have a problem hurting you." She buried her head in the crook of his neck. "I don't like it when they do."

"I don't like it, either. It makes you less confident in my continued good health."

"We didn't have much of that, did we?"

"No, we didn't."

For which he was sorry. If he had come home on two good feet, she might have been less reticent about a life together.

"I promised to love you in sickness and in health. I've done a piss-poor job of it."

"I wouldn't say that. You loved me well enough in sickness. I wish we'd had the opportunity to see how in *the health* went."

She yawned and snuggled deeper.

"What was the food like over there?"

He smiled. It seemed he'd gotten out of the exchange unscathed.

"Your favorite topic."

"Of course."

"I think I mentioned some of it in my letters. Complaining I'm sure about the detestable selection."

"I remember your telling me about the goat."

"Spicy goat. Although if I'd known that was your nickname maybe it would have gone down easier."

She eased herself back so she could look in his eyes, a sad smile on her face.

"I almost tried cooking it for you just to see what you'd do."

He wondered out loud, "Why didn't you?"

"You let me know, after the first time I served you something you didn't like, that you weren't going to eat it just because I cooked it for you. I didn't want to waste my time."

"That was pretty arrogant of me. You should have let me starve." His jaw rested on her head, her nearness doing a number on his emotions, one of which was guilt. "I didn't mean to make you cook extra."

"I didn't really mind. There was something kind of wifely about it. It made me feel good when you were happy."

His mind was on the fact she liked doing wifely things, so he didn't answer right away.

When her fingers peeked out of the afghan to tug his hair, she got his attention back.

"What else?"

"US rations, chicken, anything that came in a care package. Some of the guys got dried meat, jerky, that kind of thing. We usually shared so there was variety for a day or two. Until the next box arrived."

"Why didn't you tell me?"

"What?"

"That you wanted some of that. All I sent was boxed stuff, crackers, peanut butter along with the homemade cookies, cake. I was never sure how it would taste after being in the mail so long. But you never complained so I just..."

He tightened his arms around her, a grin taking over his face when he remembered how it felt the days the mail arrived and there would be one of her care packages.

"Are you kidding? They were the favorites. I had to hide the box to keep it safe from pilfering fingers. I still have a weakness for your sugary sweets."

And you. I still have a weakness for you.

"I liked sending them."

"If we were still married and you didn't have an aversion to my job, would you send me to work with a cooler full of good food like you do Paul?"

"Would you be able to take the ribbing he gets?"

"I think I have the stomach for that."

"Not much else."

"I like normal food, Lana."

"I'm wasted on you."

"I don't know how you can say that. You make the best normal food on the planet."

She clutched his shirt, and her yawn stifled the smile he thought he'd gotten from her.

As soon as she began breathing with light snores, he readjusted himself on the couch. He wanted to stay awake and enjoy the feel of her in his arms for as long as he could.

But her questions brought back memories, of Afghanistan, the men he'd killed. He'd been sent to fight a war on terror, and his job was to be a lethal weapon in the fight. Because the enemy knew this, snipers were targeted first. Lana had it right. He was the big yellow dot even before he took over command of the unit. That last letter had come to his parents' house, via several different locations, gauging by the postmarks, the hospital in Germany one of them. When he'd read it, he'd been back a month, had begun therapy, had begun his long fight back. And had fallen even more in love with Lana than he thought possible. It had come in increments, each letter uncovering a different aspect of who she was, smart, funny, strong. Fighting, killing and watching friends die were life-changing experiences. As snipers, their battlefield was seen at the end of the rifle scope, and each kill was magnified; creative. Lana had kept him grounded through it all, become his anchor in a sea of chaos, kept him focused on survival. He'd been less traumatized than some when he got back, her love a soothing balm that helped him weather those stormy days. Others hadn't been as lucky. Cooper, his sniper buddy, had gotten back to the States a year later. He'd spent time in a different kind of therapy, returning to Texas with PTSD.

Right before he'd gone undercover, Zach had made a trip down to see him, convinced him to get help, the trust between them built on the caked sand of Kabul. His family had been grateful, and while there, Zach re-discovered how much of a difference Lana had made in his recovery. He'd almost reached out again, to see if she'd talk, see if they could work out their differences.

With her in his arms, he wished again that he had.

⌒

When he awoke the next morning, the place beside him was vacant. Stretching, he tried to work the kinks out of a body that had no shortage of them. He lumbered to his feet and walked towards the kitchen, where he surmised Lana would gravitate.

He found her sitting at the breakfast bar, her iPad leaning against the rim of the counter, streaming last night's news about the shooting. He grabbed a mug, poured some coffee, and took a seat beside her.

"What are they saying?"

He hadn't seen the report, busy uncovering facts, meeting the boy's parents, helping Lana deal with the tragedy.

She leaned her head against his shoulder and emitted a heavy sigh.

"He...Adrian...seemed like a good kid. He was a freshman at Dorchester High School, A-student, lots of friends. No one knows who would have done this. Speculation is that it's a case of being in the wrong place at the wrong time."

Paul came in, in his night pants and a tee shirt, followed by Celia, who was already dressed for the day. She went right to work on breakfast.

Paul was rubbing the stubble on his face.

"I'm not sure it's about being in the wrong time and place."

Zach looked over and asked, "Why not?" He had his own ideas, but he wanted to hear his partner's.

"There wasn't a robbery, and the kid got shot in the back, running away. When we examined the body, Adrian still had his wallet and his phone. Why would the shooters have chased after him if it wasn't to rob him? Why would they shoot him for no reason?"

Lana offered, "Maybe he said something to piss them off."

"And then run? That would be pretty stupid."

Zach offered his opinion. "There's a piece missing, and once we find it, we'll have the why."

"Which tells us he wasn't in the wrong place at the wrong time. There was a reason."

As she closed the cover on her iPad, giving the men her attention, Lana asked, "Who do you talk to, to find out?"

Paul took a sip of his coffee before offering, "His parents gave us some of his friend's names and we'll talk to them. And I want to take another look at the brother."

Zach got up to replenish his empty cup, just as Celia set down a plate of eggs and bacon. Paul had taken the last stool at the breakfast bar and got the second plate. He dove right in.

Addressing Paul, he said as if in musing, "His brother seemed quiet when we were there. I don't know a lot about reactions, but his seemed odd to me."

"Good instincts. It did. I've been wondering about that myself. He might know something but I'm not sure he'll be willing to share."

"Why wouldn't he want to help find his brother's killer?"

"His parents might not know his secrets. And he has them. I'm sure of it."

Paul might be a dinosaur of sorts, never itching to move up, satisfied with the job he had, but he'd been in the Homicide Unit for almost fifteen years, and it didn't look like he was slowing down any even though he could probably retire with full benefits. He knew his stuff, knew how to look at the evidence from every different angle.

He'd solved nearly all his cases, and those he hadn't, he was still looking at in his spare time. If he said the brother had secrets, it was almost guaranteed that he did.

"Brother's name is Martez, seventeen." That much they'd gotten during the time spent with the family. "Gang member?"

"Maybe."

"Lana said that the shooter wore a certain brand of sneaker. Martha said it was the official footwear of the PS-15 gang. There has to be a correlation."

"Interesting and definitely something to check out."

"Same school?"

"These are questions I hope to have answered by the end of the day. We'll be heading out as soon as we're showered and dressed. There will be a lot of grunt work, talking to his friends at school, digging into Martez's life, talking to the girlfriend, canvassing the neighborhood. You up to it?"

"I'll have to be. How long until the autopsy report is in?"

"Should be on my desk before the end of the day. I'm not sure it will give us anything to go on. We'll need a gun for ballistics to match them to. We don't usually get that lucky."

Lana had grabbed Zach's hand just as he was about to get dressed for the day.

"You're leaving?"

He could feel the quiver that started in her fingers and emanated out to the rest of her body.

Holding it, he leaned in, a hair's breadth away.

"I have to, sweetheart. You want us to catch this kid, don't you?"

"Paul can..."

"I'm his partner, Lana. I want to do this for you."

Her voice broke when she said, "But I need you here." He pressed a kiss to her lips assuring her, "And there's nowhere that I'd rather be than with you, but I have a job to do."

There was a possibility that she'd feel betrayed that he was leaving her, but he needed to catch the son of a bitch who'd caused this trauma. What would he do if she shut him out again?

Celia came over to where she sat.

"Lana, he needs to do his job. You need to do yours. We can spend the morning on the renovation blueprints. You said you needed to get the website built. I can't believe you want him to sit around and watch you."

She ignored her mother, her eyes riveted to his.

"Will you come back?"

"I will. I promise."

Her hands went up to grasp his tee shirt as if not only holding him in place but holding him to his promise, as well.

"And I can stay with you again tonight?"

"From the minute I get back, until I have to leave again."

She darted her eyes around the room, taking in Celia and Paul before bringing them back to his face.

He asked in a low voice, "Are you afraid something's going to happen?"

"Yes."

"I made a promise to come back from Afghanistan and I kept it, didn't I?"

She gave him a weak nod.

"I promise I will be back as soon as I can, and I will hold you all night."

She nodded again and let go of his shirt, bringing her hand up to his face. She stood and brushed her lips against his.

"I'm holding you to that."

"I hope you do."

And with that she let him go.

Within thirty minutes Paul and Zach were on their way into the city to catch a killer.

CHAPTER TWENTY-FOUR

Lana watched him leave and didn't like how it felt any more than she had years earlier.

When she'd woken up in his arms, she'd nestled there, feeling the rise of his chest beneath her. It had comforted her and made her feel protected.

He was the only one she wanted right now. The only one she needed to help her through this. She wanted to crawl under the covers and wait for his return, crawl under his skin until the pain ebbed away. Seemed her mother wasn't going to let her wallow.

"Why don't you take a shower, and we can sit down and do a mock-up of what you want. You have to call the architect, set up an appointment to draw up some plans. You'll want them ready so that once you close, you can bring them to the town hall to get them approved, get the permit process started. You'll need to hire a construction crew. You want everything in place so when you get the green light to start the renovations, you're ready to go."

There was a moment when Lana caught the enthusiasm. "I also have to check out prices for appliances, an electronic payment system, get some insurance quotes..."

Then she remembered and her eyes filled.

"Ma. I saw a kid get shot yesterday. I can't be doing this today."

Celia came over, leaned her elbows on the counter.

"I know, Lana. It had to be awful. Staying busy will help you keep your mind off it."

She gave her mother a hostile glare.

"I don't want to keep my mind off of it. I...I...need to grieve for him."

Taking a seat on the stool beside Lana, Celia said, "We can find out where the wake and funeral will be held. I'm sure Paul will be going. Zach will probably join him. We can go, as well. It might give you some—"

"How can a burial give someone closure? Feelings of loss never go away."

Her mother's head dipped.

"No, they don't. Especially a parent for a child. Each one is a piece of your heart, and that loss is one I can't imagine." Her voice was filled with an inner anguish.

Mollified that her mother was feeling some of her suffering, she asked, "Does Paul go to all of them, the wakes and funerals?"

"Everyone that's his."

"Has he always?"

"From the first one. I always admired that about him. He took them for his own the minute he was assigned the case. Didn't matter what they were in life, drug dealers, thugs, gang members. They were his and he became their voice."

"What's it like...being married to a homicide detective?"

"You shouldn't have to ask that question. You were here right from the beginning."

"He transferred soon after you guys got married, didn't he?"

"He did. He said he didn't want another partner patrolling the streets. Sal was the best and he didn't want to settle. I often thought it was his own guilt at not being able to save him. Your father's case was open-and-shut. They knew who the perpetrator was, and Paul testified against him. The guy got life. When he went into homicide, every victim became Sal. Every killer charged and imprisoned was Paul's revenge."

"In a way, he's still working with Dad."

"He is."

"I really love him."

She was going to have to tell him. She never had. Remembering the look of agonized terror on his face when he came sliding out to her after the shooting, she was reminded how well he'd fathered them for the last fifteen years. It couldn't have been easy. Johnny was the worst, breaking curfew, drinking and getting into all kinds of trouble until Paul had faced off with him, backing Celia's rules. Her brother had slammed out of the house, refusing to speak to most of them for years before Tish turned him around. Paul was the one they called when they needed help. Not only small things like running out of gas, or needing tampons, but big things like when he'd picked Rissa up after that asshole, Jude, kicked her out of his condo, or chauffeured Tony to all his therapy sessions. He was the one who bore the brunt of their anger, their fears, their heartache. And took it, giving only love in return. Rissa had admitted to her once that she thought Paul was better at fathering than their father. And she'd been right. Lana didn't need her mother to tell her, "He's a good man."

It was easy to see why her mother had fallen in love with him, but she still didn't understand how Celia could hand her heart over to another policeman.

"Do you worry as much as you did when he was on patrol?"

"There's always worry. But I worry when *you* leave the house every day. I never know what's around the corner for any of the people I love. Your father's death made me appreciate every minute I have with those I love."

Chewing on her nail, Lana had to concede that. She worried more than was normal or healthy, didn't have the space in her head for appreciation. Maybe it was way past time to clear some out.

And if she did, what would that mean. For her? For Zach?

"I remember some nights he didn't come home. Or he'd be called out in the middle of the night. You were alone a lot."

"He worked three days straight on some cases, would come home only to be called back out with just an hour of sleep. And guaranteed if we had plans, someone somewhere would make sure they went awry. It's tough on the body, the spirit. He sees the worst part of humanity. It's tough on the family as well."

"He never brings it home, does he?"

"I don't think they can help it, although Paul seemed to have an internal switch that disconnects him from the gory details of his day. He's detached when he speaks about his cases. He bounces some things off me, but he never describes the scenes, never tells me the sordid details. My role is to give him a soft place to land when he comes home, but be his rock, adaptable, resilient, worry-free."

"That's a tough role to balance."

She wasn't sure she'd ever get the worry-free part down, no matter how hard she tried.

"Not if you love him and respect what he does."

Love for Zach wasn't the problem. She had a deep well of that. And she respected what he'd accomplished in his life. She was looking at it from a different angle since she'd gone running out to Adrian without a thought of any danger.

Death had come knocking at her door again through no fault of her own.

"That kid shouldn't have died. Not that way."

"I wish I could offer you words of wisdom like death is a part of life, but it's a hard case to make for a fourteen-year-old boy. Bad things happen Lana. I wish they didn't, but they do. And there's no rhyme or reason. I could have asked why your father died and it would have only driven me crazy. A man got drunk, beat up his wife and shot your father when he tried to stop it. It's that simple and that complicated all at the same time."

"Like being a soft place and a rock."

"That one's actually easy. You hold him after a gruesome day, a grueling autopsy, a child's death, a grizzly scene. Yet hold the fort down when he's gone, letting him know what he's doing is important. You cover all family issues. In a convoluted way, it makes me feel I'm contributing something important. The community is being served and I'm doing my share in making it happen."

Celia leaned over and kissed her forehead.

"Are you thinking...that you might be able to make it work with Zach in Homicide?"

"I don't know. I still don't trust him to stick with it. He's... I'm not sure it will suit his temperament."

"I think Zach would do anything to go back."

"Except leave the force."

Taking Lana's chin and turning so she could look her in the eye, she said, "It's where his soul sits comfortably, Lana. It would be a shame if he had to quit that."

Her soul's work was food. Would she want anyone trying to take it away? Would she let them no matter how much she cared?

She wasn't sure anymore.

Maybe she'd grown up in the last few years. Maybe she just missed him so much she had no choice but to change her thinking. Right now, he was the only one who could take her mind off the horrors of yesterday.

"I'm going to go home, get some clothes. When I get back maybe we can work on the plans, sketch out how I want it to look."

Celia stood, dumped her coffee in the sink, and rinsed out her cup.

"I'll drive over to the kitchen, get the meal ready for tonight. Phyllis is scheduled to pick it up and deliver it for us. The chef I'm ready to hire has offered to work for me over the next week or two as a trial run."

"What's her name?"

"Melissa. She recently graduated from culinary school and feels this will be good for her resume. I'm not sure what I'm going to do with the Cookery so for now it works for both of us. And you. You can put your energies into your own place without having to feel guilty."

"Thanks, Ma."

After she arrived at her condo, Lana packed jeans, sweats and sweaters, enough to last a few days at her mother's. She didn't want to sleep here, alone, wanted to be with Zach, and she couldn't afford to invite him back. Without having to make deliveries or keep appointments, she could dress down and in her present mood it was exactly how she wanted it. If she couldn't crawl under the covers and hide her head, she could at least do some of her work in comfort.

She settled in at her desk and began to do some rough sketches for the storefront. She got lost in the details and the shooting faded into the background. She didn't know how long it would last, but she was going to keep moving. After a few hours, she needed a break, her back beginning to nag, so she got up, stretched, and poured herself a cup of coffee.

She sipped at it, thinking about Zach, what he was doing, how much progress was being made on the case. She hoped it wouldn't be an eighteen-hour day. She wanted to know what they'd found out, see if they were able to uncover the brother's secret if he had one, know whether there was a gang connection. There was something disturbing about Adrian being in a gang. He was too young, too good a student to be caught up in that kind of world.

Would Zach share things with her, or would he be afraid to, given her dislike for all things homicidal? She remembered plenty of nights when Paul and her mother would sit in the family room, discussing a case, her stepfather going over the evidence collected as if something new might be uncovered in the telling. She was in high school by then, and very rarely listened in. It was Tony, also in high school and the only other kid living at home, who wanted to hear the details. He'd asked all kinds of questions, as if gearing up for the day he became part of the thin blue line. He was still in therapy back then, working through the death that had impacted them all in some way.

If she and Zach got back together, would he bring his work home, talk to her about where the case was going? Would they have a son who modeled himself after his father? Or maybe it would be a daughter who wanted to keep the line going.

She knew he wanted kids.

He'd told her in one of his letters. He'd been describing the kids on the streets of Afghanistan begging for any scrap, piece of candy, coin.

Going to her box, she riffled through to see if she could find the one she was looking for.

She knew them by heart, having read them so often. After slipping an envelope out of the sequence, she opened it up.

June 2012

Lana,

> *We started a convoy out today into no-man's land. It's a route that the Taliban is familiar with, and we'll probably be followed. Fucking awesome, huh?*

> *There's a line of Humvees and GMVs that are kicking up dust in their wake and looking back I can see it still swirling in the air miles away. It'd be great cloud cover if they want to get us, but we're moving slowly enough that we're prepared for any contingency, so if they attack, we'll be ready.*

> *We just skirted a small village, a jumble of mud huts that sit semi-circle around a water source. The residents look starved, poor, some without teeth, some dressed in rags. There are a few animals wandering around that look as ill-cared for as their owners, a muddy and decrepit goat, a couple of scrawny chickens. There's no running water, no infrastructure. The people here struggle daily for survival. It's such a sad sight to see people without hope for the future.*

> *A young boy, his face caked with grime, looked old and worn before his time. He had come out to beg for some food, and sap that I am, I dug out one of your cookies and leaned out to hand it to him. If there had been other kids around, I would have forced myself to stay seated.*

They fight over any little thing here and I would have put him danger of being hurt.

I don't know what I would do if my child went hungry like that. I might make the decision not to have any, just to keep myself from going insane. Although here, death means one less mouth to feed rather than deep loss.

I never really thought about having kids before. Maybe I was too young, too unsettled with what I wanted to do.

Now, I think I do want them. I want to spoil, love, and nurture them. I want to give them everything I can't give to this one boy or the multitudes we see in the bazaars, or on other dirt-infested roads.

Interesting how I uncover things about myself I never knew just in the writing to you.

Do you want kids?

With so many siblings it could be a definite yes or a definite no.

I don't know which way it affected you.

I loved having my sisters to comfort me, although they gave me no small amount of shit growing up. I like knowing they are waiting for me to get home. I think if you're an only child, it must get lonesome.

Like that boy we passed.

Does he have friends to play with?

Does he play at all?

We're here to save these people from this ignoble existence. I truly doubt we can achieve that end. The country is so broken it would take more than our presence to turn the tide.

Thank you for being on the other side of this letter. I like writing to you, like knowing you listen, care, and my hunch is you will be a little saddened by my description of this time and place.

I won't feel so alone.

We're approaching another village and we need to keep our focus on what's going on around us. We never know what's there, hiding in the huts or around the bend.

Take care.

My thoughts are with you.
Zach

Did she want kids?

She still wasn't sure. They demanded so much energy. She'd witnessed the sleepless nights with a newborn, the terrible twos and threes. There were women, like her sister-in-law, who had all this love inside to give, and she didn't know if she had the deep well of caring.

Had it evaporated with Zach's leaving or did she have it to begin with.

Fear could suck so much out of you.

And she'd been afraid for more than a decade.

She'd been young when she'd married Zach. Too young, it would seem. It had been impulsive, reckless. Two traits that were foreign to her. She usually weighed every option, studied every contingency, but what she felt was so invasive, so overpowering she had jumped at the chance to spend her life with him.

She obviously hadn't been ready to offer that kind of commitment. Or maybe she was afraid that he'd let her down by dying. Either way, she'd pushed him out of her life because he was bound and determined to be a cop. What she'd really wanted was a guarantee than he'd be alive to share a life with her.

Now?

She was older and maybe a little wiser and she was beginning to realize it was the depth of her love for him that scared her.

And the depth of her sorrow without him seemed to scare her, as well.

He offered a full spectrum of emotion, and for someone who liked to live life at the mid-point, the extremes were too much for her fragile heart.

How could she become a woman who seized what he gave her with both hands?

Because she wanted it as desperately as she wanted anything else in her life.

CHAPTER TWENTY-FIVE

It was late afternoon by the time Paul and Zach got to their second interview of the day.

The first one, with the victim's brother had been a struggle. Paul had used his interrogation skills with a doggedness Zach hadn't seen since the military. Over the four hours they were locked in the interview room, he'd seen Martez go from knowing nothing at all to admitting that he knew the boy in the sketch. While probing for answers, Paul never lost sight of his end goal, question after question, leading him through the maze of lies, half-truths, and truths. Throughout the dialogue, he made Martez feel as if he was on his side, that he'd forgive him for whatever it was he was concealing. He was a master at his craft and Zach watched and learned. If it had been up to him, he would have used the bad cop routine to the fullest and they'd be sitting here without anything to go on.

Martez was scared, of that he was certain. And he couldn't blame him.

The teen had been approached by the leader of the local clique, a low-level group of a powerful gang, and then been allowed to hang around for a few months before his initiation. The price he had to pay for entrance into the group, was the death of a member of the rival gang. He'd failed the test and his brother's death had been the result of a job unfinished. The boy that Lana had captured on paper was a full-blown member of the gang that Martez was associated with and had been given the task of retaliation. The PS-15 would do anything to protect their name and reputation. Martez knew he'd be facing certain death when they found out he admitted this truth.

"Please, sir, my parents don't know. Do you have to tell them?"

"You tell us, Martez, if we should leave them in the dark?"

"They'll hate me... I was trying to get out of it. I didn't know I'd have to kill people."

"Have you killed anyone, Martez?"

His face became a mask of horror, and he shook his head.

"No. No. I was supposed to...as part of my initiation, a member of the Dedham Street Gang, but I couldn't. I pointed the gun, but I couldn't pull the trigger."

He was crying now, sobbing.

"They...killed my brother— It's my fault he's dead."

According to Ed, when a gang struck back, they struck where it hurt, and his friend had worked in the gang unit long enough to know.

Zach sat forward, his arms resting on the table, taking over for Paul now that the truth was out.

"This isn't your fault. You should have come to us. We could have helped you."

"How? How could you have helped me? You don't own the streets, they do. If I had snitched, I'd be dead." Through the tears he coughed out, "Maybe I should have. At least Adrian would be alive. He didn't deserve to die."

The brothers must have been close, and he should be feeling sympathy but all he felt was sick at the senseless death of a good kid.

Zach looked up and asked, "I was taught that you protected family at all cost. Are you going to let them get away with this?"

"I don't want to die, sir."

He had no answer for that, so he didn't push any further.

Before they pulled the boy's mother in from the waiting room to go through the sad admission, the boy gave them a name.

Paul asked him to call a member of the gang unit to pick up their suspect.

"Pull up what you can on him from the computer, then call..."

"I'll go talk to Ed."

"Good. We'll have him in custody in no time."

⌒

Zach pulled up the file on Jeronimo "Tic" Glover.

The printer spit out page after page on the seventeen-year-old who'd been identified as the kid who pulled the shooter away. From the looks of it, Tic could have pulled the trigger just as easily. His rap sheet included multiple arrests for theft, drug possession, drug deals, assault, assault with intent to murder, illegal possession of a firearm. Zach compared the mug shot to the copy of the sketch drawn on Lana's observations and it matched down to the narrow eyes that held an emptiness that was chilling.

She could not have seen them that well, but she had described them with exact detail.

He quirked a smile. She would have made a hell of a cop.

After striding out of Homicide, he took the elevator down a floor to the Gang Unit Division, and found Ed. After a few slaps on the backs, glad-that-you're-heres, he relayed the information, passed along his mug shot, and gave him a list of the addresses they had on file.

Ed was shrugging into his flak jacket half-way through the run-down. "Thank you. It was getting boring around here today. Now...I have a mission."

Zach gave him a broad grin. "Drop him off as soon as you get him."

"Will do. See you later."

Zach walked away, the smile still on his face. He liked having his friends nearby. He was already beginning to see another upside to the job. The icing on the cake was that Lana was waiting for him at home.

It wasn't long before Ed and his unit returned, finding the kid outside his house, packing a .38-caliber gun. It was loaded and ready for action.

With the gun and the bullet taken from the body in evidence, they were counting on ballistics to prove whether it was the murder weapon or not.

He didn't like the fact that the wrong kid had the gun.

⌐

Jeronimo was now sitting in the same seat that Martez had sat in earlier. But the attitude was not the same.

He was slouched in his chair, a toothpick between his teeth, a smirk on his face.

Paul had brought him in a soda and bag of chips.

If it were up to Zach, he would have fed him a fist sandwich.

Instead, he sat, his notepad in front of him, his pen poised to jot down whatever Tic offered them.

An hour later, the notepad was still empty. But he'd gleaned something from the body language. He understood now where he got the nickname. His eye began to twitch as soon as the interview began. The kid was more nervous than he was willing to let on.

"Let's take a break."

Paul scooped up all his notes, his folder and exited the room.

Zach followed close on his heels.

Once they were back out in the common area, detectives who'd been watching the back- and-forth on the monitor swiveled their chairs in the partners' direction.

Paul dropped his notes on Zach's desk and addressed the audience. "We've just seen the difference between a person with a conscience and one without. He is cold."

Zach sat at the edge of his desk; his arms folded across his chest.

"What's next? Do we have enough to charge him?"

"Ballistics will check out the gun to see if it's the murder weapon. Shit for brains or cocky as hell. Don't know which and I don't care. We get him for murder if it's a match."

"How long will it take for the crime lab to tell us?"

"Weeks, maybe months. But we have the sketch. He was involved."

"According to Lana, he's not our shooter."

"He doesn't want to man up, tell us who did it, it's all the same to me. He probably has one or two kills under his belt that we haven't caught him for. Why don't you type up a warrant for his arrest?"

Zach slid into his seat and began the paperwork. He'd gotten good at this, his undercover work generating dozens of them.

Soon after he was finished, one of the assistant district attorneys came into the pen. He was the one at the crime scene right after the shooting, got the search warrant for Glover's house.

Zach escorted him into Paul's office to go over what they had so far.

"We have a witness who puts him at the scene. He was picked up with the same type of gun we anticipate might be the murder weapon. And we have a motive, according to the Cruz kid. I think we have enough for an arrest. He might not have pulled the trigger, but he was there."

The partners ambled back into the interview room, where Jeronimo was waiting, leaving the ADA to watch where part two went.

"You're under arrest for the murder of Adrian Cruz. You have—"

His face registered his panic now that things had escalated to the point of an arrest.

"I didn't kill that kid."

"The gun says you did and you're not willing to tell us otherwise."

He refused to stand for the handcuffs. There was a wild look in his eyes now that he'd been cornered.

"Okay, okay. I'll tell you the truth. The honest truth."

Paul raised his eyebrows.

"I've heard those words before and they usually tell me another lie is about to hit the fan."

"I'm not going down for a thing I didn't do."

"It's not going to be that easy, Jeronimo. The gun was in your possession, and we can't use your testimony to charge the purported shooter because you were together when the crime was committed."

"His fingerprints will be on the gun."

Paul barked, "Yours will be, too."

Zach asked gruffly, "Whose fingerprints will be on the gun?"

There was a long hesitation, the belligerence replaced by indecision.

"I don't have all day and I'm not wasting any more of our time."

Zach was staring him down. He knew who'd win and he was right.

The one word stumbled out of Jeronimo's mouth.

"Tagger."

"His name."

The pause was long enough that Zach was beginning to doubt the kid was going to make this easy. They'd find out the name associated with Tagger, but it would take them time.

"Lorenzo. Lorenzo Watkins."

"One of your brothers?"

"Yeah. Shit. This was not my idea. I didn't want to hit that kid. He's...in school with my sister. She really likes him. She was broken up when she found out he was dead. She's going to hang me for this."

"We will, too."

"No, there's got to be another way."

"We need evidence. Hard evidence that puts the gun in his hand."

"You showed me a sketch. If someone saw me, they know I wasn't the one that pulled the trigger."

Smarter than they'd originally thought.

But he didn't want Lana testifying in a gang land killing. He'd never stop worrying that they'd go for payback. It was just their way.

"I'd rather a confession. Anything we can use to get it from him?"

"Look, you got a witness. I ain't giving you anymore. I've just signed my death warrant ratting him out."

"Not if he's in jail."

"Do you know how many out on the street will be willing to take me out? They hate snitches."

"Every single one of them would do the same thing. Cold-blooded when it comes to taking a life, real wusses when theirs is on the line."

Jeronimo shoved the Coke can away.

"What do you know?"

Zach pulled out the silver bullet, fingered it before his eyes pierced into Jeronimo's.

"Know what this is?"

Jeronimo squinted against the florescent light.

"Looks like a bullet."

"It is. The military gives one of these to the snipers in the unit. The Hunters of Gunmen. We've got to go through hell to get one. You know what a sniper is?"

"A crack shot?"

"I am but a bit more lethal. I used to kill for a living. I took out the bad guys. It made me a target every time I went on patrol. I went out anyway. I know cold-blooded. I know wuss."

The kid slunk back and slouched down further, eyeing Zach with a new-found respect.

In the face of this new adversary, Jeronimo loosened his tongue.

"Tagger got word to take the kid out from one of the higher-ups, but he won't tell you anything. None of them will help me now."

"Then I'd say you picked the wrong people to be friends with. Now stand up. You're going to jail. Until we can get a confession or some more evidence, you're up for this one."

Jeronimo got up out of his seat and turned his back, finally surrendering to the inevitable.

⌒

Lana had roughed out the blueprints and moved on, now at her mother's, spending the last few hours pricing the equipment she needed, adding them to her wish list now that she knew dimensions and size. Stretching, she got up from the table and went to put on a fresh pot of coffee.

Her mother had gotten home after the meeting with Melissa at the commercial kitchen.

"How's it coming?"

"Pretty well. I called the contact for the website and we're meeting next week. I also called the architect and she'll need to get in and see the space, so I called Cookie and that's set for next week, as well. Rissa gave me the name of her attorney and she's agreed to look over the purchase and sale, as soon as I get it. I spent the rest of the morning working on the menu and brochure."

She poured herself a cup of coffee, added cream and sugar, and turned to face her mother, leaning back on the counter.

"It seems strange not to be helping you."

"It does feel different there without you. We've worked together for so long; we didn't have to think about what we were doing."

Celia opened the refrigerator and scanned the interior, riffling through the contents.

"I didn't think to take anything out."

"Not like you at all but don't worry. I'm making dinner tonight. I can't go a day without cooking something. And I need a break from the computer."

"What do you have in mind?"

"A pork roast. It's not red but it's meat. He can take it or leave it."

They both knew who *he* was.

"They might not be home until late. You should probably make something that will keep."

"Zach doesn't do one-pot meals."

Lana shuffled some paper, and admitted, "I texted him to see how it was going."

"What did he say?"

"They'd just gotten the name of the kid who did the shooting. Ed's team is out trying to find him. That could take all night."

"Want to watch a movie while we wait for them?"

"Don't you have a delivery tonight?"

"Nope. I've arranged the schedule so I can be home for the next few nights."

"You don't have to, Ma. I'm dealing."

"I know. Better than I expected, but I want to be here in case you need someone to talk to."

Lana got the roast out, preheated the oven, and began to rub the pork with a special blend of spices she'd made up, her fingers sliding over the drizzled-oil surface of the meat. The coating was a bright red mix of paprika, cumin and oregano. She wasn't sure how it would taste to Zach's underdeveloped palate, but she'd used hidden flavors before, and he never caught on. As long as she put meat in front of him, he didn't ask questions.

Standing back, she realized the bold and pungent color might give her deviousness away.

"Will Tony be by?" Lana asked.

"Probably. He'll stop in before going into work."

"Why did he pick the night shift?"

"He said more goes on in the witching hours."

She wiped her hands on her apron and placed the roasting pan into the oven. She picked up one of the potatoes out of the bag and she began to scrub it before taking another.

"He's studying for his shield, isn't he?"

"Yes. He's planning on transferring to Allston-Brighton or Downtown. He wants to be on his own."

"Maybe he doesn't want to be where Dad was."

"I think it's Paul more than Sal."

"I guess Paul's been at the father thing longer than Dad was."

"He's been a very good one."

"Oh, I know. He's always been there for us."

With the spuds sitting in the pan filled with cold water, she turned on the stove and faced her mother.

"Why do people have kids?"

Her mother's brow arched, and she blew out a breath.

"For a variety of reasons, I guess."

"Why did you?"

"I'm a nurturer. Love taking care of people. Couldn't think of a better way to spend my life."

"It's not to create something with the person you love?"

Celia eyed her speculatively.

"There is that part of it. You want a piece of that love to live on after you're gone."

"And it helped having us after Dad...died?"

"It did."

Taking a seat at the island, Celia sat back and asked, "Where are these questions coming from?"

Lana came over to sit beside her, her coffee cup back in her hand.

"I never thought I wanted kids. Didn't want the aggravation, or anything or anyone to take me away from my stove. I'm not a nurturer like you are. I don't know what I am. I'm thinking I might be too selfish."

"You've inherited my need to feed the masses. That's nurturing. That's wanting to take care of a person's body, their soul. Comfort them, sustain them." Meeting her eyes, her mother added, "Selfish? Maybe."

She felt her lips slide downward.

"Thanks, Ma. I was hoping you'd argue that one."

Rubbing her daughter's back in consolation, she said, "I remember when Rissa was at loose ends, didn't know what she was going to do with her life. She thought you had it all. You made it look that way. But she was willing to put her heart on the line, so her life got messy. You weren't. There's a selfishness in that. You made sure the people in your life had supporting roles. It wasn't until Zach that that changed."

Rubbing her face, threading her fingers through her hair, Lana admitted, "I'd never felt like that before. Never needed someone in my life that much."

"I figured that out when you accepted his proposal so quickly. It completely surprised me. It also surprised me that you were willing to let it go so easily."

Her eyes met her mother's.

"It wasn't easy. Trust me."

"If you stayed, it would have gotten messy."

"It did get messy. I was a mess. I still am."

"You're admitting it?"

"Maybe. Maybe I...maybe I was too impulsive."

"In marrying him?"

Lana stared into space.

"No...in forcing him out. The last few years have been awful."

Celia got up, turned down the heat under the potatoes, which were boiling over before returning to her seat.

"And you think they wouldn't have been if you were together?"

"They still would have been awful, but I'd sleep better at night with him beside me."

"Like last night?"

"There was just that one kiss you walked in on. So no, not exactly like last night and I'm not getting into that with you. You're my mother."

"After something that traumatic it's not unusual to want to feel alive. I think that's what he makes you feel. Alive."

"He does."

Slipping her arm around her mother's neck, she leaned her head on her shoulder.

"How can he make me feel so safe and so scared all at the same time?"

"We feel a lot of conflicting emotions when we love someone. When you were growing up, I wanted to keep you safe, but I had to let you experience life. I didn't always like the way you did it, but I couldn't lock you all away."

"By making him choose, I was trying to lock him away, wasn't I?"

"That's exactly what you were doing."

"I thought for the longest time that he just didn't love me enough to give it up. I'm beginning to see it from his perspective. That maybe I didn't love him enough to let him be who he was."

"Selfish?"

She scooted off the seat, the label disconcerting. She reached for the green beans and began snapping off the ends as if they'd offended her.

"I'd prefer to think I was too young."

"I had two children at the same age."

Her hand stilled.

"I don't know how you did it."

"I had a very normal upbringing. Two parents, four siblings, I just followed the same route. Who knows what would have happened if my father was killed when I was twelve."

Confronting her mother, she bit her lip.

"You don't mind your life being messy."

"I couldn't. Not with five kids. Are you thinking that you want them?"

"Not five. But...maybe one or two."

"With Zach or someone...else?"

"It could never be with someone else. It's a piece of his love that I'd want to live on. I never thought about having kids with Rafe. There wasn't enough there."

"He was one of those supporting roles I was talking about. You liked him being in the background."

"It's safer than being front and center."

"And that's what Zach is?"

She nodded.

He was the big, frigging yellow dot.

CHAPTER TWENTY-SIX

The men were waiting for Ed to bring in Tagger, compiling the evidence they had collected, creating a file, organizing. After they were finished, Paul asked, "Want something to eat. We skipped lunch."

Zach looked up at the clock to see that it was later than he'd thought. So much for getting back to Lana at a reasonable hour.

"Time does fly when you're having fun."

Paul went over to rummage through the cooler.

"What's in there? I doubt Lana was in the right frame of mind to help with your lunch today."

"Celia packed it before we left. Go ahead. Look. We've got to wait around for who knows how long. I don't think Tagger is as dumb as Tic. He won't be out in front of his house, waiting. It might be a while before we get home."

Paul had taken a sandwich out, peeled back the foil, and took a huge bite. Zach did the same, satisfied with the roast beef and mayo. Sitting in the chair opposite Paul's desk, he said, "We need more evidence on this kid. I don't want Lana to testify unless she has to."

Paul took a swig of his iced tea.

"I'm on that page."

After taking another sandwich out, his stomach still in protest for lack of food, Zach studied the contents before taking a bite.

"Ed told me once that these guys earn juice from a kill. Helps them earn respect, if you want to call it that. Maybe we can use that to get a confession."

"Come up with a plan. I'll back you."

As Zach fingered some corn chips, an idea came to him.

Would it work?

It sure as hell couldn't hurt.

⌐

A few hours later, Ed called saying they were bringing the suspect in, and by the time he arrived, Zach knew how he'd approach the situation. The suspect had had a gun on him when they picked him up, which they'd confiscated and would compare to the murder they were working, along with other unsolved murders in the city. Maybe they'd get lucky, and they could pin another murder on him if they couldn't get him for this one.

The kid sat down, handcuffed to the table.

"Why am I here?"

His tone was no less arrogant than Tic's had been, but he threw in a little surly for good measure.

Paul asked, "You know where you are?"

His face showed contempt for the system.

"Yeah, Homicide. You've got it written everywhere."

Paul leaned back in his chair, his pencil doing a see-saw routine in his hand.

"Been here before, haven't you?"

"Yeah. It was bullshit then. It's bullshit now."

"Homicide is never bullshit. Murder is."

"Why the hell am *I* here?"

The kid's attitude was starting to get on Zach's nerves, so he let Paul keep up the dialogue.

"I didn't just pull your name out of the air. It came up during our investigation and we need to ask you some questions."

"What investigation? I don't know what you're talking about. No way someone could have given you my name. I didn't do nothing."

"Let me refresh your memory. Adrian Cruz was killed outside the Boys & Girls Club."

Tagger's lips curled as if the topic was distasteful.

"Who the hell is he? Never heard of him."

Zach took out the sketch and passed it along the table.

"Know *this* kid?"

Zach could see the reality of the situation settling in as Tagger's expression changed.

"Maybe."

"You do. We already talked to him. He's been arrested for the murder of Adrian Cruz."

Tagger slammed his hands down on the table, but due to the restraints, didn't make the kind of statement he was going for. "What the fuck am I doing here if you already got him in jail?"

"Word on the street is that he wasn't the trigger man. Delete that. He wasn't the trigger *boy*."

Tagger sat back in his seat, fiddling with the handcuffs as if he could get them unlocked.

"Word on the street might be wrong."

Zach was up, his voice a bellow, his hands pummeling the air. The kid jumped at the increase in volume. Looking at Paul, Zach barked, "I told you this kid would be too chicken shit to admit he's the one who pulled the trigger."

Paul's voice was monotone.

"I thought he'd want credit for the kill. I figured it would grease his cred."

"Him? He doesn't care about his cred, only his neck. He's the type who'd have no problem taking a life, too scared to give up his own. Chicken shits, the bunch of them."

An angry voice cut in.

"Hey, pig, I'm no chicken shit."

Zach looked over at the now standing, swaggering teen, a smug look on his face.

"You're laying the credit on someone else's shoulders. How far will that get you in the club? In the Marines, we counted out kills. We wanted the world to know how many scumbags we got."

"This isn't the army, po-lice-man."

"I belonged to the Marines, boy. *You* belong to the army, an army of thugs. I thought there was some honor out there. Seems I was wrong."

"Anyone messes with us, they go down."

Even though he was cuffed, his finger was pointing as if reinforcing his words.

"And how did Adrian mess with you?"

"It was his brother did that. Wanted out. You don't get out, not without some pain."

Zach began to pace, in short steps, as if considering what Tagger had said.

"When someone comes gunning for your sister, for some infraction of your rules, you'll feel it?"

He knew about the sister from the bio the gang unit had on him.

Tagger's face turned ugly.

"No one would dare."

Zach leaned his hands on the desk, his body looming over the kid, wishing he could punch his lights out. Instead, he stuck to his plan.

"What would you do about it, punk? Word on the street's you got no balls. They'd get Jeronimo to take care of it."

"I fucking have 'em."

"You follow orders, like a little lamb. Baaa."

The kid was spitting mad, his eyes wild and his emotions now driving the train.

"No, I don't. I give them. I killed that kid. Me. No one gave me the orders. I made sure Martez would step back in line. Don't you tell me I have no balls."

That's not what Jeronimo had told them, but it didn't matter. Lorenzo Watkins had just admitted to being the killer. Hopefully his confession would stand in court.

If it did, it took Lana off the hook to testify which had been his overall objective.

Paul was up on his feet.

"Lorenzo Watkins, you're under arrest for the murder of Adrian Cruz. You have the right to remain silent..."

As soon as the Miranda clause was read, Lorenzo spat out, "You make sure everyone on the street knows it."

"We can guarantee it."

After the partners escorted the alleged murderer out to the waiting police car, Paul slapped Zach on the back.

"Good work, partner."

"Think it will stand up?"

"Don't see why not. I like your style. As soon as we finish up the paperwork, we can go home. Didn't even take us forty-eight hours to crack this one. We can thank Lana for that."

"The sketch helped, but the Martez kid brought it home. How'd his mother take it?"

"She started beating on him and then hugged him. It's tough being a parent. Especially here in this city."

It reminded Zach of the kids in Afghanistan. No hope for their future. It seemed it didn't matter what continent you were on or what country you lived in, there were parts of the world that offered little for a promising future.

⌐

It was close to midnight when they walked through the side door and into the kitchen.

There was a note taped to the refrigerator and two wrapped plates.

"You up for this?"

"Not really hungry. I wanna check on Lana."

Zach stepped into the family room to see her asleep against the couch cushions. He walked over and knelt beside her, just watching the rise and fall of her chest. He used to do this when they first got married, still unbelieving she had agreed to it, loving her so much he thought he'd suffocate from it.

He hadn't suffocated then. That had happened when he left.

The pain had been invasive, ripping his gut to shreds, his heart to pieces.

Now, she was inching her way back and he didn't know whether he should trust it.

Could he handle it if she decided to distance herself again?

Was it worth the risk?

Rising, he went to his room to change. He could hear Paul out in the kitchen, the beep of the microwave telling him that his partner was taking advantage of the prepared meal. He was opting out. He'd waited all day to come home to her and he wasn't going to waste any time getting to it.

He had shed his jacket, tie, shirt, pants, shoes and socks and was just stepping into his sweats when she came running into the room, catching him in the act of changing.

He froze as she burst through the door.

"You're back. You promised you'd stay with me."

It was nothing more than a broken whisper.

Seeing her standing there, his whole body tightened in need.

With a voice raw with emotion, he said, "I checked on you first thing. I thought you were asleep, and I had time to get out of my suit."

She was staring at him now, her eyes dark and inviting as they slid from his face down his body.

When she took a step towards him, he dropped his sweats to the floor and went to meet her halfway.

She slid her arms around his neck and slanted her head, fitting her lips to his. There was an electric charge that surged through his system. He lifted her, devouring her mouth in response, his tongue plundering the sweet interior, her taste something he'd never turn down.

Her hands were in his hair, on his face as the kiss deepened, as if she couldn't get enough of him, her tongue down his throat, then her teeth nipping at his bottom lip.

He held her firmly in his arms, meeting her thrust for thrust, his heart hammering in his chest, his need for this woman never-ending.

He felt it surging out of control.

He slid his hands up her back, under her tee shirt, feeling the skin, the texture acting as an aphrodisiac, and he pulsed full and thick against her. He slipped the material over her head and his thumbs found the nipples, the curve of her breast filling his hand with the lush flesh he hungered for. Bringing his head down, he kissed one, teased it with his teeth, filled his mouth with the delicacy. This was his favorite meal, all the spice he needed, and he feasted as if it was his last. His mouth slid to the other globe, and he continued to feed on the bounty she was offering.

Her moan urged him on, into a frenzy of feeling, and he slid off her leggings, finding her sweet spot, fingers finding a home there, one, then two, then three, until she was fully opened to him, and his breathing was causing pain. His thumb gently rubbed her clit in circles, pushed it up and back as his fingers slid in and out of her, his fingers now slick with her honey. She quivered beneath his hands as they gentled and aroused in equal measure. Then he withdrew the digits, marking her breasts with her own bodily fluid, his hands reclaiming them, before he rested his head in the valley, breathing in her pungent scent. This simple pleasure a mind-altering one.

She was his.

Lover, best friend, wife.

Everything he had ever wanted, denied him.

But not tonight.

He cupped her bottom and brought her up against him, his lips working against her neck, as he kissed her through his words, his touch.

"See what you do to me?"

Her lips found his again, then they found his neck, his shoulder, his chest, her fingers brushing the dark, curly hair, before her fingers found the shaft that was seeking its home.

He gasped as she applied light pressure, her hand working some kind of massage magic and he felt himself sliding to that place where only she could take him.

Her thumb rubbed the tip, and he could feel the explosion building.

With his arm around her waist, he lifted her up, closed the open door, cursing himself for his lack of awareness. Anyone could have walked in on them, Paul just down the hall, eating. But that's what she'd always done to him. Nothing else in the world mattered, just her and the driving need to make her his. He carried her toward the bed, brushing his lips over hers again, the naked desire in her eyes driving him beyond restraint. Her arms tightened around his neck, her mouth covering his hungrily. The need to consume her swamped his body and when he laid her down on the bed, he entered in one single thrust. His blood was pounding, his body on fire, having reclaimed her innermost sanctum. She squirmed under him, the friction causing an ache, the intensity raw, and he pumped in, and out, repeating the sweet torture until he felt her come undone in his arms. Only then did he let himself go, plunging deeper still, her spasms creating a vortex of pleasure that he'd thought was lost to him forever. His heart all but stopped when the release came, dying the small death in her arms.

Collapsed on top of her, he felt her fingers threading through his hair, her legs imprisoning him in place, but there was no need. He wouldn't have moved if his life depended on it. She was everything his heart desired, his body needed, his spirit thrived on.

And if only for a night, she was his again.

When he shifted, intent on moving off her, she held him, her arms becoming bands around his chest.

"No. I've wanted this for so long, waited for so long. I can't let you go yet."

He buried his head in her neck, wrapped his arms around her.

"I hope you never do."

It was like it was new again.

And yet so familiar.

The first night they'd made love had been an awakening.

He hadn't expected such raw, sexual hunger, or her willingness to be consumed. He thought it might have been because they had let the tension build, hadn't taken it to completion until the night of their wedding. But every night after, it was even more powerful. When that kind of love was gone...It had ripped him to shreds.

Tonight, there'd been the same erotic feel, the same kind of explosive reaction when their bodies became one.

Tonight, he'd been reminded how much he needed this, needed her.

And how much she needed him.

He'd just have to convince her that they were better together than apart.

⌒

They lay there, in each other's arms, all night.

She didn't sleep much, wanting to savor how it felt, wanting to fall back into the promises they'd made to one another.

This was heaven, and she reveled in it.

Always had.

Her mind relived the first night they'd made love.

It was the night of their wedding, the small ceremony held at his parents' house. Family and friends were in attendance, and the champagne flowed in celebration of the merging of these two families. Everyone was so happy. Even her mother who was disappointed she didn't get to plan a major event. Zach hadn't been willing to wait, and she'd soon learned the reason behind it. He'd been afraid she'd leave him.

She knew about fear and what it led to.

Mistakes.

Not in the marrying, but in the leaving.

Their fears had conspired against them, leaving an empty shell of a marriage.

Waiting for him to return home last night had given her time to re-evaluate where she was and what she wanted.

It all came down to one word.

Need.

When she'd awoken, found herself alone, she'd panicked.

Where was he?

Had he come home and gone to bed? Without her?

She'd flung herself up from the couch and run to his room.

When she opened the door, he'd been almost naked. His boxers were the only thing he was wearing, one foot suspended over his sweats. Her mouth had gone dry. He was the most gorgeous piece of flesh she'd ever seen. His hair unruly, his face chiseled to perfection, his shoulders broad and able to carry the world.

As her eyes slid down, she could tell he wanted what she did, the evidence in obvious view beneath the cotton material.

His invisible but powerful magnetic field had drawn her to him, and she'd felt herself moving, to taste what he offered, and there was nothing left to repel the attraction.

Opening to him had been easy, the driving need to become a part of him insistent.

With him it was spontaneous combustion and the fire that burned, singed her soul.

She'd been fooling herself all this time. She could never go back to that safe space she'd once inhabited.

Tonight, had proven it.

But how to move forward?

Maybe it was time to have that talk, the one he'd wanted before leaving that night.

She couldn't then. The pain was so deep and so all-consuming. She needed time to think, to prepare, to forgive.

But he had given her more time than she'd wanted.

That first year, she'd picked up her cell several times, but fear reared its ugly head, and she never went through with it. She was convinced he didn't love her, not as much as she loved him, and she refused to put that kind of power in his hands.

When he went undercover, he'd ignited the incendiary device that all but destroyed any chance they had.

She'd pushed all thoughts of him down deeper and deeper inside until she thought she had buried all feeling. Or so she'd liked to think. Her tattoos told a different story.

She'd stayed with Johnny and Tish for a couple of nights after Zach left, not wanting to be alone with her pain. Sitting with her brother into the early hours one morning, his tats covering his arms, she'd gotten it into her head that it was the perfect way to transfer the pain in her heart to her body.

Johnny had taken her to his artist, tried to talk her out of it the whole way over. He'd sat, holding her hand while the needle did its work. And held her when she cried.

It had become a yearly pilgrimage, every year the tattoo becoming more expressive, more personal. Johnny had never failed to go with her.

CHAPTER TWENTY-SEVEN

She was lying as she always did, partially hidden in the crook of his arm, as if burrowing in her den. His morning scent aroused her, the warmth of his flesh sending tingles through her. Her hand roamed his body, the taut chest, the flat stomach, down farther to his morning erection. Sliding down, she bent to kiss the tip and it jerked of its own volition.

Before she could enhance her exploration, hands were pulling her up and across his body, so she lay on top of him, skin touching skin, and he found her lips with his, caressing her mouth.

"Good morning."

Then his lips recaptured hers, demanding more.

And she gave it, their bodies coming together as one.

Sweaty and satisfied, they clung to each other. His heartbeat was strong and steady beneath her cheek, and she closed her eyes, more content than she'd been in years. No, not content, happy. She hadn't been happy since the day he left, had forgotten what it felt like. Overcome by emotion, it took her time to unwind herself from around him. It was only when she heard her mother in the kitchen, beginning her daily routine, that she roused herself.

"I think it's time to rise and shine."

A lazy, taunting smile slid across his face.

"I believe I've already done the rising thing."

She leaned over to brush her lips over his.

"I forgot what a glorious way it is to start the day."

Only after he'd kissed her breathless did she scoot off the bed, step into her leggings, pull her tee over her head, and tiptoe out of the room.

⌒

Lana came down to the kitchen showered and dressed for the day to find everyone else at the table eating waffles and blueberries.

She glanced at Zach, who was spraying whipped cream from the can. He looked up, arched his brow and nodded to the delicacy with an evil grin.

There was a quiver in her belly at the thought of him eating the sweet confection from her...

She spun around when the quivers began to vibrate in spasms, and she heard his chuckle.

The carafe of coffee trembled in her hands as she tried to wipe the image out of her mind.

Wanting to find a neutral zone, she asked, "How did it go yesterday? We didn't really talk about it."

Celia asked, astounded, "You didn't ask him when he came home?"

"Um, no. I was asleep when he got here. I was still half-asleep... He was tired... I..."

Her mother was giving her a peculiar look as she stumbled over the explanation.

Paul mustn't have noticed.

"Both kids are in jail. My partner here nailed the shooter but good. Everyone was applauding his technique when it was over."

She met Zach's eyes and he smiled at her.

"And it doesn't look like you'll have to testify. He confessed, and we have it on tape."

Sliding into a seat, she gave Zach her full attention.

"How did you get him to confess?"

"A combination of his stupidity, ego, and desire for street cred. He caved when he thought he wouldn't get the score for the kill."

There was an intake of breath before she gasped, "People keep score?"

Paul coughed and said, "Apparently, snipers do."

Zach's lips thinned.

"Not all. I didn't. Didn't want to know. Although they're all recorded, witnessed. But some of the guys would get greedy and be out for as many as they could get in one sitting. That wasn't how it was supposed to be."

"I don't understand how people can do that?"

"In my case, it was a question of making sure my unit was safe. Out on the streets it's a question of defending your honor."

"What honor? Do these kids have any?"

"In their world, yes."

Paul gave her evidence of how many years he'd been out catching murderers.

"Look at one of these kids wrong, they feel they've ben dissed and need to retaliate. It often ends up in someone's death. It's a friggin' shame. No regard for life."

Lana couldn't help but ask, "Don't you feel like you're shoveling...blood and guts against the tide?"

Paul gave her a pointed look.

"Some days. But it doesn't matter because the dead deserve their justice."

Lana was watching Zach, his reaction. He was finished eating and sat there looking pensive.

"In this case, there was an innocent victim. It upped the stakes for me. Made me more determined to get the killer."

"There are some who get under your skin more than others."

Lana put her hand on his arm.

"You sound like you're becoming invested in this."

He looked up and gave her a smile.

"I was in this one. Maybe because you were involved, maybe because I was pissed that someone did that to Adrian."

Paul pushed his plate away, took a sip of his coffee.

"This one was pretty straight-forward. Wait until we have a real who-done-it, then you'll have the ultimate puzzle."

"I can't say I can't wait. That means another dead."

"There'll be another dead whether you want it or not. That much I can guarantee you."

Paul pushed up from the table and transferred his plate and mug to the dishwasher.

Zach looked over at her and asked, "What do you have planned for the day?"

"Getting the menu down so I can finish the brochures."

"Are you coming with me tonight?"

It was the Mullins' turn to host their Saturday night dinner, but they were having a party for their seven-year-old son in the afternoon.

"Didn't Ed tell you?"

"Tell me what?" Zach asked.

"I offered to cook so Chris didn't have that on her plate."

"No. Ed didn't say a word."

"They probably thought you had to work. They knew about the shooting and that you were on the case."

Paul said, from across the room, "We got that case wrapped up in record time thanks to you. That sketch was spot-on. We've got to go in for a few hours this morning, meet with the AD on the finer details, then I've got to write it all up. Zach can be spared for the night."

"Are you sure? Shouldn't I be helping you with that?"

"You weren't even supposed to working this, and like I said, it's pretty clear-cut. Won't take much time at all. The notes you took were detailed, so writing the report should be easy."

"You think the DA will have a problem with my routine?"

"We got that confession fair and square. No coercion, no brutality. You didn't even lie."

"Ed told me the whole unit is more than happy those two are off the streets."

"Not sure that Glover will do hard time. It wasn't a robbery, and he didn't have anything to do with the shooting itself."

"Unless Lorenzo recants and puts the blame back on him. Then he does life."

"Innocent until proven guilty."

Lana interjected, "I don't get that. I saw that kid shoot Adrian. To me he is not innocent."

"You didn't see his face, Lana. You couldn't identify him. Jeronimo could be lying. Watkins is innocent until we can get him to admit his part in court or we can collect enough hard evidence to put him away."

"I guess. But I know that the other kid is not guilty. He could end up in jail even though he's innocent."

"It might not be the most perfect form of justice, but it's better than anything else out there."

Interrupting the silence that followed, Zach asked. "You going to be all right while I'm gone?"

"I'll keep busy. I can forget for minutes here and there, but I'm still not ready to be alone for long. Seems you help with that. Last night there were still some dark pockets of memory that came spilling out."

Sadness filled her but not the desolation she'd felt right after it happened. She surmised Zach had had something to do with getting her focused on something else.

He looked up at her.

"Why didn't you tell me?"

"You were sleeping. I didn't want to wake you. I burrowed deeper and they lightened up."

Her mother looked up at her, a half-smile on her face, but left her response at that.

"Unless we get called out, you should be free for the night. The thing about murder is it never happens at a convenient time. You'll get used to getting woken up at three a.m."

Paul shrugged into his coat and waited by the door.

"You ready to go?"

Zach got up from his place and put his plate in the dishwasher. "I'll take my car. That way I can leave when I'm ready."

"You sure?"

"I can't drive Lana's yet, but I can handle mine."

Her clutch would give him major leg cramps.

Zach glanced up, hesitating before coming over and brushing his lips over hers.

Before he could take a step away, she pulled him back as if she wanted to say something but then she pecked his cheek and let him go.

⌒

She had almost uttered those words she'd locked away.

She'd almost told him she loved him, asked him to keep himself safe, come home to her.

But she wasn't his wife anymore, not in any sense of the word.

Well, maybe in the sense that they'd made love last night.

And there was no denying it felt like love, right to the soles of her feet.

"You spent the night together. In his room?"

Her mother had been waiting until the men were gone before responding to the bombshell she'd dropped.

"I didn't intend for it to happen. When I woke up, I heard noises in the house and knew they had gotten back. Zach hadn't... I thought he... I went looking for him and interrupted him while he was changing." She closed her eyes and blew a breath out. "Let your imagination take it from there."

"Lana don't do this to him unless you intend to make it permanent. It would be...selfish on your part if you're just using him."

Selfish...

Was it selfish to want something so badly you'd be willing to sell your soul for it?

Feeling flooded through her, rushing her bloodstream.

"Is that what I'm doing?"

"I don't know. You tell me."

"I told you I was a mess. I don't know what I'm doing anymore. I want him in my life so badly I think I can overcome the fear. Then I think of him dead in an alley somewhere and my lungs seize. All I want to do at that point is run."

She looked at her internal prism and realized that the running she was doing wasn't away anymore but straight into his arms.

That was a paradigm shift of major proportions.

She wasn't opting out but re-evaluating her feelings.

Thinking, contemplating, remembering from a new perspective.

One thing she knew for certain was she was no longer dying inside.

Death might not be the greatest loss.

She was beginning to see the truth in that.

Her mother spoke for both.

"You're still here. Maybe your running days are over."

Giving her mother her attention, she admitted, "It feels too good to run from."

Patting her hand, Celia said, "I'm glad to hear that."

⌐

Hours later she was sitting at the computer in her condo, her Facebook page almost complete. This was the uninspiring part of her enterprise. Detail was not her strength.

She heard a key in the lock and stood. And began shaking. Had the shooter come to get her? She shook her head, knowing that wasn't possible, but her emotions were in shambles.

Before she could move out of the paralysis that had taken over, she saw the familiar face, heard the voice and the click of the closing door.

"Hi. I didn't want to disturb you, so I used my key."

Dropping down into her seat, she let out a breath.

"You scared the shit out of me."

"Sorry."

Zach was holding up the evidence.

"You never asked for it back, so I thought you might have changed the locks."

She hadn't.

Had hoped there'd be no need.

Hoped he'd—

She shook off the regret.

"You never tried to come back, so I didn't see the point."

Kicking off his snow caked boots by the door, he asked.

"Did you think I would?"

She raised her head at the question, meeting it head on.

"By the time you went undercover, I knew there was nothing to worry about."

Right. That's when her worry had hit the top of the meter.

He walked over to where she sat and bent down to give her a kiss.

"I've been waiting all morning to do that."

The kiss was unexpected and much appreciated.

He was here, and she wanted him to stay.

She rose and came around the desk, threaded her arms around his neck, gave a full-contact kiss that had her heart racing and her palms sweaty. His hands had come around to cup her bottom, pressing his need home.

"This warm welcome is an unexpected surprise."

"So is the visit."

"Bed still in the same place?"

Licking his lips, she answered between moist kisses, "It is."

"Can we test it out, see if it still works to our strengths?"

Her voice drifted into a whisper.

"Was that your intention in dropping by?"

"No, it was your response to my kiss that made it a possible option."

Her hands were greedy, and they stroked and petted his body from neck to shoulder to thigh to penis.

"Does this mean yes?"

His hands were busy with the same kind of work.

"It means I'm not sure I can make it that far."

Rissa had once told her that she and Luca did it on any available surface.

His body had still been bruised and battered after the wedding, so they kept the sex in the bedroom although there had been a couple of kinky moments that had caused no shortage of explosions.

All but ripping off his belt, unclasping his suit pants, she pushed both them and his briefs down. He got the idea, and her jeans and panties were the next to go.

Knowing he was still recuperating, she was going to ease him down to the floor but before she could get there, he had lifted her up and plunged her down onto his shaft, his groan lifting the corners of her mouth into a smile.

A sense of urgency drove her, her insides humming, her inner walls vibrating from the invasion.

She wrapped her legs wrapped around him and rode him up and down, the friction burning, the orgasm building. He began to stroke the nub at her apex and the involuntary shudder had her bucking against him.

He pummeled faster and faster, his need seeming to match her own, until she cried out as the spasms took control, wringing every ounce of fear out of her. He shuddered as he made one final thrust, plunging deeper, his animal growl reminding her of something long forgotten.

He was her home.

Didn't matter anymore for how long, just as long as he lived in her until the end came.

She prayed it would be a hundred years.

Pressing his lips against her neck, he walked them to the bedroom, never leaving her body. He let his bad leg buckle as soon as he reached the edge of the bed.

While he regained his breathing, she undid his tie, unbuttoned his dress shirt and denuded him before ripping her sweater over her head, unclasping her bra so she could sit skin to skin.

He cradled her close, sought out her lips with his and the ecstasy continued in more subtle ways.

His face was in the crook of her neck.

"I'm glad you didn't waste any time."

She threaded her fingers through his hair.

"It's funny. My sister once told me she and Luca rarely made it to a bed. I didn't understand why until now."

"Rissa? I think I've misread her."

"She gave me some interesting tidbits to try out...but I never got to experiment with any."

His mouth curved into a devilish grin.

They had done some experimenting of their own. Never planned, always spontaneous. One night, he'd spilled wine on her, the spot expanding out as more of the material soaked it up. The tee shirt was porous, her body so ripe, and he'd sucked up the wine along with her nipple. The combination of the nectar and her...it deserved a repeat.

He felt himself rising to the image his brain was playing with.

It got plank hard when she asked, a playful sparkle in her eyes, "How about we give the whipped cream a try? I'll pick up a can tomorrow."

His heartbeat accelerated at the thought. Wanting to see how far she'd go with this fantasy, he added, "And some cherries, with juice."

She peered up at him and asked, "Maybe some chocolate sauce?"

He gulped in anticipation.

"My very own sundae."

She kissed his lips, the anticipation of what she'd just suggested affecting her already well-spent body.

"Now who's being one-way? That's to pour on you. I think I might enjoy some chocolate on a stick."

She watched his eyes close, heard the groan.

"God, Lana."

Climbing off his lap in a slow and torturous way, she smiled sweetly and told him, "Anticipation is half the fun. No sundae until Sunday. I have to cook for tonight."

Something that was a piece of cake for her.

The look on his face was pitiful and he wasn't budging from his spot.

"You do know this is cruel and unusual punishment."

"I think it'll be fun watching you squirm. I promise it will be worth the wait."

She pulled at his hair until he got the message and stood. When he was facing her, she kissed him again, her lips pushing his mouth open, her tongue taking a full exploration of the interior.

He grasped her head, his lips grounding back against hers. Wanting to be devoured by him, taken in whole, she writhed against his body until they were rocking back and forth again, feeling the tight pleasure that she'd so long denied herself.

Her body bowed out as his lips took her nipples, covering them in his saliva, as he pulled and nibbled.

"God, how I've missed you."

The depth of her emotions at his pronouncement swelled to overflowing, and the tears that she'd kept buried since the shooting, came flooding out.

Her tears were his undoing. He'd been waiting for it all to catch up with her, wanting to be there when it did.

He'd gotten what he'd asked for and he whispered the words he'd held back, words that told her he'd always be there for her, no matter what their future held.

Before he'd made the decision to go undercover, he'd almost called, almost begged her to reconsider. He would have turned down the assignment if she'd given him a reason to. It was the finality in her words the day he left that had reverberated in his head, that had moved him forward into the nefarious jungle. A place he felt comfortable in, where nothing could touch him. Where thoughts of her had to be buried for him to stay alert and alive.

"It's going to be okay, Lana."

Her crying jag slowed to a stream, but when she looked up at him, her eyes held such sadness his heart cracked.

Then her words added another fractured vein.

"It hasn't been okay since you left."

He stilled at the implication. Taking her shoulders in his hands, his grip firm and insistent, he rasped out, "For me, either. I didn't want to leave you. I never wanted to leave you."

The irritation with herself was evident in her expression, her eyes blazing in self-recrimination.

"I didn't even give us time to talk about it. I was so angry."

"I know. I should never have held that piece of information back. I...I hoped that you'd come to accept who I was."

"I've always accepted who you are. It's what I... It's what made me..."

Her hand went to his face, and she cupped his cheek in her hand.

"It's what made me fall in love with you. I love who you are. I just have a hard time living with the consequences of that."

"The day we got that call about Adrian's shooting, I was coming out of my skin thinking you might have been hurt. It gave me a new appreciation of the word *terror*."

"I guess you could say I have a new appreciation for acting without thought. I knew that kid might need me, and I ran."

Knowing he could still get the answer he didn't want, he asked, "So where does that leave us?"

"I don't know. I don't know how to turn the fear off."

He closed his eyes, rested his forehead against hers.

A broken whisper gave him new hope.

"The only thing I'm sure of is that I love you and I want this, what we have. I need you to be patient, give me time to unpack all the baggage I've been carrying around for years. If Tony could do it, I can."

He opened his eyes to see her heart in her shadowed brown ones. He found a strange numb comfort.

"I'll be as patient as a saint."

"I don't want to be married to a saint. My flaws will stick out like a sore thumb."

He stroked her breast, his thumb grazing the nipple.

"You have flaws? I hadn't noticed."

"Oh, my love, let me count the ways. Selfish, childish, one-way." She studied him. "You are none of those things. You're already a friggin' saint."

His lips bruised hers, his possession brutal and complete.

"I'm no saint when it comes to you. All flesh and blood."

She traced one of the scars from his years in the Marines. He had so many.

"All precious to me. Remember that, will you?"

"With you waiting for me at home, I'll have all the incentive I need to stay alive."

He glanced at the clock on her bedroom bureau, not surprised it was still there.

Nothing seemed to have changed, and he surveyed the room to confirm it.

The picture hanging on the wall was new. It was a sketch done in watercolor of their wedding day. They were kissing, her in her off-white dress, him in his suit, the altar, the justice of the peace fading into the ice-blue and beige background.

"Rissa?"

He was nodding toward the wall and her eyes followed his.

"Her wedding gift."

"I like it."

"I do, too. I would look at it every night from bed. I don't know why. It made it all so much worse that I was alone there."

"I missed our bed."

Trying to lighten the mood, she smiled and said, "I can understand why. From what Paul said you lived in a flea bag."

"That's not the reason, although it's a good point. Can I move back in? The bed misses me and it's a sight bigger than the pull-out at your folks."

There was a rise of panic in her eyes, and he waited for her to process the request without saying a word.

The patience thing was going to get him into sainthood if it was this nerve-racking to wait her out.

"You just got your own place back."

"Then you can move in with me. You loved my kitchen."

"I wouldn't be moving in for your kitchen...although that does make the decision easier."

"Did you just agree?"

Kissing him lightly, she admitted, "I think so. The more I think about that kitchen..."

He picked her up and twirled her around, but his leg was having no part of it, and he barely made it to the bed before he fell over.

She was under him, his eyes telling her all she needed to know, but she didn't have time to let him have his way.

"We've got to get dressed. I've got work to do and you'll be too much of a distraction without clothes."

"All I've got is my suit. I've got to go back to your parents' house to get some clothes, then we can swing by the store and get your ingredients."

She fingered the hair on his chest.

"Some of your clothes are still here."

He was astonished and asked, still not believing it, "You kept my clothes?"

She looked up at him in a shy way.

"I liked seeing them there. It made me believe that...we'd...that you'd..."

"Come home?"

Sliding her arms around his neck, she leaned her head against him.

"I missed you so much."

"God, Lana, you're all I thought about."

The seconds ticked by as they held each other. He couldn't believe they'd wasted so much time.

Why hadn't he reached out? Why had he just assumed she didn't want him? He was never going to do that again.

Taking her hand, he led her to the closet.

"Let's see what you've hoarded away."

When he walked in, all the clothes he'd left behind were washed and ironed and hanging on his side of the closet, as if he'd never left.

He flipped through the hangers, the shirts they'd bought for him together, the jeans faded and worn. His boots and sneakers were placed side by side on the floor beneath.

"It's everything I owned."

"I never understood why you didn't call to pick them up."

He faced her; the truth so easy to tell her. Now.

"I couldn't have come back, Lana. Not if I had to leave again. It was hell walking out that door. I couldn't have done it a second time."

CHAPTER TWENTY-EIGHT

The impact of that statement wasn't lost on her.

She might not have been able to let him go again.

It was so simple and so complicated.

Like a rock and a soft spot.

She wanted to be both.

As she stood under the warm spray of the shower, she scrubbed the uncertainty away, then toweled herself off, lathering herself in confidence and moisturizer.

She had agreed to move forward, as if she was sure, it was the right thing to do.

Simple and complicated.

"Why don't you text Chris. See what time she wants us there," she called out from the steamy bathroom.

He yelled in, "I'm on it."

She was now waiting for him to finish his shower, the door open, as if in invitation. Like he had when they were living together. She had to force herself not to intrude. It would have put them behind schedule. When he came into the bedroom, a towel wrapped around his midriff, he made his way to the closet, informing her, "Chris said around seven would be fine."

It was a good thing he made quick work of dressing, or she might have done pick-up for tonight, instead of the meal she'd planned.

Now that she'd found his body again, greed was kicking in.

He was buttoning his shirt, the cobalt-blue one he'd worn to their wedding, that had a special place in the closet. She wondered how he'd found it.

"Why was this one in with *your* stuff?'

Fingering her hair behind her ear, she met his gaze full on.

"In case I ever got the urge to sweep everything of yours out, I wanted to make sure that one was spared."

As he tucked it in, sat on the bed to put his socks on, he looked up at her, a caress in his eyes.

"I like that answer."

"You must have gone through my things to find it."

"I found the dress, wrapped in plastic. This was next to it."

"I thought they should stay together."

She peered up at him to see if he thought she was crazy.

There was a glint in his eye that told her he didn't.

"I would think they were grateful for your thoughtfulness. Do you think the dress will mind that I'm wearing it?"

Her smile broadened at his playfulness.

"I think it should be fine."

"There's a good memory attached to the last time I wore this. It seemed appropriate I wear it today. Now there'll be two."

He took her hand and pulled her up off the edge of the bed.

"Are you ready?"

She thought she was. Ready to take a chance that this would work. Ready to believe she'd outsmarted her fear.

"I am."

⌒

The supermarket was packed as they wound their way up and down the aisles, Zach pushing the cart. She ticked things off the list as she placed them in the basket.

"What are you torturing me with tonight?"

They were standing at the meat counter, second in line.

"Garlic chicken."

"Not my first choice but definitely edible."

"It'll transport better, reheat more evenly than a roast beef. You'll have to wait until our turn to get what your stomach desires."

"My stomach is growling in anticipation for my sundae. I can't think beyond that."

He dipped his head to kiss her as the man behind the counter asked how he could help them.

She glanced over to him, the kiss blowing all her thoughts into snatches of words.

Hi. Help. Ma'am?

Her brain snapped back into function mode but not before she felt the heat invade her body.

"Five whole chickens, please."

When the basket was full, with two bags of potatoes, the ingredients needed for butternut squash ravioli and the sage sauce she'd prepare them with, the broccoli and pine nuts, and all the makings for her hazelnut liqueur chocolate mini cakes that she knew Zach loved, the centers oozing sinfulness, they paid for the bounty and returned to her condo, where the cooking commenced.

They spent the afternoon in companionable silence, her busy in the small kitchen, him on the couch in her family room. He found a basketball game to watch and ended up nodding off during the fourth quarter.

After she put the cakes into the oven, she went in to see him and smiled at his sleeping form. She took a minute to sit and watch him. He was at rest, not something that happened often.

His sleep had always been fitful, filled with the horrors of war, recollections of his role in the drama.

He'd bolt upright in the middle of the night, sweat pouring off him, his limbs shaking.

She had asked him for details, but he'd kept them to a minimum in person. It was the letters that had told her what she needed to know, how to comfort him.

She got up, went into her room, the sheets a tangled mess, her clothes still on the floor, and she took a minute to straighten up.

Her box was on her bedside table, and she thought to put it away but not before she slid another letter out to read.

This was the last one she'd received while he was still on duty. The next one had come after he was home, like a haunting voice in the desert.

March, 2014

Lana,

We're heading into a flat, empty wasteland this morning. It'll be good to get away from our current location, a small village on the outskirts of nowhere. We've been kicking in doors, mounting up, moving along, kicking in doors, repeat, repeat, repeat. We stayed outside the perimeter last night, but right before dawn, Coop and I climbed atop a roof to get the lay of the land. Just as our men were coming out from their nighttime positions, eight insurgents arrived, running, machine guns blazing, their suicide vests keying us in on their plans. Our intention was to stay alive while keeping everyone else in the unit in one piece.

One of the Taliban began charging, a grenade in his hand, and I got busy checking wind direction, velocity, range, and distance so that Coop could take him out before any harm was done. When the shot rang out, the grenade hit the air, the Marines freezing in place, knowing death might be only a foot away. With the bullet's impact came an explosion that sent some of the men spiraling through the air, while vaporizing the offending enemy. Not one of ours was critically injured but we were stunned they'd survived both the grenade and detonation.

Then it was my turn, my targets like ducks in an amusement park. One to the back of the head, one in the chest. The other missed due to the slight breeze that wafted through, but the second shot caught him in the face.

The remaining robe-clad men went racing in the other direction. One win for our side.

Now we go back to busting our asses getting ready to move again, prepping gear, zeroing weapons, our new LT giving us shit about our uniforms and footwear. He's out of touch with what we go through, what we face every day, and Coop and I often discuss how sick we are of the mindset.

This will be my last deployment.

Now if I can survive the remaining days, I'll get to sit across a table from you with a cup of coffee and talk of more pleasant things.

Send me details of the mundane, please. I'm in need of some.

Love,
Zach

His injuries had come a month later and once he was stable, he'd been shipped home, in one piece but worse for wear.

She placed the box in its resting place, on the top shelf of her closet. He didn't need to know she'd been re-reading them, had since he left. It suddenly became clear it had been an unconscious desire to keep the connection between them strong.

⌐

After he helped her load the car, they headed out.

Ed and Chris lived on the west side of Medford, in a colonial that they had been renovating over the ten years they'd owned it. The last time she'd been there, the kitchen demo was about to begin. As she scanned the updated space, her eyes were aglow, as only a chefs would be.

"It's beautiful Chris."

She was helping Lana and Zach by taking the stuffed bins full of food and setting them down on the granite countertop.

"I have to agree. It came out well. When Ed told me what he'd planned, I wasn't sure he was up to the task, but he did a great job with it."

Zach smiled and added, "With a little help from his friends."

Ed was just coming in, his nose in the air as if sniffing it.

"Very little, if I remember correctly. You're better with a gun than a slide rule."

"You're better with a slide rule than a gun. I'd say you're the one in the wrong profession."

"You were impressive with the sledgehammer."

"I had reason to pummel your cabinets to dust."

Zach turned to look at Lana.

"You had just forced me out. I wanted to kill something. This was the better alternative."

She raised her nose to him.

"I could say it was you who forced my hand, but I think recriminations at this point are useless."

Tucking her against his chest, he kissed her temple and said, "And unnecessary."

Andy was now taking up space in the limited area. It was getting hard to move.

"Well, aren't you two chummy."

When everyone's eyes turned to him, he put his hands up and said, "It's good. I'll say no more."

He popped some almonds into his mouth. Chris always had some in a glass container on the coffee table. They helped the men stave off the hunger they brought with them to most meals.

Chris had opened the lid to the dessert bin and asked, "What is *that?*" Ed bent down to inspect them, admitting, "I love it when you feed us."

"It's the one thing Zach eats without complaint."

"I do love her desserts. I think I might like her sundaes the best."

She gave him that look, and he gave her one back.

Yup, the greed had set in.

⌒

The men had finished cleaning the kitchen, which was the deal. Women cooked, men cleaned, although Andy often joked that it didn't seem fair. He was the one who cooked in his family, and he should be exempt from the clean-up. They were scattered around the living room, sipping coffee. It was the last course before heading home.

Julian had just taken a seat beside Lana but directed his comment to Zach.

"I talked to Norm today."

"He's the one who took over my undercover assignment, isn't he?"

"He is. Says to thank you. He likes it better than his last assignment. His wife does, too."

"His wife likes his job?"

Lana sounded surprised, although he understood why.

"He was working a now shuttered massage parlor."

"And that isn't safer than working a theft ring?"

Andy guffawed; Julian laughed outright.

It was Zach who let her in on the joke.

"It depends on how far the cop takes it. Some of the actions are prohibited. There are cops who don't mind pushing the boundaries."

"What do you mean?"

She was studying him while Julian gave her an answer.

"One of the cops got caught taking a shower with the masseuse. He took off his clothes and she sudsed and scrubbed him all over. That's not allowed. Not by the department, not by most of the wives."

Her eyes were pinpricks.

Zach put his hands up as if to ward off her Italian evil eye.

"Don't look at me like that. For one thing, I never worked a massage parlor. Number two, we were separated, and it wouldn't have been cheating."

She leaned over and pinched the underside of his arm.

"Ouch. That hurts."

"Good. I didn't like your answer."

Ed had a question mark on his face.

"It can't be easy keeping to the legality of the law. If the cop refuses to take his clothes off, it looks suspicious, doesn't it? I mean, he's there for a massage."

Rubbing the underside of his arm, Zach admitted, "That's one of the reasons I didn't accept those kinds of assignments. I liked things to be black and white."

Lana sat back, her arms tight against her chest.

"It had nothing to do with wanting higher stakes?"

"I suppose that had something to do with it. I was looking for adrenaline highs to convince me I was alive."

"Looking in the mirror wouldn't have told you that?"

"It would have told me I was physically present...I read somewhere once that something dies inside when love is lost."

She released her arms as well as the tension.

"Touché."

Mona asked Lana, "What are we missing here?"

Lana bit at her lip before admitting, "It's a tattoo I got. He got a glimpse of it after the shooting."

"You got a tattoo?"

"She has three. You should see her with a nose ring."

"Lana, you are so not what you appear."

There was a glint of humor in Zach's eyes.

"I'm finding out no one in her family is."

"Dennis is. Solid and steady."

Andy and Mona got up as one, as if it was pre-orchestrated for a certain time.

"Time to head home. My mother can only do so late, and we couldn't get anyone else to watch the kids tonight."

"We should get going, too."

Lana had gotten up, looked at Chris. "We should be going, too. You've had a very busy day. You must be exhausted."

Ed was the one who answered.

"I'd rather be out doing a gang bust than be in a room with ten seven-year-olds."

Chris agreed. "It's a good thing it only happens once a year."

As the couples leaving shrugged into coats, boots, and hats, Chris came over to hug Lana.

"Thanks. It helped, and it was delicious."

Ed was licking his lips.

"Especially that dessert. Please give Chris the recipe."

Chris laughed and said, "What good would that do? It wouldn't come out nearly as good."

"It's an easy one. Not many ingredients, not many steps."

"So says the chef."

CHAPTER TWENTY-NINE

Tuesday dawned grey and gloomy. And cold. She'd decided to skip her classes at the Boys & Girls Club, not sure she could overcome the images that still floated through her mind. It was going to be enough of a challenge going to the wake with Zach later in the day. He'd tried to talk her out of it, but she was adamant about meeting Adrian's mother, offering her condolences, maybe proving that what happened was real and not some figment of her imagination. Everyone at the club knew she'd run out to be with Adrian. No one knew of any further involvement, so she finally convinced Zach it was safe enough. Word was out that it was Martez who'd given them the lead, the sketch. No one was contradicting it, so the teen had been sent to a relative's out of state. The Cruzes didn't want to lose another son to violence.

When Zach introduced her, Mrs. Cruz hugged her, crying out a thank you.

"I will be forever grateful he didn't die alone."

"I'm so sorry I couldn't do anything more."

"A mother's worst fear is that something happens to her child. I still can't believe he's gone."

The tears started anew, and her husband wrapped his arm around her, giving his own version of thank you with his eyes.

The funeral was no better.

Seeing the coffin lowered into the ground brought back another day, another death.

Yet the residual pain from that earlier time was muted. Her father had lived a full life, had done something with it. This boy hadn't been given the chance.

It was people like her father, like Paul, like Zach who fought against that tide, trying to make the world a safer place.

It was a wake-up call that death touched everyone, not only her family. Her mother had told her often enough it was part of life, just not a particularly kind one.

Her heart filled with a new, stronger emotion.

Love had taken up so much room there was nowhere left for bitterness or regret.

That night, Zach insisted that they have a movie night. He was willing to watch one of her chick flicks.

"I want to see what all the fuss is about."

She thought it was his way of lightening up her day.

And she wanted to say thank you.

She had given him three choices before he went back to work, and he'd picked one of her favorites. He must have read the back of the video box, because it was about a woman who returned home to the South to get a divorce from her husband after a seven-year separation. Of course, they ended up back with each other.

She spent the afternoon setting the stage. Buttermilk fried chicken, mashed potatoes and corn bread. The chicken would hopefully satisfy his need for crunch. The sides were staples he'd be more than happy with.

Instead of serving Southern iced tea, she mixed up a batch of dirty daiquiris. The heroine ordered one during the movie, so she thought it would tie in. There was an underlying sexual innuendo that went with it. She hadn't known that until she'd gone on-line for the recipe.

As soon as he walked through the door, she had it ready and waiting.

After dinner, they sat on the couch and cozied up for the screening. She glanced over from time to time to see him engrossed in the comedic drama, something she hadn't expected.

There was a moment when Zach leaned into her. It was when the male lead kissed the female.

He whispered close to her ear, "You can tell he still loves her, never stopped."

Her moment came near the end, when Melanie realized she couldn't be with anyone else, that she loved her husband and didn't want a divorce.

And ran after him.

Crawling onto Zach's lap, she whispered, "She never stopped, either."

They never got to see the credits roll, too immersed with each other, too caught up in the romance and all those side benefits that came with it.

Right before they went to sleep, he pulled her close.

"I was wrong about the chick flick thing. There's no sacrifice involved."

He'd agreed to be her guinea pig, more than willing to help her refine the basket ingredients. His job was to tell her which movies worked. His measurement would be based on how hormonally incited she was after the preview.

Her job was to test recipes that any male carnivore would relish.

She planned on going through her movie collection, getting a few lined up for the next couple of weeks. When he had a free night, she'd set a stage. And hope that the performance wasn't interrupted with a late-night phone call.

⌒

Zach came awake with a start. His phone was ringing on the bedside table, and he grabbed for it to keep it from waking Lana up.

The time flashed 2:43.

"Yeah."

It was Paul informing him they'd caught another murder. Gave him the address and some specifics and told him to get there as soon as he could.

He swung his legs over the side of the bed and rubbed his eyes.

The Marines had taught him to come awake quickly so he was good at it.

Like the old days, something like excitement kicked in. He was looking forward to getting out there.

A new mystery awaited.

He'd been staying at Lana's for the last few days and they'd yet to become satiated enough with each other to get a full night's sleep. Last night was no exception. He could get addicted to this and hoped he wasn't setting himself up for another world full of pain.

When he turned to look at her, she was still lying in what would have been the crook of his arm, and his heart swelled. He couldn't say he was sorry he was sleep deprived.

He pushed himself up and walked to the closet to get some clothes. He'd brought over his suits from Celia's and added them to the wardrobe. He had better choices today and he picked one out, along with a shirt and tie, and headed into the bathroom to shower and change.

He was surprised they had gotten a second case so soon after their first. And he'd been assigned lead detective. He was surprised about that, as well. He was told he'd have to wait six months before that would happen.

"You've got the smarts and the background to handle this. I don't think you need any more time under your belt, and it'll be under my direction." Paul then went on to give him some details.

A man had gotten shot outside someone's house, on the sidewalk in a neighborhood. Another victim had been transported to the hospital in critical condition. If he died, they'd have a double to work. It would certainly keep him busy.

"Zach? What are you doing?"

Lana's voice was just outside the shower stall, and he tensed before pulling the curtain aside to tell her the news.

She seemed to shake the grogginess off before asking, "Can I make you something to eat, a coffee to go?"

"Sweetheart, why don't you try to get back to sleep. I can pick one up on the way."

"I'm up now and I'll want to say good-bye."

"If that's the case, I wouldn't turn down the coffee."

"Okay, I'll get it going."

He relaxed.

She seemed to be getting used to the flow of their lives, taking it in stride when he left for the day. Her night terrors had lessened, probably because neither of them was getting any REM sleep. His shadows had all but disappeared and he hadn't woken up in his killing fields since he moved in with her.

Life was good.

The aroma told him the coffee would be strong, just the way he liked it.

He was knotting his tie when he ambled into the kitchen.

There was a cup waiting for him, a travel mug on the counter sitting next to a cooler.

"You don't have to take it, but I wanted to give you the option."

"I think I remember asking you if you'd pack me a lunch if we were together."

"Well, I guess you have your answer."

"I'll take it. This case might end up being a cluster. There's a second victim in surgery who might not make it. It looks like it's going to be a long day."

"If you have some down time, text to stay in touch."

"I will."

He bent to kiss her good-bye, scooped up what she'd packed and headed out the door.

"Zach, wait."

He looked back to see her standing at the threshold.

"I love you. Keep yourself safe for me."

"I love you, too. I don't know when, but I'll be back."

She closed the door and leaned against it just as her phone rang.

She picked her phone up off the kitchen counter and swiped.

"Hi, Ma."

"You're up."

"I am."

"I wondered if you'd get up with him."

"I will always get up with him."

"No, you won't. You just think so now. It will become the norm at some point."

"Really? Then what are you doing up?"

"This one sounded bad. I wanted to make sure he had a good breakfast, and I packed a lunch. There's plenty for Zach, as well."

"I'm not my mother's daughter for nothing. I skipped breakfast at his request, but he'll have his own food, thank you very much."

"You had things on hand he'd like?"

"He's been here most of the week. What do you think?"

She smiled to herself. She'd even packed him a small sundae, although it would probably be melted by the time, he got to it. The ice pack wouldn't last all day.

She was hoping it would get her a text if nothing else.

"Are you back together?"

Lana hesitated. She didn't know what to say. They hadn't really planned this other than in general terms. Very general terms.

He'd been here since dinner at the Mullins', but she hadn't put her wedding ring back on. Neither had he.

They were in a kind of limbo where they were enjoying the perks of heaven, but hell was a distinct possibility on the other side.

"I don't know. We're talking."

That wasn't exactly true. They were participating in more hands-on experiments than having actual discussions, but it helped her deal with aftershocks of the murder.

It was like a bad dream she'd put behind her.

"Good. What are you doing today?"

"I'm meeting the architect at the building, so she can get the blueprints started. Then it'll be time for the Boys & Girls Club. That one's dicey. How about you?"

"A couple of appointments, and I have to admit I'm enjoying them again. Phyllis has taken on more hours and Melissa is doing a great job with the recipes. She's accepted a one-year contract, so I won't have to make a decision right away."

"I know you love your Nona role, but I can't see you devoting all your time to it. You didn't for us."

"I think you're right. I'd be bored silly in no time. Although I'm taking a week off to be with Rissa after Gabriella's born."

"Her timing was perfect. It will give them time to adjust before taking off on tour again. She's still planning on going with Luca, right?"

"As far as I know. I can't see her or Tish staying behind."

Lana laughed. Her sister and sister-in-law knew how to keep their men satisfied and they couldn't do it from hundreds of miles away. Wouldn't want to.

Separation from the man you loved sucked.

She knew that for a fact.

"Are you going to be all right? Going back? Do you want me to come with you?"

"I won't know until I get there. And no, I have to face this one alone."

"Call me if you need me."

"I will. Don't worry. I'll be fine."

And she hoped she would be.

⌒

She went back into her room and lay down on the bed. Knowing that without Zach here, she wouldn't fall back to sleep, she scrunched his pillow under her head and breathed in his scent.

Had they gotten back together?

They were playing the roles of husband and wife.

And she had to admit it was much more engaging in health than in sickness.

Glancing at the clock, she wondered what Zach had found at the crime scene and how many hours she'd have to wait before he was here beside her again. She had peeked into the room while he was dressing, seen him stand in front of their wedding picture. His eyes were closed, and she'd noticed a subtle shift in his demeanor as if he was shutting down all emotion. Gearing up for what lay ahead. Was this what he'd done in the military? He'd talked about it in one of his letters. How he'd have to detach before going out on patrol. He was more thoughtful than she'd given him credit for, less impulsive than she'd feared.

It gave her hope for their future.

⌒

Zach arrived at the scene just as Paul was pulling up behind a police car. The patrolmen were here, being the first called out, and had already secured the perimeter. The body was lying on the sidewalk, directly in front of someone's house. He could tell where the other victim had been gunned down by the bloodied clothing scattered not three feet away. Paul had his penlight on and was examining the corpse.

"It looks like a head wound."

Zach turned his on and scanned the rest of the torso.

"There's another hole here, just below his hip."

"Medium caliber?"

"Looks it. Maybe a nine-mill, or a .45?"

Zach began to shine his light on the ground, sweeping it in zig zag fashion in concentric circles around the body. CSI was already here. He could tell because there were tent markings where each casing was found, and he examined each one. Then squatted down.

"Here's a fragment, Paul. It might have come from the shot that nicked his hip bone."

With latex-gloved hands, Zach picked it up and dropped it into an evidence bag being held out by an extended hand.

He looked up to see Tony pressing the bag closed.

"Hey, bro. When did you get here?"

"I was first one on scene. Tough one. The ambulance took a kid who had more blood loss than he had blood. I can't see him surviving it."

"Any witnesses?"

"There's a guy who's been looking out that window since we got here. Maybe the 9-1-1 caller?"

Zach glanced up to see a shadow move away and out of sight.

"Thanks. I'll check it out."

Paul had come over to join them and asked his stepson, "Did you write up the preliminary report?"

"Yeah. After we got here, one of their friends came running towards the scene. Said he knew them. They'd just left a house party."

Tony took out his spiral notepad and gave them a rundown.

"The dead one is Darnell Roy, twenty-five; the one at the hospital is Kante Diallo, nineteen.

"Does he have any idea who did it? Or why?"

"None, and no. He was kind of freaked out. We put him in a patrol car. Waited to see if you wanted to interview him here or downtown."

Zach got on his phone, requesting a rundown of the victims. He wanted to know who they were and what they might be involved in that would get themselves killed. While he waited, he nodded his head in the direction of the house, telling Paul, "Tony said there might be a witness in there. He would have had a front-row seat. If he was looking."

"That would be great if he is willing to talk."

Taking out his notepad and pen, Zach jotted down the information coming across the line.

"Darnell Roy, twenty-five, runs a service station, married with two kids, no police activity to report. Kante Diallo is a mechanic who works for him. Single, with a kid. A couple of minor things against Kante."

Two hours in, they had the identifications, a third party to the shooting, a potential witness and the medical examiner had just shown up.

Not bad.

Zach assigned Leon Medino and Ray Loggia to the canvas area, with Tony participating, along with a couple of the other detectives.

As he continued to assess the crime scene, Zach asked, "Tony hoping to join the squad?"

"I don't know. He says he wants to try them all out, see what he likes."

"He'd probably make a good one. Good instincts."

"That's what I'm thinking but it's too early to tell."

The photographer was taking video as the ME turned the body over to examine it for evidence. Zach squatted down so he could watch more closely.

A wallet was extracted from the back pocket and handed to Zach. He was still getting used to working in the latex gloves and had a hard time sliding the license out. The name and age matched the friend's identification. The address listed was a surprise.

"Hey, Paul. He lives two blocks away."

During the week prior to starting his Homicide duty, he'd poured over the map of Dorchester, so he knew the area. For times like these.

Paul came over to where he was, put his hands on his hips.

"He was walking home when it happened."

"Would seem that way."

Before he could think about that in more depth, the ME gave them his assessment.

"Two bullet holes, medium caliber, first one hit the hip, second, the parietal ridge. I'd say it was at close range, two, maybe three feet away."

"From the looks of it, the shooter must have been walking toward them. Darnell didn't turn away, let him get that close. Maybe he knew him?"

"Either that or he didn't, so there was no alarm. I'll take the friend down for questioning. You see if you can get something out of the resident here."

The body was being wrapped in the bag for transport, the crime scene had been scoured and it was time to move into phase two: witness and interviews.

CHAPTER THIRTY

The meeting Lana had with the architect went without a hitch and she was excited about some of the suggestions Pam made that would make the space even more doable.

The hitch came as she was getting ready for her classes at the kids' facility. Her fingers were shaking as she snapped her jeans, her legs wobbly as she got into the car.

After pulling into the parking lot, she sat for a few minutes, the clamor of the police cars, the alarms blaring, the boy lying on the ground around the back still wreaking havoc with her emotions.

Taking a deep breath, she grabbed her bags full of the ingredients for the granola bars and slowly walked to the entrance. She'd had a month's worth of recipes planned and was grateful for her preparedness. She didn't have to think much about what to buy or bring, only what she'd face when she was inside.

Anna greeted her at the door, grabbed her into a hug, and said, "We were so afraid you would stop coming."

"I went to the wake on Tuesday. I couldn't handle attending to both. I'm not sure what I'm going to feel, so I can't promise anything."

"The children were so disappointed you weren't here. They are all so about you right now. They think you are one of the bravest people."

"I didn't do anything that required courage, Anna."

"Most people run from bullets. You went racing out as if it didn't matter."

Just like the police were trained to do...

"The body was the only thing out there. And Adrian was not about to hurt me."

"They do not have many role models like you. It is good for them to feel this."

"I know people who are brave, and I resemble none of them."

"I can disagree. It's a free country."

She gave Anna a sad smile.

But the sadness was purged as the kids came over to hug her, to high-five her, to talk to her about the incident.

And she let them.

As they made the bars, the kids vented their fears of dying, and she realized they lived with it every day, walking outside their homes, walking down the street, playing in their neighborhood.

She had nothing on them in that department.

She was glad she had moved through the fog to show up.

They were giving her examples of the kind of bravery she needed to see.

Lana had skipped lunch due to her nerves about returning to the scene of the crime. Now that she was home, her anxiety having been appeased, she opened her refrigerator to scan the contents looking for something quick to eat. She was planning on making dinner, but not for an hour or so. She broke off a piece of frittata and popped it in her mouth as the phone rang.

Picking it up, she smiled.

She'd gotten more than a text.

"Hi. How's it going?"

"You make a great detective's wife. It was exactly what I needed."

"Um, thank you."

"It was almost melted by the time I got to it, but I scooped up every bit of the puddle. The cherry was my favorite part. Or maybe it was the whipped cream."

"I'm glad it put a smile on your face."

"You put a smile on my face. Although I think I need some real sleep soon. This is going to be one long day."

"Tough case?"

"In a word, yes. Double homicide. One of them, at least, a good guy from what we can see at the surface. We're digging in, trying to find out if they were who everyone thought they were. We've got close to a dozen interviews coming up. We're just waiting for them to get here."

"What happened?"

"The victims attended a house party and were shot while walking home. Wife of one of the vics took his car to go to work because hers was at the garage getting the brakes fixed. He got a ride to the party was supposed to get a ride home but left earlier than his friend. It's kind of cold out even for a couple of blocks. Should have been safe enough."

"You're right. It should have been."

"How did it go today?"

She knew what he was asking. It wasn't about the meeting. Considering that it was more successful than she'd thought possible, she said, "Good. It's all the kids wanted to talk about. They had as much to get out as I did."

"They know it could happen to them anytime. If not directly, then indirectly."

"They never feel safe."

"The smart ones don't. Some have given up caring."

"Compared to them, I don't have anything to complain about. I'm beginning to think I'm far too insular. One of those faults I didn't think to mention."

"Very self-reflective."

"About time, wouldn't you say?"

"I'd say I better get back to work. It's going to be a long night from what I can tell. I might not be able to get home at all. Are you going to be okay?"

She took a breath in, determined to be that rock her mother told her about.

"I'll be fine. Tony called while I was on my way home. Asked if he could come by for something to eat. Did you have anything to do with that?"

"Will you get mad at me if I did?"

"Because you called me and let me know what was going on, I'll let it slide."

"I would have called with or without the sundae. I like hearing your voice."

"And I like hearing yours. It means you're alive."

"Will you sleep, okay?"

"I haven't been sleeping, remember? Maybe tonight I'll get some."

"I'll try not to wake you if I'm able to come home and grab a couple of hours."

"I'll know you're there as soon as you hit the bed, but you'll need some rest. Besides, you've had your sundae for the day."

"It was almost as good as the real thing."

His voice turned serious.

"I gotta go. They're bringing in the first of the party goers."

"Good luck."

"I'll see you as soon as I can."

"Okay."

And then the line was dead.

⌒

She sat with the phone in her hand, staring at it.

I'll try not to wake you if I'm able to come home to grab a couple of hours..
When had he started thinking of this as home?

Did she mind?

Was she rushing it? Like she had before?

The fear was muted for now. No sound of its fury rushing through her.

Would it start again?

Or was he finally in a place that could satisfy her need for safety?

She wanted to believe she could do this, wanted to believe she could be a
good detective's wife.

Getting up, leaving her doubts at the table, she took out the ingredients
for Tony's lunch. She planned on having leftovers in case Zach came home.
She might make something else so she could refill the cooler if he had another
long day ahead.

Come up with something else that would put a smile on his face.

Some kind of dessert that would imply...

She went busily about her tasks, all while thinking of a way to tell him what
she wanted, through food.

This just might be fun.

⌒

Twelve hours in, the detectives didn't have much more to go on than they had
when they'd started.

The owner of the house swore up and down he knew nothing about what
had happened. Zach suspected he was lying and planned on talking to him
again and again if need be. The second victim was pronounced dead at 1:46
p.m. while in surgery, so there was no opportunity to talk to him about what
had gone down.

The families had been notified. It was double the fun this time around and
sucked bog water, but they had no idea as to who would have wanted Darnell

dead. He had taken over his father's business when he died several years ago. He had a solid marriage, was a good father and sole support of his entire family.

They had found his phone on him and were waiting for the records, hoping they'd get a lead. They were waiting for the medical examiner's report, waiting for the people attending the party to be rounded up and brought in for questioning.

It was the waiting game he'd thought it would be, but the mystery behind it made it manageable, made working the puzzle pieces a test of his endurance and acumen.

The interviews lasted well into the night.

When they were finished, he sat with Paul to compare notes.

Darnell had stopped by a friend's house for an hour or so after work. Driven there by the guy who showed up at the crime scene while Tony was working it, one Leroy Howard. He was a mechanic who worked for Darnell. The second victim was another mechanic who was living with Darnell and family since leaving his girlfriend. Had plans of getting his own place next week. They didn't stay long, Darnell wanting to relieve his mother, check on his kids, get some sleep.

Paul was flipping through his notes.

"One of the guests told us about a problem with one of the neighbors. But his beef is with the owner of the party house. Besides, he would have been walking behind the vics, not toward them."

The hospital had called and given them the stats on Kante Diallo. He'd been shot seven times, four to the chest, three to other parts of the torso.

Zach wondered out loud, "It would seem whoever the shooter was, he was after Kante. Too many bullets to suggest otherwise. Darnell might have been an innocent bystander."

Paul looked up from his notes.

"I'm glad I gave you lead on this. You're doing a great job. I'm not used to my trainees getting up to speed so quickly."

"The Marines got me ready for detailing death. Undercover enhanced my insights. I guess this was the next logical step. Don't know why I fought it so hard."

"Hope you've stopped. Fighting it, that is."

"I'm going to like getting the bad guy for this."

"Okay, then. We'll need to talk to Kante's family again. See if they've remembered anything that can help us. He just broke up with his girlfriend. We'll have to interview her, find out if there's something there."

Zach threaded his hands through his hair before scrubbing his eyes. His exhaustion was finally catching up with him.

"I'm going to go back in the morning, see if I can't get the man in the window to talk to me."

It was past midnight. They'd been working this for almost twenty-four hours.

Paul packed up his file, leaned back in his chair, his hands behind his head.

"It might be a good time to grab some sleep. Too late to do anything else. We can pick it all up again later today."

"I'll head over to the house before the guy leaves for work."

"Then meet me back here. I'll get hold of the girlfriend, talk to Kante's parents."

Zach rose from the chair and ambled out, got his coat and cooler and headed to the elevator.

"Night."

"See you later."

⌐

He was pulling his tie off as he walked into the bedroom. He shed his suit and shirt, dumping them on the floor in the corner. No way would he wear it again until it was cleaned. Sliding his boxers off, he crawled into bed, struggling with his control, wanting to pull Lana close. He didn't need to.

Her arm snaked around his waist, her head coming to rest in the crook of his.

"Snuggle only. Glad you're home."

"Me, too. I'm going to be up early..."

"Then so will I. Now sleep."

He adhered to her command, being content to feel the warmth of her body, her embrace.

⌐

Stretching awake, he knew immediately that Lana was already up. The air was cool, her warmth missing. Glancing at the clock, he estimated he'd gotten close to five- hours' sleep. Climbing out from under the covers, he headed to the shower, hoping it would wake him up.

Knotting his tie, he stepped into the kitchen to find a plate of eggs and bacon waiting for him at the table, a cup of steaming coffee sitting next to it.

"I never asked how it went yesterday. How'd the closing go?"

"No problems. I got the key, which was kind of surreal. Thought of you when I went over there. There is a spectacular countertop that would have made a fine make-shift screwing surface."

His fork stopped half-way to his mouth. He gulped hard.

"Maybe I can get there after this case is solved."

"It will be torn out as of next Monday, and there is no way we'll be christening my sparkling new one."

"I'll make a point of finding time before that happens. I want to experience what you think of as a fine screwing surface."

"If you can't, I'm sure I can come up with another example."

"I knew you were...willing to experiment...but you never...initiated anything like this."

"If you remember correctly, while we were married—"

He glanced up from the eggs and interrupted. "Still are. Just saying."

She began again, changing the wording to stress her point.

"While we were living together, you were on the disabled list. Talking to Rissa has gotten my radar up for things like this, and now that you're healthy..."

She gave him a penetrating look.

"I want you to have reasons to come home."

He got up and took her in his arms.

"You are enough of a reason for me to come home."

He kissed her and then said, with a broad smile, "But don't shut down that radar. I like where it takes us."

He snagged up the plate and put it in the sink, shrugged into his suit coat and his winter coat and slipped on his boots.

"I'm going to try to get someone to talk to me, tell me his secrets. Any advice?"

"Sorry. Used up all my ideas on what to pack you. Cooler's there."

"Any surprises?"

"Not like yesterday."

He scooped it up off the counter, gave her a kiss and went out the door.

A half hour later, he was knocking at the door of the 9-1-1 caller. They'd traced the number back to Milton Halliday, this address.

As he stood waiting for the man to open it, he had hopes that he'd walk away with more than he had earlier in the day.

"Yeah."

"Mr. Halliday. Zach Taylor, Boston Homicide. I spoke to you right after the murder."

"I told you all I know."

"Can we please go over it again? Darnell Roy was an upstanding citizen, a father with two kids. We want to do everything we can to find the person responsible for taking him away from them. I'm hoping you might remember something about the shooting."

"I'm not inviting you in. It's not in my best interest."

"Can you come down to the station, meet me someplace else? I have a hunch you hold the key to this. Help me get the bad guys off the street."

Zach studied him as eyes shifted up and down the street.

"Look, by closing the door on me, it will give the impression you refused to talk. Meet me. Anywhere."

"If I come down to the station, I'll be late for work. I can't afford that."

"Where do you work?"

"You can't talk to me there."

He could if pressed but he didn't want to antagonize the man.

"Don't plan on it. What city, town?"

"Medford."

"There's a coffee shop in the square. Can you meet me for a cup?"

"I...might be able to do that. I can only give you a couple of minutes."

"I'll take it."

And he was glad he had.

The man had seen everything. And gave a description in minute detail, as if the scene would be indelibly inked in his brain forever.

He had a suspect.

And he'd been right.

It seemed the perp had been after Kante.

Sitting in Paul's office, Zach gave the sergeant a run-down of what he'd learned.

"The witness saw everything although I'm not sure he'd be willing to testify. He gave me a direction to go in, so I could dig for some evidence to support it."

"How'd it go down?"

"Halliday said he went to the window when he heard shouting out in the front of his house. He had gotten up to go to the bathroom. Says he doesn't usually stay up that late. When he looked out his front window, there was a guy poking Kante, shoving him back. Darnell tried to pull them apart and there was a scuffle. A gun went off, Darnell fell back, tried to get back up, when he was shot again. I'd say first shot got him in the hip, the second shot was to the head, making sure he couldn't get up again. Then the shooter aims at Kante and doesn't stop until the chamber is empty. He said the shooter began to walk down the street as if nothing happened, but he stopped a couple of houses down and dumped the gun in a trash barrel. That's when Halliday called 9-1-1."

"Son of a bitch. If he'd told us this yesterday, we could have retrieved the weapon."

Zach sat forward in the chair, leaning in toward Paul.

"I was pretty pissed, as well, but for the hell of it, I went back to the crime scene. It was garbage pick-up day, and the barrels were lined up and down the street. I began going through them, which I've got to tell you is not one of my favorite parts of the job. Look what I found."

Zach placed an evidence bag on the desk. Inside was a nine-millimeter automatic pistol.

"My very own bloodhound. Good work, Zach. We'll get that right to ballistics, get CSI on the fingerprints. I bet my life he didn't wipe it off completely."

"What did you find out from the girlfriend?"

"Seems her brother wasn't too happy about Kante breaking up with her. She was hysterical, made me think it was more than just grief causing the histrionics."

"Who's the brother?"

Paul passed over the criminal report on the person who'd just become the primary suspect.

Felipe "Ratso" Lopez.

After reading the report, Zach said, "The kid's not even eighteen and he's already been arrested several times for illegal gun possession. He seems to favor nine millimeters. So far, he's had three confiscated. Another reason he looks good as the shooter."

"He certainly does. Kante's family knew of the bad blood between them. Gave me Felipe's name this morning, right before I questioned the girlfriend."

"She might know what her brother did."

"If I was a betting man, I'd give it good odds."

"Can I assume we're waiting for him to be brought in for questioning?"

"I've got patrol out looking for Lopez as we speak. I had good reason before. Now with that gun, I'd say this might be locked up before nightfall."

Zach hefted the bag up.

"I'll get this down to the crime lab. Get an estimate on how long until they have something for us."

"It won't be today."

"Maybe I can move them along."

"Mention your father..."

"Not ever going to play that card. I'm surprised you suggested it."

"I'm never above using what I have to get the job done."

"Then you call him."

"On something important, in a heartbeat. On this case, we've got enough to go on for now. We can wait for confirmation about the gun. We'll see how the interview goes. Take it from there."

Once the gun had been delivered to the CSI lab, Zach sat down at his desk. He pulled the cooler out and slid off the top to see what was inside.

Curiosity had been eating away at him, not hunger, and he picked his way through the layers of wrapped food. A Mason jar at the bottom was filled with what looked like vanilla custard, with whipped cream and tiny pieces of cherries woven through. A rolled vanilla crisp cookie rod was stuck in its center.

A visual picture of something else slammed into his head.

Shit. She'd done it again.

His mouth was watering, but not only for the pudding. He wanted a taste of the real thing and he promised himself no matter how tired he was when he got home, he was pressing his own rod into her soft center.

Unscrewing the cover, he took the plastic spoon from the baggy Lana used as utensil storage and dug in, licking it off as if it were something else.

Dessert was always his go-to place to start. It never failed to satisfy.

CHAPTER THIRTY-ONE

Entering the small lunch place, Lana scanned the interior. She saw Mona wave and she threaded through the tables, taking a seat opposite her.

The wives met once a week to catch up and they'd asked her to join them. She'd agreed, not only because she enjoyed their company, but she intended to build the community her mom had encouraged her to. And Celia hadn't been wrong. It was good to share a meal with women who shared a lifestyle. Alone a lot, holding together their families, worrying every time their husbands left for work, they held each other up, lightened their load. They'd made it easy to form friendships that could last a lifetime.

"Glad you could make it. Rory said you weren't sure you could."

"The meeting with the lawyer went well. I signed the purchase and sale and I'll be closing at the beginning of the month."

"I can't wait. If Piatto was already open, I'd be picking something up for tomorrow night's dinner."

"Andy working?"

"Yeah. He's still dealing with that bridge fiasco. He's in court today."

"That had to be traumatic."

"The trauma came when he could save only two of the four."

Lana knew the case. The Crimes Against Children office got a call about a man with four kids standing near a bridge. By the time Andy got there, the father had thrown all of them over the side. While the father just stood there gaping down as the children flailed, Andy dove in, but he was unable to save all of them. The father was alive and well and in jail, where they all hoped he stayed.

"I don't know how he does it."

"Me, neither. The kids who died were three and six. He was the one who brought the bodies out. He's been building this case for over three months. Checked in daily with their foster care family until he found blood related. He's so low-key he makes it seem easy. I'm the only one who seems to know how it affects him."

Rory had just shown up, dropping her bags to the floor, sliding into one of the available seats.

"That's the curse of detective wives. We feel their pain."

Lana hadn't experienced that part of Zach's life yet. Unless you counted the ambush or the IED explosion. The murders he'd been working on were sad but hadn't caused the same type of psychic damage as Andy faced with that one.

She couldn't count on that being the case every time. The homicide department had been called in for those kids, but it was before Zach joined the unit. Paul had told her about it at dinner one night, saying he was grateful he hadn't been lead.

Zach's time would probably come. She needed to be ready for it.

⌒

After lunch with her friends, Lana went back to her condo and worked from there. She loved knowing that she'd soon have her storefront and that she'd be opening it to actual customers. She had to get her mailers to the printer, her logo stencil and sign on order. Rissa had given her the template and it was perfect.

It was the menu that she had to finalize.

She'd gotten some suggestions from Mona, some from Tony the night he'd come over to eat with her. They were the type of people who would be picking up supper on the fly or just refusing outright to cook.

She'd be opening in March if everything worked as planned. It wasn't an optimum time of year, at least not in New England. There'd be fewer fresh options. Things like beets, squash, kale and root vegetables would be in abundance but she knew there were only so many discerning eaters who craved rutabagas.

Clicking to her file, she opened the page with the partial menu and stared at what was listed.

Lots of soups and one-pot meals. They would reheat better than a steak or roast. It would also cut down on the number of sides she cooked every day. Lunches would consist of supper choices that she'd have available to pack and serve.

Fresh rolls, peasant bread, brioche buns could be paired accordingly.

Pizzas and calzones could be pre-ordered for pick-up. Or she could make some ahead and wrap them in plastic, store them in the cooler.

She was weighing the option of offering a main protein with cooking directions included, to be baked or broiled at home. It might not take away the task of making supper, but it would take away the decision-making process along with the grocery pick-up. One stop and she'd supply what they needed for a gourmet dinner.

Chewing on her pencil, she added that to the one-line mottos she was saving. Undecided about how best to market her storefront, she was constantly brainstorming for catchy phrases that might suit.

Desserts would always be on hand. Chocolate-frosted brownies, her lemon bars and ricotta pie, cannoli, flan, cookies, and puddings.

The only thing Zach would find appealing were the desserts.

Had he found the one she packed yet?

Making it had been fun. The cookie crisps were one of her favorite recipes. She just hoped it hadn't gotten soggy in the pudding center.

She flipped her hair back, the humming sensation that always came with thinking of Zach, was making her weak.

Later.

It would have to come later.

She had to work on the pricing piece, and she'd get nowhere if her mind was on something else entirely.

An hour later, for as much as was still up in the air, she'd gotten a lot accomplished. Noticing the time, she gathered up her things and started dinner.

She heard him coming through the door just past seven. Dinner was in the oven; music was playing low in the background and the candles were lit. She wasn't dressed in saran wrap but as close as she could come without being that obvious. The tee shirt still had a stain from the wine. She was unable to get it out, but tonight, she didn't think it would matter.

"Mm. You look good enough to eat."

"Save some of your appetite then. I didn't cook this meal for nothing."

"Let me change. It's been a very interesting day."

"You can tell me about it over dinner."

He filled her in on the interview that wasn't.

"Lopez asked for an attorney as soon as he stepped into the department, but we had enough circumstantial evidence to arrest him. Once we get the ballistics report back, we'll know whether we have the smoking gun. If so, it's a slam dunk."

"You seem to be closing these cases pretty quickly."

"I don't count working thirty-two out of thirty-six hours closing it quickly. If we spread it out over a normal work week, that's four-eight-hour days."

"I see your point, but I know Paul had several that took months to solve."

"I'm sure I'll get my fair share of them. For now, I'm just going to be grateful we wrapped them within the forty-eight-hour time frame we always set."

"You're sounding more and more like a real homicide detective."

"I am, aren't I? I've got to admit I like it."

She did, too.

⌒

Their days became routine over the next week even though Zach worked long hours. When he came home, he was full of stories, details, questions, wanting to get her perspective.

He had been getting somewhere on the cold case he'd been given access to, and he'd copied some of the materials at work so he could pour over the notes once he got home.

Things were going well, well enough that she was moving in with him, a lot of hope being packed away with some of her belongings. The tenant had moved out and they had the okay to move into the empty condo. Zach had a cleaning crew go in and it was ready for occupancy. Lana decided to begin loading up her trunk to transport boxes of her belongings. She wanted to get a jump on unpacking before his furniture was taken out of storage and delivered on Saturday morning. Running out of room in her car, she'd gotten Zach's car keys while he was dressing, planning on putting the kitchen stuff in his.

Opening it up, she stood frozen. The reality check had arrived.

Staring up at her was his Kevlar vest, his sniper rifle and an M16.

Her knees began to tremble as the chaos in her brain took over.

He had what in her mind, was an arsenal in the back of his car. Did he carry this around with him all the time? Why was he this well armed? Wasn't his nine-millimeter enough?

While her brain was scrambling for answers, his voice reached out to her, asking her what she was doing.

His footsteps echoed on the concrete walkway, and as soon as he arrived at her side, she glared up at him and asked, "What the fuck?"

He snaked his hand out to slam down the trunk before answering her question.

"I told you about the raid last night."

He had. But he'd made it sound so ordinary that she hadn't given it much thought, hadn't analyzed what it meant.

She had proof that it was more than ordinary.

"You told me you had to pick up a suspect, not that you were doing it Rambo style."

"We were out to arrest a suspect who possibly killed someone and who could be armed and dangerous. We go prepared for any eventuality."

She'd watched shows like *The First Forty-Eight*. She knew what a raid looked like. Homicide detectives, patrolmen, members of the various other squads surrounded the house, yelled for the person in question to come out with his or her hands up.

"Who knocked on the door?"

He stared at her for a moment before telling her.

"Kade. It was his case, his suspect."

"You're not protecting me from the truth, are you?"

"Promised not to hold anything back again, didn't I?"

"But it will be you knocking on that door someday, won't it?"

It was her father who had knocked at the door the night he was killed. They were the first target of a crazy person with a gun. The big yellow dot.

"Yes, Lana. It will. Do you want me to hide behind my team, so you feel safer?"

His answer made her heart begin to race.

"Yes, I do... but I also know you can't."

It was back again, the fear so strong she could smell it.

"I wore my vest. There were sixteen of us surrounding that house. The chances of getting killed were non-existent. I had better odds of dying in a car accident on the way home to you."

He was probably right but it didn't make her feel any better.

He took the Kitchen Aid mixer from her hands. She'd forgotten she was holding it. The weight of it hadn't even tipped her meter, so small compared to the reminder of what he did for a living.

"Why don't we put this is your car. I'll empty out my trunk when I get to the station, and we can pack some more boxes when I get home."

She nodded and let him guide her back to the house when he was done.

She stood stock still while he filled his travel mug, put his overcoat on.

He came over and kissed her and walked out the door.

For a few more seconds, she stood dumbstruck, and then her brain surged.

Running out after him, catching him just as he was about to close his door, she bent down and leaned in. After kissing him as if it were the last time she'd see him, she said, "Don't you ever walk away from me before telling me you love me. Not promising me that is a deal breaker."

He got out of the car and wrapped her in his arms, telling her in words and actions how much he did.

She cupped his face with her hands, her eyes taking in his features.

"Keep yourself safe for me."

He smiled a half smile and kissed the tip of her nose.

"I wore the damn vest, didn't I?"

Hugging him one more time, she let him go and watched as he pulled out of his space and out of the parking lot.

Her stomach was still lodged in her throat.

﹏

He couldn't believe she had opened his trunk.

She'd never done that before and he had to make damn sure there was never anything in there that would scare the wits out of her.

He'd gone right home after the arrest. Wanted to get back to her, so he'd opted to empty his car out the next day.

It wasn't unusual to have several weapons on hand during a raid, but he should never have left them exposed. If his car had been stolen during the night, the thief would have hit pay dirt.

He'd store his sniper rifle at the condo. Where, he wasn't sure just yet. Lana hated guns in the house, and if they ever had kids, he knew she'd become even more adamant about it.

He couldn't anticipate the kid thing.

He'd thought for sure, her face so pale in the early-morning dawn, that she was going to cancel their future. When she'd come running out after him, he'd prepared himself for the worst. Waited for her to force him out again.

But when she'd given him the rules of engagement, extracting his promise never to leave without telling her he loved her, his stomach had settled back down where it belonged.

Her plan to move in with him was still on.

To their place.

He hated leaving her with all the work, wished he could help her, but every member of the team was working on a murder, none of them easy. He had a homeless case that Tony was helping him with, on and off duty, Paul was working on a beating death, Kade a shooting, Prem and Leon drive-bys. They were all part of the team, which meant they all played some role in each of the murders. It made for some long days.

He hadn't spent a full night with Lana in almost a week, but he was hoping they could wrap up some of the cases, freeing him up to help with the move on Saturday. Lana had offered to host in their new place as soon as they were in and his friends taken her up on it without a minute to breathe, which meant the moving truck would be pulling out as his friends would be spilling in. He hadn't thought he'd be so busy it would all fall on her shoulders, the packing, the move, the furniture delivery, the dinner prep.

Tonight, he'd throw some of the boxes in his trunk and get them over to the condo before he went back to work in the morning.

He got little enough sleep as it was. Losing another half hour or so wouldn't put a dent in his exhaustion.

He spent the afternoon on his own case, contacting the shelters, talking to other homeless people, working the places where they congregated hoping to hit pay dirt on Jimmie's murder. He'd gotten an ID on the victim but there were no leads as to who might have killed him. He thought he'd have gotten a little further into the investigation by now, would have had time to help Lana. Instead, he'd left her with a dozen empty boxes and a kiss.

The street the bodega was located on, was congested, with traffic and people hanging around in small groups. Zach singled out a man sitting on the curb in front of one of the convenience stores in the area.

"I'm Detective Zach Taylor. How you doing today?"

The man chuckled.

"Zach Taylor? Like the president?"

Zach was surprised. Taylor wasn't one of the best-known of presidents and he rarely got any reaction.

"Yeah, like the president. You've heard of him?"

"Just 'cause I'm homeless doesn't mean I'm not educated. Drugs and booze can hit late in life. Mine hit after the service. Name's Ben Whipple."

Zach extended his hand. "Nice to meet you, Ben Whipple. What branch did you serve with?"

"Army."

"Marines."

"Afghanistan?"

"Five years."

"Shit. And you didn't resort to drinking when it was over?"

"No, too busy with rehab. I left a chunk of my foot back there on the desert floor."

"Sorry to hear that."

Zach pulled out a picture of the homeless man, not one of his best, seeing it showed him all. It was the only one he had.

Zach pushed the photo in Ben's hand. "Do you know this man?"

His facial expression gave Zach hope.

"That's Jimmie. What happened to him?"

"He's dead. Someone killed him."

"Shit. When did it happen?"

"Very late Friday night."

"Shit. I saw him that afternoon. He was hanging out with a guy who beat me up last year. Just for the hell of it. I declined their invitation to drink with them."

"You got a name?"

"Shark. Don't know his real one. That's what he goes by. You'll understand when you see his teeth."

"Where have you been the last couple of days?"

"My mother's birthday. It's the one day a year I go see her."

"She live local?"

"In Clinton. Not too far. My brother comes to pick me up."

"You just get back?"

"This morning. I don't get along with the family that well. They don't like my lifestyle."

"Know where I might find this Shark?"

"He doesn't stay at shelters anymore. He's gotten kicked out of all of them. One of the camps, maybe. His lady friend might be able to help you. She goes by the name Lady. That's a joke 'cause she isn't one. She was with them that afternoon. She usually sleeps at the shelter downtown."

"Thanks, Ben. I appreciate your help."

"No problem, man. Jimmie was a good guy. Little empty in the head but wouldn't hurt a fly. He'd be easy pickings for someone like Shark."

As he went to turn away, Ben asked, "You wouldn't want to buy a man a drink, would you?"

Taking money out of his pants pocket, Zach handed him a ten and said, "Have one for me."

"Thanks, man. And thanks for your service. The country appreciates your sacrifice."

"Right back at you."

For the rest of the afternoon, Zach followed up the leads Ben had given him and had Shark in his sights. Lady had been easy to find, had told her story, which included a description of the murder. She'd given the suspect up, along with his real name. Her being three sheets to the wind might have helped loosen her tongue. He'd spent time, along with one of the patrolmen, searching all known homeless camps in the area again with no success. He'd done all he could. Tony would pick it up from here, and all he could do now was wait.

⌒

Paul was out in the open area when he got back to the station, a slip of paper in his hand.

"I got it."

"What?"

"The prostitute's name."

A street walker was beaten up and left in an alleyway to die. Her pimp had been a person of interest, but he'd had an air-tight alibi. Seemed the man was with his financial adviser. They'd all had a good laugh over that one.

Over the last four days, they'd been out on the streets, knocking on doors, showing Muriel Gable's picture to anyone hanging at intersections, working informants. The police scoured the area for leads and had found a walker who'd been with the victim right before she died.

"That means there's hope we can get at least one of these cases on the closed side of the board."

"Been a rough week, that's for sure."

He glanced up, giving Paul a somber look.

"It could have gone from rough to over this morning."

"What do you mean?"

"Lana found my trunk a bit too metal heavy for her taste."

"Shit. How'd you get out of it?"

"I didn't. She kept it together better than I thought she would."

"Well, that's progress. Let's see if we can make some of our own. The woman's name is Jaira Davis, and she didn't like being roused so early this morning."

"She's here?"

"Just got here before you did. Let's see if we can shake something out of her."

Paul decided to let Jaira wait. He thought it might make her more willing to talk, just to get out of here. No one liked biding their time in a Homicide interview room, and he was sure she wouldn't be the exception.

An hour after she arrived, Paul gave him the nod and they went in, each taking a seat opposite her. She shrank back when they did.

Paul was going over his notes, didn't even bother looking up when he said, "Thanks for coming in Jaira. Can I get you anything? A cup of coffee, a water?"

"Coffee would be good. I might have gotten an hour of sleep before your goons showed up."

Paul got up to get the coffee requested, leaving Zach to keep the interview moving.

"Yeah, well, we haven't had much sleep since Muriel died. Maybe you can help us out, so we can all catch some z's."

"I don't know anything."

"From what we heard, you were her friend, walking with her right before she died. Did you see who she went off with?"

With quivering lips, Jaira pulled her coat tighter around her shoulders. He wasn't sure whether it was from the cold or from tears she was fighting off.

"Why don't you check with Bobby. She would have had to check in with him."

Bobby "Big Guy" Torres was their pimp and from what he heard, he kept a tight leash around each woman in his stable.

"We did. He said he never heard from her. Either she was trying to cut him out of her action, or she didn't have time."

"She wouldn't have dared cut him out. He doesn't like what we do, we pay."

Paul had come back in, with a steaming Styrofoam cup of joe that he placed on the table. Jaira picked it up and kept her hands wrapped around it. He waited for her to look at him again before saying, "Which means she didn't have time. She could have been killed within ten minutes of leaving. Doesn't that bother you?"

Tears filled her eyes, and he could tell they were real.

"Of course, it bothers me. Look, we're all scared right now. We don't like a killer running around the streets any more than you do."

"Then help us. I believe you saw who she left with. I'd bet my life it was her murderer."

"Look, she got a call right before she left. You should have found it when you checked her phone."

Paul interceded. "We didn't find a phone."

"Well, she had one and she took a call. Told me it was trick time. She walked towards the bodega. I got busy, didn't see where she ended up."

Zach leaned in, caught her eyes with his.

"In the alleyway, dead."

Jaira broke down then but couldn't add anything to her story. The only new information they got was that Muriel had a phone. They could request the records and hope they found something worthwhile.

CHAPTER THIRTY-TWO

Lana arrived at the condo with the final load on Saturday morning to find her mother waiting in her car. Celia shut off the motor and got out, joining her on the walk up the steps.

"I thought I'd come and help."

"Thanks. Most of it's done but I can't wait for you to see it."

The furniture had been delivered yesterday, a day ahead of schedule. Zach had made the call to the movers, guilt eating away that he'd put her in such a tough place. He didn't want her to be so stressed she couldn't enjoy their night with friends. She was relieved she'd had the breather; happy everything would be in place for their first dinner party.

She hefted a lone box out of the trunk and her mother was there to close it for her. Carrying it up to the side door, she used her shiny new key and let them in. She dumped the box on the floor, pushed her hair off her face and let out a sigh, while she pushed the container into the room with her foot.

"Last one. I thought I'd never see it. It's been tough trying to get everything done between the move, the store front, my own shit, his. Is this my life from now on?"

"I'm not going to lie. Yes."

She took off her coat and flung it over the counter.

"I'm not sure I like being a rock. I wish I'd had time to expand the role as I went along, be a pebble, grow to rock over time."

"That might have happened if you'd stayed with your husband. You'd have two years under your belt."

"Yeah, well. I can't look back now."

The sun felt good as it streamed through the slider, illuminating the kitchen.

She watched as her mother scanned the space.

"This is nice, Lana."

Celia was gliding her hand over the counter tops, taking in the pots of herbs, the pictures hung, the cookbook stand.

"I knew you'd put this room together first. It's beautiful."

"I took all my essentials, then picked up some new pots and pans for Tony just in case he gets the urge to cook for himself."

She began to laugh at that.

"Like he's ever going to stop mooching meals."

"Like I'd ever put my foot down."

"It was nice of you to give Tony the keys to your place."

Lana was letting her brother take over her condo, paying her rent in the amount of the mortgage. He was thrilled with the arrangement. It would get him out of his rental, the one he shared with several other policemen, all of whom he complained were slobs.

He'd told her it was time for him to grow up and take some responsibility for himself.

"It helped me out. I didn't have to deal with putting it on the market."

She had enough going on. The renovation at Piatto had begun and she was spending most of her time inspecting the progress, putting everything in place for her opening.

She'd been getting calls, emails, and hits on her website that made the upcoming investment look promising.

⌒

Her mother was now peeking out the slider to see what the view was like.

"While I was picking up the pots and pans, I had to pick up some things to compensate for what was missing. What Zach has in kitchen gadgets wouldn't fill a drawer."

Celia was opening one after the other, then took to peeking in the cabinets.

"You've already got some wine chilling. Hopefully the men will wrap up the cases soon and you can celebrate."

"Zach hasn't even been here yet since the furniture was delivered. I hope he likes what I've done. He dropped some boxes off yesterday morning and hasn't been back since."

Zach was assigned lead of their most recent case, the beating death of a homeless person. This one was a real "who-dun-it" and the mystery was taking all his logical thinking skills to unravel it. He seemed to be thriving, but he hadn't been home much.

The curse of a detective's wife.

And she had become his wife in every sense of the word.

The worry, she guessed, was just a natural part of it.

"Can I look around?"

"Sure, but the only other room that's in some semblance of order is our bedroom."

Celia was heading in that direction.

"It's so light and open. I can see you here."

"Thanks, I think. If you couldn't, I'd be in trouble."

She dumped the box she'd brought with her into the second bedroom where she was stashing any un-necessary items, while her mother poked her head into the master.

"You already hung up the picture."

"First thing. Zach likes it as much as I do, and I'd miss it if it wasn't there."

"Your sister will be pleased. She offered to come but she thought she'd be more of a hindrance than a help."

"There's really not much left to do right now. The only thing left that I needed help with was the clothes. Johnny and Luca picked them up earlier and should be here soon. I think they were going to stop for coffee. They were offended I didn't have any to offer them."

"They're good boys. They'll get over it."

Lana had to smile at the description. They were far from boys, had grown into men who always did the right thing. That was something about her family. It not only had lots of buds blooming on the various branches, but their tree had good, strong roots. Rissa had chosen wisely and so had she. The men they'd brought in fit the mold.

She walked over and gave her mother a kiss on the cheek.

"What was that for?"

"For what you gave us, how you brought us up."

"You brought yourself up. I was just a guiding hand. Can't take credit for who you were as people. That was in you at birth. I was lucky."

Lana studied her expression. Could it really be that easy? She doubted it. Her mother had been in their lives as much as she could, given the time she had to spend supporting them, but she'd always allowed them to express themselves and never coerced anything. She'd given them free rein to be themselves. Something she was just beginning to learn was important.

After Celia inspected every room, she came out and walked right towards the coffee maker and got a pot brewing.

The doorbell rang letting her know her clothes were here.

Johnny stumbled across the threshold, hangars of clothes thrown over his arm.

"Jeez, Louise. I didn't know you had so much. You can't possibly wear everything we brought."

"Um, your wife is the queen of closets. I have nothing compared to her."

"You're right. Her things are all over the house."

She guided him and Luca, who was more long-suffering than her brother, to the walk-in and began taking things from their arms and placing the hangers on the rods. Zach's went on the right; hers were on the left.

"Just one more batch. Then we expect some refreshments. No coffee this morning was unacceptable."

The men finished up and stuck around for coffee and leftover cake. She'd made one yesterday for Zach's travel cooler and packed up it up along with other refrigerated articles that she stuffed right into the gleaming stainless steel one here. It was the last one she'd make at her own place. This one had become theirs.

Before they left, Johnny tried to extract a promise for her to host one of their Sunday meals.

"We'll give you some time to get settled but then we're coming over."

She looked at him as if he had three heads.

"We can't possibly all fit here. You two are the only ones who can afford the mansions. And it's not my fault that our family is so big."

"Not yet but I hope you'll be adding to it someday soon."

"Let me get the store-front up and running first, please. My plates in the air are beginning to teeter as it is."

She loved her mother and siblings, but she also loved her alone time, and when they finally left, and she had the place to herself again, she breathed in the peace.

As she puttered around, snipping some fresh basil and thyme, the sun gleaming off the snow through the bay window, Lana's heart swelled at how good she felt.

Her friends would soon be filling the space, which meant she had a lot of work ahead of her if it was going to be ready for company. When she'd offered to host, Andy had asked her if she knew how to cook Portuguese food. He hadn't had anything traditional since his grandmother died several years ago, so she had planned a dinner around his request. She'd made the caldo verde soup yesterday, so she didn't overwhelm herself. It was simple enough with just potatoes, onions and kale, but it was one less thing to fuss over with all the other things she had on her to-do list.

The cod fritters were ready for frying, the rice was ready to steam, the wine was a nice dry white that the clerk at the store had suggested. Zach was the wine aficionado in the family, but he was too busy for the task. The vegetables in the soup would have to suffice for something green and healthy.

Glancing up at the clock, she untied the strings of her apron and went into their bedroom.

She stood there for a moment taking it in.

The bed was Zach's, purchased for the condo after he moved out of her place, and they'd never slept in it together before. He'd stored it with some of his other furnishings and the moving truck had picked it up after the stop at her place. She'd spent time fantasizing about how they could christen it, to make the event more memorable, but nothing had come of it with all the murders happening lately. She'd spent the first night alone in it. It was a king-size mattress, bigger than what she was used to, and it felt empty without him in it.

"Suck it up, Lana. This is your life."

If she had to sleep alone again tonight, at least she'd be swaddled in blankets. The new comforter she'd bought was soft and warm. The christening would just have to wait until Zach wasn't too tired.

She moved to the closet and stepped inside.

Pushing the hangers around, she picked out something to wear and decided to take a long bath in the soaking tub. She'd at least christen that. She put away all thoughts of some other woman getting to enjoy it. It was hers and so was the man who came with it.

As she lay there, the soap bubbles soothing a spirit that still worried far too much, she began to outline a movie night she could put into play when this case was over. Or the one after that.

Princess Bride.

It was one of her favorites. She could serve roasted pig, Fezzik's pan-fried potatoes, pea risotto, chocolate truffles. Okay, he might not touch the risotto, but she had to offer something green just for the fun of it.

Pretty Woman.

With...After a moment's pause, she scratched that. He'd never do snails, not even mussels or clams. Shaking her head, a soft smile on her face, she said, "I am so wasted on you, Zach."

She lifted the sponge and squeezed the water over herself, still thinking of options.

The Quiet Man.

John Wayne might make the movie a little more palatable. She could do a rendition of an Irish cottage pie, meat and carrots with a flaky crust, and a side of mashed potatoes.

From Here to Eternity.

A war film, that took place in Hawaii. It was famous for the scene where Burt and Deborah devoured each other on the beach. Pineapple was a must, maybe skewered as kabobs with chicken, island-style fried rice with chunks of ham and scallions, her something green just to annoy, and a parfait with a brownie base. Or rum cake.

An Affair to Remember, Titanic, Ghost, A Walk to Remember, ... All great but came a little too close to what she feared.

Eternal Sunshine of the Spotless Mind.

Pulling herself up and out of the bath, she opened the drain and wrapped a towel around herself coming up with a dozen more possibilities. She couldn't wait to test them.

⌐

When the bell rang, she was dressed and ready and she ran to answer it, the thin silver bracelet jangling on her wrist. She'd stopped wearing trinkets after her father died. It seemed so trivial to waste her time primping. But this one Zach had sent while he was overseas, and she wore it at every opportunity. She wished he'd been able to get away. It seemed kind of strange entertaining his friends, in his condo, without his presence. After greeting the couples as they arrived, all within ten minutes of each other, she showed them around, and led them back to the family room, where they all sat down. The collection of furniture was a combination of hers and Zach's and it fit nicely in the space.

As they were munching the appetizers, she heard the key in the lock and jumped up. As he walked through the door, she was there to greet him. He'd texted earlier saying he might have time to drop in, and it seemed he'd been successful.

"I'm glad you could make it."

"I got lucky. I might be called out if they find my suspect, but until then, I'm yours."

She leaned in, kissed his cheek and whispered, "You will always be mine. And don't forget it."

He couldn't return the sentiment. Andy had gotten up, shook Zach's hand and announced, "This is a great place. Nice interim that fits us all. And the food? Way better than pizza and beer."

"Interim? We just moved in, and you already have us moving out?"

"You'll need bigger once the kids start coming. Trust me. They have a way of taking over every available inch of space. You won't have room to breathe in here once that happens."

She placed her hand in the crook of Zach's arm, and they walked back towards the assembled group who were waiting for them.

"We're going to take our time with that, Andy. Let me get my bearings first, will you?"

"You, my dear, are a shining star tonight. I'll let you get away with…murder."

"I bet you say that to all the cooks who make the kind of food you ask for."

"The shrimp are to die for. I need the recipe."

"You gave me a couple of dishes you wanted; the rest I had to ad lib."

"You do it well."

He went back in for another one of the shrimp she'd made. She'd pulled the recipe up from a Portuguese food site and followed the directions. Almost. There wasn't anything she made that she didn't make small adjustments to. They had come out well.

Her head snapped in Zach's direction.

"Um, I don't have anything to feed you. I doubt you'll even be willing to taste anything on the menu."

"What do you mean?"

"Andy asked for soup...with kale. Fish fritters. The only thing you might eat is the sweet rice."

He brushed his lips over hers.

"You made Andy happy tonight by replicating one of his grandmother's meals. I certainly didn't expect you to make another one for me. I've put enough on your shoulders over the last couple of days."

He was examining the condo and she held her breath, hoping he liked what she'd done.

"It feels like a home. I missed that. Missed you. It looks great."

"Thanks. If you want to change it up, we can when we have some time. But don't go into the second bedroom. You won't get two feet in. That's where all your help is needed."

"I hope to wrap this one up soon. Then maybe I can get a day off."

"It'll be nice to have you home."

"It'll be nice to be home."

He had just enough time to sit and enjoy the camaraderie before supper was served. Then Tony called him. He'd found Shark and he was at the station. Rather than let him wait and stew, he couldn't wait to interview him. He'd gotten another tip from another source, and if he could get Shark to confess, he could put this to bed and maybe find some time for Lana.

Over the next couple of days, he solved his case and helped the team wrap up a few of the other murders. The couple that still needed resolution weren't his, so he didn't have to do much in terms of detail work. And by the grace of a higher source, they didn't get another call for almost a week.

It was a call that had nothing to do with work but threatened to destroy the cocoon they'd been living in.

CHAPTER THIRTY-THREE

As they were just about to sit down for their planned movie night, Zach's cell phone rang. They looked at each other before he answered. Lana wondered if death had come to call, altering their plans for the night. She never knew what would happen from moment to moment, but she was adapting better than she'd thought she could.

She took her apron off and was walking towards the family room when she heard a sound she'd never heard before.

Zach's voice had cracked, the deep, resonant baritone a ragged moan. She ran to where he stood, his face etched in pain, raw emotion filling his eyes.

In panic mode, she asked, "What?"

He turned his back on her, pushing his hand through his hair.

"Are you sure?"

He turned around so he was facing her.

"No, we'll be right there."

He had gone pale, his eyes glassy, as if in shock.

"Zach. What is it?"

He stared at her, through her, and didn't say a word.

"Zach, you're scaring me."

He choked out, "Andy's dead."

She felt herself recoil, away from him, away from the danger that seemed to surround him.

"What?"

He glanced at her now, tears in his eyes.

"Motorcycle accident. Someone hit him from behind. He lost control and hit a tree. Died instantly. Mona had to go to the morgue and ID him. Ed went with her. Julian and Rory are with the kids. I told him we'd get right over there."

He came to where she stood, went to put his arms around her. He needed a soft spot to land, but her heart couldn't accommodate more than her own pain, and she all but pushed him away.

"I can't, Zach. It's too close. It hit too close."

In a lifeless tone, he asked, "What do you mean you can't?"

"I can't do this."

She began to pace, her hands around her stomach, her moves jerky. "This can't be happening." She'd recently spent the night in Andy's company, cooked for him, and now...

His voice cut through her, with the same lethal precision as her butcher knife.

"It has happened, Lana. Andy is dead. Mona needs her friends right now."

"I don't know what I'd say. I can't help her right now."

"So, having lunch with them every week was building your own support group? You didn't think it might need to be reciprocated? I didn't think you were this cold and selfish."

Pushed to the limits of her restraint, she yelled, "Don't you dare call me that. You have no idea what I'm feeling right now."

His eyes became pinpricks of ice, his face creased in horror.

"No. I don't. I do know how I'm feeling right now, though. One of my best friends has died. Mona's husband is gone, but you can't get beyond your own feelings to see that."

He ground the heels of his hands into his eyes.

"You're still the twelve-year-old girl who lost her father. You haven't matured beyond that. Fuck. You almost had me fooled."

"Zach, I—"

"Your heart stopped growing, Lana. You sealed it up and threw away the key. I haven't been able to open it, no matter what I do. And I'm tired of trying."

He got his coat on and turned to leave.

She ran towards him, but the anger chiseled on his face stopped her.

"Where are you going?"

"To be with my friends. To be somewhere where I can find comfort. It seems my wife is incapable of offering it to me. She's too busy taking care of herself."

He hesitated before turning back to face her.

"I'm giving myself time to grieve him, for Andy. Then...then I'm going to file for divorce. I can't do this anymore. I can't keep walking away like this. It hurts too fucking much."

She jumped when the door slammed behind him.

And stood staring at it.

Her body was frozen in terror, her heart beating so rapidly she thought it would explode inside her chest. Seconds ticked by before she broke down. She cried, for Andy, for Mona, for their kids, for Zach, but mostly, she cried because she'd just shot another bullet, all but killing the best thing that had ever happened to her.

She gave in to the ravaged emotions, grieving for the sweet man who'd died. Out of all of them, he...didn't deserve this.

It took an hour to pull herself together.

The tears had cleansed her. The thought of Zach not ever coming home galvanized her. Busying herself in the kitchen, she hurried to prepare sustenance for the friendships she'd formed. She hoped it was enough to keep them alive, because Zach was right. Other people were feeling the impact of this death far more deeply than she was. She loved Andy but far less than his wife and children, less than his best friends. She had to get out of her own way and offer what she could, no matter how little.

She needed to become that soft place Zach could fall into to find comfort and love, regardless of what she was feeling.

She had no doubt he'd be there for her.

Always had been.

It was time for her to have his back.

She was willing to sell her soul in payment, but he hadn't asked for that, only for her to open her heart. It seemed so little to expect from his wife.

After packaging the sandwiches, salads, brownies into one of her bins, she got on her coat and started for her car.

She spun around and went into her room with hurried footsteps to retrieve something before leaving.

All the way over to Rory's, she practiced what she'd say, trying to conjure up the words that had mattered when her father died, Jeanne's words of solace. Ringing the doorbell, tears gathered as she waited to face the past with a new set of eyes.

As soon as Rory was facing her, she dropped the container and stepped forward to hug her, holding on, not needing to say anything. The comfort they gave and received said it all.

Through her tears she said, "I thought you might need some food."

Mona came over to where they stood, her eyes red and puffy. She gave her a half-smile, remembering. "Andy told me it was your way of saying you love someone. Thank you. For the food. For coming. For the love."

They fell together in an embrace, her shoulders much broader than she'd thought as Mona used them to help carry her burden.

Rory took the food and headed toward the kitchen, the other two women following in her stead. "Zach told us you weren't coming over."

A sob burned her throat, but she refused to give into it.

"I wasn't. I'm so sorry. I..."

Mona squeezed her hand.

"You're here. I know what that took. It means more."

Lana looked around, listened for the sound of his voice, the emptiness inside growing when she didn't hear it.

"Is he here?"

Rory tucked her arm in hers, led her toward the family room, where Chris was sitting with one of the kids. "They guys went to a bar. I think they are going to get rip-roaring drunk. Julian called out. So, did Ed. I know Zach spoke to Paul and he's covering for him."

She needed to talk to him, but she wasn't going to let her screw-up take precedence over Mona's grief. She sat, and they talked in muted tones, as family members showed up, funeral services were discussed, stories about Andy filling the empty spaces. The people in the house weren't the only ones who would mourn. The community had lost one of their champions. He would be missed on so many levels.

Lana spent time with the kids, knowing what they were going through, wanting to offer the kind of support she knew they needed. But they were much younger than when she'd suffered that trauma, probably too young to be so adversely affected.

They'd know he was gone, but there wouldn't be the feelings of abandonment that she'd felt for so long.

Ironic.

She suffered for years over an imagined betrayal and turned around and consciously betrayed her husband and their vows.

Could he forgive her one more time?

Or had she come to it too late?

All she could do was be present, let him know she'd be there. And hope that's where he wanted her to be.

She didn't get home until after midnight, sat and waited, praying that Zach would come home. That Rory would have told him she'd gone over to comfort Mona. That she wasn't as selfish as he thought.

She lay on the couch, drifted in and out of sleep, but every time she awoke, she felt his absence.

Her grief for Andy was a shadow of what she'd felt at the demise of her marriage.

She'd repeated the past, her immaturity driving another wedge between them.

She rubbed the ring on her finger.

All that it meant conjuring up her mistakes, her missteps.

One thing she knew for sure. She wasn't going to let it go as easily as she had before.

She reached for her phone and called Rory to see if there was anything she could do. It wasn't even six in the morning yet, but she had to know...

"Hi."

"How are you?"

"Tired, spent, out of it. I only got a couple hours of sleep. Julian came in close to dawn and passed out as soon as he hit the bed."

"Was...was Zach with him?"

There was a pause before Rory admitted, "No, honey. He wasn't. Didn't he go home?"

For as tightly as she'd held it in last night at Mona's, it now came spilling out.

"No. He said...after he got the call and I... He said he was leaving, that he was filing..."

She couldn't control the sob that erupted, letting the sentence trail off.

"Oh, Lana. He's just upset. They all were. I'm sure he didn't mean it."

She wiped her nose with a sodden tissue and gagged out, "I think he did and I...I...don't blame him."

Why couldn't she have put aside her own fears and grief to help him deal with his?

"Did you try calling him?"

Rory sounded sympathetic, her voice low and patient, and Lana didn't understand why. Rory would never have done this to Julian.

"Not yet. I'm afraid that he won't answer my calls or any text I send."

"If he doesn't, at least he'll know you're thinking about him."

"I haven't been able to think about anything else. He's hurting and I...want to...be there for him."

"If I find out where he is, I'll let you know."

"If you need me for anything, just call. Oh, and let Mona know my mother is willing to cater the mercy meal. Wherever Mona wants it. No charge."

"I will, honey. I'll be in touch."

She placed her cell in her lap, studying it, wishing it would ring, wishing Zach would call. Knowing this was on her, not wanting to repeat another one of her mistakes, she pulled his number up and hit call. When she got his voice mail, she left her message.

"Please, Zach. Call me. I need to talk to you."

⌒

By mid-morning, she knew where he was, and it told her how much he wanted to stay away from her. He'd shown up on his mother's doorstep, hung over and grieving. Jeanne had taken him right in.

She'd gotten reamed out by her mother when Celia called to ask what the hell had happened. There was no sympathy given from that quarter.

"Lana, you are so wasted on that man. Get the hell out of his life once and for all, will you?"

"Ma, I can't."

"Then you're being selfish again. This is not about you anymore."

"I know that. I don't want it to be. I'll never let it be that way again."

"I've heard this song before. Admit you can't do it. No one will be angry with you if you're just honest."

"I don't want to live my life without him in it."

"Well, it looks like you've killed whatever he felt for you. Let it go. Let him go."

With that, her mother hung up on her.

She'd hit rock bottom.

But there was only one place to go from there.

Up.

After showering and dressing, she set out for the enemy's, knowing there'd be a minefield of accusations and insults, but she was willing to face every one of them if it got her what she wanted.

She rang the bell at the Taylors' and waited until Jeanne answered the door.

The tone was crisp and to the point.

"He doesn't want to see you."

Jeanne began to close the door in her face, but Lana put up a hand to stop it.

"Please, Jeanne. I have to talk to him."

"Lana, how many more times are you going to try and reel him in only to cut the line on him?"

She wanted to argue but couldn't. Instead, she begged, "Jeanne, I just needed some time. It was too sudden."

"You're not cut out for this life, Lana. Admit it and let my son move on."

And then he was there, standing just behind his mother, and her pulse quickened at the sight of him. He looked worse for wear, his sweats old, his tee shirt worn. His eyes were blood-shot, his stubble evident. Her body shivered. There was a flat, cold look in his eyes. Was her mother, right? Had she killed what he'd felt? If she had, she didn't know how she'd live with herself.

"Mom, I'll talk to her. Can you give us a minute? I don't think it'll take longer than that."

Jeanne glared at him but backed up and disappeared down the hallway.

"We can go in there."

He nodded to the library, which was just to the right of the vestibule, and she went in ahead of him, his civility scaring her. He went to stand in front of the window, the one that looked onto the street, his back to her. Would he turn his back on her apology?

Why should he even believe that she meant it this time?

"What do you want to say, Lana? Anything that hasn't been said before?"

He didn't sound like her Zach. There was nothing in his voice that indicated feeling.

There was no flash of a smile, no gleam in his eye. No energy that filled a room.

Ashamed of herself, she didn't know how to begin.

"You were right. You were right on almost every point. I was being selfish. I climbed right back into my shell and stuck my head in."

The exhale of a sob seemed to have no effect.

"But I'm not cold, Zach. I can't love you this much and be cold. I told you you were going to have to have patience with me. I thought I was gaining on it, but this one... This one came out of the blue. This one came from nowhere and everywhere and it hit too close."

He tilted his head up, as if he were looking heavenward, as if he were waiting for her to be done with this so he could be someplace else.

Had she already lost him?

She stepped forward until she was behind him and laid her head against his back. So solid and steady, so sure of everything. She wanted to put her arms around him and never let go, but she was afraid of what he'd do.

"They usually do come out of the blue, punch you in the gut." The low vibration in his voice chilled her soul. His words didn't comfort.

"I needed some time—"

He interrupted her; his irritation evident.

"I haven't gotten much sleep and there's a lot I've got to do. Could you get to the point, please?"

That's what she'd been attempting to do. Get to the point, tell him she loved him.

But what had her love given him? Nothing but betrayal and pain. Maybe she was just being selfish again. Wanting, needing him to forgive her.

Maybe she owed him something different. She closed her eyes, deep sorrow settling in her heart. She knew what she had to do, knew the pain would be never-ending. After taking a deep breath, trying to keep her voice from breaking, she forced herself to go through with it.

"I came over to apologize, to ask, no, beg for another chance but that's not fair to you. You've given everything you are to me, and I couldn't even push through my own feelings to—You deserve better...than me. File your papers—"

Her lips were quivering, the tears ready to flow and she wanted to do that in private.

"—and I'll sign them."

She had turned to go, then stopped.

"You were right about something else. I was glad I went to see Mona. I didn't need the right words. It's more about a touch, a shared tear, a hug. Knowing that we're there for each other."

When she reached the doorway, her escape imminent, she whispered, "Keep yourself safe for me."

Before she could take a step across the threshold, she heard him call out, "Lana."

It was ragged and scarred.

When she turned back, looked up at him, he was walking toward her, came to a stop not a foot away.

His face held a tortured look. His eyes were deeply smudged with sadness.

"I needed you last night. I was back there, in the desert, picking up friends who'd died in a siege, mourning those losses as much as I was mourning Andy. It all came back in a rush of anger and grief. I didn't know what to do with it."

The weight of his admission all but crushed her. She reached out a trembling hand, placed it on his cheek, her love for him surging past any residual fear that lurked.

"I'm so sorry I wasn't there..."

He pressed his cheek into her palm.

"You've been there for me more times than I can count. Willing to listen, helping me through rehab, getting me through my nightmares, accepting I wasn't whole. It was me who screwed up, not telling you my plans, going undercover to escape the pain of your leaving when I should have done everything in my power to get you back. Maybe even quit the force if I had to. My past came rushing back last night, just like yours did. I let you down as well. I'm sorry I wasn't there for you."

She felt the tears running down her cheeks, the regret so deep it could bury her.

"You've always been there for me. And you can't quit the force. It's who you are. If I love you, I have to accept that."

She took his face in her hands, looked deeply in those blue eyes.

"And I do love you, Zach. So much. I can't stand that I hurt you. I've lived without you before and I don't...can't do it again."

He thumbed away some of the moisture from her face.

"I said that didn't I. Dumb-ass thing to say. You're my life. You're the reason I'm still alive. I should never have said that, not if I didn't mean it."

Without warning, he wrapped her in his arms, his embrace almost crushing her.

"I wanted to come home to you, wanted you to hold me...wanted to lose myself in you, forget for a minute what had happened. I didn't know if you'd take me in and I couldn't risk—"

"I waited all night for you. I called you at least a dozen times."

He loosened his grip on her, his hands taking her by the shoulders.

"You called me?"

"Yes, your voice mail is full. You never returned my calls."

"My phone died sometime in the middle of the night. The charger's at...home. I didn't know."

He kissed her, holding her face close to his.

"What did you want to say?"

"That I was sorry. That I was home waiting... I let you go too easily before and regretted it. I don't ever want to live without you again."

Her lips brushed against his, her heart filling with hope.

"I love you, Zach. I love you with everything in me. I can't promise I won't let you down again, but I'll never do it on purpose."

He gave her an upside-down smile.

"Sort of like me getting into trouble out on the streets."

She gave him a half-hearted smile in return.

"Yeah, something like that."

He enfolded her in his arms again, whispered in her ear, "You keep me safe. You make my life sane...I love you, too Lana."

"I couldn't survive if you leave again." Giving him a tremulous smile, she half joked, "I wouldn't have the body parts for all the tattoos it would take to fill a lifetime."

He slid his hands down her shoulders and arms, until he was holding both her hands in his. His thumb brushed her finger, lifted it up to see his ring there, the one he'd given her the day they got married. When she'd put it on after Andy died, she'd sworn to herself she would never take it off again.

Even if he had filed those divorce papers. He would always be her husband.

After placing a kiss on it, he asked, "What time is it?"

"I...I don't know. Maybe eleven, eleven thirty."

"Come on."

He took her hand, called out to his mother that he was going home, and tucked her into the passenger side of her car.

She couldn't miss Jeanne in the doorway, her face a scowl. There were a lot of fences to mend there, but she would do it if it took her whole life.

He was squealing out of the driveway when he said, "I took a cab home from the bar. My car's at Julian's. We'll pick it up later."

He was going a little too fast for the neighborhood and she was beginning to get concerned.

"Where are we going?"

"To the bank. I need to get there before it closes."

"Why?"

"I have a safety deposit box there."

"Can't it wait until Monday?"

"No."

Without another word, he drove until he got to the bank parking lot, jumped out of the car and hurried into the building, leaving her sitting there without a clue.

As she waited for him to return, she let the enormity of what had happened this morning soak into her bones.

She wished she could sink into the happiness and let it buoy her, but the sadness at Andy's death wouldn't let it expand, only contract.

He broke into her thoughts when he returned to the car, dropping a leather pouch into her lap.

"Can you open that up, please?"

She did as he asked, her curiosity now getting the better of her.

"What's in here?"

"My great-grandfather's watch and my grandfather's medal. And my wedding ring. Can you fish it out?'

While she was digging for the thin gold band, he was unclasping the chain with the bullet hanging from it.

He took the ring from her fingers, and slid it on, then placed the chain carefully in the pouch.

"Why are you taking it off?"

"I don't need to wear it anymore."

"Why is it one or the other?"

"The ring connected me to you. Once that was gone, I needed a connection to something else, something bigger than me. It fit the bill."

"I used to put mine on. Cry. Take it back off. I'm never taking it off again. Can we go home now? You said something about losing yourself in me and I need to be filled with your love."

He took hold of her hand and didn't let go until they were home and in bed, and she was lost in the sweet urgency of his kiss.

EPILOGUE

Life settled back into routine after those hard days of the wake and funeral.

They had lost themselves in each other, softening the edge of their grief, and were bound more securely than ever before.

Sitting in the pew with Rory and Chris, holding hands, crying together over one of the sweetest souls she'd ever meet had solidified her friendships. The church had been filled with blue, a thin blue line, a tradition that gave her goose bumps.

Solemn, heart-rendering, comforting.

As the casket rolled by, Zach, taking up a place next to it, had looked over at her, his love shining in his eyes, telling her how much he needed her.

It was good to know.

Felt more in balance.

She had been there for him, becoming the rock her mother talked about.

And they had walked away from the grave site holding hands, attended the mercy meal and found comfort in each other's arms that night.

And life moved on, at least for them.

For Mona and her children, it would take time. She knew that for a fact.

She'd taken a minute to sit with them at the house, gauge what they were feeling, offering words that might have made her feel better after her father died.

⌒

Thirty-six hours after they laid Andy to rest, her phone rang at 1:42 a.m.

She thought for a second that it was Zach's, that he was being called into work but when he nudged her, the fog lifted, and she reached over to grab it.

"Yeah?" She listened for a second and then bolted up and added, "We'll be right there."

He sat up, a look of concern on his face. She dropped the phone back down, turned to place a quick kiss on those irresistible lips, a smile on her face.

"Gabriella is finally ready to join us. Come on, we've got to get to the hospital. I haven't missed one birth yet and I'm not missing hers."

"Is this going to be a family affair?"

"Oh, yeah. The whole Scalera bunch. We like the kids knowing we're all there for each of them from the first second they take a breath."

They were dressed and at the hospital in record time, Johnny and Tish already there, Tony on his way after getting the okay to leave his shift, Dennis and Delaney waiting for Delaney's mom to get there to watch their kids. Celia and Paul were already pacing the waiting room that was about to be taken over.

A couple of hours later, Luca came out, a broad smile on his face.

"She's here."

The whole family gathered round him for slaps on the back, high fives and lots of hugs. Taking turns, they all went into the birthing area to meet the newest member.

When her turn came, she tiptoed in, Zach on her heels. Rissa was sitting there, almost glowing, Gabby already wrapped up, looking snug and warm.

Her sister, knowing her better than most, said, "Come on, Lana. She's not going to bite you. At least not yet."

Lana crept over to the bed, and she looked her fill. So small, so vulnerable. Zach asked, "Can I hold her?"

"Of course. She needs to get to know the men who'll be taking care of her."

Every male member of the Scalera clan had dedicated his life to protect and defend all the children in the family, not only his own.

Lana watched as Zach handled the new infant, his gentle movements stirring something in her heart. He needed to have one of these for himself, and...maybe she did, too. As she studied her husband, she felt a warm feeling rush through her, a feeling of peace settling deep inside. Here was a new person to love after the loss they'd suffered recently. Death and birth. All part of the rhythm of life. If anything happened to him, or to her, children would buffer them, keep them going, keep them anchored to each other. Her mother had been right.

"Can I hold her?"

They all looked surprised, which didn't surprise her. She wasn't the one who opened her heart easily, wasn't drawn to the innocence of the young. Had she been so scarred that she couldn't embrace this part of herself, mother, nurturer?

When Zach handed her over, she felt an overpowering sensation. Had she finally put the remnants of the past away? As if in answer, love came pouring out and into her at the same time. Had Zach given her this gift with his never-ending supply of patience and forgiveness?

She looked up at the three faces watching her, an expectancy in the air, mirroring her own. She wanted to love and love deeply again. She wanted to come out of her shell, wanted to embrace all that life had to offer, the good and the bad.

Smiling, she kissed her niece and said, "I think I'm ready."

Acknowledgments

I'd like to thank my editor, Amy from Blue Otter Editing, for her expertise. She has become a valued partner in my writing life, and I don't know what I'd do without her.

Jaycee DeLorenzo form Sweet 'N Spicy Designs has done it again. I want to thank her for her patience working with me on my covers.

I'd also like to thank Joan Frantschuk, from Woven Red, who not only formats my work for eBook and print but who has become a valued resource.

And of course, I'd like to say thanks to my family. Jeff, Kait, Juan, Justin, Kathryn, Jaiden, Jakob, Jon-Christopher, Dominic and Liam. They surround me with the kind of love necessary for creating novels that touch the heart.

And to all who read my books, I thank you for taking time out of your life, to journey with me.

About Faith

Faith O'Shea is a contemporary women's literature writer who loves writing about strong women and the friendships they build. She throws in a little magic, a little romance, and develops unique personalities, and what you get are characters who come alive on the page. She's found that strong women need more than a happily ever after.

Faith lives in a small town in Massachusetts with her husband Jeff, dogs Cooper and Molly, and Isis, the Egyptian feline queen. Her children live close and are a big part of her life. In her spare time, she reads, walks Coop, dabbles in all kinds of cooking, and takes time to play with her grandchildren.

You can visit her on Facebook and Twitter or find her through her website at www.faithoshea.com.

Coming Home to You

Tansy McPhail's life has never been easy and the road she's traveled has been filled with potholes. She might be dauntless, like her favorite character, but she's used up all her grit and determination looking for a home. What she could use right now is some luck or a little bit of magic.

Tony Scalera has come a long way. His nightmares are behind him, he's taken over his sister's condo, has his policeman's badge, and a family who loves him, but he's resistant to anything that smacks of relationship. He has no intention of leaving behind a widow and kids like his father did, who found death waiting behind a closed door.

But when he meets Tansy, the door opens a crack, and he's hard pressed to shut her out. He offers her a warm place to stay, food to fill her soul, and that little bit of magic she's been looking for. Will his returning nightmares crush her dreams, or will they both find out that home is where the heart is?

CHAPTER ONE

Patrolman Tony Scalera had been to the soup kitchens, the park, the T-stations, checked provisional shelters, alleyways, and doorways over the last few days and had yet to find the person he was looking for. Jamal "Shark" Jones was a person of interest in the murder of a homeless man who'd been stabbed in the neck with a bowie knife. As one of the first officers on scene that night, the body found in a back alley near a popular bodega, he'd called it into the homicide division and secured the area while waiting for the detectives to show up. Jimmie's death hadn't been his first, so he knew the protocols. Most murders took place in the dead of night and by choice he worked the graveyard shift. The city's action took place during the witching hours and he wanted a piece of it. He hadn't been surprised when his brother-in-law Zach Taylor, a Homicide Detective out of the eleventh district was assigned primary so he was the one who'd followed up on several leads and got a name for the current suspect. With Zach in the midst of several other ongoing investigations, Tony had promised to pick up the scent while he was on duty and he'd been doing some of the reconnaissance, walking the seamy side of the city, where the vagrants lived and breathed. It had been a stark realization to see how many people lived on the streets of Boston, unsheltered in the brutal cold that had swept the city.

He'd been to the tracks near the train terminal earlier that day, right after his shift ended, close to six a.m., but he wanted to give it a second look, hoping he'd have better luck this time around. Tonight, he was hitting South Station's food court, where he'd heard a group of homeless people had taken up residence, moving in from the camp that was settled out by the rail lines. He hadn't even known the camp existed before last night, had never seen the tents, the tarps, the fires burning, casting eerie shadows on the surrounding buildings. It was as if it had just materialized out of nowhere, a case of him not seeing what was right in front of his eyes. He'd never been called out there, never heard of any disturbances, so maybe the campers got along okay and were left in relative peace. The frigid temps had forced small groups into the terminal itself, putting them at risk of being picked up for vagrancy. He'd tried talking to some of them earlier, but his uniform had made them uneasy. He was back, close to twenty-four hours later, in jeans and a heavy jacket, a box of donuts in his hand as a peace offering. He hoped it would loosen some tongues.

He hunched against the cold February wind whipping the steady current of air between the buildings, glad that the interview would be taking place inside, glad that the homeless had somewhere warm to go. When he opened the glass door, he breathed in the warmth. The place was bustling, even though it was close to midnight. He could hear the murmurs of people talking, the thump of the wheels of a carry-on making *click-clack* sounds, the blare of the intercom announcing a train arrival, and the commotion could still set his teeth on edge.

That he stood here as one of Boston's finest was a miracle. The road had been difficult and filled with landmines. It had taken him years of therapy to feel confident enough to get his shield, to walk into dangerous situations without the fear of what was ahead, or behind certain doors. There were still moments when fear could immobilize him, but he'd learned over time that many of his fellow policemen felt the same thing. The difference? They worked though it and got the job done. He'd learned to do the same.

He took the escalator up to the food court, allowing it to deliver him to the designated area rather than walking up the moving stairway. When he felt the concrete under his boot, he took a step forward, scanning the area. Men and women stood at the wall of vending machines, debating choices, or sat at the tables that decorated the space, eating peanut butter crackers or packaged Danish. His gaze finally settled on the isolated corner and the group he was looking for. He hesitated before approaching. They recognized him from his earlier attempt to talk to them, and he read wariness in their eyes. The donuts might not make a difference in how they reacted to his presence.

He stopped a couple of feet away from the table.

"Hey, how you doing?"

One of the men, who looked the part of former boxer, his nose previously broken, his ear more cauliflower than human, a bald head gleaming under the florescent lights, asked, "Back again, Officer?"

Tony shuffled his feet, unsure as to how to proceed.

"Yeah. I'm hoping you can help me with something. You didn't give me a chance to ask last time I saw you. I'm hoping tonight you're more amenable."

He slid the box onto the table, and stepped back, stuffing his hands in his bulky coat pockets.

The voice rasped out, "You can't make us leave."

He shook his head. "Not trying to do that. Trying to find a guy who might have killed someone. I'd think you'd want him off the street. He stabbed one of your own to death."

Baldy sat back in his chair, an amused smile on his face. Before he could say anything, another voice carried over to where he stood.

"One of our own? So, like, we're in a brotherhood?"

The voice was female, deep and resonant, but it hadn't come from anyone sitting at the table.

He shifted to see a woman walking toward him, maybe... She looked more like a young girl, with chopped whiskey-colored hair, grey eyes, or hazel, he couldn't tell in the muted light, a rounded point of a chin, and an attitude that was ready, willing, and able to go to war with him. Combat boots told him he'd probably lose the battle. He could almost picture her as part of his brother Johnny's heavy metal band, Raging Thunder. The look suggested punk.

He tilted his head to take her in. Although the looks were completely different, there was a hint of his sister Lana about her in the way she dressed and presented herself. It was familiar in a sense and oddly disturbing.

She was sipping from a cup, the steam suggesting it was coffee, the narrowed eyes suggesting she didn't trust cops. He had no idea how she would have known he was one, never having seen her before. Unless she'd overheard baldy addressing him as Officer.

Standing his ground, he said, "Ma'am, I meant no offense."

She all but scoffed, "Ma'am? That's a good one. Do I look like a ma'am?"

The laugh was short, the tone smoky. Their eyes met and hung on until the bald guy said, "Back off, Tansy. He brought a present."

She glanced over and smiled. "No problem. I'm heading out anyway. You guys stay warm."

She went to walk past him toward the exit, giving him a sideways glance as she did, as if she didn't trust that he was who he said he was. Her appearance had pulled at his gut and his brain went numb, all thought process gone, until she was twenty feet away. Then it all came back, why he was here, what he was doing, and he called out for her to wait. He walked toward her, pulling the picture out of his inside pocket. She apparently thought he was going for something else. Her eyes turned flinty, as in dangerous, and her finger pointed at him. "Don't even try it."

The mugshot was in his hand as he raised it, along with his other one, wanting her to know he was harmless.

"It's a photo. Can't hurt you. I'm looking to find him."

He slowly extended his arm, hoping she'd take a look. After staring at him for a second, she moved to where he was standing and slanted her head. He could smell the coffee on her breath, and some other indefinable aroma. It was sweet and musky, surprising him. The homeless people he'd met lately didn't smell particularly good. Had he made a mistake in assuming she was one of them?

She backed away, a look of distaste on her face.

"That's Shark. He's a piece of refuse. I'd stay away from him if I were you."

He'd yet to hear one good thing about the man. Not that many had admitted knowing him.

"Do you know where I can find him?"

"I follow my own advice, so no, I don't."

"Have you interacted with him before?"

Her eyes turned as cold as the temperature outside, and she challenged, "As in sex, talk, drink...?"

He tried to sound conciliatory.

"As in have you been in his company."

She gave him a quick, disgusted snort.

"Once. It was enough."

"Where?"

She narrowed her eyes, as if he was pushing her generosity. He wasn't sure she was going to answer him.

"Bodega on Boston Street. I haven't been back."

It's where the murder had taken place and he'd talked to almost everyone who came and went over the last few days and had come up empty. It's where

Zach had gotten his lead, but it seemed as if Shark knew they were coming for him and had stayed away. Shit, he'd all but disappeared.

"That it, copper?" Her voice had a steely edge.

His eyes met hers and he felt a tingle down his spine.

"Yeah. Thanks."

"Good luck picking him up. You'll need it."

He watched her saunter away, her jean-clad bottom eliciting something primal. There was no way she was homeless. The jeans were clean, the boots weren't cheap, although she had on a light-weight jacket that couldn't keep her warm out there. The bald guy seemed to know her, though, which would suggest...

He turned back to the group. The four women and two men sat looking at him. One of the women told him what he wanted to know, even though he didn't want to admit it.

"That's Tansy McPhail. She drops in every now and then, to grab a coffee, something to eat. She's not a regular. More of a loner."

He couldn't keep the incredulity out of his voice, even though he'd assumed...

"She's homeless?"

The woman shrugged her shoulders, flipped her dirty hair back over her shoulder.

"She claims she has somewhere to live."

"Then why is she here at this time of the night?"

"Didn't you know? It's the witching hour."

Baldy poked her in the ribs to shut her up. The other woman offered in a more moderate tone, "Tansy's not very social. She doesn't share much."

"But you know her name, who she is?"

He wasn't sure why it mattered, but for some reason it did. He glanced back to the escalator, knowing she was long gone. To where? Where exactly did she sleep? When he turned back, the woman in need of a wash and blow-dry stated flatly, "What's it to you?"

He didn't know, so he couldn't answer. He shrugged the question off and asked one of his own.

"Can one of you give me anything else on this guy?"

He'd moved closer, handed the photo over.

The older man fingered and studied it, and told him, "We stay away from the kind of places Shark frequents. We'd rather stay here than in the shelters.

Too many rules, too many thefts, too many people who don't get along well with others. Like Shark. He's been evicted from most of the places in the area. Might find him in tent city, although from what I hear, he's close to being kicked out there, as well. He hasn't learned the art of civility."

That was a camp Tony knew about. It was like a homeless shantytown, an unauthorized housing facility, where homes were pup tents and blankets and where there was an Old West style judicial system, without the guns. People could be barred from staying there if they didn't meet the standards set by the temporary residents. And it was always a temporary situation. The clock never stopped ticking because no one wanted them in their backyard.

He knew Zach had checked it out, so he hadn't bothered to visit. He would now.

"Anywhere else I might look for him?"

"There's a woman he's with a lot. I think she goes by the name Lady."

That much he knew. Homicide has talked to her and what she told them was all they needed to make the arrest. Now they just have to find him.

The second woman smiled, revealing a couple of missing teeth. He supposed regular dentist visits weren't on their list of priorities.

"Tansy's right. We're not a brotherhood and we don't keep tabs on anyone, especially the people we don't like."

Baldy smiled sarcastically. "Actually, we do. That way we avoid trouble."

Tony pulled off his knit cap, pushed his hand across his head. He needed some advice on how to speak to the people on the streets, figure out how to deal with them without giving offense. Not that he was going to make this his life's work. He didn't want to admit it, even to himself, but they made him uncomfortable. He glanced up to study them.

How could people live like this? Not willing to give it any in-depth analysis, he said, "Thanks, for the info. I won't bother you again."

He began to leave but the man who was sitting beside the bald guy threw him a grenade. Had he picked up on the contempt?

"I'm sure you won't. Most people don't want to associate with us. And we reciprocate. You're lucky we were in a good mood tonight."

The toothless woman, powdered sugar on her lips, added, "And hungry."

He bristled because the guy in the bandana was right. Most of them smelled, had dirt caked beneath their fingernails. Some were mentally unstable or walked around in a drug haze. They carried their belongings with them in plastic bags, a shopping cart, like growths on the sidewalk. He wondered if they were lazy, on drugs or hostile. Did they even try to get a job, or did they enjoy begging for their coffee? But he'd sworn to protect and serve all members of society and he didn't want to be responsible for anything happening to them because of his questions.

"Be careful, okay? If you bump into this guy, don't stick around. You'd be at risk."

"We're always at risk and we know that better than you. Shark's got a rep for being a mean drunk."

Tony reached for his wallet, and one of his cards. Offering it over, he said, "Thanks for the information. If you ever need—"

"Don't bother. It's not the first time we've heard those words. It would be a first if you came running when we called."

He slid the card beside the box that was now open and half-empty on the table.

"Try me. I work out of another district, so it might take me a while to get here, but I don't make promises I don't intend to keep."

One of the women picked up the card and read it. "Anthony Scalera, Patrolman."

"Don't ask for Anthony. No one will know who you're talking about. It's Tony."

Baldy had finally reached for a donut, and asked conversationally, "Why are you looking for a killer? That's above your pay grade, isn't it?"

The man sounded fairly educated. The woman next to him wore her toothless smile. It was a situation of strange bedfellows, and he didn't think he'd ever understand it.

"I'm helping out the Homicide Department. If you hear anything about Shark, let me know. I'll pass it along."

He backed away, glanced up at the clock. He wasn't working tonight, didn't have to punch in, and was intent on using the time to study for his detective shield test. Before heading home, he was going to check one more place. He'd heard some of those needing shelter had another hiding spot close by, where they could stay somewhat warm and off the grid. He was going to give it at least a cursory glance.

He pulled his hat back on, bundled up against the chill that was bone-deep, still amazed that a good number of people had to resort to sleeping in the cold, and walked out to the parking garage attached to the bus terminal. After taking his flashlight out, he scanned beneath each car in the row, bending from the waist, the thin stream of light illuminating the undersides of the vehicles. He knew it was a waste of time. No way would Shark be here, but for some reason, he felt the need to check. Up and down several rows, back and forth, he finally gave it up. As he was just about to shut off his light, he thought he saw movement in a car one row over. Reaching into his jacket and putting his hand on his gun, a sliver of fear sliding down his spine, he crept over to check, wanting to make sure no one was hurt or in need of help.

The car was a black Kia, maybe a couple of years old, salt spray from driving the streets of Boston coating its sides. He tapped on the window. The figure was folded in half, as if trying to avoid being made. Getting no response, he turned on his light again, surveyed the back seat, which was stuffed with all kinds of personal items, clothes, bags, a suitcase, laundry bag, as if... He aimed the light at the driver, whose back was still toward him.

Only when he knocked again, announcing, "Police. Let me see your face," did the body unfold and turn, squinting at the light shining in her eyes.

Tansy McPhail was glaring at him from the other side of the glass.